THE
SLEEPOVER

BOOKS BY CAROL WYER

THE SLEEPOVER

CAROL WYER

bookouture

Published by Bookouture in 2019

An imprint of StoryFire Ltd.

Carmelite House
50 Victoria Embankment
London EC4Y 0DZ

www.bookouture.com

ISBN: 978-1-83888-016-3
eBook ISBN: 978-1-83888-015-6

CHAPTER ONE

SATURDAY, 30 JUNE – LATE AFTERNOON

Cathy Curtis fished the teabag from her mug and tossed it into the sink, where it splattered onto the already brown-stained chrome. She'd clear it away later; for now she wanted nothing more than half an hour's peace and quiet.

Charlie was in the bedroom he shared with his brother, Seth, no doubt glued to some video game, controller hot and sticky in his hands. Roxy was still sulking in hers. She'd been there most of the day. Cathy felt a pang of guilt. She'd not meant to be so hard on the girl but it was important she got her message across. Roxy was stubborn and single-minded, but on this occasion, Cathy had been forced to step in and dissuade her.

She poured the milk into the mug, ensuring the tea was good and milky, and took it with her into the sitting room, where she dropped onto the settee with a sigh. She kicked off her slippers and swung her legs up so she was almost lying down. Moments like this were rare. She was inevitably running around after one of her children or her partner Paul, who at times was more of a kid than the boys. She smiled at the thought. Paul was fine just as he was. He brought out the best in her.

The tea was sweet and perfect. Seth and Paul weren't due back until much later so she'd probably watch some telly or catch up on a box set while they were out. Charlie wouldn't come out of his

room until it was time to eat, so once Roxy went out, she'd have the evening to herself. She cupped the mug and let her thoughts drift again. Roxy was growing up. They all were. Soon, they'd all have left the nest, like Oliver before them. A sensation like the twanging of a guitar string resonated in her chest. Soon it would be just her and Paul and there'd be endless afternoons like this, but she'd miss them – for all their noise and arguments, she'd miss them all.

Roxy appeared at the door in skinny jeans, a T-shirt and a green baseball cap that complemented her creamy skin and drew attention to her large hazel eyes.

'Hey.'

Cathy looked up and gave her daughter a warm smile. Roxy would always be her little girl, no matter how old she got.

'Sorry about the row earlier,' said Roxy.

'Me too. You okay about it?'

The girl nodded. 'Yeah. You were right.'

Cathy put her mug on the floor and stood up, padding across the worn carpet to her daughter. 'I know you didn't want to be told what to do…'

The girl stopped her with a shake of the head. 'No, you were bang on. I was being pig-headed. I don't even think he likes me that much.'

Cathy wanted to contradict her and say of course he'd be interested in her. Who wouldn't like her feisty, gorgeous daughter who had guts and determination and knew her own mind? But she didn't want to encourage that particular relationship. Instead she brushed away a strand of dark hair that had stuck to Roxy's cheek. 'You all ready for Ellie's?' she asked, spotting the plastic bag propped by the door.

'Yeah. You still cool about me going?'

'Sure, why wouldn't I be?' Cathy knew the reason why, but she wasn't going to argue again. They'd quarrelled enough for one day.

Roxy gave a shrug and the corners of her mouth lifted slightly. Cathy loved it when Roxy smiled. Her face transformed and her real beauty shone through.

'Thanks.'

'Got any plans for tonight?' Cathy asked lightly.

'Sit around in our pyjamas eating crisps and chocolate and watching Netflix,' said Roxy with another grin.

'Sounds like my ideal night.'

'You want to join us?' Roxy asked jokingly.

Cathy laughed. 'I'll pass. Maybe next time.'

'You're on. Okay, I'm off. See you, Mum.'

'Have fun. Say hi to Ellie for me. Not seen her for a while.' Cathy dropped a kiss on her daughter's forehead, and when Roxy didn't pull away she felt much better. Their spat had been forgotten.

Roxy looked up at her mother with clear eyes. 'Bye, Mum. Catch you tomorrow.' She lifted the plastic bag and Cathy accompanied her to the front door, where she stood and watched as her daughter left for a sleepover with her best friend, who only lived in the flats behind their own. The yard gate opened with a high-pitched squeal, and Roxy bounced through, hand raised in a farewell gesture. Cathy caught a final, 'See you,' as the girl disappeared from sight, and she went back inside, glad they'd patched things up between them.

She sat back down on the settee and lifted the remote control, ready to enjoy some time on her own. It was a thought she would live to regret.

CHAPTER TWO

SUNDAY, 1 JULY – EARLY MORNING

Urgent cries rang out as more glittering flames crackled along a distorted window frame and threatened to escape the building. An intense cascade spurted from the water cannon and quenched the inferno but Jamie Bull, the watch manager, the man in charge of the crew, knew it was hopeless. The fire had taken a firm hold and ravaged the interior of the house, destroying everything in its path long before the firefighters had arrived at the stylish Victorian residence on the leafy street – one of the smartest in Armston-on-Trent. Neighbours had rung the fire brigade, panicked by the flashes and explosions and fearful for their own safety and properties. Several were currently huddled at a distance, behind the cordon, eyes wide as they observed the emergency services battle the blaze and attempt to bring it under control.

Jamie had seen enough infernos like this one to be sure there'd be nothing left of what had once been the owners' personal sanctuary. It shook him to the core every time he picked his way through the debris and smouldering charcoal remains of a building to be reminded of what the house had been like. The small signs of normal life: a pushchair, a child's toothbrush, a picture frame, plates and cups set up on a table – all the things taken for granted as part and parcel of everyday existence, melted into blackened tokens.

Worse still was when they found lifeless bodies. Jamie had been relieved to learn the property they'd been dousing for the last hour was owned and occupied by two brothers, Gavin and Kirk Lang, neither of whom had been at home when the inferno started. Gavin, a thirty-something-year-old with pale grey eyes and designer stubble, had arrived soon after the crew and now stood alone, some distance from the small crowd, with his mobile pressed to his ear, lips moving, as the twenty-five-strong crew continued to tackle the fire.

Jamie speculated about what could have caused such devastation. He knew the stats: in the UK, around 16,000 fires a year were due to faulty appliances. Maybe Gavin was checking with his brother to see if anything had been accidentally left plugged in. Jamie glanced at the man in dark trousers and a stylish black jacket with the collar pulled up against his neck; he seemed remarkably composed. For a brief moment their eyes locked and Jamie could see none of the usual signs of anguish he'd come across before in such cases. Gavin had already refused any assistance from the Fire and Emergency Support Service who'd arrived to offer practical and emotional support. He'd made alternative arrangements for the night and was now waiting to hear the firefighters' verdict as to what might have caused the destruction of his home. In Jamie's opinion the man was a little too calm, too aloof. His home and its contents had been annihilated and yet he exhibited no reaction to the huge loss – zilch. His thoughts were interrupted by one of the two crew managers, Floyd Haverstock.

'It's out, gaffer. We're sure this time. We've checked the outside too. Okay to send in the teams?' Floyd was referring to the officers in breathing apparatus.

Jamie nodded a response and watched as several men headed down the path.

With everything now under control, the last of the curious neighbours were trailing back into the comfort and security of their

own homes. Jamie noticed nobody invited Gavin to join them or offered him any comforting words. He didn't seem bothered by it. Jamie walked across to him.

'Will they be long?' Gavin asked, nodding in the direction of the firefighters who'd entered the house.

'It depends on how bad it is. There will probably be structural damage so they might have to navigate around it.'

'Reckon they'll be able to identify how it started then?' The voice was rough and at odds with the man's appearance.

'Yes. I can't tell you how long it'll take though.' Sometimes it could take days to sift through the debris and locate the cause.

'Can you work out if it was deliberate?' Gavin appeared to want immediate answers.

'The dog-handling team ought to be able to.' West Midland Fire Investigations had arrived accompanied by Kai, a Belgian Shepherd, and his handler. 'You'll need to contact your suppliers as soon as possible – gas, water, electricity,' he said helpfully.

Gavin nodded. 'Already in hand,' he replied.

Jamie nodded and moved away again. They'd needed three engines to douse the blaze and the firefighters were now clearing away equipment. The house had been soaked. Jamie didn't need to go inside to imagine the chaos or inhale the stench – a mixture of smoke, soot and whatever had been burnt that entered deep into the olfactory system and never really went away. Even at home some nights, when he was watching television, Jamie could shut his eyes and smell it. Depending on the amount of damage, the owners would either have to gut the place and start again or get some heavy-duty cleaning equipment in. His money would be on starting all over again. He hoped the brothers were well insured. However, some things were simply irreplaceable.

Hearing his name being shouted, he looked up to see one of the longest-serving firefighters, Dan Higson, by the front door. He hastened across to him, half-expecting to hear that they'd discovered

the appliance responsible for the damage, but as he drew up to the man and studied his solemn expression, a familiar gnawing began in his stomach. Dan shook his head gravely.

'We've found a body,' he said. 'It's unrecognisable.'

CHAPTER THREE

SUNDAY, 1 JULY – EARLY MORNING

DI Natalie Ward lifted her mobile phone and checked the display for the third time since she'd come to bed. It was half past four and, as usual, she was unable to sleep. She'd fallen asleep almost instantly when she'd gone to bed but been woken by loud music coming from a vehicle outside just after eleven thirty and she'd been awake ever since.

She ought to have slept like a log. It had been some time since she and her husband, David, had spent an afternoon alone together, but yesterday they'd both made a determined effort. The children, Josh, who'd be seventeen at the end of the month, and fourteen-year-old Leigh, had gone to Manchester with David's father, Eric, and his girlfriend, Pam, giving her and David the opportunity to be alone and clear the air – air that was so stale it had almost suffocated her over the last few months.

It had been one of their better days. Since April, when Leigh had run away from home, it had been a rocky road and they still had a long way to go. Natalie didn't hold David responsible for the incident but she was still struggling to accept that he had lied to her. David had claimed to be cured of a gambling addiction, but in the face of having no work, he'd returned to his bad ways; worse still, he had been more than economical with the truth.

She could have dealt with it all if only he'd been upfront about it, but the secrecy and deceit had been almost too much for her to

handle. He'd lied to her even though he knew it would be the one thing she wouldn't be able to forgive or tolerate.

Long ago, her sister Frances had lied to her. Brief snatches of the past rushed at her, threatening to drag her back there: the theft of her dying grandmother's ring, the lies, the false accusations and her parents' disappointment in Natalie when, in truth, she was blameless, and then the accident that took them before they could find out what had really happened and forgive her. She fought the memories until they receded back into the vaults of her mind where normally they remained locked away.

What trust there had been between David and her had been destroyed, and although Natalie had been putting on a brave face for the sake of her children, she couldn't reconcile herself with what David had done.

The trip to the reservoir had been David's call and a good one. They'd walked beside the huge expanse of water and watched two swans take off in noisy succession, wings beating rapidly against the water, causing vast ripples that grew in number until they splashed over the shoreline…

'They're like small, white aeroplanes,' David comments as the duo depart.

Natalie agrees. The birds make an impressive sight as they rise majestically into the cobalt sky.

David faces her, eyebrows lowered as always when he has something serious to say. 'It's been good today. We needed this time together. We've not talked, Natalie. Ever since Leigh ran away, it's like we've become strangers who share a living space. You're rarely at home, and when you are, you're nearly always doing something with the kids or you go to bed early or are too tired to talk. Neither of us talks about it. It's the bloody elephant in the room.'

'There's nothing more to say.'

'I admit I screwed up but I'm making amends.'

'I know.'

'This is driving me mad. I feel like you're there but you aren't. You're there in person but unapproachable. We've lost that connection that made us who we were.'

'You know who is to blame for that.' The hurt on his face prevents her from laying into him.

He speaks softly. *'How many more times do I have to say I'm sorry? I can't explain how much I regret what happened and I am truly sorry.'*

'I know you are. I understand why you went to the bookies and weren't at home when Leigh went missing. I've seen how unhappy you've been since you lost your job and the freelance translation work dried up. I understand it's hard for you and that an addiction is hard to get over. I get it, David. I really do.'

'Then why can't we move past this?'

There are two reasons why Natalie can't ease back into their old relationship: the first is that she simply can't forgive the lies and the second is that she no longer loves him. She's with him purely for the sake of the children. The realisation had come only a few days after Leigh's return, and try as she might, she can't find the love she once had for her husband.

'I'm trying,' is all she can utter.

'It's been two months. Two terrible long months of pretending everything is okay and knowing it isn't. How much longer before we move past this?'

She hadn't known how to respond. The afternoon had been pleasant, and for a while they'd enjoyed a familiar intimacy as they wandered along the pathways, yet as soon as they got back in the car, an invisible barrier had been erected once more and they'd avoided each other for the rest of the day.

She put her phone back on the bedside locker and lay flat on her back, eyes wide open. It was thanks to her estranged sister,

Frances, she couldn't absolve her own husband. Frances's deceit had changed Natalie forever and now she was incapable of forgiving anyone else who lied to her.

The phone buzzed and she picked it up, simultaneously kicking the bedcovers from her. 'DI Ward,' she said quietly as she crept towards the en-suite bathroom.

'Nat, it's Mike.'

Mike Sullivan was head of Forensics, and if he was calling this early in the morning, it meant bad news.

'Hey. What's up?'

'I'm at the scene of a fire in Armston-on-Trent. West Midlands and Staffordshire fire brigade were called out to it soon after one o'clock. There's a body inside the house and no one knows who it is. The fire dog hit on an accelerant, most certainly petrol, so we believe it's arson. I've taken samples. The homeowners are claiming they know nothing at all about the body.'

'Is the body still in situ?'

'Yes, we haven't moved it yet. It's burnt beyond recognition. We don't know if it's an adult or a child because bones can shrink when exposed to high temperatures.'

Natalie was aware of the effect of fire on human bodies. She'd witnessed the aftermath of a serious car accident – one in which the victims could only be identified by their teeth.

'Okay, I'll get the team together.'

'You won't be granted access to the house just yet. I've taken photographs and sent them to your email so you can get an idea. The body's in a room at the rear of the house, in what was used as an entertainment room for watching television, playing video games, that sort of thing.'

'Where was the fire started?'

'Looks like it was the front of the house. The fire dog reacted as soon as it came inside. Could have been rags or something posted through the letter box. I'm with the West Midlands FI, Nick Hart.

He's sketching out the diagrams for us now.' The fire investigator would draw out a footprint of the building, include internal plans, the rooms damaged by fire and body diagrams so the team could begin piecing together how the fire had taken hold and why the victim hadn't escaped. Mike continued. 'I've taken samples and I'll arrange to have the body moved for examination. I'm putting Darshan Singh on it.' Darshan Singh shared the laboratory at Samford with his wife, Naomi. Both were accomplished in their fields, with Naomi a top forensic anthropologist and Darshan a specialist in forensic odontology.

'And who's the pathologist on this?'

'It'll be Pinkney. Ben Hargreaves is on leave.'

Natalie had known Pinkney Watson for several years, before she'd moved from Manchester to Samford HQ, and liked the fifty-six-year-old man who lived in a Victorian house with his two cats and enjoyed his free time in his campervan called Mabel. Pinkney might be slightly eccentric but his mind was razor-sharp and Natalie found him easy to work with.

'Is there anyone about? The owner? We need to gather statements from the neighbours and see if there's any surveillance footage.'

'Yes, both the homeowners are here. They're brothers – Gavin and Kirk Lang.'

'Okay. Text me the address. See you soon.'

She switched on the light above the mirror, and as she brushed her hair and tidied it quickly into an efficient style, she heaved a sigh. It was written on her face – the disappointment and the anxiety. *Bloody hell, David. Why couldn't you have just told me about gambling instead of lying to me!* The trip to the reservoir had been a start but there was still a massive void between her and David that, at present, seemed insurmountable. However, now there were more pressing matters and she couldn't waste energy on David.

*

DS Lucy Carmichael couldn't sleep either. She'd decided to give up trying and gone out for a run instead. The streets were silent so she didn't need her earbuds and music, and it allowed her the chance to reflect on what was troubling her. She'd spent all day Saturday shopping with Bethany, her partner, and was now lost in thought about the baby that would soon be with them. She'd been very happy for Bethany to fall pregnant and carry the child, but ever since Spud had started moving about, it had all become very real, and now she was unsure if she'd make the best parent. She'd had no role models of her own, having drifted from one foster home to another and having been the child from hell.

Lucy knew having children changed so much. Her colleague, PC Ian Jarvis, had struggled to find a work–life balance and it had cost him. His girlfriend, Scarlett, sick of the long hours and fearful of the danger he was putting himself in, had upped and left, taking their baby with her. It had been different before baby Ruby had come along but becoming a mother changed Scarlett's attitude towards Ian and his job. Motherhood might also change Bethany. Maybe she too would become more demanding once Spud appeared. Her phone rang, interrupting her gloomy thoughts, and with a sense of relief she answered it. DS Murray Anderson was on the line.

'I knew you'd be awake.'

'How could you be sure?'

'You're an early riser. Always have been. Let me guess… you're running.'

She smiled. Murray had known her for most of her life and was like the brother she never had. He knew her better than she knew herself at times. She slowed down to take the call.

'Yeah, but I haven't gone far. I'm only at the kids' playground. What's up?'

'Natalie wants us to meet her in Armston-on-Trent. Firefighters have uncovered an unidentified body in the debris of a burnt house.'

'Okay. I'll meet you there.'

'Linnet Lane, number ten.'

'Have you rung Ian?'

'Not yet.'

'I'll call him and arrange to pick him up. It's on my way,' she said.

'Okay. See you there.'

Lucy raced back to the house, scribbled a message on a Post-it note for Bethany, stuck it to the bathroom door where she'd be sure to see it, and belted off. Part of her was glad to be occupied with an investigation. It took away thoughts of children and self-doubts. She grabbed her car keys and headed back out into the morning with one last thought: would this all become more difficult once the baby was born?

*

The house in Linnet Lane was a sorry sight. Once a grand Victorian mansion identical to the others in the street, it had a pillared 'coach and horses entrance' and low-rising steps up to double doors. The imposing doors led to an entrance vestibule with floor-to-ceiling arch windows that must have once been impressively grand. It was all now a blackened mess. Natalie tore her gaze away from the neighbouring house with its shuttered bay windows and imagined that this shell of a house in front of her had once looked equally splendid. She ducked under the cordon and approached the building, halting by the gates where Mike Sullivan was talking to a man in his forties with dark hair, dark eyes, a scar across his left cheek and a clipboard in his hand.

'Hi, Natalie.' Mike looked like he'd not slept for a month. She knew how he felt. 'This is the West Midlands fire investigator, Nick Hart.'

'Hi. DI Natalie Ward. What a mess!'

Nick spoke in a light Brummie accent that sounded almost musical to Natalie's ears. 'Yes, it's that all right. By all accounts,

the fire took hold quickly. They can start small but depending on the furnishings and so on, they can go wild. Did Mike tell you we found evidence an accelerant was used?'

'Yes, he did. Could somebody have thrown something through a letter box – a petrol-soaked rag perhaps?'

'That's one theory although we've been discussing it since and there's also a possibility the entrance doors were unlocked.'

'And there's another door into the house beyond those front doors?' she asked.

'That's right. Those doors lead to a large vestibule and another door which goes into the house. I'll make sure you get a layout and sketch of it all,' Nick replied.

Mike spoke up. 'We're removing the body shortly and then I'll head back to Samford.'

Nick nodded. 'And I'll finish documenting the scene and send notes and sketches across to Mike later today. I spoke to the homeowners and it seems the body was in what they refer to as an entertainment room. It contained three large round sofa chairs and a widescreen television and gaming equipment. Nothing else. The body was found in the middle of the room and we suspect the victim was on one of the chairs and didn't move or try to escape.'

'Unconscious?' Natalie asked.

'Possibly, or they'd inhaled carbon monoxide while asleep… or were already dead. The pathologist will hopefully be able to confirm that.'

Natalie screwed up her face in concentration. Who was this mysterious person and how had they got in? She thanked Nick, who headed off to continue his work, leaving her with Mike. 'Where are the owners?' she asked.

'They're in the Vintage Tea Room at the end of the street.'

'It's open at this time of the day?'

'They're friends with the owner, Daisy Goldsmith. She opened up for them.'

'Oh, okay. I'll go and talk to them. Ah, there's Murray,' she added as he pulled up in his Jeep Renegade.

'And I need Darshan to start work on identifying the body. I'll be in touch later today.'

'Isn't it your day to have Thea?' Thea was Mike's daughter, who had just turned five. He only got to see her every other weekend, and Natalie knew any time with her was precious to him. His marriage might have failed but he still adored his little girl.

'Yeah. Bastard, isn't it?'

'Can't you swap for another day?'

'Let's just say Nicole and I are in negotiations regarding that subject.' He pulled a face and lumbered away.

Murray waited for her to cross the road and then greeted her. 'Lucy's on her way with Ian. They shouldn't be too long.'

'I'm not sure how much we'll get out of people at this time of the morning but we need to make a start. The homeowners are in the tea room at the end of the street so we'll begin by talking to them.' Murray's phone interrupted them. It was Lucy.

'Murray, Ian's not answering the door or his phone.'

'Have you tried Scarlett?'

'Yes, and she bit my head off for waking her and Ruby. He's not there.'

Murray relayed the information to Natalie, who shrugged and said, 'We'll try him later.'

'Natalie says leave it for now. We'll be in the Vintage Tea Room on Linnet Lane.'

'Roger that.'

Natalie strode up the hill, past the houses with their drawn curtains and sleeping occupants. Each house seemed to be fitted with security cameras that might have captured the person or persons responsible for the attack, but the street itself didn't have any CCTV. She hoped that somebody inside one of the mansions had spotted the arsonist.

*

Natalie peered through the window of the quaint tea shop, with its net curtains that hung halfway down the window and empty china cake stands waiting to be filled. Inside was bright and cheerful with a dresser containing a variety of ceramic teapots and ten square wooden tables. The brothers were the only customers, both standing in front of a counter, talking to a woman in her late twenties. They looked up as the doorbell sounded and Natalie and Murray entered the shop. They flashed IDs and introduced themselves to the men.

Gavin and Kirk Lang looked nothing alike. Gavin was a good five inches taller with thick, quiffed hair, combed over to one side, and deliberate facial stubble; his brother was squat, bull-necked and sported a high, tapered fade cut with a messy top of wavy dark hair and a soul patch beard which was sculpted into a neat rectangle the size of a postage stamp directly under his lower lip.

Kirk nodded towards a table. 'Mind if we sit down? It's been a long night,' he said.

'Go ahead.'

'Any chance of a black coffee, Daisy, love? Make it strong.'

The woman threw him a warm smile. 'Sure. I'll bring it over. You want anything, officers?'

'No, we're fine, thanks.' Natalie walked to the nearest table, pulled out one of the chairs and sat down. Murray took the seat next to her and withdrew his notepad and pencil.

A coffee machine hissed and bubbled in the background as Gavin, last to join them, wandered across and sat down beside his brother, his eyes fully focused on Natalie.

'I'd like you to run back over a few things you'll have already discussed with the fire investigator. As you know, a body was found.' Natalie glanced at both men as she spoke.

'I want to make it absolutely clear that we don't know anything about that,' said Gavin quickly. 'We left the house at the same time, eight thirty, and I alarmed the place and locked the doors like I always do. We've no idea how anybody could have got in.'

'You alarmed the house?'

'I'm fairly certain I did.'

'Did you, or didn't you?'

'I'm sure I did. Some things you do automatically, don't you? Yes, I put the alarm on. I always do.'

Natalie gave a brief nod. If he was telling the truth, then whoever had broken in had disabled the alarm. Added to that, Mike and the FI had told her they believed the entrance doors weren't locked. Somebody had managed to unlock the doors and turn off the alarm, and had been inside when the fire took hold. Was it the arsonist?

'Does anyone have a spare house key? A cleaner perhaps?'

Kirk sat in silence while his brother did the talking. He rubbed at his eyes and stifled a yawn.

'We use a cleaning agency – Top to Bottom. They have a set of keys.'

'Can you give us their details, please?'

'Sure.' Gavin brought up the information on his mobile and slid it across to Murray, who noted the name and numbers.

'Which days do they work for you?'

'Monday and Friday.'

'Does anyone else have a key?'

'Daisy.' He indicated the woman who was placing cups on a tray. She looked up at the sound of her name and cleared her throat, ready to speak, but he continued.

'She's my girlfriend,' he added by way of explanation.

Natalie directed her next question to Daisy. 'Did you go to the house last night?'

'No. I stayed here all night.'

'Where is the key?' Natalie asked.

'On the key ring with the shop key. I usually keep them behind the counter.' Daisy glanced at Gavin but he didn't respond in any way.

Natalie continued, 'I see. Do you run the place on your own?'

'Yes.'

'And you prepare everything here, behind the counter? You don't have a separate kitchen?'

'No. There's only this room and the customer toilet over there.' She nodded in the direction of a door.

'And you're always here?'

'I never leave the shop when we're open. I sit behind the counter if it's quiet. Or if I go upstairs, I always lock the front door and put up the "back in five minutes" sign.'

Natalie had at least determined it wasn't likely that anyone might have taken the key, even for a brief time, to make a copy of it. She waited while Daisy brought the coffees across and placed them on the table then said, 'Do you live here?'

'Yeah. In the flat upstairs.'

'And you didn't hear or see anything unusual last night or in the early hours of the morning?'

Daisy dropped her gaze. 'I'd been rushed off my feet all day so I had a long soak in the bath, turned in about ten thirty and fell asleep until the commotion woke me up.'

It struck Natalie that Daisy was sliding the now empty tray between her hands nervously and was sure the woman was with-holding something. 'What happened then?'

'I looked out of the window and saw blue flashing lights heading up the street. I pulled on some clothes and ran in that direction.'

'Why?'

'Why?' Daisy repeated.

Natalie recognised the delaying tactic. Often people would repeat a question to buy them time. 'Yes.'

'Because the fire engines were going towards Kirk and Gavin's house. I had to check out what was happening.'

'But the fire engines might have been attending a fire or an accident elsewhere.'

She shook her head. 'No. I saw the sky lit up and people running down the road. That's what made me follow them. As I got closer, I could smell smoke and people were standing on the street and I saw it was Kirk and Gavin's house on fire. I rang the club and spoke to Kirk.'

'What's the name of your nightclub?' Natalie asked Gavin, whose eyes were trained coolly on Daisy. The young woman didn't look at him.

'Extravaganza. It's near the railway station, next to the old cinema.'

The nightclub was only about ten minutes away by car. Murray made a note of the name but didn't interrupt Natalie, who'd turned her attention to Kirk.

'And Kirk, what did you do after that phone call?'

Kirk leant forward, removed a slim packet of sugar from a ceramic pot on the table and slowly ripped it open. He tipped the contents into his cup before replying. 'I told Gavin the place was on fire and he belted off to see what damage had been caused.'

'You didn't go too?'

'I stayed at the club. It was heaving and one of us had to make sure everything was running smoothly. It didn't need both of us to come back.'

It struck Natalie that neither man seemed stressed or upset by the news their home had burnt down. Shock came in many forms and it was possible they hadn't fully comprehended the enormity of what had befallen them, but that idea seemed unlikely. 'What time did you leave the club?' Natalie looked at Kirk but Gavin spoke for his brother.

'I rang Kirk when I got there, told him the place had been totalled and the fire brigade were trying to get the blaze under control. I said I'd wait around and sort out insurance, accommo-

dation and so on, and to stay put at the club until closing time.' Gavin crossed his legs, half the size of his brother's meaty thighs, and cocked his head to one side, waiting for her response. It irked Natalie. She was trying to do her job. A body had been found in a house belonging to these two men, and yet she was under the impression they didn't care.

'And what time was that, Kirk?'

'Not sure. I left the bar crew to lock up. Four thirty, I think.' He casually lifted the coffee cup and slurped noisily at it.

Daisy cleared her throat. 'Can I carry on? I've got to set out everything.'

'Sure,' Natalie replied.

Daisy beetled off back to her counter.

'He joined me at four fifty,' said Gavin.

'You seem remarkably composed. I'd be distraught if I'd lost all my personal belongings in a house fire.'

Kirk put down his cup and said, 'At the end of the day, it's only stuff. Possessions can be replaced.'

'But it wasn't just stuff, was it? Somebody died in your house,' said Natalie.

'But *we* didn't let them in and *we* don't know who it was. Could have been a burglar or the stupid bastard who burnt the place down.' Kirk's icy glare made him look even more menacing. Of the two brothers, he looked like the one who was handy with his fists and who worked out regularly in the gym.

Murray glanced quickly at Natalie, who nodded briefly at him. He had something he wanted to ask Gavin.

'You said you contacted the insurance company? How did you know their number?'

'I keep all emergency numbers in my contact list,' Gavin replied.

Murray spoke again. 'What other emergency contact numbers do you have in your phone?'

'Garage, dentist, doctors, plumber. The usual,' he drawled.

Natalie waited in case Murray had anything else he wanted to add, but he appeared satisfied with the response so she continued. 'I'd like to get back to the question of who might have had access to your house.'

Kirk glanced up over his cup. 'No one else we can think of.'

'Have you no thoughts as to who might have got into it?'

'Like Kirk said, probably the shithead that burnt it down,' said Gavin.

'If that's the case, can you think of anybody who might want to set fire to your house or wish you any harm?'

'Plenty of jealous gits out there,' Gavin muttered. 'They don't like to see anyone do well for themselves.'

'Have you received any threats?'

Kirk gave a quiet snort but it was his brother who spoke. 'We get threatened regularly by drunks or punters who think they've been unfairly turned away from our club. Look, I'll level with you. We pissed off a load of people when we bought the warehouse and turned it into a nightclub. Plenty thought it had some historical value and should have been preserved instead. But we don't give a shit what anyone else wants because clubbers love it and we do very nicely out of it. So… we've ruffled feathers. Need I say any more?'

Natalie understood his meaning. These brash young men had upset the locals and it was possible one or more of them had decided to retaliate – but why now? 'How long have you been in Armston-on-Trent?' she asked.

Gavin answered, 'Just over two years. We moved from London to Birmingham in 2012 and then to Derby in 2014. We were hunting for the right place to set up our own club. When we heard the old indoor cattle market was coming up for sale, it seemed the perfect opportunity. We took it on in March 2015 and it opened in June 2016.'

'And the house?'

'We moved into it in February 2016.'

If the fire had been started because of some hate campaign against the pair for buying what was now the nightclub, then it was strange it had occurred now and not sooner. Something must have triggered it. Of more concern to Natalie was the body in the house. She needed it identified quickly and then to work out why that person had been inside a burning house. The fire had started in the entrance and yet the body had been discovered in a room at the back of the house. To her mind that meant it was unlikely to be the arsonist unless there had been two or more intending to set the fire and one had been left trapped inside. They were questions she couldn't answer for the time being. At present, they only had the contact details for a cleaning company, a girlfriend who'd claimed not to have seen anything and two unperturbed victims of arson.

The door opened and Gavin's head snapped up at the sight of the person striding towards them. Lucy always made an impression. It was due to a mixture of rock-chic elegance – even in the black trousers, white blouse and jacket she wore today – and an air of confidence. She introduced herself, pulled a chair from the adjacent table across and dropped lightly onto it, then pushed away the blue-black fringe that hung low over her forehead, revealing the scar that ran across the bridge of her nose. She looked at Natalie, who continued talking to the two men. Gavin's eyes were now on Lucy and he studied her like she was a tasty morsel on a plate in front of him. Kirk, less interested in her, put his elbows on the table and waited for more questions.

'Have you ever received any hate mail?'

Kirk shook his head.

'Is there anyone you can think of who might have wanted to set your home alight?'

'Nobody at all. If I could think of somebody, I'd have probably already hauled them in to the police by now.' His jaw flexed and Natalie believed he'd be more likely to bash the truth out of the arsonist first.

'And apart from Daisy and the cleaning company, nobody else could have gained access to your house?'

'No one,' Kirk answered again.

Natalie looked at Gavin, who agreed. 'Can't think of anyone.'

'You didn't leave your house keys anywhere?' Natalie asked.

Gavin said, 'They were on me all the time.'

'Mine were in my jacket pocket hanging behind the office door,' said Kirk.

'Was the office unlocked?'

Kirk nodded.

'Do you share it with anyone?'

'Only Gavin. Hardly anybody comes in unless they're looking for us, but mostly we're mingling out front.'

'Is there any CCTV there?'

Gavin took over again. 'Not in the office. There's nothing worth stealing, only the computer, and nobody's likely to try and walk out over the dance floor with it shoved up their jumper.' His flippant remark made his brother smirk.

Natalie ignored him. 'Can the office be accessed from the rear of the building?'

'There's a fire door and it only opens outwards, so no.'

'Can anyone reach your office via the dance floor or do you have security preventing them?'

'They can pretty much go where they like: the party room upstairs, the bars, anywhere apart from the VIP rooms.'

'Why not the VIP rooms?'

'They're only for private parties and are locked unless in use, and then we keep a bouncer on the doors.'

'Did you have any private parties last night?'

'Yes. One.'

'What about the toilets?'

'They're in the same corridor as the office,' said Kirk.

'Even for the private partygoers?'

'There are facilities in the VIP rooms. Everyone else uses the toilets downstairs.'

'And your office was unlocked?'

'Yes.'

'Then there's a chance your keys could have been taken from your jacket and replaced later, and you wouldn't have known.'

Kirk pulled a face – a sneer that contradicted his words. 'I suppose so. I didn't spend any time in the office last night but I definitely had the keys when I left the club.'

'Okay, let's back up a bit. What time did you arrive at the club?'

Gavin answered, 'Eight forty or thereabouts.'

'Is that usual?'

'Yes. We open at nine every night.'

'How many employees were working last night?'

'One on reception, four working behind the bars, four hostesses, two hostesses in the VIP lounge, two bouncers and the deejays – DJ Crush, and upstairs in the party room, Dimension. Fifteen in total.'

Natalie nodded. 'We'll need the names and contact details of everyone who works for you.'

Gavin tapped his phone and began reeling off the information to Murray. There were twenty-five names in total. They'd have to interview all of them to determine if any of them had a grudge against the two men. It was likely those who'd worked the night before would be in bed by now, but the neighbours would be waking up and she needed to determine if any of them had seen any suspicious activity near the Langs' house. The sooner they got started the better. With all contact details now written down, she terminated the interview with a final question. 'Where will you be staying?'

'Here in Daisy's flat,' Gavin replied.

'Both of you?'

'Just for the short-term. Obviously, we'll need to make other arrangements as soon as possible. Place isn't big enough for all of us,' said Gavin.

Natalie picked up on a swift look that passed between Daisy and Kirk. She didn't know what it meant but they made eye contact and broke it almost immediately. Daisy lowered her gaze and continued setting cupcakes onto a stand.

'Okay. We'll be in touch as soon as we have any news,' said Natalie.

As the team stood up, Gavin eased his hands behind his head, stretched and released a heavy sigh before asking, 'Any idea when we can get into the house and have it assessed for damage?'

'You'll have to ask the fire investigator. We're concentrating on the death of the person found inside your house.'

Gavin blinked lazily. 'Yeah, sure.'

Daisy still had her head down behind the counter and quietly acknowledged Natalie's goodbye as the team headed for the door.

Once away from the shop and out of hearing, Murray was the first to speak up. 'Am I the only one to think it's odd that Daisy went to bed so early at ten thirty? She's only in her late twenties and it was Saturday night – she ought to be out clubbing with friends, especially since her boyfriend runs a nightclub. I was always out on the razz at her age.'

Lucy agreed with him. 'Unless she'd been out the night before and was knackered.'

'Nah. She said she'd been busy all week and was tired,' said Natalie.

Murray continued, 'There was a weird vibe going on in there too.'

'I noticed that when I came in,' said Lucy. 'Daisy kept looking over at Gavin.'

'She's his girlfriend,' Murray explained.

'No. It was a cautious look – almost nervous – and she dropped the cupcakes not once but twice. She was edgy and not just because we were there. I think she's hiding something.'

Natalie agreed. 'She was certainly nervy about something. I picked up on a few signs.'

'Like her shuffling the tray when you were asking her questions about the fire,' said Murray.

Natalie nodded in agreement. 'Yes, she seemed pretty anxious then, didn't she? We should try and talk to her again alone. She might even have had something to do with the fire.'

'The brothers are certainly playing it cool,' said Lucy.

Murray snorted. 'Aren't they just? And that whole insurance business. I don't have contact details for my insurance company on my phone. They're in a file on my computer. If I needed to contact them, I'd have to look up the number. They might have deliberately set fire to their own place for insurance purposes.'

Natalie had already considered the possibility. 'That's something we definitely should look into. Ask Ian to get hold of the nightclub finances. See if they're doing as well as they make out they are. There's one more thing that's bugging me. Those guys weren't the least bit concerned that a body's been found in their house, and I can't ignore the possibility it's because they put it there and then set fire to the place to eradicate all traces.'

Murray nodded. 'It would certainly account for their offhand attitude.'

'Okay, we'll discuss this later. Best to wait for the body to be identified. Let's start by canvassing the street.' She turned back towards the café and watched as Gavin leant in close to Kirk. He was talking quickly, hands waving. They were definitely acting suspiciously. They might be from London and think they were in some little backwater, but they were no match for her or her team. If they were guilty of any crime, she would find out.

CHAPTER FOUR

SUNDAY, 1 JULY – MORNING

Natalie thanked the woman she'd been talking to and returned to the pavement, where she waited under one of the many lime trees offering dappled shade along the street. Finches chattered noisily above her head, an avian argument that she was not party to. Natalie had drawn blanks. Most of the people she'd spoken to had either been in bed or inside with their curtains drawn at the time of the fire, and nobody had seen any unusual activity leading up to it. Moreover, no one had expressed any sorrow. She'd sensed the brothers were unpopular.

Murray came into view, head high, shoulders swaying, like a heavyweight fighter approaching a boxing ring.

'Anything?' she asked as soon as he was within earshot.

He continued his stride until he was level with her. The birds fell silent at once. 'Only a fair amount of hostility towards the Lang brothers, nothing of any use whatsoever on any of the security cameras in the area and one neighbour, Lincoln Wild, who said he wasn't surprised the house had burnt down. Reckoned there were a fair number of comings and goings – mostly women. He said the guys often held random parties and even went so far as to speculate drugs were involved and suggested somebody had probably set fire to the place by accident when they were high.'

'Did he have anything to back that up?'

'Nothing whatsoever. In my opinion it was just idle speculation on his part. You want to talk to him?'

'You think I'd get a different response?'

Murray cocked his head. 'I don't think he can tell us a lot more, and nobody else I spoke to mentioned women and parties. He could just be a bit of a shit-stirrer.'

Natalie knew what he meant. Some people used such opportunities to besmirch others, or maybe Lincoln had seen women going into the house once or twice and jumped to conclusions. It wouldn't be abnormal for the brothers to have female visitors. 'No one's said anything to me about any parties or women. We'll wait to see what Lucy's uncovered. If there's any cause to delve further, we'll interview him again.'

Murray patted his pocket. 'I wrote it all down anyway, even though I'm sure he was venting.'

'Okay, let's wind it up then and get back to Samford. Has Ian contacted you yet?'

'Not heard from him.'

'What the fuck's he playing at? He ought to have picked up the message by now. It's gone nine.'

'Maybe he rang Lucy.'

Natalie cast about looking for any sign of Lucy but couldn't spot her. 'Perhaps he has. We could do with him turning up soon. Okay, you go back to the station and start by checking out the nightclub's finances. Find out whatever you can about Gavin and Kirk Lang. See if you can get hold of any of their staff too. I'd like to know what their employees think of them.'

'Will do.'

Murray headed back to his car. Natalie marched back to the Langs' property, where she checked in with the officer protecting the premises from intruders. She ducked underneath the cordon to stand in the entrance, turning a full 180 degrees to take everything in. The house was elevated and set well back from the road, hidden

from view behind a brick wall. A security camera, blackened and cracked, had been set up above the main doors and overlooked the driveway. Any footage it might have taken would have been destroyed in the blaze. She tried to imagine what the house had been like before the fire. The front of the house had fared marginally better than the rear, with exterior brickwork surrounding the bay windows now charcoal-black. The back of the house was a different story. Frames had fallen around windows, devoid of glass, and brickwork crumbled beneath them. The roof had collapsed in part. A gentle breeze got up and flakes of ash fluttered about her like skeletal leaves. She took a step backwards away from any possible danger. Who had entered the Langs' house and died there?

She made her way back down the slope. A car drove by and slowed down, the occupants craning their necks to see what had happened. She ignored the vehicle and, spotting Lucy, called out to her. Lucy spun on her heel, acknowledged Natalie and walked towards her.

'The brothers don't appear to have many friends on this street. No one saw a thing and I got the impression not one person I interviewed gave a damn about the fire. Not a single security camera fitted to the houses I visited picked up suspicious movement – nothing apart from the odd cat,' said Lucy.

'We got similar results and reactions. The brothers don't seem to have won over the residents. Any of them mention parties or visitors?'

'Funnily enough, the last bloke I just spoke to. He lives four houses down. Said the brothers kept themselves to themselves but he had heard loud music coming from their house on a couple of occasions when he was out walking his dog late at night.'

'Loud music? Could simply have been the brothers.'

'He said it was party music – techno or garage – he didn't know what exactly, something with a heavy, repetitive beat and the house lights were all off.'

'Did he remember which nights?'

'No.'

'We've not gleaned much, have we? Only that they're two fairly unpopular men who live in a swanky house and maybe hold the occasional party. They certainly haven't won any friends. What about their immediate neighbours?'

'Didn't hear or see anything last night and have never spoken to them.'

'Not even a "hello"?' Natalie had known her own neighbours on either side of her house for years. They weren't very close but they always sent each other cards at Christmas and had each other around for drinks. She'd stop and chat to them if she saw them in their gardens or on the street. Still, she didn't live in a Victorian mansion on an exclusive street.

Lucy shook her head. 'Nothing. They never even introduced themselves.'

Natalie let it drop. If the neighbours didn't know anything about the brothers, then there wasn't much to gain by staying in the area. 'Murray's gone back to the station. We ought to get going too. Have you heard anything from Ian?'

'He hasn't rung me.'

Natalie's eyebrows knotted. This was most unlike Ian. He was normally conscientious and the first to arrive on the scene. 'Okay. We'll manage without him. You done here?'

'Yes. That was my last house.'

'I'll see you back at base then.'

The police headquarters at Samford was a modern-day landmark. Designed and commissioned especially to house police specialists, Forensics and terrorism squads, it was one of only four such headquarters in the UK. It overlooked the main road that passed through the town centre, and those not in the know might easily

mistake it for a modern arts centre or similar. The building was accessed by automatic glass doors, leading into a bright atrium. Natalie and Lucy acknowledged the reception staff behind the curved front desk, passed through the ID recognition Perspex gates that swung open simultaneously and then took the stairs to the first floor where their office was located. Many of the special police units could be found on this floor, each housed in a glass-fronted office that overlooked the lengthy corridor. Natalie's office was halfway along it, with a large patterned settee, supposedly for guests but rarely used, directly in front of it.

Murray had his back to them but his voice was clear as he shouted at somebody at the other end of a phone. Natalie swiped her pass again to gain access and caught the tail end of the conversation.

'Stop fucking about and man up!' He ended the call and tossed his mobile onto the desk.

Lucy threw him a look but he gave an almost imperceptible shake of his head. Natalie noticed the movement but didn't draw any attention to it. He clearly didn't wish to discuss the conversation. Instead, he picked up some notes he'd made.

'I've got information on both the owners and on Extravaganza. The Lang brothers were born and brought up in Dagenham. They're the youngest of five foster children. Dad was a London cabbie and their mum used to work in a fish and chip shop. They're both retired now but still live in Dagenham. The brothers rented a place in Shepherd's Bush in 2010 and worked at Green Pineapple nightclub. In 2012, they moved to Birmingham and worked at Starstruck on Broad Street and then Platinum 123 in Derby. They definitely rattled a few cages when they bought the warehouse that was the indoor cattle market and transformed it into a nightclub. The locals drew up a petition to try and prevent them but it was too late. The brothers had already been granted planning permission and licences to run the nightclub before they actually moved to Armston-on-Trent.'

'That goes some way to explaining their unpopularity. How's the nightclub doing?' Natalie asked.

'I'm still waiting for that information although I spoke to one of the employees – Lindsay Hoburn – who's looking for another job because she hasn't been getting the shifts she was promised. She's a "reserve" bar person and called into work when it gets really busy and they need backup bar staff, but she only worked once last month and that was only because two staff members were off sick.'

'Did she tell you anything else?'

'Only that the Lang brothers are okay to work for and she hadn't noticed any particular bad feeling towards them. I haven't spoken to any of the other staff yet.'

Natalie pressed the point between her eyebrows as she often did when she was organising her thoughts. She soon spoke up. 'Okay. Let's work through the staff list and talk to everyone we can. Are either of you or your friends familiar with the club?'

Murray shook his head. 'Nightclubs aren't my thing. I'm more of a pub person.'

'Not been to Extravaganza. We tend to go to Derby or Nottingham for a night out,' said Lucy.

'Well, toss a coin and one of you can check out the place tonight. Have you got the number for the cleaning agency the Langs used?'

Murray scribbled it down and passed it to Natalie. As she walked to her desk to ring it, Lucy pointed a finger at him and mouthed, 'You go.' He shook his head.

Natalie dialled the number, and with her back turned to her officers she spoke to the cleaning agency owner.

Lucy took the opportunity to whisper, 'Who were you speaking to when we came in?'

'Ian,' he hissed. 'Stupid prick is having a major meltdown. Thinks he might jack it all in so Scarlett will take him back.'

'What?'

'I told him to get his arse here and I'll take him out for a beer later and talk to him.'

Murray and Ian had never really seen eye to eye although recently they'd been more tolerant of each other. The fact Murray was willing to listen to his younger colleague and offer advice was a surprise to Lucy. 'Is he coming in?'

'I don't know.'

'Shit!' She turned to her desk. If Ian quit the team and the police force, he'd be throwing away everything he'd worked for. He'd come back to work soon after being stabbed and had thrown himself wholeheartedly into every investigation. He couldn't throw it all away. Would he really be willing to give it all up for Scarlett and Ruby? Lucy wasn't sure she'd make a similar sacrifice if Bethany ever wanted her to leave the police force. Besides, she could never leave the team short-staffed.

Natalie ended her call. 'Top to Bottom cleaners definitely didn't go to the house yesterday. I've asked the company owner, Rachel Stevens, to come to the station all the same. She might be able to tell us more about the brothers.' She dropped onto a seat and stared out of the window. The brothers appeared to be very close. They'd lived and worked together for quite a few years. They'd worked in nightclubs and looked to no one but themselves. They were driven to succeed, and lived in an expensive house, yet claimed material goods didn't impress them. Both brothers had looked very smart, and although she couldn't be certain, their clothes looked expensive.

'What cars do the Lang brothers own?' she asked.

'An Audi RS5 and a BMW 6 series,' came the reply.

'Financed?'

'Not sure. Waiting for confirmation of that.'

Natalie continued staring ahead, processing the information she had. They drove quality cars. Even if they'd purchased them on finance, they were prestigious vehicles.

'According to the Zoopla website their house cost £750,000,' said Lucy.

'Shit, that's treble what we paid for our place,' said Murray.

'And it's a huge amount for two guys who own a nightclub to come up with. Imagine the mortgage payments on that place.' Natalie tapped a fingernail against the desk and said thoughtfully, 'They'll pay out a fortune on the nightclub too: running costs, wages, not to mention how much it must have cost to buy and renovate the place in the first instance. They must be stretched financially. The more I think about this, the keener I am to find out about their finances.'

'I'll push for some information,' said Murray.

There was a shuffling outside the door and it opened. Ian, unshaven, walked in wearing a wrinkled shirt. He halted by Natalie.

'Where the fuck have you been?' Natalie snapped, steely gaze on the young man who faced her.

'I was at a friend's house.'

'Why didn't you call in to let us know?' Natalie knew immediately there was more to it than that. Ian's eyes were bloodshot and she could smell sour alcohol on his breath. He dropped his gaze. She waited for him to lie his way out of it, and her heart sat heavy and solid in her chest.

'He did call in. He rang me earlier to let me know he was on his way,' said Murray. His voice was flat. Natalie spun to face him, one eyebrow raised. He continued, 'With all that was going on, it slipped my mind. I should have told you.'

Murray's face was blank. Ian glanced quickly at him.

'If you're covering up for him—' she began.

'I'm not. Ian phoned me before you came back. I didn't mention it because we were discussing the Lang brothers. Sorry.'

There was little point in pursuing it. They had an investigation to conduct and she needed all her team behind her. She gave a brief nod. 'Next time, make sure you keep me in the loop.' She

looked from Murray to Ian and then let the subject drop. 'Okay, I'll bring you up to speed. Murray, I want those financial records.'

No sooner had she finished going through the investigation with Ian than her mobile rang.

Mike's voice was low and sombre. 'We've identified the victim. It's a fourteen-year-old girl by the name of Roxanne Curtis.'

Natalie swallowed back the bile that rose rapidly and stung the back of her throat. The girl in the house was the same age as Leigh. Mike continued with, 'She lives in Clearview.'

Clearview was a suburb – the ugly part of Armston-on-Trent with high unemployment, cheap housing and an unsavoury reputation. Gang culture, knife crime and violence were rife there.

'Where exactly?'

'Stockwell Estate.'

Stockwell was regarded as one of the better estates that made up the vast area but that didn't say much. Natalie's team had been called out to it on one of their early investigations when a teenager had been stabbed during a brawl outside a convenience store.

'That was quick work.'

'We had a spot of luck, if that's what you can call it. The poor kid had metal pins and a metal plate screwed into the elbow hinge joint. Darshan got hold of her medical records and we were able to identify her from them. He's sending them across to you to look at.'

'Thanks, Mike.' Her voice was quiet, her mind suddenly elsewhere. What possible connection could the Lang brothers have to a teenage girl who lived on the far side of town? She placed her phone on the desk. She already had the attention of her team, who were waiting to hear what she had to say.

'The body belongs to fourteen-year-old Roxanne Curtis.'

'Oh, shit!' Murray rubbed a hand over his head. 'I wasn't expecting that.'

'Me neither.' Natalie blinked away the thoughts of her own daughter, who'd gone missing earlier that year. She'd been terrified

that something terrible had befallen her. This poor girl's mother would be going through a similar living hell. 'She lived on the Stockwell Estate. Ian, drag up whatever you can find on her from social media. Murray, I still want you to chase up those financial records for the nightclub, but first, find out whatever you can about Roxanne's family. She had internal metal fixings in her elbow so she might have been in some sort of accident or even been attacked and beaten up. Forensics are sending over medical records. Lucy, take a closer look at them. Maybe they'll give us an indication as to what happened to her. I need to update Superintendent Melody and then you and I will go and inform her parents.'

There was a renewed burst of activity. Murray and Ian both dived towards the computers on the bench at the far side of the room. Natalie headed towards the stairs, leaving the trio working in silence. There was no sound other than the tapping of keys and then suddenly Ian spoke quietly. 'Cheers for that.'

'What?' said Murray, keeping his eyes on the screen.

'Speaking up for me.'

'You did ring in. It was the truth.'

'Yeah, but I called to tell you I wasn't coming in. That I'd had it with all of this – that I was giving it up to get Scarlett back.'

'Well, you're here now, so stop wittering and get some details on this family.'

'I really wasn't going to come in, you know? I was at an all-time low. I only changed my mind because of what you said.'

'Which bit? The "don't be a total fuckwit" or "man up"?'

'Both.' Ian turned his attention once more to the screen, fingers dancing across the keyboard.

Murray left it a minute then added, 'That drink's still on if you want it later.'

Ian looked across. 'Cheers. I'd appreciate that.'

Lucy looked at them both from across the room. 'For crying out loud, can you two quit the whole *bromance* thing and give me

something useful to act on? You know what Natalie's like. She'll want to know everything about the family before we speak to them, including the names of their bloody pets and shoe sizes.'

'We're on it,' said Murray. 'Give us a fucking chance.'

Lucy grinned then tutted loudly. 'Does this sound normal to you? Roxanne was admitted to hospital on three separate occasions between 2012 and 2016 for fractures: clavicle, wrist and elbow.'

'Didn't all those breaks ring any alarm bells?' Murray asked.

'I can't see anything to suggest so. There are no reports filed for suspected child abuse.'

'Maybe she was accident-prone or sporty,' said Ian. 'I broke my shoulder and my leg and dislocated my thumb when I was a teenager all through playing rugby.'

Murray squinted at him. 'You played rugby?'

'Left wing.'

'Makes sense. You look like you could be one of those lanky speed merchants.'

'That's me.'

'She could have been sporty. I'll ask the question,' Lucy replied.

Murray slipped back into work mode. 'Lucy, I've found some information on her family. Her mother is Cathy Curtis, born 11 April 1979, aged thirty-nine, and works at Argos. Married Aidan Curtis in January 1998 – divorced 2010. They have three other children: twenty-year-old Oliver, eighteen-year-old Seth and seventeen-year-old Charlie. The two youngest boys live at home but Oliver is in the army – the Royal Engineers, currently stationed at Chetwynd Barracks in Nottingham.'

'Roxanne was the youngest then?' Lucy said, jotting the information down in her notebook.

'Yes, and she was the only girl. In 2011, Cathy moved to 114 Pine Way on the Stockwell Estate, with Paul Sadler. He was born 19 July 1988 so he's a fair bit younger than Cathy – by almost ten years.'

'That's not a massive age gap,' said Lucy. 'But it's quite a responsibility to take on four kids when you're only twenty-three. Does he own the place?'

'No. It's rented.'

'He'd still need to earn a fair bit of money to feed all those mouths.'

Murray grunted a response and then continued. 'According to our general database, he's worked for CAT Aerials since he left school.'

'Nothing untoward then?' Lucy said.

'Ah, possibly. His ex-girlfriend, Sarah Raleigh, reported him for domestic abuse back in 2008 but dropped the charges, and again the following year in 2009 when she dropped the charges again.'

'Were there any further charges made against him?'

'Hang on a sec. No more but police were called out to his house in 2016, following a phone call from a concerned neighbour who claimed he heard Cathy screaming for help. The couple refuted it and said the person was mistaken. According to the report, Cathy had injuries to her face but she insisted they were caused by a fall in the bathroom.'

Lucy tapped her pencil against her notepad. 'More suspicious injuries. I doubt Roxanne's mother was accident-prone too. Roxanne was first admitted to hospital in 2012, the year after she and her family moved in with Paul.' She cocked her head to one side. 'I know… we shouldn't jump to conclusions.'

Ian swivelled on his seat. 'We ought not to but a young girl who sustained three fractures in four years and whose mother had facial injuries rings alarm bells for me.'

Lucy grimaced in response. 'Me too. I'll see if we can get to the bottom of it.'

Murray sucked his teeth noisily. 'You could be right. There's something else you need to know. Roxanne was reported missing twice: once in April 2016 and again in January 2017. She came

home of her own accord the first time but it took a week to locate her the second time. She was found on the streets in Stoke-on-Trent.'

Lucy's eyebrows lifted. 'That definitely smacks of an unhappy teenager.'

Ian had returned focus to his screen. 'This is her Instagram account. It's not set to private. She's got 850 followers.'

Lucy crossed the room in three strides and peered over his shoulder. An unsmiling Roxanne looked defiantly back at her. With full lips, slightly upturned nose and clear, hazel eyes, she was an attractive girl. She had attitude: the way she posed with hands thrust in the front pockets of her jeans and chin lifted, the studs in her upper earlobe, the black T-shirt bearing a studded skull, and her dark brown hair styled in a dramatic shoulder bob with a perfectly straight fringe that rested just below her eyebrows. In many ways she reminded Lucy of her younger self: rebellious and hateful of the world.

'What do you make of her?' she asked.

'It seems she only posted a couple of times a month. Captions are simple, mainly emojis and a couple of kisses. She's only got pictures of the estate, presumably where she lived – quite arty ones of kids milling about, graffiti on walls, empty playgrounds. There's only this one selfie of her.'

'That's quite unusual, isn't it, for a teenage girl?' Lucy said.

'Not really. This generation isn't uploading like we do. Scarlett posts four or five pictures a day but her little sister who's fifteen only posts once a month. She told Scarlett it was passé to post so often and to use loads of hashtags. Apparently, it's different for Snapchat, where they post more frequently, but the trends are changing all the time. Teenagers are becoming cagier and more cautious about what they put up on social media. It wouldn't surprise me if this account is a Rinsta.'

Murray screwed up his eyes. 'What the fuck is a Rinsta?'

'Fake Instagram account. It's a polished version, that parents can see, and usually has loads of likes. Teenagers have got wise to

parents tracking them down so they have Rinstas and Finstas. The Finsta is actually their real Instagram account and the one their close friends can access. The fact this one isn't set to private makes me suspect she has another, a Finsta.' He continued tapping at keys.

Natalie appeared from nowhere. 'You got some information for us to work with?' she asked.

Lucy gave a sharp nod.

'You can go through everything while we drive. Murray, we're taking a communications unit with us. Let us know if you uncover anything else you think's important,' said Natalie.

Murray lifted a hand in acknowledgement and Natalie strode away, Lucy hot on her heels. Natalie turned her head slightly as she bounded lightly down the wide staircase. 'When we've finished with Roxanne's family, we'll ask the Lang brothers to come in for further questioning. I have no idea what their connection to a teenage girl might be but I suspect they know more than they've so far been prepared to share.'

'I'm with you on that. What about Gavin's girlfriend, Daisy?'

'I was getting on to her. I'd like to talk to her again when Gavin and Kirk aren't about. In fact, if you get the brothers to the station, we'll use that opportunity to question her at the tea room.'

CHAPTER FIVE

A row of bollards stood between the disused shops and the road. Litter had collected at each of the bases and crept up the sides of the concrete posts. *Like paper snowdrifts*, Natalie thought. The whole area smacked of poverty: a bus shelter barely functional with the protective side panels missing; grey shutters down on all the abandoned shops, now covered in nonsensical graffiti and tattered posters advertising a gig that had taken place in 2016. All that was left was the overhead signage of what had once been here: the Indian Palace takeaway restaurant, Zadiq's barber shop and a charity shop. Above each neglected premises were flats with dirty windowpanes and satellite dishes attached to the grimy brickwork. The family they were about to visit lived in one above what had once been a post office.

'No entrances visible from this side. We'll have to go around the back,' said Natalie, turning her gaze towards a couple of teenagers squatting in the bus shelter. One looked up as they drove past and nudged his mate. Natalie could feel their hostility as they watched the squad car go by.

Lucy spotted a turning that led directly into an area used for parking and drew up near a faded purple Ford Ka. 'Which flat is it?'

Natalie craned her neck and studied the backs of the buildings, hidden behind fence panels and wooden gates. 'I think it's the

third one along. The one with the "For Let" sign appears to be number 116.'

Lucy unbuckled her seat belt and opened the car door. The car park was overlooked by a huge block of flats about fifty metres away. 'Not much privacy, is there? Everyone up there will be able to see the comings and goings here.'

'Maybe somebody over there noticed something out of the ordinary,' Natalie replied.

'There must be at least thirty windows that face in this direction.' Lucy sounded downbeat and Natalie knew how she felt. Investigations like this one required manpower, not to mention a lot of time and effort, and she only had a small unit. Countless requests to get another member on board had fallen on deaf ears.

She slammed her door shut and marched towards a shabby gate. It wasn't locked and opened into a yard, little more than an empty concrete space. A dark blue-black Yamaha motorbike was leaning on its stand; spatters of black oil stained the ground beneath it. Concrete steps with crumbling edges led to the first floor and a white door that had yellowed with age. Natalie was struck by the contrast in this property where Roxanne had lived and the one where her life had ended. A large tabby cat was curled asleep in front of the door on a dingy mat and ignored them when they knocked. Music was playing inside and Natalie had to knock a second time, more loudly, to get the attention of the occupants. A bare-chested man dressed only in tracksuit bottoms came to the door. His hair was fashionably shaved at the sides while on top it was longer and slightly curly. His face was littered with stubble and he rubbed at his eye and yawned. Natalie and Lucy lifted their identity cards and Natalie introduced herself and Lucy.

'Are you Paul Sadler?'

'Yes.'

'Would you mind if we came inside?' Natalie asked.

'What's this about?'

'Please, could we come inside?' Natalie repeated.

The man opened the door wide and rubbed a hand over his flat stomach. The cat didn't move so Natalie stepped over it into a living room cum dining room where a slim woman with her back to them was tugging at a vacuum cleaner. Paul shut the door behind Lucy and shouted, 'Cathy!'

The woman's head jerked up and she turned off the appliance, releasing the attachment too quickly so it clattered against the wall and fell on the carpet. She faced Natalie, blue eyes open wide. Natalie introduced herself and confusion washed over the woman's sharp features, tugging at her thin eyebrows and creasing her forehead. 'What do you want?' she asked.

Paul burst into sudden action. 'I'll turn off the music. Where's the remote, Cathy?'

Her movements were jerky like a marionette's as she hunted for the control. It was resting on a shelf next to a photo of a young girl, Roxanne, and three boys: two with shaved heads and wide shoulders sandwiching the third, who was taller and slender with thick wavy hair, and who stood immediately behind Roxanne, hands on her shoulders. Cathy aimed the control at a speaker next to the television. The sudden silence was deafening and Paul blinked several times.

Cathy took a few tentative steps towards Natalie and asked slowly, 'What's going on?'

'It'd be best if you sat down for a minute,' Natalie replied gently.

Cathy froze. No matter how many times Natalie had to break news like this to parents, she never felt she had the right words. What could one say to somebody whose world was about to blow apart? 'I'm truly sorry. I have some bad news about your daughter.'

The woman's eyes widened in horror. 'What's happened to her? Is she in hospital?'

Natalie shook her head as she spoke. 'I'm afraid she's dead, Mrs Curtis.'

'Oh, God! She's dead?' Her face morphed into a mask of pain and agony like Edvard Munch's *The Scream*. 'No. No-oh!' The second 'no' became a wail that reverberated through the flat. Paul rushed to her side but she balled her fists and beat them against his naked torso as he attempted to encircle her in his arms; he grabbed them and held them tightly in his own hands and made soothing noises until the anger morphed into dismay and soft whimpers filled the room. 'Please… no… no.'

A young man with earbuds hanging around his thick neck rushed into the room.

'Mum? What's up?'

Cathy's shoulders shook as she sobbed into Paul's chest and she sank further into him as if the strength was ebbing from her body.

'Why's she crying?' The young man spoke again. He had the same shining eyes as his mother. 'What's going on?'

'I'm really sorry—' Natalie began again but Paul interrupted her, his voice full of emotion.

'Roxy. She's dead.'

'What?' The boy's voice cracked. He looked at Natalie, who answered him.

'I'm afraid so. Her medical records confirmed it was her.'

'Records? I don't get it?' Paul said, still comforting Cathy. 'Why did you need her medical records?'

'She died in a fire.'

His brow furrowed deeply and he shook his head. His voice dropped. 'Fire? Where was it?'

'In a house in Armston-on-Trent.'

'What?' His voice was incredulous.

Cathy pulled away from him and wiped the back of her hand under her nose. The words were ponderous and punctuated with sharp intakes. 'No. She was having a sleepover with Ellie. It must be someone else. There's been a mistake. Roxy's with Ellie.'

'Where does Ellie live?'

Cathy sniffed back more tears. 'In the block behind the car park. Third floor. Number seventy-two. That's where Roxy is – you'll find her there. Wait, I'll prove it.' She leapt to her feet and disappeared only to reappear moments later with her mobile glued to her ear.

'Jojo? It's Cathy. Is Roxy with you?' There was a pause and her eyes filled with tears. 'She isn't? Are you sure? Could you check?' She chewed on a thumbnail and stared hard at the carpet, not daring to look up, and then said, 'She didn't sleep over? No. She's… something's happened to her… the police are here. Yes. I will.' She rang off, her eyes fixed on the screen as if her daughter might suddenly call her.

Natalie moved towards her and put a hand on her upper arm. Cathy's eyes were liquid and her voice thick as she allowed Natalie to guide her back to the settee. 'She isn't with Ellie. She didn't sleep over with her. Jojo doesn't know anything about any sleepover. Roxy isn't there. Where was she?'

'We found her in Linnet Lane, in Armston,' Natalie replied softly.

'I don't understand. Why was she there? Why wasn't she with Ellie? Did she say anything to you?' Cathy glanced at her son, who shook his head vehemently.

'She said nothing to me. I honestly thought she was with Ellie too.'

'Cathy, I understand this is a very difficult time for you but we have to ask you some questions to help us find out what happened to Roxanne. Please sit down. Let's talk,' Natalie urged, nodding at Paul, who seemed to be rooted to the spot, confusion written all over his features.

'What the fuck was she doing in Armston?' he asked Natalie.

'We don't know. Why don't you all sit down? You've had a dreadful shock.'

'Roxy. She hated being called Roxanne,' said the boy. He blinked several times, his eyes moist with tears.

Natalie couldn't work out his age. He had only light hair growth above his lip and on his chin but a closely shaved head and a neck tattoo that made him appear quite mature. When Paul spoke, she realised this was Charlie, the seventeen-year-old.

'I need to put a shirt on. Charlie, can you sit with your mum for a few minutes?' He wiped tears from his cheeks and left quickly.

Natalie felt sorry for the suddenly awkward teenager who dropped onto the settee beside his mother, unsure of how to comfort her or how to deal with his own emotions. She talked as he patted his mother's hand clumsily.

'Are your brothers here?'

'Oliver doesn't live here any more. He joined the army.' His voice trailed away and his shoulders slumped.

'What about Seth?'

'I don't know. I've only just got up. He's not in our room. Mum, where's Seth?'

Cathy closed her eyes and drew a breath. 'He left about an hour ago. He didn't say where he was going.'

Paul chose that moment to reappear. Now wearing a long-sleeved top, he swapped places with Charlie, who slid onto the other settee without a word. Natalie continued with her questions.

'Talk me through what happened yesterday. What time did Roxy go to Ellie's?'

'About five thirty, I think.'

'When did she arrange to stay there?'

'Only yesterday lunchtime. She said Jojo was working late and asked if she could keep Ellie company. I agreed. She and Ellie have been friends for years and she stays over there quite regularly. I didn't think there was anything odd about it.'

'Did she seem different in any way? Anxious to go?'

'No, but I should have checked she was actually there, shouldn't I? I never thought…' She bent forward, sobs shaking her upper body. Paul shushed her gently. Eventually she tried speaking again,

a spluttered sentence that took a length to articulate. 'I… must… sound like… such… a… crap mother.'

Natalie spoke up. 'No, really, you don't. I'm a mother of a teenage girl too and I know how hard it is to get through to them some days.'

Cathy inhaled ragged breaths. Paul gave her a wan smile. 'Of course you're not a bad mother. This isn't your fault. No way.' The sobs abated briefly.

'You believe she fully intended to spend the night with Ellie? You don't think she planned on running away?' Natalie had to ask the question although she was also considering other possibilities – that Roxy had been snatched or taken against her will to the house in Linnet Lane.

'She was definitely going to Ellie's.'

'What did she take with her?'

'Just a small plastic bag with a change of clothes.'

'You saw what was in it?'

'I assumed it was her pyjamas and overnight stuff. They were going to watch films and eat crisps and chocolate in their pyjamas – a girls' night in…'

'Roxy has run away on a couple of occasions, hasn't she?'

Paul looked up sharply. 'What exactly are you getting at?'

'I'm only trying to establish why Roxy might have gone to Armston and not to Ellie's flat. Was she upset about anything? Anxious in any way?'

'No, and when she ran away then, it was different. She sneaked off,' Cathy said.

'And why did she run away?' Natalie kept her eyes on Cathy, who chewed at her bottom lip.

The silence lengthened until, finally, Paul answered. 'Last year, she ran away cos of some lad.'

'Who?'

'We don't know. She wouldn't tell either of us.' Paul kept an arm around Cathy's shoulders, concern etched across his features.

'And what about the first time she left home, in 2016?'

'She was having a hard time at school and fell out with friends. She came home after a night of roughing it on the streets in Birmingham.' Paul squeezed Cathy's hand and she nodded in agreement.

'What's Ellie's surname?' Lucy asked. Her interjection seemed to rouse Cathy, who was drifting off in a private world of misery.

'Cornwall.'

'I know this is a really tough time for you, but could you tell us what you were doing yesterday?'

'You don't think we had anything to do with her death, do you?' Paul asked.

'Not at all. We just have to ask these questions. It's normal in these situations.'

'That's stupid. We haven't done anything! We're not fucking responsible for this,' Paul insisted.

'It's only procedure, sir. Cathy, can you remember what you did after Roxy left?'

'Nothing much. I watched telly… waited until Paul and Seth got back and then we sent out for a takeaway.'

'We were at a motorbike event – BMPS North Wales Classic Motorcycle Show. We got back at about eight o'clock,' said Paul, wiping a hand across his face.

'You didn't join them, Charlie?' Natalie said, turning her attention to the boy in the chair.

'No. I was with my mates all afternoon. Came back in about five. I went to my room and messed about online until Paul and Seth came home, and then we had dinner.'

'And what did you all do after you'd eaten?'

'We watched television.'

Lucy, who'd been making notes throughout all this, looked up and asked, 'All of you?'

Cathy shook her head. 'No. Charlie and I did for a while. Seth and Paul played on the PlayStation in the boys' room.'

'Yeah. That's right,' said Charlie. 'I joined them when Mum went to bed. We packed it in soon after midnight.'

Cathy nodded slowly. 'I went to bed at about half past eleven and fell straight asleep. I woke up when Paul came to bed and that was at quarter past twelve. I didn't even think about her, you know?'

'Hey, it's okay,' said Paul as the tears tumbled over her stained cheeks again. 'You weren't to know.'

'Why did Roxy go to Armston?' Cathy asked.

'I don't know, love,' he replied quietly, eyebrows knitted together.

Natalie waited until they were receptive to further questioning then asked, 'Do either of you know of Gavin or Kirk Lang?'

'Who are they? Did they kidnap her? Who are these people?' asked Cathy, her voice tight with anxiety.

Paul patted her hand to calm her. 'I've never heard of them,' he said.

'Charlie, do you know them?' Lucy asked.

The boy shook his head. 'No.'

'You're sure you've never heard of them?'

'Never.'

'Why are you asking about them?' Paul asked again.

Natalie returned her attention to Cathy. 'It was their house that burnt down, where we found Roxy. Would it be possible to talk to Seth at all?'

Cathy swept the backs of her hands across her cheeks, smearing her mascara. 'I can't… Will you ring him, Paul?'

The response was a heavy, 'Sure.' He took Cathy's mobile, flicked through the contact numbers and lifted the phone to his ear. After a couple of seconds he said, 'Answerphone.'

'Leave it for the moment, then. We'll try him later,' said Natalie, catching the look of despair in Cathy's eyes. 'Would you like us to contact your son Oliver for you?'

'No. We'll ring him. He should hear about this from us,' said Cathy.

'What about Roxy's father? Do you want to talk to him too?'

Cathy's face changed in an instant – her mouth a thin line of disapproval. 'I haven't spoken to Aidan for years, not since he buggered off to the south of Spain.'

'Was Roxy in contact with him?'

'You're joking. Not after the way he behaved. He walked out on us back in 2009. He went off with his girlfriend and left us all to get on with it. Roxy was only five years old at the time. She hated him for abandoning us. It broke her heart. He tried to get back in touch with the kids a few years later, but none of them wanted to know about him. Roxy wouldn't even speak to him. My poor girl.' Her voice lurched and she fumbled in her pockets for a tissue.

'That's fine, Cathy, we can take care of that. Aidan hasn't contacted you or the children recently?'

'He fucked off without so much as a goodbye. They haven't seen him in years,' mumbled Paul.

'It might be better then, if we inform him of Roxy's death,' Natalie said.

Having retrieved a tissue, Cathy snivelled into it, her words muffled as she spoke. 'This can't be happening. Please tell me you've got it wrong and you've found somebody else.' She shook her head in despair, not really expecting an answer.

Natalie gave her a minute then asked, 'Can you tell me a bit about Roxy? What sort of things did she like?'

Cathy rubbed her eyes and sighed wearily. 'Make-up… television, clothes… and video games like the boys.'

'Was she sporty?'

'Not really.'

'Tell me, how did she break her elbow?'

Cathy swallowed hard. 'She fell off her bicycle.'

'I understand she was admitted to hospital for fractures on two other occasions – a broken wrist and her collarbone.' Natalie studied Cathy's face hard. It crumpled before her eyes.

'Look, do we have to do this now? You can see how upset she is.' Paul was indignant.

'I'm sorry but these are relevant questions.'

'I don't see how. She had a couple of accidents in the past – fell off a climbing frame and tumbled off her bike, that's all.'

Natalie left it at that. If there was more to it, she'd find out, but pressing the issue now wasn't going to help matters. She needed to talk to Ellie as soon as possible but she also wanted to check Roxy's room in case there were any clues. She changed tack. 'It would help if I could see her room. Is that possible?'

'I suppose so,' said Paul.

'I'm going out. Will you be okay, Mum?' Charlie twisted a plain silver ring on his right hand as he spoke.

'Hey, mate, don't you think you should stay here for a while longer?' Paul replied.

'But I'm no help and I don't know what to say or do.' He blinked away the tears. 'Gonna see Zara.'

'Who's Zara?' Natalie asked.

'My girlfriend, Zara Walters.'

Paul shrugged. 'Cathy?'

She waved a hand in response and he gave the boy another sad look. 'Yeah. Okay, I suppose. He may as well be with his girlfriend as moping about here,' he said to Natalie as Charlie disappeared from view.

A tap at the door announced the arrival of Tanya Granger, the family liaison officer assigned to the family. Natalie had spoken to Tanya on the phone earlier and had been expecting her. Lucy let Tanya in, and after introductions, Lucy and Natalie headed upstairs to examine Roxy's bedroom. No sooner had they reached the bedroom than Natalie heard the gate outside open with a squeak and then the front door rattling. She stood at the top of the stairs and heard a voice ask, 'Why's there a police car outside, Mum? What's happened?'

Natalie told Lucy to check the room and made her way back downstairs.

Paul was speaking. 'Roxy's been involved...' He couldn't find the right words.

Cathy took over, her voice little more than a whisper. 'She's dead, Seth. She died in a house fire.'

There was no response and Natalie walked into the sitting room to find a slim young man standing by the doorway, his back to her.

'Seth?' she said.

He spun on his heel and stared at Natalie, his face impassive.

'I'm DI Ward and that's PC Granger. We're here to help you.'

He turned back to his mother. 'Mum?'

'That's right. They're trying to find out what happened to her.'

Natalie tried again. 'Seth, why don't you sit down. It's a lot to take in.'

'I don't want to sit down.'

Tanya was standing by the settee and facing him. She tried to assist. 'We're here to help,' she reiterated. Her words didn't have the desired effect.

'Fuck off,' he said, and catching Natalie off guard, he barged past her, pushing her against the wall before marching out of the house. She took off after him and charged down the steps. The gate let out a squeal as it opened and then slammed shut, and she opened it again in time to see him stride towards a black Honda CB125 motorbike, parked near the squad car.

'Seth. Wait up!'

The young man strode on ahead without looking back. He reached the bike, pulled on a full-face motorcycle helmet and prepared to mount.

Natalie got to him before he kicked the bike from its mount. 'I must talk to you.'

He straddled the bike, hands on the handlebars. His reply was slightly muffled. 'What about? I don't know anything.'

'I know this must be a dreadful shock for you but we need as much information as possible to help us find out what happened. Do you have any idea where Roxy was headed yesterday or who she was seeing last night?'

He lifted his visor slightly, revealing tawny eyes and lengthy, curling eyelashes, and answered, 'No idea at all. I didn't even know she'd gone out until we were eating takeaways and Charlie said she'd gone on a sleepover. She never told me anything, if that's what you want to know.'

'Did you get along?'

'Sure we did. She was my kid sister.' His voice cracked. 'Look, I just need to be alone. This is a lot to take in.' He dropped the visor again and shifted position to start up the bike but Natalie held up a hand.

'Just a few simple questions. That's all.'

He sat back, bike balanced between his thighs, arms folded. He didn't raise the visor again and Natalie didn't know if that was because he didn't want to reveal how upset he was or if he wished to hide something. She could ask him to remove the helmet but he might take off instead, and she had succeeded in getting him to stay long enough to answer her questions.

'Can you just quickly tell me what you did yesterday evening after you got back from the motorcycle event?'

'I had tea and then Paul and I played video games until quite late.'

'Any idea of what time you finished?'

'After twelve. I don't know exactly.'

'Have you heard of or do you know Kirk or Gavin Lang?'

'Nah.'

'What about a nightclub called Extravaganza?'

'I know of the place but I've never been.'

'What about Armston-on-Trent itself? Do you ever go into the centre of town?'

'Not very often.'

'And did Roxy ever mention the nightclub or those names to you?'

'Never.'

'I understand this is tough for you but I'll probably need to talk to you again.'

'Yeah. Okay. Can I go now?'

'Yes. Thank you.'

She took a step back and he took it as a sign that he was free to leave. He hunched forward, started up the engine and pulled away. As Natalie watched him depart, Lucy joined her. 'He took off quickly, didn't he?'

'Yes, he didn't want to hang about.'

'I expect he's in shock.'

'Maybe so. He doesn't appear to know anything useful. You got anything?'

'Nothing unusual in her room. I've got her laptop. I'll check it back at the station.'

'Okay. Not much more we can do here. Best visit Roxy's friend, Ellie, then. I'll just make sure they're okay first. You wait here. I won't be a minute.'

Back inside the flat, Cathy was sobbing uncontrollably, head in her hands. Paul was rooted to the spot beside the window that looked out onto the backyard. The emotional fallout had begun. This family would experience more anguish before they could begin rebuilding their lives. Natalie headed in the direction of the kitchen, where Tanya was searching through a cupboard for tea. 'His mum says he's like that – can't handle stress. People react to and handle such news in very different ways. He needed to put some space between him and home.'

'The other brother, Charlie, did pretty much the same. And Cathy said Roxy was moody. They seem to be quite a volatile bunch.'

The kettle bubbled, releasing noisy puffs of steam that masked the sound of their voices. 'Do you want me to let you know if Seth comes back?'

'No. I don't have any more questions for him at the moment. I'll get off. You okay here?'

Tanya pulled out a box of teabags and set about making drinks for Cathy and Paul. There was something comforting about her friendly face and wide eyes. 'Of course. I'll let you know if anything useful crops up.'

'Cheers. I'll catch up with you later.' Natalie returned to the main room. Paul was now back on the settee next to Cathy.

She addressed them both. 'I'm going to leave you with PC Granger. She'll help you through this. If there's anything you need or want to ask, you just tell PC Granger.'

The sobs subsided for a moment and Cathy managed a small nod. Paul shook his head and looked at his feet. It wasn't going to be easy for either of them.

Back in the car park, Natalie spoke to Lucy, who'd put Roxy's laptop away in the car. 'I'd like to get some more info on Paul, the stepdad. You mentioned he was reported for domestic abuse although charges were dropped. I think we should speak to his ex-girlfriend about it. What was her name again?'

Lucy flicked through the notes she'd taken down in the office. 'Sarah Raleigh.'

'Get contact details for her and we'll follow that up. I thought Paul was a bit quick to deflect my questioning when I was asking about Roxy's injuries. Might be worth seeing what Sarah has to say about him. Right, let's talk to Ellie and see if she can shed any light on what happened to her best friend.'

CHAPTER SIX

SUNDAY, 1 JULY – MID-AFTERNOON

Natalie and Lucy located the entrance to the block of flats, discarded McDonald's wrappers and empty cigarette packets tossed carelessly by the door. A skinny dog with its tail firmly between its legs scurried nervously away as they approached, watching balefully from a short distance until they entered the building. Inside was dingy even in daylight, with grey walls that seemed to close in on Natalie. She waited for her eyes to become accustomed to the gloom before walking past a lift sprayed with a crude image of a penis, found the staircase and climbed the wide concrete stairs. Lucy was directly behind her, and as they emerged onto the third-floor landing, a girl flew past them on a scooter, almost knocking them both over. Number seventy-two was close by. Natalie rang the bell and waited. The child returned and drew to a halt beside them, staring but not speaking. Lucy gave her a smile, which wasn't returned.

'Do you live here?' Lucy asked.

The child shook her head.

Natalie rang again and was rewarded with a scuffling behind the door and the scraping of a bolt. A girl with tousled hair clung to the doorframe as if the effort to stand unsupported was too great.

'That's Ellie,' said a small voice. The child was still there.

Ellie snapped, 'Clear off, Boo.'

Boo stuck out her tongue and then scooted back down the landing. Natalie and Lucy showed the girl their ID cards.

'I'm DI Ward and this is DS Carmichael. Could we come in, please?'

'Do you have to?' The face was pure concern.

'It really would be best if we came inside.'

A voice called out from inside, 'Whoever it is, tell them to fuck off. It's Sunday, for crying out loud.'

'It's the police,' Ellie shouted back.

The scooter zoomed towards them and Boo slowed down. 'Are they policewomen? Have you done something bad, Ellie?'

Ellie scowled at her. 'No… now go away, Boo. Come in,' she hissed to Natalie.

A woman swathed in a large towelling dressing gown appeared in the hallway.

'Mrs Jojo Cornwall?' Natalie asked.

'Yes. Are you here about Roxy? Is she okay? Her mother was on the phone half an hour ago asking if she was here.'

'I'd really like to insist we go to the sitting room.'

Ellie's mother padded barefoot into the room to Natalie's left. It was compact but tidy, and mother and daughter sat together on a pale blue settee.

Natalie began, 'I'm afraid I have some bad news regarding Roxanne Curtis. She was found dead earlier this morning.'

Ellie's face blanched and her eyes grew so wide they seemed to fill her face.

'Oh, Ellie, I'm so sorry, love. When Cathy rang me, I didn't think…' She groaned. 'I don't know what I thought. I certainly didn't imagine anything like this had happened to Roxy.' She put an arm around her daughter's shoulder.

'I'm truly sorry. I understand you were good friends,' Natalie said to Ellie.

Jojo kept her eyes on her daughter, whose shuddering was intensifying. She stroked the girl's hair, making soothing sounds, then said, 'They were tight – best friends.'

'Cathy thought Roxy came over here yesterday evening for a sleepover.'

The woman shook her head. 'There was no sleepover. I was at work and Ellie was at the youth centre. Roxy didn't come over while I was out, did she, Ellie, honey?'

The girl managed a weak, 'No.'

'Did you see Roxy at all yesterday?' Natalie asked the girl.

'No. I didn't see her at all.'

'Did you talk to her or have any contact with her?'

Her bottom lip quivered. 'We were on Snapchat first thing but I didn't talk to her after that. Mum and I went out.'

'What did you talk about?'

'Nothing much.'

Natalie smiled gently, mindful that the girl was only fourteen. 'I expect she shared a lot of secrets with you?'

'Uh-huh.'

'She'd have told you where she was going.'

'No. She didn't tell me. Honestly.' The shuddering intensified. Jojo gave her a squeeze and then shook her head sadly.

Natalie nodded. 'I know this is really hard for you, but we need to find out where she went. Have you any idea where she might have gone? Did she go to meet somebody?'

The girl shook her head. 'I… don't… know. She never said.'

'Did she talk to you about a nightclub in Armston-on-Trent?'

'No-oh.'

'Did she ever mention the names Gavin or Kirk to you?'

Again, she shook her head.

'Have you heard of them?'

'No.'

'What about a house in Linnet Lane?'

'No.' Ellie's eyes became glassy with tears and suddenly she jumped to her feet and raced out of the room, brushing past Natalie. Her mother stood up to pursue her then halted as the sound of heavy retching filtered through to them.

'I'm sorry but I need to talk to her. She probably knew Roxy better than anyone,' said Natalie.

'No! Listen to her. She's throwing up. Give her a chance to recover first.'

'Mrs Cornwall, we have to act as quickly as possible. Imagine how you'd feel if something had happened to Ellie. You'd want us to investigate immediately, wouldn't you?'

Jojo threw her head back and stared at the ceiling for a few seconds then heaved a sigh. 'Let me have some time with her. I'll see if she's up to talking to you. If she is, I'll bring her back in.'

'Thank you. Before you do that, what can you tell us about Roxy?'

'She was a nice enough kid and Ellie loved her.'

'Did she ever talk to you about her home life, concerns, issues, anything?'

'She used to come around to see Ellie, not me. I got on with her but we didn't have any deep conversations. In truth, I don't know much about her other than she preferred chocolate ice cream to strawberry, and cheese and onion crisps to plain, and she could sing really well and wanted to be a beauty therapist.'

'Did she often spend nights here?'

Jojo cocked her head to one side. 'Probably once a month. I often work late. Ellie would have her over to keep her company and Roxy was always welcome here. They'd watch films, YouTube videos, get takeaway pizzas, have girly evenings, try out each other's clothes, spa nights – you know, face packs and stuff – and paint each other's nails. All sorts of girl things. I was happy for Roxy to sleepover.'

'Did she ever seem troubled?'

'You're asking me? I don't know. All teenagers are troubled, aren't they? They don't want you to be their best friends. They shut themselves away when they hurt and talk to their friends. I don't know when Ellie's troubled half of the time, let alone Roxy. She could be moody or quiet and hardly talk some days but Ellie's the same.'

'And you're sure Roxy didn't suddenly decide to come over and stay while you were out?'

'If Roxy had been here last night, Ellie would definitely have said so.'

'Does Ellie ever discuss Roxy with you?'

Jojo tucked in her chin and frowned at Natalie. 'I get on well with my daughter, and if there's anything important she wants to share, I listen, but she doesn't tell me everything. Do you both have children?' she asked.

Lucy shook her head but Natalie replied with, 'I've got a daughter about the same age as yours.'

Jojo narrowed her eyes. 'Well then, you should know better than to ask me that. Does *your* daughter discuss her friends' problems or lives with you?' She didn't wait for a response but instead moved towards the door. 'Now, I'm going to check on mine.'

Once she'd gone Lucy whispered, 'Ouch! I think we crossed some line. She's going to hold out on us now, isn't she?'

'If she can calm Ellie down, we might find out something else, but I can't see her giving up any of Roxy's secrets, even if she knows them. This could be a wasted trip. Listen, why don't you have a go at questioning her. She might feel more at ease with somebody who's closer to her own age.'

'If you think so, but I'm not exactly a teenager.'

'You look young enough for her to feel more at ease with you and she might open up if she's speaking to you rather than me. I'm too much of an authoritative figure. I might be putting her off.'

The sound of voices drifting in their direction silenced them, and when Ellie came back into the room, Lucy gave her a smile. 'Thanks for helping us. Do you want any water or anything?'

The girl refused the offer and sat down again. Her mother dropped down beside her and Lucy took the chair opposite them, brushing the fringe away from her face and uncovering the scar that ran across the bridge of her nose for a second.

Ellie noticed it. 'What happened to your face?'

'I got in the way of somebody waving a smashed bottle,' Lucy replied.

'Oh.'

'Could have been worse.' She waited a heartbeat then casually said, 'Roxy suffered a few injuries too, didn't she? I bet she had a few scars too.'

The girl shrugged a response.

'Tell me about her. What was she like?'

Ellie blinked. 'Funny. Brave.'

'Brave?'

'Yeah.'

'In what way?'

'Lots of ways. She wasn't scared of much.'

'And she was a good friend?'

'Yeah.'

'You knew her better than anyone, Ellie. Can you think of who she might have gone to see yesterday?'

Her head swayed like a slow pendulum.

'Did you see Roxy often?'

'Most days.'

'But not yesterday?'

Her eyes filled up again. 'No. I was with Mum all day. We went shopping in Derby, and after we got home, I went to the youth centre to hang out like usual. I thought Roxy might be there but she didn't show up.'

'Were you a little surprised she didn't show up at the youth centre?'

'Not really. She only came along when she felt like it. It was too babyish for her. We play table tennis and mess about. She didn't enjoy it much.'

'But you do?'

'Yeah. It's okay.'

'Did you text her last night from the centre to ask if she was coming?'

'No. There's no signal in there and I lost track of time.'

'You can't think where she might have gone, then?'

'No.'

'Did Roxy have a boyfriend she might have visited?'

'No.' The reply was a little too quick and accompanied by a further lowering of the head. Ellie wouldn't meet Lucy's eyes.

'Thank you, Ellie. You've been really helpful.' Lucy waited for the girl to lift her gaze, and when she did, she asked casually, 'What time did you get back home from the youth centre?'

'I dunno – nine thirty.'

Ellie's mother butted in. 'Ellie's responsible. She's always back at about that time. She goes every Saturday, and I messaged her on WhatsApp at about ten to check she was at home.'

'You answered?' Lucy asked Ellie.

'Yes, I was watching telly.'

'She did,' said Jojo.

'And this youth centre is the one on Park Road?'

'That's the one. Most of the local kids go there. There's not a lot else for them to do,' Jojo added.

Lucy stood up. 'We're really very sorry about Roxy. If you can think of anything at all that would give us a pointer as to where she might have gone yesterday, will you let us know? I'm going to leave my card with your mum. Just call me if you think of anything at all. It might be more important than you think and it could help us find out what happened to Roxy.'

Ellie wriggled under her regard but nodded.

Natalie thanked them both and added, 'I'm sure the school will be offering counselling to fellow students once the news is broken, but if you'd like, I'll ask one of my colleagues to drop by and visit you.'

'We'll be fine,' Jojo replied, putting an arm around her daughter. 'We don't need anybody else around here.' The guard was back up and a hardness had crept back into her eyes. It was time to leave.

Boo was standing with one foot on her scooter next to the staircase as they walked towards it. 'Is Ellie going to prison like her dad?' she asked candidly.

Natalie shook her head.

'She does lots of naughty things.'

'Really?' Lucy halted and studied the girl with curly dark hair and large brown eyes who seemed very pleased with the sudden attention.

'Uh-huh. She and her friend were smoking downstairs with boys. I came in with Mummy and she told them off for it. They shouldn't smoke inside a building. It's dangerous. They said rude words back. That's naughty, isn't it?'

'Yes, but not bad enough to be sent to prison. Is your mum home, Boo?' Natalie asked.

The curls shook side to side. 'She's out. Nanna's looking after me.'

'When will she be home?'

'Don't know. Later,' she replied, then hearing her name being called, she suddenly took off, speeding along the landing again.

Lucy's brows lifted at the rapid departure and commented, 'She's quite something, isn't she?'

'I wonder if Roxy was the other girl smoking downstairs. Hang on a sec.' Natalie followed after the girl and rapped on her door.

A thin-faced woman in her late sixties answered, her hand on the door handle in preparation to shut it quickly. Boo materialised, squashed in beside the woman and the doorframe, and looked up keenly at Natalie, who introduced herself and asked if the woman knew Roxy.

'I don't live here. I don't often come here. I'm only here to look after Boo while my daughter's at work. Normally, Boo comes to our house, but my old man's got a nasty stomach bug and I didn't want her to catch it. I don't know any of the kids around here by name.'

'Not even Ellie?'

'Course you know Ellie, Nanny,' Boo piped up. 'Her dad robbed a shop and had a gun.'

The woman's face scrunched up in disgust. 'Oh, her.'

'Roxy was her best friend. You might have seen them together.' Natalie showed her a photo of Roxanne. The woman squinted hard at the picture. 'I might have but they all look the same to me.'

'What time is your daughter due back? I'd like to ask her about Roxy.'

The woman's demeanour was frosty and her hand remained on the door handle. 'Teatime – about five.'

'Well, thank you for your time.'

The woman nodded once and shut the door quickly. Natalie joined Lucy, who was waiting at the top of the stairs.

'No joy there. Might ask Boo's mum,' said Natalie as they clattered down the stairs.

'I think Ellie's holding back on us. She couldn't look at me when I asked what time she got in.'

'I noticed that too. She might have been out later than nine thirty, maybe even with one of the boys Boo saw her with, or just hanging about with friends. She was adamant she didn't see Roxy yesterday so we'll leave it for now and see what else we can uncover.'

'She could have been lying and was with Roxy,' said Lucy.

'I'm definitely not ruling out that possibility. We'll talk to her again if we need to. I'll check with Murry and see if Gavin and Kirk are on their way to the station. If so, we'll try Daisy at the tea room.'

As they crossed the street to the squad car, Natalie glanced back towards the block. Ellie had seemed truly shocked by the news of her friend's death but there was, as Lucy had pointed out, something else suspicious. It came to her in a flash: Ellie hadn't asked how Roxy had died.

The Vintage Tea Room was jam-packed when Natalie and Lucy arrived. Several bicycles were propped against a lamp post and the shop window, and a group of cyclists had taken residence inside, tables pushed together. The noise of their laughter carried outside. Natalie opened the door and walked in, ignoring the warmth and the sour smell of sweating bodies. Daisy, in the middle of balancing two plates of cakes and a pot of tea on a tray, looked up. 'They're not here. They've gone to the police station.'

She slid out from behind the counter and around the tables with practised ease, and after placing the food and drink on the tables, she exchanged pleasantries and gave a warm smile that faded as she returned to the counter where Lucy and Natalie were standing.

She wiped the tray over with a cloth, placed it back in position and rearranged some cups. When neither woman moved off she said again, 'They're not here.'

'Yes, I know. I'd like you to answer a couple of questions for us.'

'You're kidding. I've got work to do,' she replied, wiping her hands on a plain beige hand towel.

Natalie craned her head and looked around the room. 'It appears everyone's been served. If you could step outside with us for a few minutes, you'll still be able to see if you're needed. It won't take long.'

Daisy tossed the towel onto the top and marched to the front door. Once outside, she folded her arms and waited for Natalie

and Lucy to join her. They stood in a huddle in front of the door. One of the cyclists who'd been observing them made comment to another, who twisted around briefly to stare at the women. A blank-faced Lucy returned the look until both men went back to their tea-drinking. She pulled out her notebook and Natalie began the questioning. 'Daisy, you told us earlier you had a bath and went to bed at about ten thirty last night.'

'I did. I'd had a long day.'

'You didn't fancy joining Gavin at Extravaganza?'

'You're kidding! I never go there these days.'

'I see,' said Natalie and added, '"These days". I take it, then, you used to go there?'

Daisy grimaced. 'You'll find out anyway, I suppose. I used to work there. I was one of their hostesses. I worked in the private rooms – served drinks, made sure everyone was happy and spending plenty of money.'

'How long were you there?'

'Over a year.'

'And when did you leave Extravaganza?'

'Two months ago.'

'The Vintage Tea Room is a fairly new venture, then?'

'Yes. It opened in May this year.'

'I don't suppose a nightclub hostess earns a huge amount. How did you finance it?'

Daisy shifted from one ballet-style shoe to the other. 'I got some help.'

'From?'

'Gavin. He loaned me the money for the shop lease and the apartment above it.'

Lucy interjected, 'That was good of him.' She was rewarded with a scowl.

'It was a business arrangement. I'll pay him back.'

'How much do you owe him?' Lucy asked.

'None of your business,' snapped Daisy.

Lucy made a note before responding. 'Not a problem. I'm sure we can find out the exact details.'

Natalie pressed on, 'It must be hard to find time to spend together, what with Gavin at the nightclub until the early hours and you working days in the tea room.'

'He doesn't work every night. I'm not being funny but what's this got to do with their house burning down?'

Natalie side-stepped the question with a quick, 'Do you know anyone called Roxanne Curtis?'

Daisy's mouth turned down as she appeared to think over the question. 'Can't say I've heard of her. Does she work at the club?'

'No. She's a schoolgirl.'

Daisy pulled a face. 'I'm not likely to know her then.'

'Don't you get any schoolkids coming into the tea room?' Lucy asked.

'It's not the sort of place they hang out in, not unless they're with their mums.'

'Do you know Cathy Curtis? Roxanne's mum?' She pulled out a photograph to see if Daisy recognised her face, but she stared blankly at it.

'No. I've not come across her.'

Natalie paused a second and then asked, 'How long have you and Gavin been a couple?'

The woman's reactions changed subtly; she covered the front of her throat. Natalie had seen such tell-tale signs before in courtrooms when a defendant would suddenly cover their face, throat or abdomen during questioning – a protective gesture and sure sign that the lawyer had hit a nerve. It was human instinct to cover a vulnerable part of the body. Gestures often told a different story to words spoken. Such was the case with Daisy.

'Eight or nine weeks.' The fact she couldn't be sure of when they'd started seeing each other struck Natalie as odd. Couples in

fledgling relationships usually knew when they met and had their first date.

'So you've been together since May?'

'Yes.'

'Was that after you left the nightclub?'

Daisy rubbed her throat unconsciously as she spoke. 'It's complicated.'

'What do you mean?'

'We've been an official couple since May. Unofficially, we've been hanging out for a lot longer.'

'How long exactly?' Natalie asked.

The woman shuffled her feet but kept her hand in position. She was clearly uncomfortable with this new line of questioning. 'Almost a year. About two weeks after I started working at the club, he and I got chatting. He said he fancied me and asked if I'd like to get to know him a bit better.' She fixed her gaze on the pavement, her hand still in position covering her throat. Her shoulders had risen and her voice had weakened, becoming shallow: more signs of nervousness and feeling tense.

When she'd first started working for Manchester police, Natalie had attended a course on how to spot obvious lies. She'd learnt that people telling lies could often run out of breath because heart rate and blood flow increased when they were lying. No matter how much somebody could try and convince you with words, their bodies might tell a different story, and such physiological indicators had helped Natalie recognise liars quickly. Daisy was anxious about her relationship with Gavin, but why?

'You didn't have a boyfriend at the time, then?'

'I'd just come out of a relationship.'

'And Gavin was single?'

'Yes.'

'Did Gavin ask you out then?' Natalie kept her questioning light.

'Yes – the first time was to a pub for a lunchtime drink.'

'And after that?'

'We started seeing each other whenever we were both free, about once a week – meals out, films, trips out – the usual. Then, after about six months, we went away for a weekend in Edinburgh.'

'Why keep it unofficial? It sounds like you've been going out together for a long time. Who were you hiding your relationship from? Your ex-boyfriend?'

'No. It wasn't like that at all. We kept quiet about seeing each other while I was working at the club. Gavin didn't want anyone, especially the other hostesses, to hear about it and that suited me.'

'Why?' asked Natalie.

'Some of the girls are right bitches. They'd have said I was chasing after him for his money or some shit like that, and would have made life difficult for me... for us both. You know how women can be.' Her head cocked to one side, and her fingers rubbed at her throat again.

Natalie suspected Daisy had been the one who'd really wanted to keep a lid on their relationship. The hostesses might have been right that Daisy's reasons for cultivating the relationship had been purely financial. She pushed further to expose the truth.

'But they'd be wrong, wouldn't they? He came on to you and invited *you* out. It wasn't the other way around,' Natalie said.

Daisy's head bobbed up and down but her eyes weren't lifted to meet Natalie's. 'Yeah, definitely.'

'You don't sound so sure.'

'Of course, I'm sure. What the hell does it matter anyway? We're a couple now – an official couple.'

'But you don't live together?'

Daisy sighed. 'I'm not ready for that sort of commitment yet.'

Natalie gave her a long look. 'When did he suggest buying you this place?'

'He's invested in it, not bought it. There's a difference.'

'When did he suggest investing in the business?' Natalie said.

'When we were in Edinburgh, six months ago. I told him it was my dream to own a tea shop and he laughed at first then said it was a good dream to have. I didn't want to always work as a hostess and he knew I was saving up. He said he'd help me find and finance a place, and once I packed in working at Extravaganza, we could become an official couple.' For someone whose boyfriend had helped her achieve her ambition, she didn't seem especially happy or content with her lot. Natalie was more certain than ever that Daisy had chased after Gavin for his money, and was now regretting being with him. Could Daisy have set fire to the house, and if so, what motive would she have for doing so? She tested the woman with a fresh question.

'Daisy, can you think of anyone who'd want to burn down Gavin and Kirk's house?'

She kept her eyes on the pavement. 'No idea at all.'

'Can you run through exactly what you did after you shut up the tea room?'

'Why?'

'We need to establish your exact whereabouts to eliminate you from our enquiries.'

'I didn't do it! Why would I? This is insane!'

Natalie waited for the woman to calm down, which she did. She removed her hand from her throat and folded her arms. 'I went upstairs at about six, ate a chicken salad, poured a glass of wine and watched some television, messaged some mates on WhatsApp and then had a bath. It's hard work being on your feet all day, seven days a week and sorting out orders, books and so on. It'd been a really busy week and I didn't feel like doing anything much afterwards.'

'Did you talk to anyone online afterwards?'

'No. I wasn't in the mood. I came on yesterday. I always feel shit when my period starts.'

'You didn't text or talk to Gavin?'

'No.'

'Who did you message on WhatsApp? Friends, relatives? Somebody who can confirm your whereabouts?'

'I was tired. I went to bed. I was tired.' She'd avoided the question.

'Who did you talk to?'

Daisy shook her head. The hand was back at her throat.

A customer tapped on the window.

'I have to go.'

Natalie took a step back. 'I can have your call log checked.'

'I messaged Kirk.'

'Why?'

'To ask him to tell Gavin I wasn't going to the club as planned. Gavin wasn't answering his phone.' Her eyelids fluttered. More lies.

'You messaged Kirk rather than try Gavin again?'

'I don't see what any of this has to do with last night. I didn't burn down their house.'

'Daisy, have you ever had a relationship with Kirk Lang?'

Daisy's face became guarded and her eyes flashed. 'What sort of question is that? Of course not. I'm going out with his brother. Anyway, my private life isn't any of your business. Now I'm needed inside.'

Both women watched as Daisy stomped back inside.

'Do you think she was seeing Kirk before she started seeing Gavin?' Lucy asked.

'Maybe, or she is certainly interested in him now. She doesn't seem that bothered about Gavin, which strikes me as strange, especially as he gave her the money for the tea room. She's only officially been with him for two months. She should be a bit more loved up than she seems, shouldn't she? Considering they're supposed to be a couple, they don't seem to spend much time together

and she didn't ring Gavin's mobile to tell him the house was on fire. She rang Kirk at the club.'

'And she was definitely nervous about something when we last spoke to them all. We all picked up on that,' said Lucy.

'It could be that she and Kirk are seeing each other behind his brother's back, and she's only with Gavin because of the loan, or there could be something more to it. Anyway, I didn't get the impression she knew Roxy or Cathy. There were no tells that I could spot. There's something else going on though. Why do I keep getting the impression people are keeping things from us?'

'Because the fuckers are,' said Lucy as she opened the car door.

Natalie glanced back at the tea room and caught Daisy staring at her. The woman dropped her head as soon as she'd been seen. 'I reckon you're right on that. Time to talk to Gavin and Kirk.'

CHAPTER SEVEN

SUNDAY, 1 JULY – MID-AFTERNOON

David Ward dragged a crusty, yellowed sock from the bottom of the washing basket and tossed it into the washing machine before shutting the door with such force it didn't catch and sprang back open. He tried again, this time more gently, and waited for the click that told him the door was securely fastened. Reaching down beside it, he lifted and slammed the box of washing powder on top of the appliance. He scooped the requisite amount into the drawer and closed it too, then twisted the knob, listening to the solid click… click… click as it turned into the usual position for a forty-degree wash. It grumbled into action as water spat into the drum. He rested his palms on it and stared at the calendar on the wall. It was covered in his neat handwriting, essentially filled with their children's busy itineraries, so he knew when he'd be required to ferry them about, and red crosses when Natalie was at work. Today was blank. It ought to have been a family day but Natalie had been called into work, leaving him with two teenagers who were holed up in their respective rooms, unwilling to join him.

What the fuck am I doing with my life? Here he was, a man in his late forties with a first-class degree in languages and a career in translating law documents, who couldn't get a job of any description, let alone an interview for one, and instead of feeling fulfilled and relaxed at the weekend after a busy but productive week at work, he

was stuck inside on a Sunday afternoon, cleaning up. He didn't mind doing household chores. He was happy to help out and take the load off Natalie, but oh lord, how he despised himself at the moment.

He'd always been an achiever. He'd striven to succeed and had been proud to get a position translating legal documents at a top law firm in Manchester, and he'd been diligent and hard-working. In fact, he'd been bloody good at it. It had defined him. It had earned him respect. The first blow had come when he'd been made redundant. He hadn't seen that coming. Suddenly, he'd gone from a high-flyer to a nobody. His work colleagues had shunned him and his world had come crashing down through no fault of his own. The Internet had taken over his role and he'd found himself hunting for employment, only this time it was in a different world: one crowded with graduates who were as good as him but more dynamic, more tech-savvy, a better fit than him at the up-and-coming companies where he stood apart like an ageing relic.

However, he'd got over it and had tried to make it on his own as an online translator but once again had failed. More recently, since Leigh's attempt to run away, he'd thrown himself back onto the job market. He was willing to take up any employment offered to him, anything that allowed him to earn a salary, regain some self-esteem and not rely on Natalie to be the breadwinner. It wasn't that he was jealous of Natalie, who had risen up the ranks and been promoted to DI. God, no! He admired her and loved the very bones of her, but he needed to feel useful and he yearned for respect again. He wanted to be a father that his kids looked up to, not the weak-willed, hopeless, bloody mess he'd become.

He pushed away from the machine. Standing there feeling sorry for himself wasn't going to make matters better. The drum droned as it churned and he watched as the clothes toppled over each other. No, he had to do something.

He wandered into the kitchen and picked up his mobile. He'd known Mike Sullivan for years and he was one of the few people

who understood him properly. It was Mike's day to have his daughter, Thea. He rang him.

'Hi, Mike. Wondered if you fancied popping around for a few beers. You could bring Thea. I know Leigh would love to see her.'

'Oh, mate, I'd love to but I haven't got her today. I was called into work in the early hours.'

'You working the same investigation as Nat?'

'Yes. I saw her earlier at the crime scene. Have to take a rain check. We'll reschedule when I'm next off.'

'Sure.'

'Everything's okay, isn't it?'

'Yes, of course. Just thought we could catch up. Not seen you for a while.'

'Bloody work. Stops you having a social life,' said Mike, who paused before saying, 'Sorry, that was thoughtless. It just came out.'

'Forget it! It's fine. We'll grab a drink soon.'

'Defo.'

David hung up, replaced the phone on the table and ran a hand over his chin. He felt like a leper. Nobody wanted to know him. *Fucking hell!* He took the stairs with purpose and, drawing a deep breath, rapped on Josh's door. Not expecting a response, he opened it and stuck his head around, fake enthusiasm all over his features.

'Hey!'

Josh was sitting on the end of his bed, games control in his hand and a microphone attached to his head. He paused the screen, freezing a soldier who was aiming a machine gun at a dark corner of an abandoned building. He looked up at his father.

David didn't give him a chance to speak but went straight in with his suggestion. 'Thought you might like to go to Costa. You could see if they've got any jobs going like we discussed, and then we could maybe go bowling or something afterwards.'

'Nah, you're okay. I don't fancy working there anyway. I'd have to serve a load of mates and they'll take the piss.'

David kept the artificial smile fixed to his face. 'It's a job, Josh. You could do with the money.'

'I'll find something. Not there though.'

'You won't find anything sitting in here all day,' David began, then checked himself. Natalie had already told Josh he needed to find a job for the long school holidays. Josh didn't need two of them nagging him. Besides, David was a fine one to talk. He changed tack. 'Well, how about going out anyway? We haven't bowled in ages.'

'It's a bit… lame,' said Josh. 'The place will be filled with kids.'

Josh glanced at the screen, making David feel he was being dismissed. He persisted.

'Okay, how about you and I have a game on that?' He nodded at the screen.

'You won't understand the rules for this one. I'm levelled up on it already and you won't be able to keep up.'

'Okay, what about that car game we used to play? We could have a game together. Go on. It'd be more fun than playing by yourself.'

'I'm not playing by myself. I'm online. I'm playing with my mates,' said Josh, pointing at the headset.

'Yeah. Sure. Okay. It was just a suggestion.'

Josh nodded at him and he backed away. As he drew the door to, he heard the rat-a-tat of rapid gunfire once more. His son was back in the zone with his online companions. That was it these days: kids didn't go out to meet their friends, they hung about inside and talked to them online. David didn't get it. He wasn't useless when it came to technology but he still didn't understand what made teenagers want to hide away in their rooms and only communicate via the Internet. It made him feel old. Leigh's room was opposite and he tried it.

'Yeah?'

Again, he pushed open the door, a smile on his face. 'Fancy a banana smoothie in Costa? Just you and me… and a cake of your choice.'

Leigh put down her magazine. 'I'm not hungry. Besides, I'm meeting Katy and Jade soon.'

'Where are you going?'

'Jade's house.'

He was at a loss as to what to say next. It seemed only moments ago that they spent time together, watching films or comedy shows, or sharing a pizza. They'd had such a special father–daughter bond and had enjoyed time together. Then Leigh had run away, and now she could barely manage to talk to him.

'Okay. Well, another time, maybe.'

'Sure.'

He plodded back downstairs to the kitchen. Was this it? Was this all there would ever be in his life? Last week, he'd updated his personal information on the job agency websites, and even though his CV read well, he'd still not even been offered an interview. He opened the cupboard above the sink and lifted out the bottle of whisky he'd bought at Aldi. He undid it, poured a large glass and knocked it back in one then poured another before taking it into the sitting room and dropping onto the settee in front of the television. The kids didn't give a shit about him, so why should he keep making the effort? He swigged the alcohol, allowing the warmth to flood his veins. *Fuck it!*

CHAPTER EIGHT

SUNDAY, 1 JULY – EARLY EVENING

Kirk Lang leant forward, arms on the table, and asked Lucy, 'Why exactly am I here?'

Lucy dropped down onto the chair opposite him, threw him a tight smile and said, 'Because we need to ask you a few questions.'

'You could have asked me at the tea room. You didn't need us to haul our arses down here. We're busy men – and where's Gavin?'

'Thank you for coming down. I'd like to go back over a few details. Firstly, can you confirm you were at Extravaganza all night?'

'I asked you about my brother.'

'He's in another interview room.'

'Why?'

'Because I wanted to talk to you separately.'

'We haven't done anything wrong.'

'I didn't suggest you had. I want to get a clear picture of what happened, and last time we spoke to you, your brother took the lead. I'd like to hear what you have to say. So, can you confirm you were at the nightclub last night until the early hours of this morning?'

He sighed. 'Yes. I told you that already.'

'And you took a phone call from Daisy, who told you your house was on fire?'

He blew out his cheeks. 'Yes.'

'Why didn't you return home with your brother to see what damage there was?'

'I already explained. The nightclub was heaving busy and we didn't both need to see the state of the house. Gavin's the one who looks after all the paperwork and insurance and shit like that, so it made sense for him to go. I wouldn't have been any help, would I? It's not like I could've put out the blaze myself.'

'And you went about business as usual?'

'Pretty much. Gavin kept me up to speed with what was happening.'

Lucy tapped her notebook. 'Now, here's the thing. You and Gavin seem to have quite an unusual attitude with regards to the property. I have yet to meet anyone who was as laid back as you two are about losing everything they owned in a house fire.'

'You know why. We aren't like everyone else. It isn't that big a deal. Besides, the insurance money will put everything to rights.'

'But a person was found dead in your house.'

'And I don't know who the fuck they are. It has to be the bastard who set fire to it.' He narrowed his eyes, and once again, Lucy was aware of how menacing he could appear.

'Do you know this girl?' Lucy slid the photograph of Roxy towards him.

Kirk glanced at it and pushed it straight back. 'No.'

'Look again, Kirk.' Lucy pushed it towards him again.

He stared at it for a full minute before placing his forefinger on it and sliding it back across the table. He released a sigh and said, 'No.'

'You are saying you don't know this girl and have never seen her before in your life?'

'That's exactly what I'm saying. Who is she?'

'Roxanne Curtis.'

'Not heard of her.'

'She's a fourteen-year-old schoolgirl from Clearview.'

'Clearview? That shithole!'

'You know the place?'

'Who doesn't? It's a run-down eyesore filled with druggies and wasters.'

'That's quite a sweeping statement to make.'

'I don't need to defend my thoughts. Everyone who lives in Armston avoids that area. You only go there if you're looking for trouble, and sometimes it comes looking for people in Armston. Clearview kids come into town to get into fights and smash up shopfronts and cause fucking mayhem. We've had loads of trouble outside the nightclub. Clearview is a shithole,' he repeated, hissing his words.

'What sort of trouble?'

'Kids trying to score, get into fights – all sorts.'

'You report them to the police?'

'What's the point? By the time you lot would have arrived, they'd have scarpered. We doubled security on the doors and keep the fuckers out.' He clenched and unclenched his fists, and Lucy wondered if he'd taken any of the troublemakers on himself.

'Did you take matters into your own hands?'

'Never.'

'You expect me to believe that?'

'If I took any of them on, I'd probably kill them. Lethal weapons,' he said, holding up his wide hands.

Lucy stared hard at him, and he realised he'd said something that could incriminate him. 'I train – I never fight. It's all about image. If you look scary enough, people usually behave for you.'

Lucy digested his words. Could he have attacked Roxy and killed her with those fists? She tapped the photograph to draw his attention back to it. 'Roxanne is also the girl whose body we uncovered in your house.'

'*She* set fire to our house?' His eyes widened in genuine surprise.

'We don't know that yet, but it would help if we could find out how she got into your house and what she was doing there.'

'I'm fucked if I know. I've never set eyes on her.'

'You're completely sure you haven't heard of her or seen her anywhere? Look again at the photo, Kirk.'

'I don't need to look. I don't know who she is.' He leant even closer towards Lucy and looked her in the eye. 'I don't know who the fuck she is.'

Lucy didn't move a muscle.

He pushed his chair back suddenly and stood up. 'You can't keep me here. Where's Gavin? We're leaving.'

'I'm afraid that's not possible for the time being. DI Ward is talking to him. What about her mother, Cathy Curtis? Do you know her?' She showed him a photograph of Cathy.

He shook his head. 'No, I don't. I've never seen her and I haven't heard of anyone called Curtis. I can't for the life of me imagine why this girl would be in our house, how she got in or why on earth she'd set fire to it. Has she got a criminal record?'

'No, she hasn't, and we don't know that she did set fire to your house, just like we don't know if she was already dead when the fire started.' She looked pointedly at Kirk, who gave a soft groan.

'I've not seen her before,' he repeated. 'She's never set foot in our house before last night.'

'You said yourself, your hands are weapons.'

'No… no. I wanted to explain that I never set on troublemakers. It's enough to look like you can hurt somebody. I'm not a violent man. Not at all. Ask my brother.'

The macho image had fractured. His eyes pleaded. She let it drop for the moment.

'What about the name Paul Sadler?'

'No idea who he is.'

Lucy picked up the photographs and put them in her file. Standing up, she said, 'If you wouldn't mind waiting for a while, I'll be back shortly.'

'Can't I go? I don't know anything.'

'If you could just wait until we've finished talking to your brother, it would be most helpful.' She walked off, ignoring the loud huffing behind her.

*

Natalie was finding Gavin hard going. Not only did he not recognise the photos of Roxy and her mother, he was stomping about the interview room, demanding to leave or to have a lawyer. She was rapidly running out of patience.

'I'd like to remind you that a teenage girl was found dead at your property. We have no way of knowing how she died or how she got into your house. It's imperative we establish those facts. We need your full cooperation.'

'I've never clapped eyes on her and I've no fucking idea why she'd be in my house other than to torch it. Maybe she was some sort of crazed drug addict who broke in and accidentally set fire to it. I don't know. It's for you and the fire investigators to sort out, but let's get something clear: I am not in any shape, way or form responsible for her death.' He squared his shoulders, waiting for her retort, but she had none. Until they could prove that Roxy was known to the men, they couldn't do a lot. She thanked him for his assistance and told him he could wait for his brother at reception.

*

'Bollocks!' Lucy, perched on the edge of her desk, scowled into the distance. 'I don't believe for one second that Roxy got her hands on a door key, disabled their alarm and strolled into their house with a can of petrol and set fire to it. Besides, according to the FI, the

fire was started at the entrance and she was in the entertainment room to the rear. It makes no sense at all. Gavin and Kirk are hiding something. I'm bloody well sure of it.'

Murray flicked through his notes and gave them what he'd got. 'Got to agree with you on that. While you were out, I interviewed Top to Bottom cleaning agency's owner, Rachel Stevens. I showed her photos of our victim, and Rachel's definitely never met or heard of Roxy. She cleans the house in Linnet Lane herself. It's closer to her own home so it's convenient for her to do it. She confirmed what she told you, Natalie, that Roxy isn't related to or known by any of her staff, and when it isn't being used, the house key is kept in a locked cupboard in her office. She's only spoken to the brothers on a couple of occasions. They tend to be out when she's cleaning. She didn't have anything bad to say about them. Reckoned they were fine to work for, paid on time and was sorry she couldn't help us any further.'

'Fuck! Another dead end.' Natalie dragged her fingers over her scalp. They were getting nowhere. 'We're running around in circles. We'll have to try Roxy's friends.'

'Fat chance of any of them cooperating, even if they know something. Clearview kids are a tough bunch. Remember that drugs case we had last year when five kids on the Denton Estate were beaten senseless?' Murray mumbled.

Lucy groaned. 'God, yes. They wouldn't say a bloody word. Murray's right, Natalie. They won't be any use.'

'I don't see what other choice we have. We have to establish if she was involved with somebody who set fire to the house or if she actually knew the Lang brothers.' Natalie rested her fingers against her temples and released a lengthy sigh. 'Fucking hell. This is a nightmare.'

Murray picked up his notes again. 'I spoke to Sarah Raleigh. She's Paul Sadler's ex-girlfriend. She agreed to come to the station to be interviewed. I'm expecting her soon.'

'Paul's got an alibi. He and Seth were at a motorcycle event all day and he wasn't even at home when Roxy left. After eating, he spent the night playing games with Seth,' said Lucy.

Natalie shook her head. 'We'll still find out what we can about Paul. It might take us in a new direction.'

'I can't see it myself. Seth confirmed what Charlie said. They were in the bedroom until midnight, and Cathy woke up when Paul went to bed. They all flatly denied knowing Gavin and Kirk, let alone where they lived. Besides, how would Paul even know Roxy was in the house?' Lucy argued.

'He could have been the arsonist,' said Ian from his desk, where he was hunched over his screen.

Murray lifted and drained a plastic cup then asked, 'You think he and Roxy planned to destroy the Langs' house?'

Lucy let out a derisory snort.

'Why not?' Ian responded. 'Weirder things have happened.'

Natalie shrugged and added, 'People lie all the time. It's possible. Maybe they're all lying. Everything's bloody possible at the moment. We need some facts. We're shooting in the dark at the moment.'

Murray scraped back his chair. 'I'm going for another coffee. Anyone want one?' He was met with headshakes.

Just as he reached the door, Ian spoke loudly. 'Natalie!' He spun to face the trio, looking somewhat perkier than when he'd first arrived. 'The financial reports for Gavin and Kirk Lang arrived a few minutes ago and they make interesting reading. The brothers took out a substantial bank loan to purchase the nightclub, and, get this… they used their house as collateral. If the nightclub goes under, they lose everything: their house, business and the two cars which were also bought on finance. They're stretched to the limit.'

Natalie dropped her hands from her head and sat up. 'What about that tea room and flat above it?'

'Mortgaged. It's written down here as a buy-to-let property and is solely in Gavin's name. Does Daisy pay rent to him?'

Lucy joined in. 'She told us she was paying him back every penny so maybe she is paying him some sort of rent each month. Those brothers were definitely holding back during their interviews. Something about this isn't right. I bet what they said about the club being packed with people was just bullshit to throw us off the scent. Is there any CCTV so we can find out?'

Ian shook his head. 'Only one camera overlooking the downstairs till. It doesn't matter how busy a place is – it could still be haemorrhaging money. I've only received their personal finances so far. I'll chase up the business accounts. If they are having financial difficulties, it opens up other possibilities.'

Murray agreed. 'And if the nightclub is in trouble, it'd also help explain why that part-time bar person, Lindsay, couldn't get any stand-in shifts. They might have been cutting back on staff. I'll follow it up later when I go there, and find out what staff morale's like. Could be one of them bore the brothers a grudge and this was payback.'

'Or the shifty bastards set fire to the place themselves simply to get the insurance money to help pay their way out of the shit they're in,' said Lucy.

Natalie said, 'I'm with Lucy on this. The fire could well be linked to insurance money. Gavin was very keen to get a report to the company so he could get a payout. They might well have set fire to their own property or even paid someone else to do it while they were out and had plenty of witnesses as to their whereabouts. That would be logical. However, none of this explains what Roxy was doing in that entertainment room at the time the house caught fire.'

Ian offered his thoughts. 'She might have known the arsonist and went along with them to help burn the place down. It could still be Paul or her brothers.'

Natalie pressed the spot between her eyebrows as she often did when trying to concentrate. Why would Roxy agree to be Paul's accomplice, and why would he torch their house anyway? 'Okay, let's look at that possibility. How might they know each other?'

'Paul fits aerials. Could he have fitted one to their house or nearby?' Ian offered.

Natalie agreed that was possible. 'Follow up on that.'

Murray gave a grunt. 'Maybe we're trying too hard to link the Langs and Paul Sadler; maybe it's simpler – Gavin and Kirk murdered Roxy, panicked and tried to dispose of her body by burning it beyond recognition, unaware she had metalwork inside that could help identify her.'

Natalie agreed that could be the case but added, 'Let's not get ahead of ourselves. What we need is solid evidence so we can charge somebody, and unless we find some, we're stuffed.'

'I'll start on Roxy's laptop and see what I can find. Do you want me to begin contacting her friends?' Ian directed his question at Natalie, who rubbed her dry lips together as she pondered her answer. Talking to all of Roxy's online and school friends and those from the youth centre would be a mammoth task.

'Not yet. If Roxy didn't tell her best friend Ellie what was going on, it's unlikely she'd have shared secrets with any others,' she replied.

'One of those friends might be the arsonist,' Murray suggested.

'That's possible but there has to be an easier way of doing this. By the way, has Roxy's father been informed of her death yet?'

'An officer was dispatched over an hour ago.'

'Okay. I doubt he's seen her recently, but we'll ask the question anyway. We'll wait for Nick Hart's report on the fire and see if we can glean anything new from it, and tomorrow we'll try Ellie again. In the meantime, check through Roxy's laptop and trawl through footage from any CCTV cameras in the vicinity for any suspicious activity. I know it's a ball-ache and a long shot but we don't have many other options for the moment. Can somebody talk to Oliver Curtis? I'd like confirmation that he was at his barracks in Nottingham and nowhere near the house in Armston yesterday. Murray and Ian, why don't you both go to Extravaganza when it

opens later. Let's chase the insurance fraud and unhappy employees angles for a while. They seem the most logical, although I still can't work out why Roxanne was in their house.'

The desk phone lit up and Natalie answered it. It was the desk sergeant, who had Sarah Raleigh, Paul Sadler's ex-girlfriend, in reception.

'Murray, you want to come and interview Sarah with me?'

'Sure.'

Sarah was nothing like Cathy. She was considerably younger to look at with a fresh complexion, fuller figure and short dark hair and chestnut-brown eyes. She sat with a large handbag on her lap but didn't release the handles and kept her eyes on Natalie, who sat opposite her. Natalie gave her a warm smile.

'Thank you for coming in. You've already spoken to DS Anderson on the phone.'

'That's right.'

'We're conducting an investigation into the death of Paul's partner's daughter, Roxanne Curtis. We're talking to everyone who knew the family,' Natalie explained.

'Yes, Sergeant Anderson told me, but I haven't seen Paul since we split up and I don't know his new girlfriend.' Her tone belied a bitterness.

'But you lived with Paul for a while. What can you tell us about him?'

Sarah's hands gripped the handles more tightly. 'It was a long time ago now – nine years ago. It was great to start with. We met at a bar in town in January 2008. I was a barmaid in those days and I served him. Paul chatted me up and after a week, he asked me out. It was a proper whirlwind romance. Everything was perfect. Paul was great – attentive and fun. We saw each other every day and I moved in with him two months later. About six months after that, things changed.'

'In what way?'

'In the early days, whenever we had a day off, we'd spend it in bed together – all day – eat, watch telly, have sex. It was so romantic. We stopped doing that and then he started being picky. He'd criticise me – the way I speak, my hair, my clothes – and he didn't care if he upset me. Then he started going out evenings on his own and wouldn't tell me where he'd been. I'd complain and we'd argue. I didn't want to give up on us though. We'd been so good together but he didn't really want to make any effort. He used to deliberately start an argument so I'd snap back. The arguments became worse. He'd push me about and threaten to hit me if I didn't shut up. He slapped me a few times. Eventually, I left him.'

'I understand you called the police on a couple of occasions because you were frightened. Once in 2008 and the second in 2009.'

'It seems stupid now when I look back on it. The first time, he'd been out without me and when he came home he was steaming drunk and in a shit mood. I had a go at him and he went mental. He slapped me really hard and then put his hand around my throat and squeezed. I thought he was going to kill me. I was petrified but he took his hand away and said he was sorry – that he'd had a terrible day at work and needed to be left alone not yelled at.'

'You brought charges, didn't you?'

'I did but I dropped them.'

'Why did you do that?'

'Because he was in bits after it happened and told me he was truly sorry and it was a one-off and he would never ever hurt me. He said he hated himself for hitting me.'

'And did he keep to his promise?'

'Sort of, but a few months later, in early 2009, he grabbed me by the hair. In those days, I had really long hair. He wrapped it around his fist and said he was going to smash my face against the wall but I screamed really loudly and he let me go. He said he was sorry

but I ran to the bathroom, locked myself in and rang the police. A few minutes after I called them, he banged on the door, crying and begging for forgiveness. When the police arrived, I told them it had been a mistake – that I'd overreacted. I didn't press charges. Paul was completely different afterwards – so sad and genuinely sorry – that I wanted to forgive him and believe him when he said it wouldn't happen again. I was confused and it was easier to drop charges and forget about the whole thing and go back to normal.'

Natalie kept her eyes on the woman and offered her another smile. 'It's usual in these circumstances. The abused feels guilty and backs down, but he hurt you, didn't he?'

'He bruised my face, that's all.'

'Did he threaten you again?'

'No. I didn't give him the chance to. My best friend, Annie, knew what was going on and she told me I really had to get out of what she called a toxic relationship, that he'd never change, and there'd be more times when he'd think it was okay to hurt me. She said I ought to get away while I was still strong-willed enough to and before he started to get properly violent. After we split up, I was so confused by it all, I went to therapy sessions. They helped me to understand what happened and that's why I can speak more openly about it now and understand what went on. A year ago, I met somebody else, Leon, and I'm much happier – happier than I thought possible.'

'I'm glad to hear it. Paul injured you on two separate occasions, is that correct?'

'Yes.'

'Did he threaten you on any others?'

'No. We bickered a lot.'

'And what led up to the episodes when he hit you? Did you argue about something specific?'

'It was dumb really. He accused me of flirting with one of his mates and being disrespectful to him.'

'Was there any truth in that?' Natalie asked.

Sarah shrugged. 'A little.'

'So, he was jealous about other men paying you attention?'

'When he was drunk, he'd get really possessive.'

'He never threatened you for any other reason?'

'No.'

'Did he lose his temper a lot?'

She stared at her bag and sighed. 'Only after drinking. He wasn't a big drinker but if he had a few pints, he'd change – become loud and pushy.'

Natalie was fully aware of the effects of alcohol on people – it wasn't unusual for anyone to exhibit aggressive behaviour after too much of it. 'Was he aggressive towards others?'

'No. He got on well with people. Look, it was only those couple of times and I suppose I wound him up a bit. My therapist and I talked about this. I was much younger then, only a kid myself. We were both a bit hot-tempered at times and I taunted him a little. I flirted with other guys to wind him up and make him pay me more attention, but if we'd drunk too much we'd argue and fight. I was to blame as much as him but that doesn't make it right, does it? He should never have hit me. My therapist said that wasn't acceptable.'

'No, he shouldn't, even if he felt he was provoked,' Natalie replied. 'You left him because you believed he'd hit you again and that the next time he might not be able to control himself. You had good reason to go.'

'At the time, I thought I did. My friend painted such a bleak picture of what could happen but now I look back and think I could have handled things differently. It takes two, doesn't it? Paul could be very sweet at times – a lot of the time. Maybe if I hadn't been so quick to leave, things would have been different. I didn't go because I thought he'd hit me – that was almost an excuse. I left because I wanted him to come after me and beg me to come

home – to notice me again. I wanted things to go back to how they'd been before he lost interest in me.' Tears sprang to her eyes.

'Have you ever met his partner, Cathy Curtis, or her children?'

'Never. I don't know anything about them. I only found out because one lunchtime, a few months later, I bumped into Paul in the supermarket. He'd popped in to buy some lunch and was doing a job near where I worked. It was really awkward. He asked how I was and if I'd met anybody new. I hadn't and I think part of me hoped he was going to invite me out but he didn't. He said he was really sorry things hadn't worked out between us and hoped I'd be happy. He told me he'd met a woman – that she had four kids but they were getting on well with him. I wished him luck and we parted. I haven't seen him since, or his family. Seemed funny thinking of him as a dad. He always wanted a big family.'

'Did you talk about having children?'

'We did more than talk; we tried hard for a baby but it didn't happen.' She hesitated a moment before adding, 'If you believe Paul had something to do with this girl's death, I want to say, I think you're wrong. He likes kids. He and I used to take my six-year-old nephew out regularly to help out my brother and his wife and give them some time together. We'd take him to the zoo or the park. Paul always looked forward to it and was really good with him. Maybe having a baby would have changed us both. I know he wouldn't hurt a child.'

'Sarah, can I ask about your movements Saturday evening? Where were you?'

'At work. I'm a nurse at Burton Hospital. I was in A & E all night until seven this morning.'

'And your boyfriend?'

'Leon? He's a hospital porter. We were on the same shift.' There was nothing to indicate she wasn't being open and honest. The only emotion Natalie could detect was regret.

'Does your friend Annie work there too?'

Her brow furrowed in confusion. 'No. She's a primary-school teacher but she moved to Colorado three years ago with her husband. We've kind of lost touch with each other.'

'Thank you, Sarah – I think that's it for now. You've been most helpful,' Natalie replied.

The woman slid her arm through the handles of her oversized bag and stood up. 'I don't want you to think he's guilty of hurting anyone based on what I've told you.'

'We're talking to everyone involved: family, friends and those who know them. We're not making any assumptions.'

The woman gave a quick nod and, accompanied by Murray, vacated the interview room. Natalie mulled over what they'd learnt. If Sarah was telling the truth, Paul wasn't quite the bully they first suspected, but she could be lying to protect him for a number of reasons – maybe even because she still cared about him and hoped there was a chance for her.

Natalie was still in her seat when Murray reappeared. 'She's gone. What do you think?' he said.

'He's a scumbag for hitting her and I reckon she still has a thing for him. She could be covering for him,' said Natalie. 'Check her and Leon's whereabouts. Should be simple enough to verify they were both at Burton Hospital last night into this morning. Might be an idea to see if she's telling the truth and hasn't seen Paul since then. Look into her story, will you? I'm still not completely convinced about him.'

'She seems to think he was happy with Cathy.'

Natalie grunted. 'She had a few minutes of awkward conversation with him in a supermarket. I'm not reading a lot into that. The only thing I'll admit is that he appears to have an alibi for his whereabouts last night. We'll stick to the facts and keep an open mind for the moment.'

*

Upstairs, Ian had news for them. 'I've been talking to the vice squad. They had Extravaganza under investigation for drug dealing and prostitution late last year. They were tipped off in September and sent in undercover agents but didn't find anything. They reckoned either they were rumbled or the information was wrong. Two weeks ago, they pulled a local dealer in nearby Kingston-on-Trent who confirmed there was drug dealing going on inside the club but he wasn't party to it. He wouldn't give them any other information but said there was more going on than just dancing and partying.'

'Are they going to check out the club again?' Natalie asked.

'Yes.'

'Then we'd be stamping on their toes,' said Lucy.

Natalie said, 'Kirk and Gavin know we're investigating the fire and looking into Roxy's death. They're not fools. If anything's going on in the nightclub that they're party to, they'll make sure it isn't happening at the moment, not while we're sniffing about. I say we give the vice squad the heads up and go in regardless. Our priority is to investigate Roxy's death, not drug dealing and prostitution… unless the two are related. I'll talk to the senior officer there and tell him Ian and Murray are going to the club tonight.'

'Fine by me,' said Murray.

'And me,' Ian added.

'While you're there, ask about Daisy Goldsmith, Gavin's girlfriend. She was a hostess there until May. There's something strange about her. I can't put my finger on it but I don't buy the whole "we fell in love at work and kept it secret" business. See what her work colleagues have to say about her.'

By eight o'clock the team hadn't uncovered any fresh evidence to assist them. Sarah's story had checked out. Both she and Leon, her boyfriend, were at work as she'd said, and there was nothing to suggest Paul Sadler or his family were part of her life. Natalie

wound it up for the day, allowing Ian and Murray a couple of hours off before they headed to Extravaganza. She was last to leave, and as she darted towards the stairs she almost ran into Mike Sullivan.

'Hey. Sorry it's late in the day but I've literally just received the fire investigator's report and spoken to Pinkney.'

'Damn, I sent everyone home. It might have to wait until tomorrow now. Did they uncover anything useful?' She took the files from Mike and began thumbing through them as he spoke.

'In brief, the fire was started in the entrance as we first suspected, and spread throughout the house, front to back. The entertainment room was one of the last rooms on the ground floor to be engulfed by flames. Pinkney's found smoke inhalation damage to Roxanne's lungs, which explains why she appeared to have made no effort to escape.' He turned a page in the file and pointed to a sketch. 'Nick's plan of the entertainment room shows she was on one of the round chairs close to the television at the time.'

'So, what was she up to there? Watching television?'

'On her phone, smoking, on social media, asleep or all of those, I suppose. Whatever she was doing, she wasn't aware of the fire until she was overcome by fumes.'

Natalie pulled a face. This was a revelation. 'That's really odd. She was alive but didn't move from her chair,' said Natalie thoughtfully. 'That suggests she didn't hear anything. Even with the television on or engrossed in social media, she'd hear noises: popping, small explosions, roaring all caused by a fire of that intensity, so my guess is she didn't move because she couldn't – maybe she'd been drinking or had taken drugs and was fast asleep. Has he run any drug tests on her yet?'

'They're ongoing.'

'No matter what they show, I still have no frigging idea why she was in that house.'

'The door might have been unlocked and she simply let herself in.'

'It's not bloody *Goldilocks and the Three Bears*, Mike. Besides, the door was locked. Both Gavin and Kirk confirmed that.'

He gave her a wry grin. 'I know. Just chucking it out there for you. Anyway, maybe they lied and the door was left unlocked for her.'

She gave him a begrudging smile. 'That's a fair assumption. I'll accept that as a possibility but this is all so damn frustrating! A teenage girl, supposedly with her friend on a sleepover but instead in a house occupied by people who claim not to know her, in their entertainment room, and who doesn't try to escape when it's set on fire! It makes no sense.'

'Sleep on it. It'll clear your head. I'm clocking off. Fancy a quick drink before you head home?'

She shut the file and hesitated. It was tempting, really tempting, but her family hadn't seen her all day. 'Got to head home.'

'I understand. How's Leigh doing?'

'Being a bit of a pain, to be honest.'

'Normal then?'

Natalie gave a quick laugh. 'I guess so.'

'Can't wait for Thea to become a teenager. I'll have all this fun to come.'

'Enjoy her while she's this age. It soon passes.'

Mike patted his pockets and pulled out a packet of cigarettes. 'Right. I'm off. See you in the morning. I'm going to grab a pint and ring Thea before she goes to bed.'

Natalie shoved the file into her briefcase. 'I'll walk down with you.'

As they headed towards reception, for a brief moment she wished she didn't have to go back home and face David and the kids – especially David.

CHAPTER NINE

SUNDAY, 1 JULY – EVENING

Cathy Curtis waited as a group of rowdy teenagers dismounted the bus before dropping silently to the pavement.

'You got a light?' One of the swaggering youths was in her face. He was about the same age and height as Oliver, her eldest, but more menacing, with large rings on all his fingers and a neck tattoo. She thought back to the conversation she'd had with Oliver earlier…

'Mum, it's Oliver. You okay?'

'No, love. I'm not but I'm coping.'

'My sergeant's just told me about Roxy. It's true?'

'Yes… it is.'

There's a heavy pause and then, 'What happened to her?'

'We don't know. She was in a house in Armston that burnt down and she died in the fire.'

'Fuck! Mum, I really don't know what to say.'

'I know. We can't believe it.'

'I'll come home – Sarge said I can take compassionate leave.'

'No, don't do that. There's nothing you can do.'

'I can be with you.'

'It's fine, love. I've got your brothers here. You can't do anything. She's gone.'

There's no sobbing, only silence followed by, 'I did care about her, you know?'

'I know you did.'

'I care about you all.'

'And we care about you.'

'I ought to come back, Mum.'

'No, don't. Come back when we know more. We don't even know if we can have a funeral for her yet. Wait until I ring you. There's no point taking leave until you need to.'

'You sound weird. You sure you can manage?'

'I've got help from a nice liaison officer called Tanya and we'll all get through this. It's hard but we'll manage.' She bites back stinging tears and her heart aches at the lies she's telling her eldest son, but he doesn't need to return to Clearview to share in the suffering. He's left this place and made a life for himself – a good life – and she's so proud of him. She doesn't want to drag him back to his past. Her children are all so different: Roxy, ballsy and demanding; Seth, needy and unsure of himself; Charlie, trying to be like his big brother; and Oliver, the strongest and bravest of them all, the boy who became a man – a good, solid man. She can't talk any more or she'll give away how much she really wants him to be by her side, so she tells him she loves him and that she'll ring him again tomorrow.

'I love you too, Mum. I'm absolutely gutted about Roxy.'

'We are too, love. We are too.'

Cathy wasn't intimidated by the boy on the pavement. She'd brought up three of her own and knew all their friends. This one, Logan, had been in the same class as Charlie and had been around to the flat on a few occasions. She pulled out a disposable lighter and handed it to him. 'Here. Keep it.'

'Sweet. Thanks.' The boy rejoined the group and she moved in the opposite direction. She was no longer in familiar territory. It was

funny to think that Clearview was a suburb of Armston-on-Trent. In reality, they were two completely different towns: Clearview with run-down estates, crime and squalor, and Armston, which oozed privilege and wealth. Checking Google Maps, she crossed the street from the bus stop and followed a road to St Mary's church, passing a terraced row of picturesque houses with neat doorsteps and hanging baskets either side of painted wooden doors: Ivy Cottage, Primrose Place, The Glades. She read each oval nameplate and speculated about what it must be like to live here rather than the far side of town. The church bells began, a rippling musical melody that reminded her of a music box she'd owned as a child. Loud cries made her turn in time to spot the youths who'd travelled on the same bus chasing after two others, hurling abuse at them. They'd no doubt come to town to cause trouble. It would be an evening's entertainment to them. The group disappeared from view and she continued down the street to the sound of chimes that appeared to resonate through her body. She counted seven and then increased her pace, keen to reach her destination.

Tears threatened again but she swallowed them back down. Now wasn't the time to mourn. She needed to make things right first. She'd let Roxy down and not for the first time. She wasn't a good mother. Not at all. She was a shit mother and she knew it. Even though it was a warm evening, she shivered. A woman in a summer dress as yellow as meadow buttercups appeared from a doorway, a plastic can in her hand. She lifted it and carefully dripped water into a blue ceramic pot filled with blooms beside her front door.

'Lovely evening again, isn't it?' she said brightly as Cathy passed by. Cathy didn't answer. She didn't belong here, talking to people like this. She checked her phone. Linnet Lane joined this road. It wouldn't take five minutes to reach it, and once she'd seen the house, she'd ring DI Ward. She'd copied the detective's number from the Samford Police website and slipped it into her purse.

She reached the rear of the sandstone brick church that was impossibly clean. There were no churches in Clearview and most of the public buildings were covered in graffiti. There was nothing this neat or impressive. Lives were different here. Evening sunrays bounced off a stained-glass window, seemingly setting it alight so it burnt deep crimson, and gooseflesh crept along her bare arms as she scurried past it alongside the stone wall. She halted by a wooden gate, where she contemplated going inside to pray for her daughter. The thought had no sooner surfaced in her conscious than it popped and evaporated. Cathy had never been religious and she'd come to Armston for one sole reason: to see where her daughter had died. She wouldn't rest until she'd at least seen the house.

Her wedged sandals made no sound along the pavement. She was struck by the utter peace, the lack of cars, motorbikes, barking dogs and loitering teenagers. It was a far cry from the daily hubbub she was used to, with traffic streaming past the flat, sirens at all times of the day and night, revving engines or the sound of squealing tyres as people raced along the main road. It was rarely quiet, let alone calm like this. There was always some activity outside, crowds of youths fighting or yelling. She couldn't even imagine what it must be like to live in such serenity with only birdsong and the occasional rumble of a distant engine.

She'd come to the end of the street and, turning to her left, she spotted the sign: Linnet Lane. One side of the road had a pavement running past hedgerows and fields; the other was tree-lined with enormous mansions set back from it, each partly hidden from view by leafy foliage. *What the fuck had Roxy been doing in an area like this? Nobody she knew could afford to live here. What had my daughter been up to?* Cathy stared at the flashing icon that showed she was almost upon the property, and even before she reached it, she knew she was in the right spot. Crime-scene tape like yellow-and-black party banners decorated the deep olive-green bushes and her heart began to race. This was where Roxy died.

A police vehicle blocked the driveway to the property so she walked past on the other side of the street where there were no houses, only fields, to gaze at the ruined shell opposite her. Burning tears that stung her eyes filled and clouded them. One of the most precious people in her life had been killed in this house. This should never have happened. If only she could turn back the clock… but she couldn't. All she could do now was assist the detective. She fought back more tears. She'd uncovered some information that might help bring the monster who'd killed her child to justice.

A movement startled her. A man with a clipboard under his arm emerged from the property. She blinked hard and shuffled onwards, head bowed, shoulders slumped. It was time to ring DI Ward but she wouldn't do it here, not in the middle of this street where anyone could hear her – and besides, she needed some time to compose herself before she spoke to the policewoman. She knew where she could go. She'd been there before on a couple of occasions although she'd never realised it was so close to this street.

The weight in her chest was physical, like her heart had turned into lead and was tugging at all the veins, arteries and nerves that supported it, making them scream in agony. Each step that took her further away from the house caused such anguish she could hardly breathe. She walked, unable to think any more, her movements robotic. She needed a place where she could unburden herself from the emotional pressure that threatened to explode at any given second, and finally her eyes alighted upon a wooden sign that pointed towards the canal, some distance from the place where her child had taken her last breath. The pain intensified but she dragged her feet forward, driven to find the secluded spot where she could release the agonising build-up and make the phone call.

The path was flanked by tall hedges and cool green foliage and opened out onto a towpath. The canal was empty of boats, and a pair of ducks swam past, pausing only to bob upside down momentarily. A bench stood only a metre ahead of her, and she

sped up and dropped onto it heavily, only seconds before her legs would have finally given out on her. She deserved this anguish. She deserved all the pain. She wished she and Roxy had never argued earlier on Saturday. That was surely what had made her lie about the sleepover and take off. She understood how volatile her daughter could be. If she'd only given Roxy a hug instead of shouting at her, it would have been enough to have prevented the girl from leaving.

Her mouth dropped opened slightly as she inhaled shallow breaths. Her heart was being prodded by a thousand needles. *Torture.* She rooted in her bag and pulled out Roxy's toy black cat. She clutched it to her chest and allowed her tears to dampen the soft fur. What she would give to see her girl sitting cross-legged on her bed with the cat beside her. The tears tumbled, and wrapped in her own grief, she didn't hear the crunch of leaves underfoot, the rustle from the bushes, didn't hear the person approach from behind her until it was too late.

CHAPTER TEN

SUNDAY, 1 JULY – EVENING

'Anyone home?' Natalie shut the front door and listened for a reply. When none was forthcoming, she continued with a mumbled, 'Hi, Mum, we missed you.' She shook her head. The days when Leigh would bound downstairs like an exuberant Tigger, eyes bright and full of enthusiasm about her day, were long gone. She left her briefcase beside her shoes and wriggled her toes in her comfortable slippers, musing that some manufacturer ought to make shoes that felt as comfortable as slippers but still look smart. Hers had begun to rub on her little toe. *Old age*, she reflected.

She started in the kitchen in the hope David had decided to cook something, but it was empty with no sign of any activity. 'David?' She spun on her heel and made her way to the sitting room but no one was there. She walked slowly towards his office. The door was shut and a familiar thudding in her chest began. *He wouldn't be online gambling, would he?* She tapped on the door, and when no one answered, she pushed it open. It was empty. She had seen David's car in the drive so he couldn't have gone far.

It was unusual for the house to be so quiet. Maybe they'd all gone out with David's father. She padded silently upstairs and onto the landing towards Josh's room and was relieved to find him lying on his back on his bed, earbuds in, listening to music.

'Hi. Everything okay?'

He removed the earbuds and pushed himself into a seated position. 'Sure.'

'What have you been up to?'

'Stuff.'

'You got anywhere with a holiday job?' she asked.

Josh screwed up his face. 'It's really hard. Not much about. None of my mates have got jobs.'

'Did you go into town and ask about?'

'It's Sunday,' he said.

'I know but shops and cafés do open on a Sunday. I thought you were going in to see what was available.'

He gave a half-hearted shrug. 'I'll try tomorrow. Dad was a bit busy today.'

'Was he?'

'Yes.'

'You eaten?'

'Not yet.'

'What about lunch?'

'Finished the leftover macaroni cheese from last night.'

'Okay. I'll sort out something.'

'Cheers, Mum.'

She shut the door and ambled to Leigh's room. She wasn't in. She was going to ask Josh where his sister was when she heard a deep rumbling coming from her bedroom. It didn't take long to work out what it was. David was lying on the bed, fully clothed and fast asleep. She shook him roughly until he stopped snoring and his eyes snapped open.

'What's going on?' Natalie asked.

He sat up in one movement. 'Nothing. Must have dozed off.'

She wrinkled her nose. The smell of alcohol was strong on his breath. Instead of chastising him she asked, 'Where's Leigh?'

'Chilling with Katy and Jade.'

'Oh. When's she due back?'

'I agreed to collect her at ten.' His tone was light but she knew instantly there was more to it. He rubbed a hand across his chin, a tell that he was buying time.

'Everything okay?'

'Sure. Why wouldn't it be?'

'Well, you're asleep at eight, Leigh's gone out on an unplanned visit to friends and Josh didn't go to town to drop off his CV as we planned.'

'He didn't want to go.'

'He said you were busy.'

'That's bullshit. I was ready to take him but he was playing some online game and didn't want to do anything.'

'We discussed this, David. We were going to all go to town, let him ask about and then spend the day together.'

'We were until you went to work.'

'Just because I'm not around doesn't mean you can't carry on without me.'

'They didn't want to go to town, okay?'

'No. Not okay. Josh needs a job. He can't sit around here all school holidays doing nothing. Besides, work experience will be good for him.'

David stood up. 'Don't boss me about, Natalie. I'm not one of your minions. I asked if they wanted to go to town and neither of them did. Leigh was in one of her moods and flounced off to see her friends. What am I supposed to do in those situations?'

She clamped her mouth shut and mentally counted to ten. 'Okay. Let's leave it at that. What do you want to eat?'

'There are pizzas in the fridge.'

'Right. I'll go and collect Leigh. You put them in the oven.'

His eyes flashed. 'Don't, Natalie.'

'Don't what?'

'Talk to me like that.'

'Oh, grow up. I'm being practical, that's all.' Even as she spoke the words, she knew she was in the wrong. She was treating him with disdain and she knew how fragile his ego was at the moment. However, she didn't really care whether he felt hard done by or not, and she stalked away, feeling his eyes on her departing back.

*

It was just before ten when Ian arrived at the large brick building that was now the nightclub Extravaganza. There were no windows or openings to be seen from the street, and any apertures that might have existed in the past had been blocked up with fresh brickwork. Subtle signage was all that alerted the public to the fact this was a nightclub, and Ian walked along the street to an alley, where he encountered Murray waiting near an innocuous door.

'Been here long?' he asked.

'A couple of minutes. Long enough to watch a group of pissed-up blokes go inside and come straight back out again. The price of the drinks probably put them off.'

'You'd think they'd want a clear head for tomorrow,' Ian muttered.

Murray laughed. 'Do you know how ancient you sound? That's the sort of thing my dad used to say. Life's for living. Carpe diem and all that shit. They're young enough to get up tomorrow with no hangovers whatsoever. I used to be like that. You should give it a go yourself. Loosen up a bit.'

'Fat chance. What with work and all the other bloody pressures at the moment.'

'Come on, where's your party mojo?' Murray retorted.

'I'm not really in a partying mood. I'm in a bad place at the moment.'

'Want to talk about it before we go in?'

Ian hesitated before saying, 'We'd better do this first.'

'Come on, then.'

Murray rapped on the door, which was opened immediately by a man all in black, with a pointed beard and ebony eyes that oozed hostility. Murray and Ian held up ID cards and were met with a scowl.

'What do you want?'

Murray spoke. 'Just a few questions. The club owners' house was burnt down last night.'

'Yeah. We heard about that. Kirk's in the back office.'

'We'd like to take a look around first, chat to the staff.'

'I'll get somebody to show you around then.'

'We can manage on our own,' Murray replied.

The bouncer glowered again and responded with, 'How about I take you through to the bar and let Kirk know you're here?'

'Is Gavin in?'

'Not that I know of.'

'Okay. Cheers.' Murray kept his tone casual and light. The guy showed Ian and Murray into the dimly lit room, where a woman in a tight red dress that emphasised her curves was sat on a stool beside a tall round table. Thumping music was coming from somewhere inside, its frantic beat heavily muted here in the entrance.

'Two, is it?' she asked, picking up a rubber hand stamper, ready to brand them with the nightclub's logo.

'They're police,' said the man, walking past the table towards a black door.

Murray and Ian didn't follow him; instead, they both halted in their tracks.

Murray gave her a warm smile. 'How long have you worked here?'

'A year or so.'

'Must get really hectic some days,' Ian said.

'Only at weekends. Mostly Fridays and Saturdays,' she replied, eyeing him through thick eyelashes.

'How many times do you use that on a busy night?' Murray asked, pointing at the hand stamper, the smile in place.

'Don't know, really. Lots,' she replied and replaced it on the table.

'What about on an average Sunday?'

'Depends. Anything between twenty and two hundred. Can never tell.'

Ian continued. 'You enjoy working here? It must be rubbish hours.'

'It's okay. It's a job. Like yours. Must be shit hours too.'

Ian agreed.

The man with the beard opened the door, and a wave of electronic pop rushed in, killing all further conversation. Murray followed the man through the door, Ian by his side.

The room opened out before them and technicolour lights strobed across the ceiling, bathing the numerous open-fronted booths around the dance floor with fluorescent pinks, greens and purples. Two imposing floor-to-ceiling onyx pillars stood either side of the dance floor. To the rear was a raised podium on which, almost hidden from view behind a black curved screen that resembled a church pulpit, stood a wiry individual, casually attired in a T-shirt and wearing headphones, his head lowered over hidden electronic equipment.

A black leather-fronted bar ran almost the full length of the left-hand wall. Two members of staff in white polo shirts and black trousers were in a huddle, talking to each other.

The bouncer nodded sharply in the direction of the duo and then crossed the dance floor, disappearing behind a black curtain, above which was marked 'Toilets'.

Murray put his lips close to Ian's ear. 'Talk to the bartenders. I'm going to nose about.'

Ian headed across while Murray darted off to the right and through another door that was lit by a neon sign: 'Party Room'.

The door led to a wide staircase and a dark corridor lit dimly with floor lights. Framed pictures of groups of revellers raising glasses, wearing party hats, waving sparklers adorned the dark green-black walls. To both his left and right were doors marked 'Private' but ahead of him, wide double doors that were open led into the party room. The music playing was familiar to him: eighties classic pop rather than the modern electronic sounds he'd left behind. The room was a throwback to the disco era, with a giant disco ball hanging over a dance floor and curved leather settees, striped black and white, each capable of seating up to eight people, facing it. The bar was smaller in this room and also curved, taking up one corner while the deejay equipment was packed tidily in the other. There was no one behind the decks, and apart from a young woman with auburn hair in a high ponytail, there was no other staff. She greeted him as he approached.

'Hi. Is it always this quiet?' Murray asked.

'It might pick up but Sunday isn't the best day to be here. It was busier last night. What can I get you?'

'I'm okay, thanks, just having a look about. It's my first time here.' He casually dropped onto one of the stools to continue his conversation.

She looked him up and down and asked, 'On your own?'

'Nah. My mate's downstairs. I thought I'd see if there was more life up here but there isn't and there's no deejay,' he added.

'Dimension was our permanent resident deejay up here but now he only comes in for special parties, themed nights or special events like Valentine's Day. The rest of the time we run playlists through the system.'

'You choose this one?'

She grinned. 'What can I say? I'm a pop diva.'

'What's your name?'

'Lola. You?'

'Murray.'

'You been here long?'

'Since it opened.'

'I guess it's a lot busier than this other days.'

She shrugged. 'Sometimes.'

'There's not a lot of party atmosphere at the moment,' he quipped.

'It's only ten. It'll liven up later.'

'Fair point. But usually I like to be in bed by ten,' he replied with a twinkle.

A smile tugged at the corners of her mouth.

'What goes on in the private rooms?'

The smile vanished. 'They're for VIP guests.'

'What do I have to do to become a VIP guest?' he asked with a grin. It was too late. She wasn't succumbing to his innocent charm any longer. Her face took on a guarded look.

'Why do you want to know?'

He laughed. 'Just curious. I've not been to a nightclub with rooms like that before. What happens in them?'

She suddenly picked up a glass and held it to the light to check for smears. 'It's just for private parties, nothing more than that. Look, I have to get on, okay?'

'Sure. Thanks for chatting. Oh, just one second. You haven't seen this girl around at all, have you?'

'What are you? Police?'

'That's right. DS Murray Anderson. I'm investigating the death of this girl.'

He passed her the picture of Roxanne, and Lola studied it before returning it to him. 'She's not been here.'

'Have you ever seen her around the nightclub?' He looked carefully for any signs the woman knew Roxanne but her face remained impassive and she gave an involuntary light shrug of apology.

'No. Sorry.'

'I take it you've heard about the fire at Kirk and Gavin's house.'

'Of course. I was here last night when they got the call to say it was on fire. Gavin shot off to find out what was going on. I heard it's a right mess.'

'Have you ever been there?'

She shook her head. 'I only work here. I'm no more than bar staff.'

'You know Lindsay Hoburn? She's one of the bar staff here.'

'Sure.'

'Does she still work here?'

'I don't know. I haven't seen her in a while but she only works stand-in shifts. Unless somebody's off sick and none of the regular staff can stand in, we don't need her.'

'What about Daisy Goldsmith?'

'What about her?'

'You know her?'

She let out a snort. 'Course I do – gold-digging Daisy.'

'What do you mean?'

'I don't need to spell it out, do I?'

'Best if you did.'

'She chased after Gavin from day one. She was a shit hostess and never pulled her weight but she sucked up to Gavin and got away with it. We were all pretty glad to see the back of her.'

'And do you get on okay with the club owners?'

'I wouldn't be here if I didn't. I wouldn't work for people I didn't like. They're good bosses.'

'You're not involved with either of them, are you?' Murray threw it out there to watch her response.

Her eyes widened. 'No way. I'm married – to the guy on the door, Clark.'

'What about the other employees here? Has anyone complained lately about Kirk or Gavin, or has anyone been fired recently? Or maybe you've overheard something that could help us?'

'You're joking, aren't you? We don't get a chance to sit around talking to each other, and by the time the shift is over, we're all fit to drop. I haven't heard anyone bad-mouthing them. We're all pretty happy with our lot here.'

'Okay. Thank you. I'll leave my card in case you want to contact me.'

'I can't imagine that happening.'

'Take it. You never know.'

She yanked the card from between his fingers and slapped it on the counter near the till. She turned her back to him and placed the glass she'd been holding on a shelf, then bent down to rearrange some bottles. She wasn't going to open up to him or answer any more questions.

He retraced his steps down the corridor, crossing paths with a group of women and men all in their early twenties. Once they'd disappeared into the party room, he paused by one of the other doors and quickly pushed on the door handle. It was locked. He tried the door opposite but it too was locked so he headed back downstairs. It had filled up a little and two girls were dancing side by side, arms around each other's waists. Ian was in conversation with Kirk. He joined them, and Kirk greeted him with, 'Your colleague here said you'd gone to the toilet.'

'I took the wrong door, ended up upstairs in the party room,' said Murray.

'The toilets are over there,' Kirk replied, indicating the curtain.

'Thanks. We're following up enquiries and would like to talk to your employees, if possible.'

'We don't have many staff on shift tonight but go ahead. You've probably met Lola in the party room.'

'Yes, I did.'

'It'll get busy in the next hour so I'd ask your questions now if I were you.'

'Thanks. Is Gavin coming in later?'

'Not tonight. He's spending some time with Daisy.' He glanced across the floor and raised his hand. Murray turned to see a group of four men at the door with the fork-bearded bouncer.

'Who's that guy?'

'Which one?'

'The bouncer that showed us in.'

'Clark. Been with us since we opened.' His response was automatic, attention now on the men who radiated confidence in outfits that looked, to Murray's eye, stylish and expensive.

'I'll leave you to it. Don't annoy any of the punters, though, will you?' Kirk said and strode off. Murray watched as he fist-bumped each of them and stood in earnest conversation. One man lifted both hands, palms up, and another spun on his heel, clearly irritated. Kirk patted him on the shoulder and spoke again. The first man nodded, and making large hand gestures, he spoke to the others before they all trooped after Kirk.

'You get anything?' Murray asked Ian.

'I didn't get a chance to speak to both of the bar staff before Kirk appeared. I had a few words with one of them but he was a bit cagey.'

'The girl upstairs, Lola, was like that too. Let's split up, talk to anyone we come across and meet up again outside.'

Ian headed back to the bar. Murray moved towards the podium and spotted Kirk and the men going through the door that led upstairs. He mounted curved steps towards the deejay, and as he did so, he became aware of Clark, who now stood in front of the door, legs planted wide, eyes trained on him.

Murray stood close to the wiry guy in headphones. From this position he could keep an eye on Clark and anyone coming into the club. The music was loud and he had to shout to make himself heard over it. DJ Crush was a ball of energy, talking and pressing buttons on his mixing decks at the same time.

'How long have you worked here?'

'Since it opened. Before that I gigged in Ibiza.'

'So, you know the brothers well?'

'Sort of. We share a beer and a laugh after work sometimes.'

'Do other members of staff do that too?'

'Mostly they go home but I'm usually too pumped from the music, so I hang back. The bros sometimes join me.'

'What do you talk about?'

'Man talk.'

'Such as?'

'You never talked man talk, officer? Football, dirty jokes, women, you know?'

'They tell you much about themselves?'

'Sure. I know they came from London. I have friends down there too. We talked about the nightlife down there.'

'What about personal things?'

'You kidding me? I'm a deejay not a psychiatrist. We just chat and drink beer.'

'What about Daisy? You ever talk about her?'

'Oh, man! Daisy was hot. She only had eyes for Gavin though. She was sex on legs and she sucked him right in.'

'Did he often talk about her?'

'Mentioned her quite a few times. You would, though, wouldn't you? A hot chick like that after you.'

'She was after him?'

'For sure. She had him in her sights and went full pelt for him. He didn't stand a chance. Kirk and I used to take the rip out of him. She wanted him to keep it under wraps while she was working here but it got out. She might have thought she was being subtle but she was not – no way! He's still crazy about her but she won't move in with him and it's driving him nuts. I don't get it. She was all over that man and she won't move into a nice house with him…

Maybe she's holding out for a ring on her finger first.' He stuck his headphones to one ear and pressed some buttons. The tempo changed as a new track began playing. His head and shoulders moved to its rhythm.

Murray had to shout even louder. 'You ever hear anyone complain about the brothers?'

'No way! The bros are great guys. We all get on really well. Like one big happy family!' His sentences rattled like rapid gunfire, accompanied by jerky movements to his music as he spoke.

'You got any idea who might have burnt down their house?'

'Nah,' he said.

Lights strobed quickly across the darkened room, lighting corners then turning them instantly back into darkness, and Murray caught sight of Clark talking to two women. He maintained his questioning while keeping one eye on the women. Both were dressed in tight, strappy dresses and killer heels. One had two-tone hair with the top section blonde and the bottom half red or a deep brown. Murray couldn't be certain of the actual colour but there was something furtive about them both and her in particular – the way she cast anxious looks in his direction as they spoke.

'You can't think of anyone who had a problem with Gavin or Kirk?'

'I'm usually focused on the vibe on the dance floor. That's my chief concern. I speak to my bros when I get here and when I leave, but I don't know anything about any grievances or problems. I just spin the decks. I don't pay any attention to what's going on anywhere else. Got to keep the crowd happy.'

Murray glanced at the two women. They were still by the door, deep in conversation. Judging by the head shakes and hand gestures, they were arguing. The shorter one tugged at the other's hand. The other woman pulled back.

'You ever seen this girl?' Murray showed him the picture of Roxy.

'I have no idea. If she was here, I'd never know. When that floor is thumping, you can't see anyone's face… it's just a giant mass of bodies. Sorry.'

'You heard of her – Roxanne Curtis, known as Roxy?'

'Doesn't ring any bells. What music are you into? Hip-hop? Garage?' DJ Crush asked.

'I'm a bit out of touch. I listen to playlists of modern pop and some rock.'

DJ Crush grinned, revealing the gap between his teeth. 'I figured so. You should come in one night and listen to some real music.'

Murray looked over to the door again but the women had vanished. He thanked the man, and casting about as he descended the steps, he spotted them disappearing through the curtain in the direction of the toilets.

Clark had vanished too and Murray seized the opportunity to pursue the women. Pushing the curtain aside, he found himself in yet another dark corridor with arrows pointing towards the toilets. He hovered outside the ladies', straining to hear any sounds from within, and when none were forthcoming, he knocked on the door. There was no response so he pushed it open and walked into the room that smelt of jasmine or some other summer scent he couldn't identify coming from a perfumed air freshener plugged into the wall. The cubicle doors were ajar and the place empty. The only sound was a dull rhythmic thudding of music.

He tried the men's toilets to no avail so he continued along the corridor, where he rapped on Kirk and Gavin's office door, simultaneously calling out as he pushed it open and walked into a small room furnished minimally with two back-to-back desks and some filing cabinets. A computer was switched on; the screensaver, a picture of a party night at the club. There was nowhere to hide, so where had the two women gone? He tried the room opposite, 'Staff Only', which was fairly small with lockers and benches, much like those found in gyms, but to the rear of the room was a

set of stairs. He took them and came through a fire exit door that took him into the party room. Twenty to thirty people had turned up since he'd last been in here and were milling about in groups, some shoulder-swaying in time to the Fun Boy Three track that now played. A man was serving at the bar alongside Lola, who was engaged in making cocktails. He moved along the dimly lit corridor and waited outside one of the private rooms, wondering if the women were inside.

Lola appeared with a tray of drinks and stopped short when she recognised him.

'Hi again,' he said.

She threw him a dark look. 'What are you doing here?'

'I already told you. I'm investigating the fire at Kirk and Gavin's house. I'm checking the whereabouts of everyone who knows and works for Gavin and Kirk. I was hoping there'd be someone I could talk to inside this room.'

'There's no staff other than Clark and Kirk in there and I can't let you disturb the guests. They pay a lot to use the private rooms.'

'Why? What's special about them?'

'They're private. That's what's special about them. Now, would you excuse me?'

'Sure.'

He moved aside to let her knock on the door, and as soon as her taps were answered, she slipped into the room quickly before the door closed again. Murray moved off. He hadn't been able to see much in that brief moment, but he'd spotted the blonde and red hair of the woman who'd stared at him and who had tugged at her friend's hand.

While Murray was talking to the deejay, Ian was engaged in conversation with Bryan, a twenty-something bar attendant. He didn't have anything to say about Daisy, who he claimed he barely

knew, and didn't recognise Roxy's photo or her name. Ian asked about the brothers.

'I only really pass the time of day with both of them,' he said, leaning on the counter. 'They're usually busy with the guests. They might come over and ask if everything's okay or request some drinks be sent over to a table, but generally I don't spend time with them. I can't think of anyone who hates them enough to burn down their house. In fact, I don't think I've ever heard a bad word about them.'

'No grumbles about pay or work conditions?'

'I've worked in much worse places. It's a decent atmosphere here.'

'Pretty busy though.'

'Some nights it's madness, others it's not too bad.'

Two women had been hanging by the door, like they couldn't make up their minds to come in or go out again.

'You know those two women?' he asked Bryan.

Bryan looked around the room. 'Which two?'

'By the door.' As soon as he'd spoken, the women slipped away towards the toilets.

Bryan shook his head. 'Can't see who you mean.'

'Never mind.' Ian had finished his questions and headed back to the entrance. The girl there might know who the women were.

She was alone. 'Hi,' said Ian.

'Hi.'

'We're investigating the fire at Gavin and Kirk's house but also seeing if anyone knows this girl. You didn't tell us your name earlier. What is it?' He held the photo back and waited for her to respond, which she did.

'Olga.'

'That's a pretty name. I've never met an Olga before.'

'You have now.' She gave him another smile, which he returned.

He revealed the picture, and as she looked at it, her lips rubbed together and she swallowed hard.

'No, sorry. I can't help you. I don't know her.'

Ian wasn't sure he believed her. 'The name Roxanne Curtis or Roxy doesn't mean anything to you?'

She swallowed again. 'Nothing. I've never heard of her.'

'You sure?'

'Honestly, I've never heard of her or seen her.'

He waited for more but she had nothing else to add. He offered her a smile before asking, 'What are Gavin and Kirk like to work for?'

'They're good to work for.'

'You get along well with them?'

'I'd say so but we're not like friends or anything. They say hello and pay me. That's about it.'

'Can you think of anyone who would be angry with either of them for any reason?'

'Staff members?'

'Yes, or anyone else you can think of.'

She rubbed her lips together in thought and then shook her head.

'You never heard anyone complain about them?'

Again, she shook her head. There was nothing to suggest she was lying when she said, 'I really haven't.'

'Do you know Daisy Goldsmith?'

She cocked her head to one side. 'Yes, I know Daisy but I haven't spoken to her since she left. She was a bit up herself so we didn't have much in common.'

'You knew about her relationship with Gavin?'

'Who didn't? It was obvious. She was all over him like a rash. She thought we didn't know, but we all did.'

'One last question: the women who came in a few minutes ago. Do they work here? Kirk asked us to only interview staff members.'

'They're regulars. They don't work here.'

'Thank you. I don't want to annoy any of the guests.'

'Guests!' She giggled.

'What? What have I said?' he asked, his teeth flashing.

'It sounds so funny. Like they booked into a hotel or something.'

'Do you know their names? I guess you must do if they're regulars.' He'd backed her into a corner.

She gave a light shrug. 'I don't know their full names. The one with the coloured hair's called Crystal, the other's Sandra B.'

'That's an odd name.'

'They have another friend who comes in with them sometimes, also called Sandra – she's Sandra M.'

'That's very helpful. Thank you.' He'd finished his questions in time. More clubbers turned up and waited to be stamped. He went back inside and bumped into Murray.

'Not found out anything about Roxy or who might have burnt down the house,' Murray said.

'Me neither but I did find out Daisy chased after Gavin and everyone here knew they were in a relationship.'

'Yeah, I got that info too. Funny cos she told Lucy and Natalie differently. You didn't happen to spot a pair of women in strappy dresses, did you? One had her hair in a sort of two-tone effect.'

'Crystal and Sandra B. They're regular clubbers.'

'How the fuck did you find that out?'

'Charmed it out of Olga on reception.'

'The babe with the big eyes? Kudos to you.' He grinned before adding, 'I'm sure those women were both in one of the private rooms upstairs with a group of guys. I can't be sure, but the way Lola clammed up about the private parties and the fact they kept me shut out of the room makes me suspect something was going on.'

'Lap dancing?'

'Yeah, most likely. Still, I can't see how it's relevant to the fire or to Roxy's death, so we'll call it a night.'

'Suits me.'

*

Natalie lay flat on her back, her eyes tightly shut. Judging by the sighs he periodically made, David was also awake, but there was no way she was going to engage in any conversation with him. Leigh had been in a foul mood all the way home, angry that her mother had come to collect her.

'You made me look stupid,' Leigh says as they drive away from Katy's house.

'How did I do that?'

'Dad said I could stay until ten. I felt like some little kid being told to come home.'

'I think you're exaggerating. I was friendly. I apologised to Katy and Jade for taking you away.'

Leigh ignores her and stares out of the window.

'Don't let's fall out over this. You have school tomorrow. You haven't finished term, even if Josh has.'

'It's only just gone eight.'

'And I bet you haven't done all your homework for tomorrow yet. You know you always leave it until the last minute.'

Leigh folds her arms. Natalie has hit a nerve.

'Leigh, can we not argue about this?' Waves of tiredness wash over Natalie as she slows down and waits at the traffic lights.

'Dad said I could go to Katy's. I wasn't doing anything wrong.'

Natalie sighs inwardly. David's caused this problem. If only he'd made proper arrangements and agreed an earlier pickup time, this ridiculous squabble wouldn't be happening. She makes one more attempt.

'I know, sweetheart, but you'll see them both tomorrow at school, won't you?'

'If they still want to hang out with me and don't think I'm some sort of loser.'

'They won't think that at all because you're not,' she says.

'Why couldn't Dad come and fetch me?'

'I volunteered and he's sorting out pizzas for supper,' says Natalie, unwilling to say anything that might alert her daughter to the cracks in her parents' relationship. Leigh is sensitive, and having already run away once because of her parents' arguments, Natalie doesn't want to raise suspicions now.

'I'm sorry if I embarrassed you. I didn't mean to.' She hopes her daughter will back down and stop sulking but she doesn't. Instead, she picks up her mobile from her lap and texts the friends she's only just left. Natalie bites her tongue and puts the car into gear. Handling tetchy teenagers is a skill and she's not sure she's really got the hang of it.

Natalie let the thoughts rattle around her head for a while. She should have tried to defuse the tension between her and David but she had no energy or inclination to talk, and the tightness in her chest prevented her from making any comforting gestures towards him. Instead of looking after the children, he'd sat around drinking and feeling sorry for himself. She knew she ought to have more compassion and understanding – after all, she knew why he was unhappy – but she didn't want to expend any more emotion in this direction. She shut her eyes and Mike's face appeared. *No. You mustn't even go there.*

She directed her thoughts back towards the investigation. That was safer ground. What was the link between Roxy and the Lang brothers? She brooded on the subject for a long time, going back over what they'd discovered and coming to the same conclusions until she gradually felt herself drifting, sleep beckoning her into its bottomless abyss.

CHAPTER ELEVEN

MONDAY, 2 JULY – MORNING

'Come on, Leigh!' David's voice was edgy. Of their two children, Leigh had always been the sluggish, slow-to-respond one in the mornings, and now Josh had finished his examinations and no longer had to attend school, it was a marathon getting her ready on time. 'Leigh! It's quarter to eight. Breakfast's ready. Get a move on.'

David rolled his eyes at Natalie and was about to say something when their daughter finally appeared, eyes still heavy with sleep and school tie draped around her neck.

'Come grab some toast. Josh!'

Josh emerged from the sitting room, a folder in his hand.

Natalie gave an approving nod at her son's appearance: gelled hair, neatly ironed shirt, black trousers and polished shoes. 'You look very smart. Good luck.'

'I'm only handing out my CV, Mum, not starting work today.'

'I know, but appearances count and you'll impress them.'

'We'll see you later,' said David, and he leant in to kiss her on the cheek.

She accepted it with a smile, fully aware her children were watching. 'Have a good day,' Natalie said breezily.

'Sure. Maths and double science,' said Leigh moodily.

David ushered them into the kitchen, and as Natalie slipped on her shoes and heard Leigh complaining loudly that her brother

had eaten the last of her favourite cereal, she was glad she could escape to work.

Murray concluded his report on the previous evening's activities.

Lucy sat back in her seat and said, 'Daisy chased after Gavin cos she thought he was a wealthy catch, and now she's got him, she's no longer interested in him?'

'That'd be my take on it,' said Murray. 'She doesn't want to move in with him although DJ Crush thinks she's holding out until Gavin proposes to her.'

'Do we still keep her in mind?' Ian asked.

Natalie's head moved up and down slowly. 'I think so, if only because she doesn't have an alibi for the night Roxy died.'

Lucy asked, 'What do you think was happening in the private room that the hostess and bouncer didn't want Murray to see?'

'Could have been lap dancing. A group of blokes turned up and Kirk took them upstairs, then the women arrived soon afterwards. I didn't want to rattle any cages by insisting they let me in,' said Murray.

Natalie unfolded her arms and agreed with him. 'You did the right thing. You were there to ask about Roxy, the fire and Daisy. If whatever the Lang brothers are up to is relevant in any way to this investigation, then it's a different matter and we'll act accordingly. For now, we're still trying to work out how and why Roxy gained access to their house on Linnet Lane. I've not yet received the full pathology report but it is almost certain she died of smoke inhalation. We can assume she was asleep, unconscious or completely unaware that the house was on fire. Pinkney is still running tests on her and we're waiting on toxicology reports. I suggest we try her friends today. Lucy, Ellie knows you, so would you speak to her again? Maybe she knows more than she said she did. Talk to Boo's mum too. Boo said they saw Ellie smoking with another girl and two boys. Let's see if we can find out who they were. Tanya

Granger is on her way around to see how Cathy's doing before we interview her again.'

A muffled ringing interrupted them. Ian fumbled in his pocket and pulled out his phone, glancing at the screen with a frown. He excused himself and walked into the corridor.

Natalie carried on. 'We really must establish a connection between Roxy and the Lang brothers. Until we do that, we can't really move on.'

'We know she died in the fire so we can rule out the idea she was murdered and the fire was set deliberately to incinerate her remains,' said Murray.

'No, I'm afraid we can't. If somebody thought Roxy was dead, and set fire to the house to incinerate her remains, that's essentially the same as murder and then covering it up. We can't rule out the possibility this was murder and arson.'

'By somebody, do you mean Gavin and Kirk?' Lucy asked.

Natalie glanced at the photograph of the dead girl now attached to the large whiteboard at the front of the office. 'It could be them or somebody else altogether. Whoever it was either had a house key or was let in. For now, we'll refer to them as the perpetrator.' She gazed past the board and out onto the landing. Ian had ended his call and was headed back towards the office.

He stood in the doorway and spoke. 'That was Olga from Extravaganza. She's a sort of receptionist cum hostess there. She wants to talk to me about Roxy. She's got some information but she doesn't want to come to the station or tell me over the phone. She only wants to talk to me. I'm meeting her at Starbucks in town in ten minutes.'

'Looks like your charm worked overtime,' said Murray.

'Yeah, whatever,' Ian replied. 'I'll call in the information, Natalie.'

'Hope she really does have something for you and isn't just after your body,' Murray called as Ian withdrew.

Ian raised his middle finger.

*

The liaison officer, Tanya Granger, pulled into the car park and parked behind 114 Pine Way. She'd arrived shortly after lunch and spent Sunday afternoon with the Curtis family before leaving them early evening. She'd seen many reactions to death but the Curtis family had troubled her more than most. Cathy had broken down at the news of her daughter's death, as had Roxy's stepfather, but both Charlie and Seth had dashed off, abandoning their mother and stepfather to their pain. Oliver, the third son, stationed in barracks in Nottingham, would have found out about his sister from his senior officer or chaplain. She wondered what his reaction had been. He certainly hadn't raced home to be with his family. Tanya had three children of her own and she hoped they'd all stand by her if ever she needed them.

She picked up her briefcase, full of information to help the family, from the passenger seat and steeled herself. This wasn't going to be easy. It never was. Cathy hadn't wanted to talk to her yesterday. It was understandable. The woman was grieving and in shock. Tanya could only offer tissues and tea. Today, she'd try to help them make the first steps towards accepting Roxy's death.

She locked her car and stood in front of the gate to the flat. The cat that had been asleep on the doormat the day before bounded towards her, winding itself around her ankles and arching its back against her shin, pleased to see her. She bent and scratched its head. 'You're a friendly chap,' she said. She eased herself back up. The animal accompanied her through the gate and into the yard with a motorbike perched on its stand. Her fifteen-year-old son wanted a motorbike. *Over my dead body.* She wasn't letting him ride one. As far as she was concerned they were death traps. She'd visited families whose children had died in accidents on motorbikes. Her kids accused her of being too strict, with old-fashioned views, and

to an extent she was, but she prided herself on her morals and the fact she'd brought her children up single-handedly, and done a bloody good job so far.

The feline shot up the steps ahead of her and squeezed through the cat flap. She caught a glimpse of its fluffy tail before the cover shut with a clatter. She rapped on the door and waited. Gooseflesh rose on her bare forearms as a cool breeze tickled them. She ought to have brought her jacket with her. The day wasn't looking as promising as it had done when she'd got up.

Her meanderings were interrupted by the door opening. Charlie – the teenager with a neck tattoo and shaven head – peered out. She reintroduced herself. 'Is it okay to come in and talk to your mum? She's expecting me.'

He looked at her blankly. 'She's not here.'

'Where is she?'

'At her friend Megan's.'

'Okay. I'll give her a call and see if she's on her way.'

'She's not picking up. I tried ringing her ten minutes ago to ask when she was coming home.'

Tanya dialled Cathy's number and got the answerphone. Charlie hadn't moved from the doorway.

'Have you got Megan's number?' she asked him.

'No. I don't know it.'

'What's her full name?'

'Megan Dickson.'

'Where does she live?'

'Queens Road, Oldfields.' Oldfields was a small town about ten miles from Armston.

'Okay, I'll get her number and ring your mum. Is Paul in?'

'He went to work first thing.'

'You alone then?'

'No. Seth's here.'

'Could I come in for a minute? Just while I get Megan's number and talk to your mum? We arranged to meet this morning. I'm surprised she's not here.'

He nodded and she entered the flat. Seth, in light ripped jeans and a hooded sleeveless top, was watching television, a mug of tea in his hand and a piece of toast on a plate balanced on the arm of the chair.

'Morning, Seth,' she said.

'Hi.' He stood up immediately and slouched off into the kitchen, where he was joined by his brother; they drew into a huddle and talked in low whispers.

Tanya rang the station for Megan's phone number, and as soon as she received it, she called her. Megan picked up immediately.

'Hi, I'm PC Tanya Granger, a liaison officer from Samford HQ. I'm supposed to be meeting Cathy Curtis at her flat right now but I understand she's with you.'

'Cathy? She's not here. I'm at work.'

'She didn't spend the night with you?'

'No. I haven't seen her in over a week. She rang me yesterday to tell me about what happened to Roxy, but she didn't want to see me – or anyone, the poor love. She was in bits. I said I'd go over today after work.'

'You didn't see her at all yesterday evening?'

'I was in all day and all night. She didn't come by.' Her voice sounded concerned.

'Okay, thank you. If she turns up, would you please ring me back?'

'Sure. Has something happened to her?'

'I really don't know but I wouldn't worry too much yet.'

Tanya caught Charlie staring at her with furrowed eyebrows. She sat on the chair without asking and pulled out her file. Paul's number was in it and she tried it, but it went to answerphone.

'Have either of you any idea where else your mum might be?'

When neither boy could help her, she rang the person who needed to be told immediately: Natalie.

*

Ian had left the office to meet Olga at Starbucks.

'What was that all about?' Lucy asked Murray, who'd been teasing Ian.

'Oh, nothing. I was merely boosting his flagging ego,' Murray replied.

Natalie's phone rang and she missed the conversation between the pair.

'What? When did she leave? Oh, for fuck's sake. Okay, leave it with me. What's her number? Right. Got it.' She spun back to face Murray and Lucy. 'That was Tanya. Cathy's missing. Paul got a text last night from Cathy saying she was staying overnight with her friend Megan, but she hasn't come home yet. Paul's gone to work and the boys can't get hold of him or their mother. Tanya's spoken to Megan, who hasn't seen Cathy in over a week.'

Murray offered a suggestion. 'Maybe she just needed time alone. After all, she found out her daughter had been killed.'

'That sounds alarmingly like her daughter. Roxy was supposed to be on a sleepover, and now Cathy…' Lucy cocked her head and left her unfinished sentence deliberately hanging.

'Let's hope it's that and not something more serious. Ring CAT Aerials and find out where Paul is. I need to talk to him urgently. Lucy, get hold of Cathy's phone provider and see if they can triangulate the location when it was last used.' Natalie rang the number, and as she expected, it went immediately to answerphone, a sign it might be switched off. She tried the other number Tanya had just given her. A concerned voice answered immediately.

'Megan Dickson?'

'Yes.'

'It's DI Natalie Ward from Samford Police. I'm checking up on Cathy Curtis. We're trying to locate her and I understand you are friends with her.'

'She's my best mate. We've known each other for years. I just spoke to another officer. She thought Cathy stayed with me last night, but she didn't. Is she okay?'

'We won't know until we find her. Did she contact you yesterday?'

'In the afternoon. She told me about Roxy. She was in such a dreadful state. I could hardly hear what she was saying and I wanted to go around straight away to see her but she told me not to. She was crying so hard it broke my heart. She said she couldn't face anybody, not even me, and that she had Paul and the boys, and she needed some time to let what had happened sink in. I promised I'd visit her today. It's a bloody tragedy. Poor Cathy.' Her voice trailed away to be replaced by the sound of nose-blowing.

'I don't suppose you could come down to the station to talk to me a little later, could you?'

'I'm at work at the moment. I don't finish until three. I can come by after that.'

'That would be very helpful. Thank you. I take it you knew Roxy?'

'Of course. I've known them all since they were little kids. They used to live in Oldfields.'

'Have you any idea where we might find Cathy?'

'I wish I could help you but I haven't a clue. I hope she's all right and hasn't done anything stupid. She was in a really bad way yesterday. You don't think…?' Her voice cracked.

'We'll let you know as soon as we find her.'

'Thank you.'

'Does she have any special places she might like to visit? Somewhere that reminds her of happier times, or maybe where she and Roxy used to go?'

'I can't think of anywhere.'

'And when did you last talk to Roxy?'

'It's been a few months. Not seen her since Christmas.'

Natalie became aware of Lucy trying to attract her attention and thanked the woman. She'd extract more information from her later. For now, they had to locate Cathy.

A map of Armston-on-Trent was on Lucy's computer screen. She used her forefinger to trace a rough triangle on it. 'The phone company has pinpointed the last message sent at seven twenty last night. Her phone emitted a signal that was picked up by this mast here,' she said, pointing at a red dot. She indicated a second and third dot. 'It was also located here, and at twenty past seven it pinged and was picked up at this mast. That must have been when she sent the message to Paul. That means she was somewhere in this vicinity at around that time.'

Natalie screwed up her eyes and squinted at the area Lucy had invisibly traced out, then stabbing at the screen, she exclaimed, 'There's St Mary's church and that street is Linnet Lane. I reckon she went to the Langs' house.'

'She said she didn't know them.'

'She lied. I'm sure of it.'

Natalie's phone rang, interrupting them. It was Ian.

'Natalie, I'm trying to convince Olga to come into the station. She's got some useful information for us. On Saturday evening, she spotted Roxy talking to the two women who Murray and I saw come into the club. They're called Crystal and Sandra B. She thinks her surname is Bright or Brighton, something like that. She was on her way home to get changed for work when she spotted them all in Armston-on-Trent, about three streets away from the nightclub.'

'Have you got an exact location?'

'Bishop's Close.'

'Thanks. We'll look into it. See if you can get Olga to make a statement.'

'Will do.'

'Also, Cathy Curtis is missing. She sent a text message last night at about seven twenty from somewhere close to Linnet Lane. I'm going to ask Superintendent Melody to provide us with assistance to search for her.'

'I'll be back as soon as possible then.'

'Don't rush back. Make sure you squeeze as much information as possible from Olga.'

She ended the call. 'Right, Murray, find out details on Sandra Bright or Brighton. She's one of the women you saw last night. She and her friend, Crystal, were at Bishop's Close with Roxy on Saturday night.'

The office phone lit up and Murray answered it. Covering the mouthpiece with his hand, he said, 'Natalie, I've got Cathy's partner on the line.'

She paced towards him and took the receiver. 'DI Ward.'

'It's Paul Sadler. My boss said you've been trying to get hold of me.'

'That's right. Cathy isn't with her friend Megan. Can you think where else she might be?'

'She isn't with Megan? But she said… No. I've no idea at all where she is. This is mental. She said she was with Megan.'

'Has she been in contact?'

'I haven't heard from her since she texted last night to say she was staying over with Megan.'

'Weren't you concerned?'

'Not really. She said she needed to get out for a few hours and digest what had happened, so she went to Megan's. They've been close friends for a very long time. It was only natural she'd want to spend some time with her. I sent her a couple of messages, but when she didn't reply, I figured she'd turned off her phone so she could be left alone.'

'Surely, she'd have left it switched on in case the boys needed her?'

'They had me. I was at home. She wanted some space and a female shoulder to cry on. That's understandable, isn't it?'

Natalie gave a nod but continued. 'What about this morning? Didn't you try to contact her to see how she was?'

'Yes, obviously I did. I messaged her first thing, to let her know the boys were okay and to say I was going to work and would come home at lunchtime, but if she wanted me before then, to ring me or the office, and I'd come back. When she didn't respond, I thought she might still be asleep or even hungover. Listen, I only gave her what she needed – time out with her oldest friend. Cathy needed a girlfriend – another woman who could understand what she was going through – probably better than me in some ways. Women feel things differently, don't they? Cathy needed Megan.'

'Paul, how did she seem when she left?'

'Still a bit teary but okay – not hysterical or anything. As soon as the liaison officer left, she shut herself in the bedroom and wouldn't come out for ages. Eventually, when she did, we talked for a while, but I didn't know what to say to her to make it better. About half past five she said she couldn't cope hanging around the house and was going to visit Megan, maybe even have a few glasses of wine to numb the pain. She asked if I was okay to look after the boys and I told her I was. I thought it was a good idea she went. She looked so… empty, like the life had been sucked out of her!'

'And did she drive to Megan's?'

'No, she doesn't drive. She caught the bus. It's only a fifteen-minute journey.'

'You didn't offer to drive her there?'

'Course I did but she wanted to catch the bus like she usually does. She insisted she needed normality in her life, carry on like any other day or it would drag her down. I didn't get it but I let her have her own way. I don't understand why she isn't with Megan. None of this makes any sense. This is like Roxy all over again. What the hell's going on?'

Natalie continued without speculating as to what might have happened. 'Is there anybody else in her life that she'd go to, a relative, an old friend, a male friend, maybe?'

'A boyfriend? Not Cathy. She's not like that. She's got an aunt in Gloucester, but she's not seen her for years. Shit! I really can't think where she'd have gone.'

'It would be helpful if you could come to the station and talk to me in person. Would that be possible?'

'Sure. I'll let my boss know I won't make my next appointment. I'm about ten minutes from Samford.'

'Ask for me at reception.' Natalie collected her thoughts for a minute then said, 'Lucy, Cathy must have travelled by bus. Find out the times from the stop closest to her and see which buses went into Armston-on-Trent. Some of them have cameras on board. Get the footage checked out. See if she was on board and alone.'

Natalie then rang the technical department to request they check through CCTV footage in and around the area they believed Cathy to have walked the evening before. It was a huge task and she didn't have the manpower to do it herself. She got affirmation and was about to ring Superintendent Melody when Murray announced, 'I've found a Sandra Bryton who lives in Bishop's Close. Think that's her?'

'Got any photographs of her?'

'I've only just fed her details into the general database. Hang on a sec. Okay. Here we go.' He squinted at the picture of the dark-haired woman with wide, almond-shaped eyes. 'That's her. Says her profession is dancer. She was charged with soliciting in 2014.'

'We need to talk to her immediately.'

'I'll do it.' Murray sprang to his feet and grabbed the car keys from his desk.

Lucy, who'd been engaged in a telephone conversation, also stood up. 'The bus depot is looking into it. Want me to stay here or interview Ellie?' she asked Natalie.

'Ellie, and while you're in the area, talk to the Curtis boys about their mum. When Ian gets back, I'll send him to Linnet Lane to ask around and see if anyone noticed Cathy in the area last night. Where the fuck can she have disappeared to?'

'Beats me, and why? I can't fathom out why she'd go off like that, unless she really was grieving so badly she wandered off aimlessly,' said Lucy. She threw on her jacket, picked up a folder and slid in photographs of Cathy and Roxy.

Natalie was still puzzling it over. 'It makes little to no sense. Why leave her family at such a difficult time? Megan wanted to dash around to comfort her but Cathy kept her at bay, claiming she wanted to be alone. That's weird too. And what was so important she made up an excuse to go out and stay away from home? You don't suppose she'd have gone to see her other son, Oliver, do you?'

Lucy tucked the file under her arm and thought for a second. 'All the way to Nottingham? It's possible, but why not tell them that's where she was headed?'

'I'll ring him anyway. Grief does strange things to people although I have a bad feeling about this.'

'Hope you're wrong.'

'Me too.'

It was difficult to get hold of Oliver. He'd left in the early hours on a training exercise and was not due back at the barracks until later.

'Is there no way of contacting him?' she asked the major who'd taken her call.

'Unfortunately, not until the squad's returned.'

'We're searching for his mother and trying to establish if she visited him last night.'

'She'd have had to pass through security, and I can see, looking at the visitor log, that there were no visitors at all to the barracks yesterday evening.'

'How did Oliver take the news of his sister's death?'

'I'm afraid I can't answer that. His sergeant would have passed on the sad news.'

Natalie had no option other than to try again later. 'What time do you think I could get hold of Oliver?'

'After six. I do hope you find Mrs Curtis before then.'

She thanked the man and rang off. They had no way of knowing if Cathy had gone in search of her son and met him outside the barracks. A small voice in her head said it was highly unlikely. What concerned her most was that Cathy had gone to Armston-on-Trent. Had she gone to confront the Lang brothers?

Using the office phone, she called Superintendent Aileen Melody, still brooding over the facts. Would a mother leave her other children so soon after they'd found out their sister had been killed and not stay in touch with them? It didn't seem normal to Natalie, and that was what worried her most. Cathy ought to have rung Seth and Charlie by now, if only to assure them she was okay. Invisible ants crawled across her scalp. Cathy had to be found quickly. Her life could well be in danger.

She listened to the purring of the phone then a click and Aileen's calm voice. 'DI Ward. How can I help?'

*

Ian lifted the paper cup to his lips and tried not to wince as the now cold tea slid down his throat. He couldn't leave the café without trying one more time to persuade Olga to come into the station.

She looked at him with liquid eyes and shook her head. 'If word gets out I told you about Crystal and Sandra, I'll be fired, and I can't lose my job. I've got a little kid to support and they're really big friends with Gavin and Kirk.'

'How come they're so friendly? They're only club-goers.'

'No, they're what we call VIPs – they get special privileges like permanent use of the private rooms and free drinks.'

'Why do they get that?'

'For bringing in business – people who pay a fortune to rent the private rooms – and they dance, of course.'

'Is that what goes on in those rooms – lap dancing?'

She shrugged. 'I'm always on the door so I've never been to a private party. All I know is the guys who book them are usually loaded and happy to spend whatever it costs on a good time, so Gavin and Kirk look after them. Crystal and Sandra know all the big-spenders in the area and are always invited to the private parties.'

Olga looked as good in the daylight as she had done on the door. Today she had her hair pinned back and dangling green earrings that matched her thin-strapped vest top, exposing an unblemished alabaster décolletage.

She gave him a long look before shaking her head again. 'I can't come to the station. You have no idea how hard it is to find work that lets me spend time with my three-year-old. She's my life. I can't risk losing my job.'

Ian felt for her. His girlfriend, Scarlett, was in a similar position, trying to look after their daughter, Ruby. She'd chosen to leave Ian and bring up Ruby alone but she found it difficult, even with Ian's financial support. He'd never let down his family.

'What's your daughter's name?'

'Maisie,' she replied and her eyes lit up at her name. 'You got kids?'

He nodded. 'Ruby – she's still a baby.'

She gave an approving nod. 'Children make you complete, don't they?'

He didn't want to go into his private life and was relieved when she continued talking.

'That's why I wanted to tell you I'd seen that girl, Roxy. She's somebody's daughter. I hope Crystal and Sandra can help but you can't let them know I saw them.'

'We wouldn't reveal your name. You can make a statement and that'd be that?'

She pushed her cup away and shook her head. 'I'm not doing it so don't try. I wasn't even sure I wanted to talk to you here. It was only because you had a kind face and seemed so worried about Roxy. I've done my duty so don't ask for more.' She scraped back her chair and stood up.

'Olga, it would really assist us if you'd make a statement.'

'How? I've told you everything I know.' With that she moved off towards the door.

Ian returned without Olga only minutes after Natalie had persuaded Aileen to send officers to Armston to search for Cathy. He explained the situation to Natalie, who dragged her fingertips along the back of her neck, teasing the knots and easing tension that was building up in her muscles. Eventually she nodded. He'd managed to get some useful information they could act on.

'We've established Sandra Bryton was charged with soliciting in 2014. See what you can drag up on Crystal. I'm going to interview Paul Sadler. When you're done, leave any info on my desk and head to Linnet Lane. Cathy was in that area last night. Find me a witness who saw her. There's a small unit hunting for her in that area. Let me know if there are any developments.' She raced down the corridor, aware that it was now gone ten in the morning and Cathy had made no attempt to contact her family. Natalie was more convinced than ever that something dreadful had happened to her.

*

Murray parked in a side street off Bishop's Close and walked to Sandra Bryton's flat, one of four above a fish and chip shop that wasn't yet open for business. He pressed the buzzer and waited for a response. There was none. He pressed again and this time held

his finger in position until a voice on the intercom below the worn buttons snapped, 'Take your fucking finger off my buzzer.'

'Morning. I'm DS Anderson from Samford HQ. Could I have a quick word with you, please?'

'What about?'

'I'd prefer to discuss it inside.'

'I'm not dressed yet. You woke me up.'

'I'm sorry but we're investigating the death of a young girl.'

The intercom fell silent. Murray pressed the buzzer repeatedly.

'Will you stop that?' The voice was back.

'Just let me in for a minute. We have reason to believe you might know this girl.'

There was silence again then, 'Go away and don't press my buzzer again or I'll have you for harassment.'

'I'm not harassing you. I'm doing my job. If you won't answer my questions, I'll have no choice but to insist you accompany me to the station. I'll be waiting for you to decide. I won't be going anywhere.'

There was more swearing and finally, 'Okay. Come up. Second floor.'

The door opened with a loud click and Murray walked into the dingy hallway. The smell of stale grease clung to the darkened walls and caused him to wrinkle his nose as he clunked up uneven wooden steps.

Sandra stood in the doorway in a kimono dressing gown that reached the top of her thighs. 'Come in,' she said and stalked ahead of him. He followed her down a narrow corridor and into a galley kitchen with barely enough room for two people to pass each other. She walked to the far end and filled a kettle before turning to face him. The night before he'd put her in her mid-twenties, but in the daylight and without make-up he saw she looked in her late thirties. He held out a photograph of Roxy and showed it to her. She made a big show of taking it from him, staring at it and returning it to him. 'Never seen her before.'

Murray waited a beat before saying, 'That's not true, Sandra. We have a witness who saw you with Roxanne Curtis on Saturday evening, here on this street.'

'What witness?'

'I'm not at liberty to disclose that information; however, we're investigating this girl's death and we'd appreciate your cooperation.'

Sandra stared at him hard, and for a moment there was something in her expression that suggested she knew more than she was willing to say.

'Roxy was killed in a house fire.'

Sandra blinked rapidly and looked away briefly, causing Murray to be even more certain she knew something.

'The fire at Kirk and Gavin Lang's house. You must know about it. I heard that you're good friends with them.'

'I wouldn't say *good friends*. I go to their club a fair bit, do some partying, do some dancing, but you already know that, don't you? You saw me there last night.'

'You knew their house had caught fire.'

'Of course I did. I was at the nightclub on Saturday night too. I heard about it. I don't know anything about this girl though.'

'Yet you were with her the day she died.'

'Your information is wrong.'

Murray tried a different approach. 'Sandra, she was only fourteen. We need all the help we can get. Give me something. Please.'

His words caused a reaction. She moistened her lips and appeared to be about to speak, then ran fingers through her fringe and lifted it away from her eyes.

Murray looked at her for the longest minute but she didn't respond. 'Where does your friend Crystal live?'

She remained silent.

'You may as well tell me because I'll find out one way or the other, and all you'll do is waste my time. Time I could spend finding out exactly what happened to Roxy.'

'Crystal's upstairs. Number fifteen, but she doesn't know anything either.'

'You seem very certain of that fact.'

'I am.'

'If anything springs to mind that might help the investigation, please contact me.' He held out a business card, levelling his gaze on her. He'd have to bide his time. She wasn't going to crack. He took his leave and climbed the stairs to the next floor, where he knocked on the door and hoped he'd fare better with Crystal.

It took several attempts to get Crystal to answer her door. She was older than Sandra but looked younger, with a neat figure, clear skin and large, dove-grey eyes. Her hair was cut into a long bob that had been dyed red from halfway down to the ends. She frowned at him in bewilderment.

'DS Anderson,' he said, holding up his identity card. 'I need to discuss Roxanne Curtis with you.'

She opened her mouth then halted mid-action, the frown deepening. He took a chance and said quickly, 'Don't deny that you know her. We have proof you do. I've been talking to Sandra.' He hoped she'd assume Sandra had confessed to knowing the girl and it worked. Befuddled with sleep, she stepped back to allow him to enter. As he was about to, he sensed movement behind him. He turned and faced Sandra, who'd followed him upstairs.

'Please return to your flat immediately,' he said coldly.

Sandra looked past him and at her friend. 'I never said anything, okay?'

'Immediately,' Murray said, raising his voice.

Sandra backed off but she'd already done the damage. Crystal now regarded him differently and held onto the door with one hand. 'I don't know what you're talking about,' she said.

'You do, Crystal. A teenage girl, Roxanne Curtis, died in a house fire in Linnet Lane in the early hours of Sunday morning. She was last seen talking to you and Sandra. Now, you can either talk to

me or come with me to the station. I can even have you charged with perverting the course of justice.'

'Oh, *please*!' She tilted her head back as she spoke, a gesture of irritation. She stared at the dingy ceiling for a minute before lowering her head.

'Or you can tell me what you know and make it easy for yourself. Given you were the last people to set eyes on her and you know the homeowners, you could even find yourself under suspicion for her death.'

'I haven't got time or energy for all this shit. Come in,' Crystal said and moved away.

She led him into a small, tidy sitting room and pointed at a chair. He sat down and waited while she dropped onto another and reached for a packet. She sparked a lighter, lit a cigarette and wouldn't speak until she'd inhaled and exhaled very slowly. Only then did she fix her eyes on him.

'Tell me about Roxanne,' he said.

'Poor little cow. We met her a few months ago on our way home from the nightclub. It was about five in the morning and she was huddled under a bridge in tears, hardly any clothes on and shivering like crazy. It was bloody freezing that day. We felt sorry for her. We brought her back here to warm up. I made her a hot chocolate and she told us she'd run away. She hadn't taken any clothes or money with her – it was a last-minute flee after some row with her folks. We didn't pry. She was a tough little cookie, but shit, she was only thirteen at the time and we couldn't let anything happen to her. She reminded me of my kid sister – all hard on the outside but vulnerable inside. We eventually convinced her to go back home. It's a bloody dangerous world out there and she could have got into all sorts of trouble.'

She crossed her legs and studied her cigarette before continuing. 'We didn't see her again. Not until Saturday. She'd come looking for us. She needed a place to stay for a couple of days. Things were

really bad at home and she was scared. I said she could stay in my spare room. She seemed really panicky but she wouldn't open up. She just looked at me with really big, frightened eyes and I knew in a heartbeat she was telling the truth. I'd seen that look before. Something had scared the shit out of her. I didn't ask any questions. I told her Sandra and I were working at the club, but I gave her my number in case she needed anything and left her here. When I got back, she'd gone. Simply vanished. That's it. That's all I can tell you.'

'Did she mention Kirk or Gavin to you either Saturday night or the first time you met her?'

'No.'

'And you had no idea she'd gone to their house?'

'None whatsoever. Last night was the first I heard of it when Kirk told us. He reckoned she was the one who set his place alight but I don't think so. I think that Roxy was frightened of someone.' She stared at the cigarette and sighed then snuffed it out by pinching the end of it together with long, painted nails before dropping it onto a saucer. 'What a waste.'

'Would you be willing to come and make a statement at the station?' Murray asked. He'd dropped the hard act. Crystal was clearly upset by what had transpired.

'Yeah. I don't know anything else though, okay? I've told you everything.'

'Sure. I understand. Could you do one more thing for me?'

'What?'

'Persuade Sandra to talk to me and make a statement too. It would help the investigation. Roxy was only a teenager. A girl with her whole life in front of her. We need to find out who did this. For her family.'

CHAPTER TWELVE

MONDAY, 2 JULY – MORNING

While Murray was in Armston trying to persuade Sandra to talk to him, Lucy was back in Clearview at the Stockwell Estate, mounting the stairs to the landing where she and Natalie had first encountered Boo. She walked past Ellie's door and made her way around to the far side where she'd spotted the child's grandmother when the woman had called Boo in. She rang the bell and heard shuffling and a woman's voice the other side of the door.

'Boo, shift yourself!'

She opened the door and her mouth opened in surprise. 'Oh, I thought you were someone else. Hang on.' She turned away and called, 'It's okay. It's not Molly.' A small voice shouted a reply that Lucy couldn't hear. The woman faced her again, both hands on the half-closed door.

Lucy showed her credentials. 'I'm part of a team investigating the death of Roxanne Curtis. You might know her as Roxy. Could you help me out?'

'Roxy?'

'Do you know her?'

'I think I know the name but I can't place her.'

'She was one of Ellie's friends.'

The woman pursed her lips as if she'd suddenly got a sour taste in her mouth. 'Oh.'

'We were here yesterday and we came across your daughter on the landing. She told us Ellie and some friends were downstairs smoking the other day, and I wondered if you'd be able to identify them.'

'That was last Thursday. I don't know who they were, apart from Ellie. Two lads, Ellie and another girl. They were a lippy bunch. I told them smoking wasn't allowed inside the building but they gave me some right backchat. If Boo hadn't been with me, I'd have given them a proper mouthful but...' She shrugged.

Lucy pulled out the photograph of Roxy. The woman's head bobbed up and down. 'She was one of them. Cheeky little mare. Is that Roxy?'

'Yes.'

'Oh, I see.'

'Can you describe the boys?'

'Not really. One had dark hair, I think. Roxy was really gobby. Like a lot of the kids around here, but to come out with all that filthy language in front of a five-year-old was too much. I told her to cut it out and she gave some sarky reply so I grabbed Boo's hand and left them to it. If I'd been alone, it would have been a different story.'

'Had you met her before?'

'I saw her a couple of times, coming out of Ellie's flat, but I didn't know who she was. She was a rude madam but I'm sorry to hear she's been killed. No mother wants to get that news.'

'How do you get along with Ellie and her mum?'

'Don't have anything to do with them. I know them and Ellie's father, Jack. Since he went to prison, she and her mother haven't mixed much. Jack was trouble. He was a bully and a thief. He robbed the local store and shot the elderly owner, who was unarmed, so not many people have time for either of them.'

A woman's voice drifted over and Boo's mum looked up at her name being called. 'Sorry. That's my friend arriving. I have to walk Boo to school.'

'Thanks for your help.' Lucy backed off and walked past the woman holding a small girl's hand. The child smiled up shyly at Lucy as they passed and she returned it. Soon she'd have her own little girl's hand in her own. The thought was warming.

Ellie answered her door. Her ghost-white face reflected no surprise at seeing Lucy.

'Hi. Can I chat to you again?'

'Mum's out so I can't let you in.'

Lucy knew she couldn't officially interview the girl without an adult present but rather hoped she'd feel able to open up. 'How are you?'

'Shitty. Really shitty. I feel sick. Mum said I didn't have to go to school.'

'I'm sure you feel awful. It's a massive thing to lose your best friend. It'll take time. You ought to talk to somebody though. You shouldn't bury this. There are people – trained professionals – who understand exactly what you're going through. They'll listen and help you.'

'Nobody can help. They can't take the pain away, can they? They can't make me stop feeling like this.'

'They can help you cope with that pain until it eases a little,' said Lucy with a small smile. 'Have you talked to any of your friends?'

'Yeah, a few. They didn't know Roxy like I did. They're all like, "Oh no!" and they're all in tears and saying how great she was and how they'll miss her, but none of them can feel like I do. I loved her so much. We were really good friends.'

'I understand that. She meant the world to you, didn't she? I wouldn't be here if it hadn't been for my best friend.'

Ellie surveyed her through narrowed eyes. 'What do you mean?'

'Let's just say she helped me through a really bad time in my life.'

A silence hung between them before Ellie said, 'That was like Roxy and me. We helped each other. She was there for me when Dad was sent to prison and everyone here was saying all sorts of shit about us.'

'And you were there for her too,' Lucy said quietly, hoping the girl would take the bait. She did.

'Yeah. She went through some really crap times and there was no one she could tell but me.' Lucy waited for more and it came. 'About how she got hurt.' As soon as she'd spoken the words, she looked up, eyes wide. 'Don't say anything, will you? That was her secret. She didn't want anyone to know. It would kill her mum.'

'Why?'

Ellie shook her head. 'I promised I wouldn't tell a soul. I'm keeping that promise. She was my best friend.'

'Would you tell me if you thought it would help me find out what happened to her?'

The girl straightened up and shook her head. 'I can't. I have to go. I don't feel well.' She took a step back and shut the door before Lucy could say another word. Lucy knocked on the door a few times but there was no response.

*

Back at police headquarters, Natalie was in interview room B with Paul Sadler, who cradled his head in his hands. 'Fuck, I can't think straight. This is madness. I mean, what is Cathy thinking of, going off like this? She must know how worried we are about her.'

'Take a second and try to think of anyone she might have gone to. She was in an emotional state. Who would she be likely to run to?'

He lifted his head with effort to respond. 'Me.' His features were screwed in pain and he swallowed several times before attempting to speak further. The effort to do so was too great and he couldn't prevent tears from spilling over his lids and trickling down his face. 'It should have been me she ran to. I understood. I was hurting too.' His shoulders began to shake as the sobs intensified. He reached for the glass of water he'd been offered and sipped then swiped at the tears and tried, with difficulty, to compose himself. He made

another attempt to explain. 'I was Roxy's dad. Not her biological father but still her dad. I don't understand why Cathy's gone. We need her, all of us need her.'

'We believe she went to Linnet Lane.'

'To the house where Roxy died?'

'It seems that's possible. Does she know Gavin or Kirk Lang?'

'No. We'd never heard of them until you mentioned them.' His face stretched and lengthened as he fought confusion and despair.

'Can you think of anywhere in that area where she might have gone?'

'No. I don't get sent to jobs in Armston very often. I did one near the arts centre once.' Natalie was aware of that fact. They'd already checked with his employer to see if he'd carried out any work near Linnet Lane and discovered the arts centre, a kilometre away, was the closest he'd been to it. He released a painful groan. 'I wish she'd phone. This is fucking torture.'

'We'll do everything we can to locate her. It might be best if you went home in case she returns.'

'Sure. The boss isn't expecting me back. I shouldn't have gone in at all. I don't know why I did. I should have stayed at home with the boys.'

'I don't think it would have made any difference. You'd have been expecting her to return and none the wiser that she was missing until PC Granger turned up. I'll take you to reception, and as soon as we have news, we'll let you know.'

*

Charlie Curtis was on the settee, in the same position his mother had occupied the day before. He was staring unfocused at a spot behind Lucy's head. The strain was beginning to show on his face and his biceps flexed from time to time as if he had a nervous tic. Hunched over a mobile in the chair next to the settee was Seth, his hair flopped over his face, long pale fingers swiftly moving over the

screen as he played a tile-matching game. Tanya Granger waited by
the door while Lucy faced the pair, notepad and pen in her hand.

'Would you mind if I sat down?' she asked.

Charlie answered with a half-mumbled, 'Go ahead.'

She dropped onto the chair opposite and leant towards him.

'Have you heard from Mum?' he asked.

'We're still looking for her. Tell me when you last saw her.'

'When you came to tell her about Roxy.'

'You left to visit your girlfriend, Zara, didn't you?'

He unclamped his hands from his armpits and rested his hands
on his thighs. His ripped jeans were so shredded, Lucy could see
a great deal of muscular flesh through the slits. He studied his
ragged fingernails. 'Yeah. I stayed there all afternoon. Didn't come
back until nine. Mum had gone out by then. Paul was on his own
watching telly. I joined him for a while.'

'How did you know she'd gone to Megan's?'

'Paul told me Mum had texted him and was staying over with her.'

'Seth, did you see her before she left?'

The boy paused his game and looked across. His golden eyes
were dull and bloodshot, and dark bags had formed under them.
He might have been the elder of the two, but he somehow appeared
frailer than his brother, who sat with legs apart and an air of
confidence. Seth shrank into himself and spoke quietly. 'I didn't
come home until late either.'

'What time would that have been?' Lucy asked.

'Dunno. Late. Everyone was in bed.'

'You share a room with Charlie, don't you?'

Charlie answered. 'Yeah. I heard him come in. We didn't talk
though.'

'Any idea what time it was?'

'It wasn't long after I'd gone to bed, about ten thirty. I went to
sleep soon after that. This all feels really weird. I can't believe it's
really happening.'

Lucy gave a quick nod. 'Losing Roxy will take some getting used to.'

Seth had dropped his head again, fingers tapping his mobile's screen in rapid movements, not participating in the conversation.

'Which one of you spoke to Paul this morning?' Lucy asked.

Seth replied, 'He was about to leave for work when I got up. He said he'd try and get back at lunchtime.'

'Do you work, Seth?'

'Yeah. Same place as Mum – Argos. We're both pickers but we're not due in until tomorrow.'

'What about you, Charlie?'

'I'm a trainee plumber. I work for Calvin Unwin Plumbing in Clearview. I told Calvin about Roxy and he gave me the week off.'

Lucy turned her attention back to Seth. 'Did Paul mention your mum this morning?'

'I asked him where she was and he said she was at Megan's and she'd be home soon.' He finished his sentence with a light shrug.

'Okay. I'd like to ask you both about Roxy again. Did she ever mention going to Armston?'

'Not to me,' said Charlie.

'Seth?'

The boy responded with a shake of the head.

'Did she talk to you about anyone she knew there?'

Seth's mouth turned downwards as his head moved slowly this way and that. 'Nope.'

'Did Roxy talk over problems or share secrets with either of you?'

Charlie gave a light snort. 'No way. Not Roxy.'

'But you're her brothers. Surely, she'd talk to you.'

'Only about normal, boring stuff.' He lifted a well-chewed thumbnail to his mouth and worried the skin around the edges with his teeth.

'Seth, what about you?'

'No. She used to talk to Mum, not us.' He turned his attention back to his game and Lucy suspected it was a ploy to distance himself from the conversation. She kept up her questions.

'Didn't she ever complain about your mum or Paul to you? I know I moaned about my folks to my brothers all the time.'

Seth spoke without looking up. 'Roxy didn't like being the only girl in the family. She said we ganged up against her but that was rubbish. She got moody a lot, didn't she, Charlie?'

Charlie pulled his thumb away and sighed. 'Yeah. She was really sulky at times, and if we got on her nerves, she'd get proper bad-tempered. She argued all the time, not just with us, but Mum and Paul too.'

'That's normal in families,' said Lucy. 'I used to fight with my brothers a lot too.' She omitted the fact they were foster brothers and she'd hated most of them. 'What did she argue about?'

'Anything that made her mad.'

'Did she ever mention the names Gavin or Kirk Lang?'

'Not to me,' said Charlie.

'Did she say anything about a nightclub called Extravaganza?'

'Nah. Never,' Charlie answered.

'What about the names Sandra and Crystal?'

Charlie looked completely stumped. 'Are they her friends?'

'I don't know whether or not they were her friends. I thought maybe you could help me.'

'She never said anything to me about them. Seth?'

'Nor me.'

'Roxy didn't really tell either of you much at all, then?'

'She was my sister not my best mate. Try her friend Ellie. They were tight.'

Lucy noted the anguished look that crossed Charlie's face. He was putting on a hard front but his trembling hands gave away the fact he was beginning to understand the enormity of what had happened.

Lucy had only a few more questions, and after winding up the interview, she left the boys with Tanya. She was no closer to knowing why Roxy had gone to Armston on Saturday evening or where Cathy might be.

*

Natalie paced the office, troubled by the lack of evidence. Her interview with Paul Sadler had only highlighted his misery, confusion and anxiety. She was musing on her next move when the communications unit sprang to life and she leapt for it.

'Ian? Receiving.'

'We've found Cathy Curtis.'

'Where?'

'In the canal. She's dead.'

'Oh, fucking hell! Does it look like suicide?'

'I can't call it but there appear to be suspicious ligatures around her neck. She might have been murdered. I've sealed the area.'

'Okay. I'll report it and get Mike's team over immediately. I'm on my way.'

CHAPTER THIRTEEN

Natalie crouched beside the lifeless form. Cathy's wet hair glistened, caught in a shaft of light that escaped between the clouds now clumping together above them. The golden ray caressed the woman's cheek before disappearing altogether. *An angel's kiss*, thought Natalie. Cathy seemed smaller and frailer than she recalled. Her body lay on the towpath where it had been deposited by a dog walker who'd spied her and attempted to rescue her. The man, Lyndon Harvey, a well-spoken individual, was currently talking to Lucy, who'd joined them by the canal.

'What are your thoughts about those marks on her neck?' Natalie directed the question to Mike.

'On the one hand, she might have got entangled in something in the canal. On the other, that's the less likely option. My money's on foul play. I suspect she was strangled.'

'It looks that way to me too. Pinkney will be able to confirm it but the signs are there: petechiae in both eyes, bruising around her neck. This is purely hypothetical, but Cathy left home last night for a reason, probably to meet somebody, and I have a nasty feeling the person she intended meeting was her killer.'

'You reckon her death is linked to her daughter's, then?'

'I do. I can't see the connection yet but I'm going to uncover it.' She pushed herself upright and moved closer to the edge,

peering into the gloomy water. The last time she'd been beside a canal, she'd been fearful that her daughter had been murdered and left on board a narrowboat used by a killer to first hide and then murder young girls. Death and canals now went hand in hand for her, and she couldn't feel any of the joy or calm associated with them. The water appeared to be fairly clear and she saw nothing beneath the surface that could have managed to wrap itself around Cathy's neck and choke her. Cathy had been devastated at Roxy's death and undoubtedly felt guilty for not ensuring the safety of her daughter, but would she jump into the canal and kill herself? Natalie couldn't imagine that was possible. Cathy had three other children. Surely, she wouldn't have turned her back on them? Something caught her eye.

'Mike, what's that?'

She pointed at the object – a wig, black hair or similar, sitting towards the centre of the canal.

'Hang on. I've got something that'll fish it out.'

He returned with a flexible pole and net that he submerged until he could scoop up the article. Natalie recognised it immediately. It was a black toy cat – probably Roxy's. Her heart sank. Poor Cathy had brought a memento of her daughter with her. Natalie could fully comprehend the woman's grief. She'd almost gone out of her mind with worry when Leigh had disappeared, and she had feared the worst. The distress had been physical. If Leigh had been found dead, Natalie was sure she would have been suffocated by her own guilt. Had Cathy taken her own life? It was beginning to look possible.

'Natalie, did you want to talk to the man who found her body, Lyndon Harvey? He's asking to go home. I've taken a statement from him,' Lucy said.

'Actually, I wouldn't mind asking him a couple of questions.' Natalie accompanied Lucy back to the man, who was fussing a large English setter that tugged at its lead.

'I'm sorry to have kept you, sir,' said Natalie.

Lyndon reminded Natalie of her science teacher back in the day, with his wire-framed glasses and shock of white hair that stood up on his egg-shaped head. He half-bowed in her direction.

'I'm DI Ward. I'm sure you've gone over this a few times already but could you tell me how exactly you came across the body?'

'It was Albert here who found her. He loves a morning swim and he launched into the canal as usual to chase off some ducks. Then all of a sudden, he stopped over there, in line with the bench, and began diving under the water and worrying something. I thought he was badgering an injured duck and rushed over to intervene and then saw it was a person. Somehow, he'd managed to push her upwards and I leant over and hauled her out. It was too late of course. There was no pulse at all and I could tell she'd been dead a while. I laid her out where she is now and called the police immediately.'

'Have you seen her before?'

'Alas, no. I told DS Carmichael that I've not come across her before, and Albert and I walk this route every morning and evening. Mind you, I rarely see anyone. This is a disused part of the canal so there are no boats and only the occasional jogger or dog walker.'

'You walked along here last night?'

'Yes. We came out at about seven.'

'Did Albert go into the canal for a swim last night too?'

'He always needs a good wash afterwards so I only let him go in once a day if the weather's nice. No, I kept him on his lead and just walked the towpath.'

'And you didn't notice the woman's body last night?'

'I'm afraid not. I was rather engrossed in an audiobook and not paying any attention to the canal.'

'Did you happen to see anybody else while you were walking along?'

'I believe I did. The trouble is I can't say whether they were male or female, young or old. I only caught a glimpse of a person. I was

further up the canal at that point, headed in this direction, and by the time I reached the bench, there was no sign of anybody.'

'Do you recognise this girl at all?'

Natalie showed him the photograph of Roxy and he pursed his lips thoughtfully before saying, 'No. I can't recall seeing her around here. Or anywhere for that matter.'

'Do you know Gavin and Kirk Lang?'

'Ah, now those *are* familiar names. They're the duo who bought the old cattle market for a song and transformed it into a trendy club. I'm one of the old fossils in this town who tried to oppose it. Not that it made a blind bit of difference to the outcome. I highly suspect some backhanders were given to the planning department on that one. It was a travesty. The old cattle market was part of the town's heritage. I'm not against change, but a nightclub! Surely there were numerous other possibilities for such a magnificent building: an arts centre, a theatre; anything that would have been more beneficial to the entire community?' He tutted. 'Sorry, I shouldn't be ranting about such matters. It isn't appropriate for the circumstances and I'm being deeply disrespectful. Poor woman. Do you think she committed suicide?'

'We don't know how she died yet.'

'No, of course you haven't had a chance to establish that yet. Would it be all right if I left? I've spoken to your officer and I'll happily talk to you again, but Albert's becoming fretful and requires feeding.'

'Of course. Thank you for all your help. Are you sure you're okay after such a terrible experience?'

'Oh, I'm fine. Thank you for asking. I spent many years as an orthopaedic surgeon so I'm not squeamish. I'm very sorry I was too late to help this unfortunate lady.'

'Had you and Albert not come by, we might not have found her for a while, so thank you again.'

Albert tugged again at his lead, and Lyndon moved away without looking back at the body on the path. Natalie caught sight

of Pinkney approaching. The two men passed on the narrow path and acknowledged each other with a brief lowering of the head.

'Morning, Natalie… Lucy. Who have we got here?'

'Roxy's mother,' said Natalie.

'Really? Her mother? I'm no detective but I'd say that was very interesting – if, indeed, interesting is the right word.'

'Not sure it's *interesting*. It's certainly suspicious,' said Lucy, who was good friends with the pathologist.

'"Suspicious". See, that's why you're the detective and I'm merely an old sawbones.'

'Sure you are. You do know a sawbones refers to a doctor or surgeon not a forensic scientist, don't you?' Lucy replied as Pinkney got ready to examine Cathy.

He raised his eyebrows in mock surprise. 'Really, gosh, aren't you terribly loquacious today?'

Lucy gave a small grin. The light banter was purely to keep up morale. Natalie had heard the pair making similar exchanges on several other occasions.

'I shall now retreat from any further verbal swordplay with my worthy adversary and examine our unfortunate victim.' Pinkney lifted the mask that had been dangling round his neck and covered his mouth.

The man was very likeable with his eccentric mannerisms and fashion sense. One of his most endearing qualities was his sensitivity towards all of those he examined. Natalie observed him as he knelt beside Cathy: holding her hands gently, he first patted them as if she was one of his patients he was merely comforting before checking her over for rigor mortis.

Mike, who was squatting in front of the wooden bench, said, 'There's evidence of a struggle here. Come and see.'

Natalie bent down and checked out the small markers placed in four spots where the grass had been scraped and scuffed-up patches of earth were visible, like four small troughs.

'Those are shoes marks. Cathy's wearing wedged sandals, and although they've been in water, there are still traces of mud on the heels. I think she was sat on the bench and attacked from behind. These marks,' he pointed out two of the longer gouges, 'are roughly the same length and commensurate with somebody digging in their heels. The others are from repeated movements.'

'She was trying to escape.' Natalie pictured Cathy struggling to loosen whatever was around her neck, her feet kicking wildly.

'The signs definitely point in that direction. We've also discovered fibres under her fingernails.'

'From the toy cat?'

'Unlikely. They're not black.'

'Could they have come from whatever was used to strangle her, then?' Natalie asked.

'Possibly so. That's supposition at this stage, but to my mind, it's looking increasingly like she was murdered.'

Natalie looked from the bench to the water and back again. 'According to the man who found her, she was more or less in line with this bench. Could her assailant have pushed her into the water while she was alive?'

'If that had been the case, we'd have probably found some signs of resistance, but there's nothing. The evidence is here around the bench. I think she was killed here.'

'So, you agree that she could have been thrown in?'

'I'd say that's the most likely scenario.'

'Have you located a purse, phone or handbag?'

'Not around here although it might be somewhere in the canal.'

Natalie walked up and down for a few metres in either direction, eyes scanning the water, but she couldn't spot anything. The other forensic officers were combing the bushes and grassed banks, searching for any evidence. She halted again beside Mike. 'Maybe the killer took it with him. I suppose it could have been a random mugging.'

'Sure, it could have been, but I can tell by your face that you think that wasn't the case.'

'You know me too well,' she said drily and spun on her heel. 'I'm going to break the news to her family. Find her bag and phone for me please.'

'Will do.'

Natalie hovered close to Pinkney, who looked up. 'I know. You want an answer. I can't be completely sure until I've examined her thoroughly but I reckon she died of asphyxiation due to strangulation.'

'Thanks, Pinkney. That's what I needed to hear. Lucy, come with me. We have some questioning to do.'

Paul had his arms around Charlie, whose shoulders trembled violently as he sobbed. Paul wasn't in a much better state. His face was lined and his cheeks soaked with tears. Both had collapsed at the news that Cathy was dead. Tanya Granger was with them and another colleague, a male liaison officer who was sitting with a dazed Seth, who kept shaking his head and repeating, 'No.' Seth glared at Natalie as if she'd murdered his mother.

'What are you doing about it?' he asked.

'Everything we can, Seth.'

'Like what? First Roxy and now Mum. You're bloody useless.'

'Mate, that'll do,' said Paul, quietly.

Seth marched across the room and stood in front of his stepfather, who had to lift his head to meet the young man's gaze. 'You can't tell me what to do,' he hissed, raising a finger and pointing it at Paul.

Paul's eyes flashed. 'Drop the attitude.'

'Fuck you!' Seth stalked out of the room. Paul hugged Charlie more tightly and said no more.

Natalie knew all their movements from the day before but had to ask them again to state where they'd been after Cathy had left. 'Paul, you received a text message from Cathy at seven twenty. Could you show me it, please?'

He pulled away from Charlie, who flopped down in a heap, covering his face with his hands. Paul reached into his pocket and extracted a mobile, which he handed to Natalie, then sat next to the boy. Natalie flicked through the messages he'd sent Cathy that day and the night before and found the one from her that he'd mentioned. He'd been true to his word.

Hi, sweetie. Staying over with Megan. Really can't face coming home yet. I'm sorry. Look after the boys, will you? See you all tomorrow. Love you x

It was brief and to the point. Why she'd lied to Paul was still a mystery.

'You were on your own after Cathy left, weren't you?'

'Erm, yes, for a while. Charlie came in about nine and we watched telly.'

'What did you do during the time Cathy left and Charlie came home?'

He rubbed forefingers across his cheekbones and under his eyes, wiping away the wet residue. 'I kept busy. I worked on Charlie's Yamaha.'

'Is that the motorbike outside?'

'That's the one. I had to remove a nut to get to the oil leak but it was completely stuck and I couldn't shift the bugger. Took me forever and I got fucking oil everywhere and all over myself. After I fixed it, I cleaned up the mess, had a shower and then a bite to eat, and Charlie came in soon after that.'

'Did anybody see you working on the bike?'

'I doubt it. If anyone was about, they might have heard me cursing it. I think I turned the air blue. It was a bitch to work on.'

Natalie would check with the neighbours to verify that. 'Charlie, I know this is a really difficult time but can you remind me of where you were yesterday?'

'I was with Zara all day until I came home.'

'I'll need her contact details so we can confirm that,' said Natalie.

'This is such bullshit!' he said miserably, wiping his nose on the back of his hand. He searched through his mobile for the details and passed it to Lucy, who took note of Zara's number.

After assuring them they would do everything possible to find out what had happened, Natalie and Lucy took their leave.

'When I spoke to the boys earlier, Charlie was the one who was putting on a brave face and Seth was meekly cowering in the chair. Now, Charlie's in tears and Seth's full of anger and bravado,' Lucy commented. 'Seth could barely manage to talk to me earlier.'

'He lived and worked with his mum. They could have been really close for all we know. He's having an extreme reaction to the news. He was angry and upset and raced off when he heard about Roxy yesterday too. Let's try next door, see if anyone there can confirm Paul was at home yesterday,' she said.

In sharp contrast to the suffocating gloom and misery inside the flat, outside the sun shone, warming Natalie's face as she stood momentarily outside the gate to 114 Pine Way. A car horn blared loudly, answered by another higher-pitched honk, and traffic rumbled by on the road the other side of the flats. She and Lucy went into the yard next door – tidier than their neighbours' yard and filled with plastic toys, a mini slide, a child's trampoline, a red sit-on toy car and several balls – and up the steps to the front door, where they rang the bell. A woman with a toddler in her arms answered. Natalie identified herself and explained the reason for the visit.

'Can you confirm seeing Paul Sadler outside yesterday evening?'

'I didn't see him but he was definitely there. It was warm so we were playing ball outside. There was all sorts of clattering and banging going on, and he let rip with some pretty foul language a few times. That was when I brought Tommy back inside. I didn't want him to hear all the bad language.' She jiggled the toddler on her hips to indicate that was who she meant.

'Any idea what time that would have been?'

She puzzled over the question. 'I can't be certain. Quarter to seven… maybe seven. It was definitely after half past six. Tommy ate his tea at quarter past six and then we went outside to play before bathtime.'

'How well do you know the family next door?'

'I don't have anything to do with them. They're an aggressive, noisy bunch, always shouting and carrying on. You can hear them through the wall most days. I stay clear of them.'

'You haven't met or spoken to Cathy?'

'I've lived here almost a year, and in all that time, she's never spoken to me once. I said hi to her a couple of times but she ignored me.'

'And what about the daughter, Roxy?'

'Same thing. Never spoken to her.'

'Right then. Thank you for helping us.'

'S'okay. Come on, little one. Let's go watch *PAW Patrol*.'

Standing next to the car, Lucy told Natalie about Ellie and the secret she refused to share.

'We need to uncover whatever it is she knows. She wouldn't open up to me. Maybe she'd respond better to somebody else. I thought about bringing Tanya in but then we got the call about Cathy and that sidetracked me, so I haven't contacted Tanya.'

'I agree with you. This is too important for Ellie to play around with us. If you think she'd respond better having Tanya around,

then sort it out, but I think you can crack her alone. Got any idea what she's hiding?'

'Only that it is probably to do with Roxy's injuries and how she didn't want it to get out because it would kill her mother. Do you think, given Cathy's now dead, she meant it literally?'

Natalie wasn't sure. 'If that's the case, we need to find out sharpish what this bloody secret that's costing lives actually is. We've no choice other than to try Ellie again. We'll do it now.'

Natalie hammered on number seventy-two's door but got no answer. It was Boo's mother who shouted out from her doorway, 'There's nobody at home.'

Natalie and Lucy walked across to her. Natalie asked, 'How do you know?'

'I saw Ellie ten minutes ago. She was headed downstairs and she wasn't in uniform so I guess she's skipped off school.'

'What about her mother?'

'No idea where she is. Just telling you I don't think anybody's in. That's all.' She shut the door again before Natalie could respond.

'Friendly,' muttered Natalie.

'At least she spoke to us.'

'See if you can track down that girl, Lucy. I want to find out what she knows. No more treading lightly. Bring her in if you need to.'

They didn't see another soul as they descended the staircase and marched back outside and to the cars. Natalie hesitated before getting in, her head lifted towards the flat where the devastated family lived.

'The neighbour said the family was aggressive. While you're in the neighbourhood, can you try and dig up some more info on the boys? See if you can unearth anyone else who thinks they're hotheads.'

'Will do.'

'I'll get Murray to check out Seth and his claims that he was in Scarborough. See if we can pinpoint his whereabouts. If you could be back at headquarters by one thirty, we'll catch up then and see where we are with this.'

Natalie pulled away from the small car park and back out onto the main street. The traffic rolled past the flats as usual and a woman pushing a buggy strolled along the street, chatting animatedly into a mobile. The world was carrying on as normal, oblivious to the double tragedy that had befallen the flat above the Indian restaurant.

There was more to this investigation than met the eye, she knew there was, but exactly what was still a mystery. She was up against it because people were lying to her and Natalie hated nothing more than lies. She squeezed her steering wheel so tightly her knuckles turned white. God, how she hated liars!

CHAPTER FOURTEEN

MONDAY, 2 JULY – AFTERNOON

Natalie had called for a brief meeting to see what they'd found out so far. Lucy had joined them and was the first to provide input. 'I couldn't locate Ellie. Phone provider can't help and she isn't answering her mobile. It could be switched off.'

Natalie made a *tsk tsk* sound of exasperation. 'When we're done here, head back out and try her schoolfriends. They might have an idea of where she is.'

Lucy continued. 'Will do. I didn't find anyone else who thought the Curtis boys were hotheads but I spoke to Charlie's girlfriend, Zara Walters, and Charlie was definitely with her and her family until nine last night. They all confirm Charlie was with them. According to her, he was cut up about Roxy and was reluctant to go home to face up to what had happened. I checked his mobile provider and his phone wasn't picked up by any masts, so it appears to have been in Clearview all night.'

Natalie put a question mark beside Charlie's name on the board. 'Unless he sneaked out of the house after Seth came to bed, found his mother and killed her, I'd say that takes him out of the frame. Murray, how are you getting on?'

'I interviewed both of the women, Sandra Bryton and Crystal Marekova, who we spotted at the nightclub. They confirmed Roxy was scared of somebody and asked to stay at Crystal's flat on

Saturday. She told them she desperately needed a place to stay until she could work out what to do about her situation. Wouldn't tell them any more than that but they suspected she was frightened of somebody in the family.'

'Are they still at the station?'

'Sandra walked out of the interview and said she didn't know anything else, but Crystal is downstairs. I got the impression she might be willing to say more, so I left her with a cup of tea and said I'd be back.'

'I'd like to meet her. She probably knows something else or she'd have left with her friend.'

Lucy interjected with, 'Crystal might be able to throw some light on the secret that Ellie is keeping – about Roxy's injuries.'

'If we could find Ellie, she might tell us exactly what she knows now that Cathy's dead. We've got to have answers and we can't let a fourteen-year-old screw us about. Right, where are we on Seth Curtis?' Natalie directed the question at Murray who'd been dealing with it.

'The tech team are checking ANPR cameras along all routes into Scarborough for Sunday. His mobile was switched off and not transmitting so we have no way of pinpointing him using cell towers. He might have deliberately turned it off so it couldn't be tracked,' Murray suggested.

Natalie dropped onto her seat. Her feet had begun to ache. Another sign of getting older. 'That's certainly possible or, as Paul told us, it could be because he keeps it switched off most of the time. It was off when they tried to reach him about Roxy.'

Lucy rubbed the scar across her nose in an absent-minded fashion as she sometimes did when puzzling over facts. 'What young person keeps their phone switched off?'

'Those that don't want to be contacted or tracked,' said Murray.

The comms unit crackled loudly on the desk next to Murray, who responded.

Ian, who was still in Armston, was succinct. 'We've been canvassing streets leading from the bus station to Linnet Lane and I've found a witness who saw Cathy just after seven. She lives at Rosemary Cottage on St Mary's Mount and was watering her hanging baskets when Cathy walked past her doorstep. She made pleasantries but Cathy didn't respond. Said she appeared nervous and anxious. I'll let you know if there's anything else.'

'Good job, mate,' said Murray.

Natalie stubbed the map on her screen with her forefinger. 'At least we know Cathy's location at seven o'clock.' She traced her finger down the road where it joined with Linnet Lane. 'How long would it take her to reach number ten, the Langs' house – two, three minutes?'

'Definitely no longer than five minutes if she dragged her feet,' said Murray.

'I have a hunch she went to their house, and we should question Gavin and Kirk as to their whereabouts yesterday evening.'

Natalie felt her phone vibrating in her pocket. She'd forgotten to turn on the sound. She hauled it out and answered Mike's call.

'We've made a couple of discoveries: first, some footprints in bushes close to the bench where we believe Cathy died. We've taken impressions and sent them back to the lab. Should be able to give you make and size soon.'

'Cheers. That's encouraging. What else have you found?'

'Cathy's handbag.'

Natalie's pulse sped up at the news.

'There was identification in her purse and something else. She wrote down a phone number on some paper and slid it into a credit card slot. Luckily it was still legible. It's your number, Natalie.'

Natalie shared the news with the team.

Murray was quick to offer his thoughts. 'Sounds like she had some information she wanted to share with you.'

Natalie wasn't convinced. 'She could have had it for a very different reason – she could have been scared for her life and wanted our help. Right, this is how we're going to play it. Lucy, get hold of Gavin and Kirk – I want them brought in and questioned as to their whereabouts yesterday when Cathy went missing – and then find Ellie. Murray, you and I will attempt to coax more out of Crystal.' She was halfway out of the door before either could respond. Murray chased after her, throwing a look at Lucy as he did so. There was no slowing Natalie down when she was in such a determined mindset. They could only try to keep up.

Crystal had one elbow on the table and was propping up her head with her hand. She shifted into an upright position, her half-red hair swinging into position to frame her face, as soon as Natalie marched in and introduced herself.

'I'm sorry you've been kept hanging about. It couldn't be helped,' she said as she slid into her seat. 'Can we get you something to drink?'

'I had a tea already.'

Murray dropped into position next to Natalie, adopting a non-threatening pose, arms loosely on the table. 'Thanks for staying.'

'Yeah, well, I was about to go, actually. I don't think I can help you any more. I sort of wondered if you'd got any updates about Roxy.'

Natalie spoke up. 'I'm afraid there's been another development, which is why we needed to talk to you again.'

Crystal rubbed at a shiny ruby-red thumbnail. 'I don't see how I can help.'

'You've given DS Anderson a statement but we were hoping you could tell us more about why Roxy was afraid when she came to you Saturday afternoon.'

'I don't know why she was.'

'Crystal, you're clearly a kind-hearted person. You took in a frightened young girl and gave her somewhere to stay. You wouldn't have done that unless you knew why she was scared. You didn't know her at all and it's quite something to allow a stranger into your home.'

'She was only a kid,' said Crystal. The rubbing intensified.

'Can you go back over what you told DS Anderson for me?'

'But I already told him.'

'It would help me if you could repeat it. Tell me about Saturday afternoon when you met Roxy?'

Crystal moved onto the opposite thumbnail, making tiny circular movements over the shiny scarlet surface. 'Sandra and I were coming back from shopping. When we got back home, Roxy was slumped against the railings close to our block of flats. She was all huddled up, arms around her knees, and she'd been crying. I asked her if she was okay. It was obvious she wasn't. She looked… terrified. That's the word. I couldn't leave her there so I invited her inside.

'Sandra came in with us and we chatted about what we'd bought and kept it light, so she'd open up and tell us what the problem was. She didn't. She just kept staring with great big eyes and I was worried for her. Sandra left and I told Roxy she could tell me anything and I wouldn't breathe a word about it. That she could rely on me.'

Natalie waited for more but Crystal had hit a stumbling block and didn't continue. 'Did she tell you then?'

Crystal studied her nail and whispered, 'Yes, she did, and I insisted she stayed over. I offered her my spare room. It was only going to be for a night or two until we could figure out how best to deal with the situation. I showed her where everything was in the flat and left her watching television. We were going to sort everything out the following day but when I got home, she wasn't there. I didn't see her again.'

'Did she have a bag with her?'

'Yes – a plastic one.'

'She didn't leave that in your flat, did she?'

'No, it wasn't there. She left a black zip-up top behind – the one she'd been wearing when I last saw her.'

Natalie guessed the bag had been consumed by the fire.

'Crystal, we need to know what she told you. Roxy is dead. Her mother is dead. It's now critical that you tell us.'

Her jaw dropped at the news. 'Her mother's dead too?'

'I'm afraid so. Her body was found earlier, so you see why I need to know.'

The response was hesitant, the truth emerging little by little. 'My little sister, Lida, and I went through something very similar to Roxy. I was powerless to rescue Lida, but I could try and help Roxy.'

Natalie gave her a small smile of encouragement. 'Help her again by telling us why Roxy was afraid.'

Crystal dropped her hands to her lap then lifted them to her forehead, where she pressed her fingers firmly against her brow until finally she gave a sad sigh of defeat. 'Okay. Maybe I should tell you.'

A rap at the door interrupted them and Murray got to his feet. Crystal began rubbing her thumbnail again and Natalie hoped she wasn't going to change her mind. An officer at the door passed a note to Murray, who glanced at it, dismissed the man and returned to the table. He gave the message to Natalie.

Not contacted Lang brothers. Got waylaid by Cathy's friend Megan Dickson. She is waiting in interview room A with an officer.

She says Roxy argued a lot with family recently, especially with mother.

Believes Roxy's brothers bullied her.

Roxy was upset the last time Megan saw her but wouldn't explain why.

I'm now leaving station to look for Ellie.

Lucy

She read the contents and then, folding it back up, turned her attention once more to Crystal.

'Who was Roxy afraid of?'

Crystal wet her lips but struggled to answer the question.

'I'm going to make it easier for you. Was she afraid of somebody in her family?'

'Yes.'

'Was it her stepfather?'

'No.'

'Her mother?'

'No!'

'Her brothers, then?'

'Yes.'

'Was she was scared of all of them or just one in particular?'

'One. He hurt her a few times.'

'Did he break her elbow?'

'Yes.'

'Did he threaten her?'

'Yes. She was scared rigid he would actually kill her.'

She lowered her voice and spoke urgently. 'Crystal, which brother was Roxy most afraid of?'

'Seth.'

Seth, the brother who had been quick to get away as soon as the news broke about Roxy's death, who'd displayed the least emotion and who'd claimed to be in Scarborough when Cathy was wandering the streets in Armston.

'Why didn't she want this to get back to her mother?'

'Her mother doted on him and wouldn't stand up for Roxy. Seth had been getting increasingly aggressive and her mother wasn't able to calm him down or control him any longer. That's all I know. Honestly, that's all. I ought to leave now.'

'Thank you. I appreciate your help. I'll arrange for somebody to take you home. Could you stay with Sandra or somebody else for

the time being? We'll need to arrange for a forensic team to check out your flat, especially the room she stayed in, in case there's any evidence she was taken from it against her will.'

'Really? How long will they be? I have to go out tonight. I need my clothes and make-up and all sorts of things.'

'Where are you going?'

'To work.' She dropped her gaze.

'To Extravaganza?' Natalie asked and immediately knew she'd crossed a line. Crystal's concern for Roxy had been born from personal experience in a similar situation, but asking about the club was a different matter and off limits. Crystal's demeanour changed instantly and she was once again the tough young woman with attitude.

'I don't have to agree to this. I haven't done anything wrong. I've even helped you out with your investigation, and I didn't have to. You can have the top she left behind but I don't want anyone in my home. Got that?'

'You were one of the last people to see Roxy alive. We have to examine your flat. You don't want to be implicated in her death, do you?'

'That's crazy talk! Why would I come here and tell you all this if I knew anything about how she died? This is utter shit. I wish I'd never come.'

'But you did and you helped us. Now you have to do the right thing again and grant us access to your flat. There might be a clue as to why she left it while you were out. Come on, Crystal, you've seen it through to this stage. You want to know you've helped us find whoever is behind her murder, don't you?'

'No. I don't. If you want to get into my flat, you're gonna have to get permission. This is the last time I help you out.' She stood up in one swift movement and stalked to the door. 'And you can't stop me leaving. I haven't committed any crime.'

'Crystal—' Natalie began in vain. The door slammed shut.

'There must be something in her flat that she doesn't want us to find,' said Murray.

'It looks that way. She's probably on her way back now to hide whatever it is. I hope she doesn't screw up any evidence. Give me a few minutes to arrange a search warrant and then we'll talk to Megan.'

'Sure. I'll wait in the corridor.'

'While you're there, think about this, will you? Why did Cathy protect Seth and allow him to hurt Roxy? Why didn't she step in or at least make him pay for his actions? I can't get my head around that.'

'Favouritism? Scared of him herself? Maybe Seth hit her too – that would explain the screaming that was reported back in 2016, and Cathy's injuries to her face that she said she caused herself.' He paused for a second then added, 'If I had to place a bet which one was the more aggressive brother, I'd have put it on Charlie. He's got more physical presence, he's more muscular and he looks like he's spoiling for a fight all the time. Still, they say you should watch out for the quiet ones, don't they? Maybe Seth's just very good at hiding who he really is.'

Natalie thought briefly of David and his attempts to cover up his deceit. It was a woeful fact that people were capable of enormous duplicity. 'Yes. I think that's quite possible.'

CHAPTER FIFTEEN

Natalie held her wrists under the tap, allowing the cold water to cascade over them. She was hot and bothered and the investigation was getting to her. Megan was in the interview room, awaiting her arrival, and Lucy was out looking for Ellie. Forensics were on their way to Crystal's flat and Ian was still in Armston, making door-to-door enquiries. On the surface, it seemed as if they were closing in on a suspect – Seth – yet Natalie was unsure he was the perpetrator. Plus, Roxy being scared of her brother wasn't reason enough for them to arrest him. There were too many other factors that didn't add up: why Roxy had left Crystal's flat on Saturday night to go to Linnet Lane; how she'd got into the house; why, if she'd been as terrified as she'd made out she was, had she not kept her head down and stayed in the flat. Then there was the question of Seth's connection to the Lang brothers – he didn't seem to have any, so why burn down their house?

There was another angle they needed to look at: the nightclub. Both Sandra and Crystal went to Extravaganza regularly – they were clubbers and lap dancers there. Vice squad were certain prostitution and drug dealing were taking place there. Further searches on Crystal had revealed she too had been charged in the past for soliciting. For a brief second, Natalie chewed over the prospect that somehow Roxy had become involved in either prostitution or

drugs. Anything was possible. She turned off the faucet, her wrists now numb, and shook her hands dry. She was feeling cooler and more in control.

Back in the corridor, she instructed Murray to bring in the Lang brothers rather than join her then headed to interview room A to speak to Megan. Cathy's friend was loud, brash and very upset.

'What are *you* doing to find her killer?' she demanded as soon as she set eyes on Natalie.

'We're all doing everything we can to find out what exactly happened to Cathy. We aren't certain yet how she died but we're examining several possible lines of enquiry.'

'That's police talk bollocks. Tell me straight. Do you think she was murdered?'

'I can't answer that until I've read the pathologist's report.'

'Crap! You know she was murdered, don't you?' Megan was on her feet. 'She wouldn't have killed herself. Cathy was strong and stood up to people and she loved her kids – all of them. She was a bloody warrior.'

'You voiced concern about her state of mind when we spoke earlier,' Natalie said.

Megan's brows lowered. 'I was confused when we spoke. Roxy had died in a fire and Cathy was missing.' She put her hands over her face and breathed in several times. When she pulled her hands away, her face was damp with tears. 'What the fuck is going on? First Roxy and now Cathy. What's happening?'

Natalie encouraged her to calm down. 'Come and sit down, Megan. There's a lot for you to take in.'

Megan returned obediently to her chair. 'God, I wish I'd gone round to see her last night as soon as she rang me about Roxy. What a horrible mess this is.'

'Have you any idea who Cathy might have gone to meet last night?'

'No.' Her head moved slowly side to side.

'Do you think there's any chance she was seeing somebody on the side?'

'Cathy? Absolutely not. She loved Paul. He turned her life back around after Aidan walked out on her and the children.'

'Would you say Paul is a good father?'

Megan lifted her head. 'Yes, I would. He's been terrific with all of them. Gets on so well with them.'

'What about Roxy?'

'All of them,' she repeated. 'Roxy too.'

'You told DS Carmichael that Roxy argued a lot with her family.'

'She was always sassy, even when she was a little kid, but she got worse as she got older, and recently…' She rolled her eyes. 'Cathy said it was down to hormones but she was always a handful. She didn't see eye to eye with anyone.'

'Do you happen to know how she broke her elbow in 2016?' Natalie asked.

'She fell off her bike.'

'Is that what she told you?'

'It's what Cathy told me and I had no reason to doubt Cathy. Roxy tried to copy her brothers a lot and was a right tomboy when she was younger.'

'Yet you believe Roxy was bullied by her brothers.'

'Bullied, picked on… teased. I might have used the wrong word.'

'Then can you explain what you meant?'

'Seth, Oliver and Charlie were such a tight band – really close. They always hung about together and excluded Roxy. A couple of years ago she became argumentative, which only made the boys behave worse towards her. In their minds it was horseplay, but some of the things they did really upset her, like the time they tied her to a tree and left her there for hours until Cathy managed to get it out of them where she was.'

'They didn't do anything more sinister to her?'

'What are you suggesting?'

'They didn't abuse her in any way?'

'I seriously doubt that. Roxy would definitely have said something if they had. She wasn't one to keep quiet about anything. She could stand her ground.'

'But they might have. Victims don't always speak out.'

'Look, I've known those children since they were toddlers, and Cathy for years. There was nothing going on other than the usual squabbles between them. Cathy would definitely have suspected if there'd been anything like that taking place, and I don't like you even mentioning such things.' She glared fiercely at Natalie, who deflected the look with another question.

'Roxy argued a lot with Cathy, didn't she?'

'The boys are a handful. Cathy would get pissed off and knackered by them all and Roxy didn't help matters. She wound everyone up and Cathy would always have to deal with the fallout. There were some pretty heated exchanges but Cathy also argued a lot with the boys. She'd often come to my house to get away from them and have some peace and quiet.'

'The last time you saw Roxy, she was unhappy. Have you any idea why?'

Her eyelids fluttered and she shifted uncomfortably in her seat. 'I feel really terrible about this now but she was always such a drama queen, I didn't really pay much heed to it at the time. Around Christmastime, I met them both for coffee in town, and when Cathy went to the loo, Roxy grabbed my arm and hissed, "Tell Mum to make him stop." I told her not to be so melodramatic and asked her what she meant by that, but she instantly changed, became defensive and said to ignore her because she was just feeling shitty on account of her period starting. Roxy was like that: one minute up, the next down. I thought maybe one of the boys had done something to annoy her and it was her way of trying to get him into trouble, so I didn't pursue it, and

after Cathy came back, she didn't mention it again. In fact, she seemed to forget about it.'

'And you don't think she was talking about being abused?'

'No! I really don't think the boys would do anything to her. Charlie's been going out with Zara for a long time, and Oliver left home three years ago, and Seth... well, Seth just wouldn't.'

'What do you mean?'

'He's really quite gentle.'

This sounded at odds with the boy Natalie had met who had argued with Paul in front of her, and who'd been aggressive on a few occasions.

'Can you expand on that?'

'He's a real Mummy's boy. Worshipped Cathy. Always has done. He struggles to be as macho as his older brothers. He puts on a front but underneath the bravado, he's very sensitive. Too sensitive at times. Cathy was worried he was too clingy. A lad his age should be spreading his wings and thinking about forming new relationships, but Seth was happy at home, being around Cathy.' She'd dropped her voice as if someone might hear.

Natalie nodded and let it drop. There was still a possibility that Roxy had been a victim of abuse. She'd gleaned something more about the family and Seth. However, it still didn't link to the nightclub owners.

'Do the names Gavin and Kirk Lang mean anything to you?'

'I think I might have heard of them.' Megan screwed her eyes tightly in concentration but opened them again with, 'No, I can't think where I've come across them.'

'Did Cathy mention them to you?'

'I don't think so.'

'Roxy?'

'Maybe. Maybe she said something about them. Are they in her class at school?'

'No, they run a nightclub called Extravaganza.'

'Oh, I know which one you mean. I've been there. Cathy and I went there the first Saturday in December – girls' night out. They were offering free entry to all women.'

'You were at Extravaganza?'

'We didn't stay for long. It was full of young people and the drinks were way out of our price range. We caught a bus back to Clearview and went to the pub.'

'Did you meet the owners?'

'What do they look like?'

Natalie pulled out photographs of Gavin and Kirk from a file. Megan peered at them before saying, 'I remember him. He chatted up Cathy. She dragged me off to the toilets to get away from him. Said he was a right creep. Couldn't tear his eyes away from her tits.'

Natalie looked at the person she'd indicated – Gavin Lang. 'Did he tell her his name?'

'No. She didn't want to talk to him. He was really intense. We left soon afterwards.'

'You never went back to the nightclub?'

'No. We only went along because it was free entry but it wasn't what we expected. We didn't return. It was a one-off.'

Back in the office, Natalie went back over her interview with Megan. It put Gavin Lang in the frame although Natalie wasn't going to discount any of the Curtis family.

Murray appeared. 'Gavin and Kirk are downstairs and I'd better warn you, they're like a pair of angry bulls. Seriously, that Gavin looks like he's going to deck somebody.'

'Then it'll give us good reason to charge him if he does.'

'They're refusing to cooperate until they have a lawyer present.'

Natalie threw her pen onto the table. 'Bloody hell! I'm getting sick of that pair. Okay. Let me know when somebody turns up and then we'll talk to them.'

Ian's voice came over the comms unit.

Murray scooted across and answered. 'Go ahead, Ian.'

'There's been a development. A black motorbike was spotted travelling along Linnet Lane yesterday evening around seven. Witness says it was going very slowly as if the biker was hunting for an address. He went out into the road to speak to the rider but they tore off once they spotted him. He didn't get the entire registration but he's certain it ended in "N" for November, "F" for Foxtrot.'

'November, Foxtrot...' Murray scrabbled for the case notes and flicked through the pages. 'I'm sure Seth Curtis owns a black motorbike with a number plate ending with those letters. Yes! He does. I'll chase up the tech team immediately and see if they spotted his bike on any ANPR camera.'

Natalie didn't need to reply. She was certain Seth had not ridden his bike to Scarborough, and it was obvious what they had to do next: locate and bring in Roxy's brother.

CHAPTER SIXTEEN

MONDAY, 2 JULY – LATE AFTERNOON

David Ward slammed the notepad hard against his desk. *Fucking waste of time!* He'd been confident, calm and enthusiastic. What more did these people want? He stared at the white Skype logo on the blue background, and with the touch of a key he banished it from sight.

The company had been looking for somebody with a background in languages to assist with overseas sales, and although David didn't have much background in actual selling, he had a wealth of knowledge in law from his previous occupation that would have greatly assisted the young company hoping to expand into Europe. He should have guessed he wasn't going to get the job when they asked to interview him via the Internet. He tapped another key and stared at the webpage he'd studiously examined prior to the interview. He'd researched T-Zone Enterprise Ltd thoroughly, even running searches on the founders to show he was keen. He typed in a fresh web address, one that was now incredibly familiar to him – the local employment website – and swore under his breath.

Stephen, the guy who'd interviewed him, was his polar opposite: casually attired in a T-shirt and relaxed, leaning back in his chair as if watching a dreary film. David, dressed in a shirt and tie, had spent the entire interview bolt upright like a soldier waiting for

instructions. Little wonder the guy didn't want him to be part of the new company. He had to face it – he was an out-of-touch has-been compared to the entrepreneurial guys who were making their marks on the world. He looked at the display on the computer. It was almost five and Josh was in his room, lost in an online game, and Leigh was at Katy's house. Heaven knew what time Natalie would finish work. It could be midnight. How he hated it when she was working a tough investigation. *You didn't mind her hours when you were working, did you?* said a small voice in his head. He told it to fuck off.

He loosened his tie, yanked it from around his neck and tossed it onto the desk. He clicked the mouse button and pored over the available positions. Nothing new had been added since yesterday when he'd last checked.

He interlocked his fingers behind his head and rested back into them, eyes closed. What the fuck was he supposed to do next? He'd promised Natalie he'd find a job, that he'd mend his ways. He'd not been at home the day Leigh had run away because he'd been at the bookies. Not only that, he'd lost the money he'd borrowed from his father, Eric. He'd had a gambling problem. It had taken a while to admit it but eventually he had, and although he'd received treatment and made a recovery, he'd had a setback, brought about by a feeling of failure. He picked up the business card he kept propped against the computer monitor. It bore the name and number of the Gamblers Anonymous group he'd been attending each week since the dreadful day Leigh had run away. He turned it over, rubbing his fingers over the glossy surface and reminding himself he was not weak. He didn't need to be that person who had almost ruined everything.

He flicked the card onto the desk next to the tie and pushed back his seat. What could he do to make it all better? Natalie was still being distant with him and they hadn't had sex in weeks. It wasn't going well, and in spite of his efforts, he could sense it all

spiralling out of control. He ambled to the kitchen, checked the fridge and pulled out some tomatoes and ham. He couldn't face cooking anything for him and Josh. Sandwiches would do. He lifted two plates from the top shelf in the cupboard and stopped, his eyes resting on the three bottles of red wine stashed at the bottom. *Fuck it!* He deserved a drink. He uncorked the bottle and poured a large glass, dropping onto the kitchen stool and staring out of the window. Was this what it had come to? Would he ever find any self-worth again?

The first glass was soon emptied, and the second, and he took the third back into his office, the ham and tomatoes still on the kitchen top. He figured if Josh was hungry, he'd come downstairs for some food and could bloody well fix his own sandwich. He stabbed at the keypad and brought his screen to life. His fingers hovered over the keys. He shouldn't. A look wouldn't hurt. He could delete his browsing history so Natalie would be none the wiser. It wouldn't harm anyone to take a quick look. He typed in the address and sat back, glass in hand, as the bright flashing lights of the casino page flickered across the screen. He didn't have to play. He could look and imagine what it was like to be a winner, couldn't he?

CHAPTER SEVENTEEN

MONDAY, 2 JULY – EVENING

Natalie was in limbo waiting for the Lang brothers' lawyer to turn up. Lucy was still out searching for Ellie but Ian was on his way back to the station with Seth. She stomped back to the office from the vending machine, two lukewarm coffees in her hands. Murray, the only member of her team in the office, spoke as soon as she walked in.

'Mike's team has examined Cathy's mobile and there's nothing on it that can help us. The last text message was sent at seven twenty yesterday to Paul's phone, as we already know. Pinkney has sent through the pathology report on her. In brief, there was tissue damage associated with strangulation, pinpoint haemorrhaging on the skin and in the conjunctiva, and a superficially incised curvilinear abrasion, caused by the victim's fingernail, where she struggled to release her assailant's grip.'

'She was definitely strangled then?' She passed him a plastic cup and he thanked her.

'Yes, and there was no water in the lungs or in the trachea so she was dead before she hit the water.'

'Any inkling as to what was used to strangle her?' Natalie asked.

Murray shook his head. 'Pinkney thinks it was some form of material. The marks on her throat and neck are suggestive of something softer than a rope, belt or cable.'

'Crap! That hardly narrows it down, does it? Could be anything from a pair of tights to a scarf. We still can't interview Gavin and Kirk for the moment. They're holding out for lawyers. Where are we with Seth Curtis?'

'Tech team have just finished hunting through footage of the routes from Armston to Scarborough. They couldn't find his motorbike on any ANPR cameras or CCTV footage in Scarborough, as we suspected. There's an outside chance he took back routes and avoided most of the cameras, but it's highly unlikely, especially once he entered Scarborough. There are numerous cameras in town and there was no sign of him near any beaches.'

'Okay. We're getting somewhere and that's good.' She sipped the coffee and pulled a face. 'I'm sick of bloody coffee. You eaten?'

'Not yet.'

'Phone the Lotus Flower, will you? Get a selection for us all, and noodles. I really fancy some noodles.'

She grabbed her phone and hurtled upstairs to the roof terrace, where she conducted most of her private phone calls. One side overlooked the main road into Samford, and from the other, endless rooftops sprawled way into the distance, towards and beyond the town centre, which was marked by a church spire. The terrace was where the smokers hung out or those who wanted a few minutes away from the hustle and bustle going on inside the building. A makeshift bench had been erected in the centre next to a metal waste bin which was almost filled with empty cigarette packets and sandwich wrappers. This was the place she did a lot of her thinking, especially when it was empty, as it was now. The rush hour traffic droned like a hundred enormous bees below her. She rested lightly against the low concrete wall, briefly savouring its coolness that permeated her blouse and lowered the temperature of her flesh. She dialled home and Josh picked up.

'Hey.'

'Hi.'

'Just checking to see if everything is okay.'

'Fine.'

'What are you up to?'

'Making a sandwich.'

'Where's your dad?'

'Watching telly, I think.'

'I wanted to let you know I'll be late home.'

'Okay.'

'There's some moussaka in the freezer. I put it into Tupperware tubs and marked it up. You only need to microwave it.'

'It's okay. I've got a sandwich now.'

'What about Leigh?'

'She wasn't hungry. She's gone for a bath.'

'Oh, okay. How did your interview go?'

'Fine.'

'Do you think you got the job?'

'Dunno.'

'I'm sure they liked you. You looked the part.'

She was met with a brief silence then an ambivalent, 'Yeah.'

'We'll have to see, won't we?' She hated her false cheery tone and wished she was at home where she could at least measure her son's response from visual clues. His monotone conversation wasn't telling her anything. 'Can you put Dad on for me?'

'Hang on.'

She heard a muffled, 'Dad! It's Mum.'

David's voice was sleepy. 'Hey.'

'Hi. I'm sorry but I'm held up. I don't know what time I'll get in.'

'Okay.'

'How do you think the interview went today?'

'The interview?' He sounded suddenly wary.

'Yes. Josh's interview.'

'Oh, that! Yes. He seemed confident, although we won't know for a couple of days whether or not he got it.'

She picked up on the confusion he'd tried to hide. 'Is everything okay?'

'Why shouldn't it be?'

'No reason. Just making sure.'

'It's all fine so don't worry.'

'I told Josh there's some moussaka in the freezer. Don't worry about me, I'll get something here.'

'Great. Thanks. I'll see if they fancy it. So, I'll see you when I see you, then.'

'I'll try not to be too long but you know how it is.'

'I certainly do. Hope you get a result. Take care.'

He ended the call and Natalie pocketed her mobile with a frown. David had sounded overly upbeat and at the same time vague. She had little time to dwell too long on her thoughts because Mike appeared.

'Must stop meeting like this,' he said with a grin. 'Fucking shit day, what about you?'

'I'd say "fucking shit" just about covers it. A second victim, two uncooperative suspects, a third equally unhelpful suspect with attitude on his way to be interviewed, and far too many people keeping secrets.'

'Welcome to policing,' he said with a laugh. He kept his hands in his pockets and stared at his feet. 'Some days I wonder what on earth I'm doing. The world's such a fucked-up place with millions of fucked-up individuals causing mayhem. We're fighting a losing battle all the time.'

She gave him a moment to speak. Something was really bothering him. It wasn't like him to be so downhearted. He pulled out a packet of cigarettes. It was only after he'd lit one and taken his first drag that he spoke again. 'We got called to a traffic accident earlier. Wanker was completely stoned and slammed into an SUV driven by a young mum and three kids. She was only twenty-eight and the little ones all under the age of four. They all died on impact and yet the bastard walked away without a scratch on him.'

'Oh shit, Mike! I'm sorry. That's really terrible.'

'Isn't it? I couldn't handle it, Nat. Not today. I left the others to deal with it. I had to distance myself as quickly as possible. I wanted to smash my fist into that guy's face and break every single bone in his body and make him suffer. Shit! To think I was within a hair's breadth of losing control.'

'But you didn't. You walked away.'

'Yeah.' He snorted then added, 'It's Thea's birthday next week and…'

'I get it completely. It's almost impossible not to think of your own loved ones in those situations.' She reached out and squeezed his shoulder. He reached up and circled her wrist with his hand. He held onto it and stared into her eyes. She gave him another gentle squeeze. 'I have to go. My suspect will be here. Ring Nicole and talk to her and Thea. Reassure yourself that they're both fine and well. You'll feel better if you do.'

'I was going to. That's one of the reasons I came upstairs – that and a quick fag. Thanks, Nat. It's good to have somebody who understands what you're going through.'

'I've got your back,' she said with a smile.

'And I've always got yours,' he replied.

She broke away and headed downstairs, heart racing. The magnetic pull she'd been fighting had almost propelled her into his arms. She couldn't allow that to happen. Not again. She'd succumbed to his charms in the past. Their brief affair had taken place because her marriage had hit a low point and now that it was struggling again, she couldn't afford to weaken this time. If she did, she'd never be able to face David. Back in the office, she refocused her energies. She was sure Seth hadn't travelled to Scarborough, and she'd have to present all her facts to coax his actual whereabouts out of him.

Her stomach grumbled and she squashed it with the flat of her hand. She couldn't remember when she'd last eaten. It was easy to

lose track of time when an investigation was as complex as this. 'How long will that food be?'

Murray flashed a smile. 'Not long. I told them it was urgent.'

'Good. I need to eat something before I interview anyone or the sodding recording device will pick up my stomach growling every two seconds. I'm going to talk to Seth before we start on the Lang brothers. They've kept us waiting so we'll return the favour. Any news on their lawyer?'

'Nothing yet. Maybe he's eating his dinner and is too tied up to come.' He gave a wry smile before answering an internal call then jumped up and headed for the door. 'Grub's here. I'll nip down and get it. You okay with chopsticks?'

'If you asked for chopsticks, you know where I'll shove mine,' she shouted after him.

Some twenty minutes later, having wolfed down her food, Natalie put down the office phone and neatly tucked her blouse back into her skirt. Ian observed the act, sucked up the last of his noodles and jumped to his feet.

'Seth's been assigned a lawyer and is ready,' she said. 'Murray, when the Langs' lawyer turns up, let him know I'm busy, will you?'

Murray quickly swallowed a mouthful of food and replied, 'Yep. Will do.'

The building had quietened with many of the offices now empty, and Natalie didn't spot another soul on the way back down to the first floor. It always felt strange to be here out of hours when only night-duty staff were around – like a hospital when all the staff and visitors have left for the day, or a school empty of children and teachers. Somebody coughed loudly – a repetitive, hacking cough, the sort a smoker might have – but she couldn't locate the person who might be in one of the numerous rooms along the corridor or in reception. She and Ian marched to the interview room without

speaking. Ian knew the procedure as well as she did and she gave him a brief nod of assurance before opening the door to the room.

Seth Curtis sat hunched in his seat next to an elderly man in an ill-fitting suit. The legal aid lawyer was known to Natalie and was, in spite of his appearance, a sharp cookie.

After introductions and an explanation of what was about to happen, Ian started the recording device and they reintroduced themselves officially.

Natalie asked all the questions. 'Seth, do you own a black Honda CB125 motorbike with the registration ending in LNF?'

'Yeah.'

'You claimed that on Sunday afternoon, following the news of your sister's death, you rode that bike to Scarborough and did not return until late that same night. Is that correct?'

'Yes.'

'Seth, I have to inform you that your motorbike didn't pass any ANPR cameras along the motorways to Scarborough that afternoon or evening. Nor did it appear on any cameras along the A64, A170, A171 or A165, which are the only main roads leading into Scarborough.'

'I took the back roads.'

'Even if that is true, there are cameras along the main road to the beaches and you didn't appear on any of them.'

'I was there. You just didn't see me,' Seth replied.

'We have double-checked. Your bike was not spotted in, around or near Scarborough.'

Seth kept his head lowered. His lawyer wrote something on a pad and kept his focus on Natalie.

'I'd like to talk about Roxy. We have a witness who claims you hit Roxy, sometimes with such force that you broke her bones.'

The lawyer lifted his pen and spoke firmly. 'I must interject at this point and remind you that my client has suffered a tragic double loss. He's not in a fit position to answer such probing questions based

on supposition and hearsay. Furthermore, I'd also like to mention that you're investigating the death of his sister and mother, not what domestic issues might or might not have transpired in the past.'

'Mr Matthews, my questions are relevant to the investigation, and I would appreciate it if Seth would cooperate. If he can explain himself, then he'll be eliminated from our enquiries.'

Mr Matthews shook his head. 'I suggest you keep it relevant to the case, DI Ward.'

'Then I would like to discuss your whereabouts yesterday evening between seven and eight, Seth.'

'Scarborough.'

'I think we've established you weren't there unless you can prove otherwise.'

His response was a light lifting and dropping of the shoulders.

'Okay, let's play it your way. Which route did you take to get to Scarborough?'

'I don't know. I just drove until I reached it.'

'Have you been there before?'

'No.'

'Did you use a satnav?'

'No.'

'Then how did you know where to go?'

'I didn't know where I was headed. I didn't realise I was in Scarborough until I got there.'

'We have another witness who saw a bike matching your bike's description and with a similar registration in Linnet Lane yesterday evening. How can you explain that?'

'Can't. I wasn't there.'

'What did you do when you got to Scarborough?'

'Sat on the beach. Thought about things. Came home.'

She watched his eye movement, looking out for a slight lift to the right that came when people were recalling incidents. There was nothing. His amber eyes remained fully focused on her as he responded.

'Scarborough is about three hours away. Did you stop off for food or fuel?'

'I got some petrol and a sandwich but I can't remember where.'

'Do you have a receipt for it?'

'No.' Still his eyes stayed fixed on her.

'Did you pay cash or use a credit card?'

'Cash.'

'Did you see anyone when you sat on the beach?'

'No.'

'You have no witnesses who can place you there?'

She was met with another shrug.

'Could you please answer the question for the recorder?'

'No. No witnesses.'

'Which beach did you go to?' Natalie happened to know the town from having holidayed there on numerous occasions with her children. The South Bay was the more touristy of the two beached areas and housed the arcades, cafés and attractions, whereas the North Bay was regarded as more peaceful and was home to Peasholm Park. The twelfth-century ruined castle, high on the promontory, divided the two bays. Anyone who'd visited the town would know that. Seth seemed to know very little.

'I didn't pay much attention.'

'You travelled all that distance and don't know how many beaches there are? Did you drive past the castle?'

'I guess so.' A blink followed swiftly by another. Seth was beginning to show signs of becoming flustered and dropped his gaze.

'You *guess* so?'

'I wasn't there to sightsee. I wanted time alone. My sister was dead. I was sad. I just wanted to be alone, okay?' He turned his anguished eyes back onto her, and for a fleeting moment she believed him. Then she spotted something else – anger – and she again doubted he had driven all that way to be alone.

*

After a further frustrating half hour with Seth, Natalie called for a break to the interview. She needed it, and outside the door she paced back and forth in front of Ian, face contorted with annoyance.

'I know Seth's lying. I just know it!'

'Can't we press him again about Roxy's injuries?'

'No. His lawyer won't let us go there. We'd need proof he was responsible before we could try that tack again. Damn! There must be some way to get him to talk.'

'How about trying Charlie again?'

'He won't give him up. They're as tight as tight can be. Charlie already said Seth was at home on Saturday night when Roxy died.'

She pressed her fingertips against her temples. The noodles and sweet-and-sour she'd gobbled down earlier were repeating on her. She swallowed the sour taste and lifted her head as Murray rushed along the corridor towards them.

'Mike's given me details on the footprints found by the bush at the canal. They're from Adidas Alphabounce trainers, size thirteen and a half. The word Traxion is visible on the sole but the top of the letter "T" has worn away on the left shoe.'

It was the boost she required. Seth Curtis had unusually large feet, a fact she'd noticed as she'd sat opposite him. This could be the break they needed.

'Excellent. Let's see if we can make some headway now,' she said and marched off to organise a warrant for the flat in Pine Way.

CHAPTER EIGHTEEN

MONDAY, 2 JULY – EVENING

An hour later Natalie received what she'd hoped for – Seth's Adidas trainers found at the bottom of his wardrobe. One quick look at the bottom of them and she knew she had Seth over a barrel.

'He's not getting out of it this time,' she said to Ian. 'Is he back in the interview room?'

'Yes, he and his lawyer are there.'

'Right, let's nail him this time,' she said, picking up the evidence bag and her folder and striding through the door.

Downstairs Seth sat with his head hung low, unable to meet Natalie's eye. Ian once again started the recording machine and they began where they'd left off. Natalie pushed the transparent plastic bag containing the trainers across the table.

'Are these your trainers, Seth?' Natalie asked.

He glanced at the bag and shrugged. 'Dunno.'

'We found them in the bottom of your wardrobe. Look carefully at them.'

The boy stared at the bag and blinked several times. He was either buying time – waiting until he had to tell her what she needed to hear – or frightened.

'For the tape recorder, DI Ward is showing Seth Curtis a pair of size thirteen and a half Adidas Alphabounce trainers. Both shoes

bear the word Traxion on the sole. The top of the letter "T" has worn away on the left sole,' Ian said clearly.

'Are these your trainers, Seth?'

'My client doesn't need to answer that question,' said Mr Matthews sternly.

'I'm afraid he does. Seth, are these your trainers?'

'Yes.' His voice was little more than a puff of air.

'Then can you explain what you were doing in the bushes close to the wooden bench where your mother was killed?'

The lawyer's head snapped round as he looked at Seth. The young man dropped his head.

'Seth, when were you at the canal?'

He refused to answer.

'Seth, your lawyer will explain how this looks to us. We must establish when and why you were hidden in the bushes there. You need to tell us the truth.'

'I didn't kill her,' he whispered.

'Then how can you account for the fact we found footprints most certainly made by your trainers at that site?'

'I had a pee in the bushes.'

'What were you doing by the canal?'

'I went looking for Mum.'

'Did you find her?'

'No, and I didn't kill her.'

Natalie sighed. 'Okay, tell me what happened.'

He shot a look at his lawyer, who nodded…

Seth doesn't know where to go or what to do next. Roxy's dead. It doesn't seem possible. He shuts his eyes and thinks back to Saturday morning when Roxy was alive.

*

He's in his bedroom, trying on a new top he's bought for the motorcycle event he's going to with Paul. It looks really stylish with an animal print that makes him look more macho, like his brothers. He ought to shave his head like Charlie does or even get a tattoo. He tries to imagine himself with a tat, except the thought of going through with it turns his stomach. He hates needles. She's flounced into his room while he's studying himself in his wardrobe mirror, and he catches sight of her sneering face. Roxy can piss him off instantly with her jibes and sulky looks, and today she lands a sucker punch to the stomach.

'You need a sparkly tiara to go with that top,' she mocks.

He tugs it back over his head and she laughs at his pale, hairless chest. 'You're such a bitch! What do you want?' he asks.

'I'm looking for Charlie,' she says.

'You can see he's not here so bugger off.'

She laughs again, spins like a ballerina and disappears. He drags out an old grey T-shirt to wear with his jeans and tosses the new one onto the floor of his wardrobe. 'Bitch!'

*

The memory is sour. It was the last time he'd spoken to his sister, and although they wound each other up, he feels a gaping hole in his heart put there by the knowledge she's gone. He can't bear to think of the happy times spent together when they'd mess about and laugh wildly, or were tight as brothers and sisters can be, like the time she stood up for him when a gang of lads had made comment about his feminine looks. She'd told them to piss right off or her brother would flatten them, and that he had a bigger cock than all of them. He'd loved her for that. He'd loved the confidence she exuded and craved the same. Oliver and Charlie are equally self-assured and comfortable in their skins, yet he isn't.

The trouble is he struggles with who he really is – one minute he's up, the next down. Life is so fucking hard. He tries to be as badass as his brother Charlie, swaggering about and flexing his muscles, but he

knows it's all a big act. He isn't at all like his brothers. After their dad walked out on them all, Charlie and Oliver had carried on as if it didn't matter. Even Roxy had managed to get along without Dad, but it had been so different for him. He'd hidden away and cried and cried for days. He'd wanted his father to come home again and no matter how often his mother told him it wasn't his fault it had happened, he believed it was. He stares at his reflection and scowls. He hates himself. He hates his long eyelashes and soft skin and the fact he has almost no body hair, even at eighteen. He's not gay but he finds it really hard to attract girls. They are put off by his looks and even when he behaves more macho, like his brothers, they still don't seem to fancy him. He's really confused and mega sick of it all. Mum understands and it's his mother he wants to talk to right now, except she's swamped by a blanket of grief and he doesn't want to go home and see her in tears, broken by what has happened. She's his rock – the person he shares his fears and concerns with. She's the person who looks out for him and makes sure he doesn't get so overwhelmed by it all that he turns to very dark thoughts of taking his own life.

He's been on the move ever since he found out about Roxy. He's been trying to outrun the pain. He's swung his bike around sharp bends and down tiny lanes at top speed, all the way to the Peak District to try and shake off the darkness that descended almost immediately after learning his sister was dead. It came on quickly but even the usually exhilarating thrill of pushing his bike to its limit, or the pint of beer he drank in the pub beer garden, didn't help. In truth it made him feel nauseous, and after it, he'd sat with a pint of orange juice that squelched in his belly.

He doesn't know how long he was there, but he smoked five cigarettes and waited for the dense black fog that swirled around him to lift. It didn't and he remained there until the arrival of a group of hillwalkers who joined him in the garden sent him slouching back to his bike. Then he took more endless country lanes, heading in no particular direction until his arse bones hurt and he found himself close to Ashbourne.

Now it's coming up six fifteen and he still can't face returning to the flat, so he heads to Armston and the spot he knows well. He goes there when he's feeling really bad. There's never anyone there and the silence and the water help him. He's been gone a long time and his mother will probably be concerned about him. She'll know where to find him. He hopes she'll come. The fog is suffocating him and he's scared of himself.

He reaches the canal and sits down near the bench, his back to the cool wall, and rests his arms on his knees. He lowers his head and cries... cries not for Roxy who has gone, but for himself, still trapped in a body he despises.

Time passes but his mother doesn't appear. She's too wound up in grief to make the journey to sit and talk to him as she usually does. He's been selfish coming here and hoping for her attention. This is the one day when Roxy deserves it. He's not been to the toilet since he stopped off at the pub and now his bladder's full to bursting so he stands and moves towards the clump of bushes nearby and relieves himself. When he finishes he looks one last time up the towpath but there's no sign of her, so he plods up the path to the road, clambers back onto his bike and rides away again. He has no idea where he's going. He chooses a road that leads into a wider one, with fields to one side and houses to the other. A sign indicates he's in Linnet Lane. His blood freezes. This is where Roxy died. He takes it slowly, driving up and then down the road, searching for the house. Some nosy parker comes outside and makes for him, probably to demand what he's doing, so he scarpers before the bloke thinks he's responsible for burning down the fucking house.

He just can't face going home because going home means he has to accept Roxy's dead and he can't do that.

Seth shook his head in horror. 'I didn't see her. She didn't come.'

'Have you any idea what time you left?'

His head drops again and he emits a quiet, 'No.'

'How often did you meet your mother at the canal?'

'A few times. I can't remember exactly.'

'How did she know to find you there?'

'That's where I always go when I'm really low. Sometimes sitting by the water helps me. If I was gone too long, she'd come and find me.'

Natalie shook her head. It was possible, but equally, he could be making it up. She certainly couldn't ask his mother about it.

'What about the others – Oliver, Charlie and Paul – do they know you go to the canal when you feel depressed?'

'I don't talk to them about it. It's really hard. They're so… normal! Mum knew. She tried to help me!' He turned towards his lawyer.

'I want you to think very carefully before you answer this,' said Natalie. 'Do you know Gavin or Kirk Lang?'

He shook his head. 'I don't know them.'

'Have you ever been to their house in Linnet Lane?'

'Never.'

'But you used to go and sit by the canal very close to their house regularly – in fact, every time you felt low.'

His mouth flapped open. 'I didn't know the house existed until I drove past it yesterday. I didn't know it was so close to the canal. That's the truth.' He dropped his head, sprinkling tears over his lap. 'I didn't kill my mum!' he wailed.

The lawyer interrupted the proceedings with a gruff, 'I think it would be prudent to pause the interview to give my client a chance to recover and allow me to talk to him.'

Natalie gave a curt nod. She had other suspects to interview and no time to waste.

*

Lucy had been in the Cornwalls' flat for well over an hour. The beat of a bass drum coming from a flat above had thudded continuously ever since she'd arrived, and in the last ten minutes a baby's piercing

cries had added to it. She marvelled at how thin the walls were and wondered how anyone here ever got any sleep or peace.

It had taken a lot of persuasion to get Ellie to open up.

'I understand how you feel. You made a promise to Roxy, but you aren't breaking it. When you made it, she was alive and you were protecting her. She doesn't need that protection now. You aren't hurting her. In fact, you'd be helping her. You'd be helping *us* to find out what happened to her. You want us to find out how she died, don't you?'

Jojo Cornwall stood protectively over Ellie, hands on the girl's thin shoulders. 'Ellie,' she murmured. 'Maybe you should tell her what you know.'

'I promised Roxy,' she spluttered between sobs.

Lucy held her peace. She'd tried everything and was now placing her trust in Ellie doing the right thing. Gradually, the words came.

'She begged me not to tell anyone about it. It was her brother Seth. He used to bash her up. She got so scared of him. He'd wait until she was alone then attack her.'

The words became thick as Ellie's sobs intensified again.

'You're doing really well, Ellie. Did Roxy explain why she didn't tell her mum about this?'

'She wouldn't have listened to Roxy. Seth's really good at pretending he's innocent; besides, he threatened her and said if she breathed a word about him to any of the family, he'd kill her, and she believed him. She told everyone she fell off her bike. Seth's proper scary. I keep out of his way. Roxy said if he found out I knew about him, he'd probably kill me too.'

Lucy thought it sounded a little dramatic. Megan had said Roxy was prone to being a drama queen – so had she duped her friend, or was she genuinely terrified of Seth? She needed more than hearsay.

'Ellie, did Seth ever threaten you?'

She bit her bottom lip, tears forming. 'Yes, once. I was with Roxy at her place and only Seth was about. We were in the kitchen

getting drinks and he came in, stopped, looked at me and walked straight out again without speaking. I didn't think he'd heard me but he had and he freaked. He rushed at me and grabbed me by the throat. Roxy told him to shove off or she'd tell her mum. He let go and went away but I know he was steaming angry. That was when she told me to keep away from him.'

Lucy was curious as to the catalyst for the sudden angry outburst. Had he been offended? 'What exactly did you say about him to make him so angry?

The girl lowered her gaze, 'That he ran off when he saw me in the kitchen cos pussy scared him and he was probably gay.'

'Did Roxy tell you he was gay?'

The girl gave a quiet, 'No. He isn't. I was only joking. I stayed away from their house after that. Roxy always came here. Seth hurt her a few times and she always came and hid here afterwards. She knew she was safe here.'

Her mother's mouth was a thin line of disapproval, but sorrow made her shoulders slump. She stroked her daughter's hair, her eyes on Lucy. 'I'm sorry Ellie didn't speak up before.'

'Roxy was her best friend and she'd made a promise. It's understandable she didn't want to go back on her word. Ellie, did Seth ever hit Roxy's mum?'

She nodded miserably. 'Roxy told me he lashed out at her a few times, bruised her face once. I think Mrs Curtis hit him back when he was younger, but when he got older she was scared of him. He could fly off the handle very quickly.'

'I'm going to call my boss and pass this on. Is that okay?'

Ellie sniffed and nodded.

'Thank you, Ellie. It'll help us.'

She headed outside to call it in. The baby's cries had intensified and could be clearly heard on the landing. Below, a gang of youths was jeering and shouting, egging on two motorcycle riders who were racing around the car park, engines revving loudly. A dog was

going ballistic at the noise, adding its loud barks to the kerfuffle, and Lucy edged towards the stairwell to make her call, grateful she didn't have to live in a hellhole like this.

CHAPTER NINETEEN

The hands on the clock on the interview room wall indicated it was a few minutes after nine. Natalie had spent the last twenty minutes attempting to extract information from Kirk Lang, who insisted he'd never met or heard of Cathy Curtis. His lawyer was only marginally less intimidating to look at than Kirk. The pair looked like gym buddies with their matching wide shoulders and thick necks. Kirk hadn't recognised the photograph of Cathy, and he'd left the interview room with a disdainful expression on his face and the words, 'I'm not too impressed with your investigating methods. If all you're going to do is keep hauling us back in, you'll not make any progress at all.'

Gavin Lang was next to be interviewed, with the same lawyer present, and doubts were swirling in her mind. So far, she'd only succeeded in pissing off one of the victims of the arson attack, had a potential suspect who insisted on his innocence, and had no evidence to lead her to Roxy and Cathy's murderer.

Lucy had left a message for her. Seth had apparently attacked his sister on numerous occasions, broken her elbow among other injuries and even threatened to kill her should she speak out about him. Natalie had challenged Seth but he had denied it, claiming it simply wasn't true. He hadn't deliberately hurt Roxy. Roxy was an out-and-out liar.

Natalie was bone-weary. She'd been on her feet all day, and apart from the recent takeaway, hastily consumed with a bottle of water, she hadn't eaten. Ian had left the interview room to go to the toilet, and she leant back in her seat and stretched her arms above her. She could do with calling it a night yet she still had to carry on. Cathy had been to Extravaganza and Gavin had shown interest in her. It was a link she wasn't going to ignore. She yawned loudly then forced herself up onto her feet, tucked her blouse back into her skirt and braced herself for the next interview.

The overhead lights crackled like dry paper and she wondered how many hours of her life she'd spent in rooms like this, dealing with criminals and innocents, going over and over facts until she was able to find a hole in somebody's alibi or statement. The answer was too many. She ought to be at home with her kids, being a mother, and still there were people to interview. She should also talk to Paul Sadler and Charlie Curtis to find out who was lying. Was it Seth or Roxy? She plodded to the door, aware of her little toe now pressing hard against the inside of her shoe, causing needle-prick pains each time she placed her foot on the ground. She eased her swollen foot out and rubbed the tender area, wincing. Outside, raised voices drifted closer towards her. She forced her foot back into the shoe and opened the door to find Ian restraining a young man with cropped hair and bright blue eyes – an identical colour to Cathy's. One look at his face told her who he was.

'It's okay, PC Jarvis, let him go.'

The young man shook himself free of Ian's hand and faced her.

'I'm DI Ward and you must be Oliver Curtis.'

'That's right.'

'I'm very sorry about your mother and sister.'

He ignored her platitude. 'Where's Seth?'

'He's helping us with our enquiries.'

'What have you done with him?'

'He's in a holding cell for the moment.'

'Why haven't you let him go yet?'

'When we're satisfied he had nothing to do with the deaths of your sister and mother, then we'll release him. At the moment, we have evidence that places him at one of the crime scenes.'

'He didn't kill Mum. Can we talk?'

Natalie opened the door wide, allowing him to enter. He strode in, head high, and took a seat. He didn't wait for her or Ian to take up their positions. He sat confidently, hands resting on beefy thighs, back straight. This was clearly a man used to military ways and behaviour. He showed the right amount of deference, making eye contact as he spoke. 'Seth wouldn't have killed either of them.'

Natalie returned to the seat she'd recently vacated. It was still warm from her body. Oliver looked a lot like Charlie, except his jaw was squarer and he had no visible tattoos. His eyes looked heavy from lack of sleep and he had a five o'clock shadow covering his chin. He continued speaking without being invited to. 'Why is he still here?'

'I've explained why.'

'He's not guilty of anything.'

'What makes you so certain?'

'He absolutely adores Mum. He'd never, ever hurt her.'

'And Roxy?'

'He wouldn't hurt her either. He loved her to bits.'

'We've been told that he harmed her on several occasions. In 2016, he even broke her elbow.'

Oliver gave a sad shake of his head, keeping his eyes trained on Natalie. 'I was on leave and at the flat when that happened. It was an accident. They were both at fault and he was cut up about it afterwards – really upset. In tears.'

'That only points the finger of blame further in his direction. If he's prone to explosive behaviour, he could well have attacked your sister and mother.'

'He wouldn't.' He shook his head again to emphasise the point.

'His footprints were found near a bush close to where your mother was murdered.'

'Where?'

'By the canal in Armston.'

Oliver nodded. 'He goes there when he has a major freak-out. It was Mum's idea. She read some new-age theory about water and depression, how sitting by water can help lift the mood. She found that spot and that's where he goes when he's feeling really bad. The footprints could have been there from ages ago.'

'He admitted he was there yesterday afternoon.'

He shrugged. 'There you are. He wouldn't admit it if he'd killed Mum, would he?'

'How long has he had depression?'

'It started after Dad left home and got worse when Seth started senior school – that would have been about 2014.'

'All of you knew about his depression, even Roxy?'

'We did, and when Roxy was in a bitchy mood, she'd torment him about it. That's how she ended up with a broken elbow. She could be as bad as him at times.'

'What did she say that got him so mad?'

'She told him he was gay because he didn't have a girlfriend.'

This was the second time Seth's sexuality had come up. 'Is he gay?'

'No, he isn't. He's only had one girlfriend though and she dumped him after a few dates. He hasn't really had any success with girls since then.'

'Why did she dump him?'

'She went off him.'

'You never talked to him about his depression?'

He shook his head and she noted how thick and knotted his neck was. He gave a tight smile. 'I'm not the sort of person to sit about talking about feelings. I get on with it.'

'You don't think Seth is aggressive, then?'

'Not really. He can lose his temper now and again. We all can.'

'Roxy told her friend she was terrified of him. She even said he'd threatened to kill her.'

Oliver released a sigh. 'I seriously doubt that. Roxy would say whatever she felt like to shock people.'

'You don't believe she was frightened of him, then?'

'Roxy wasn't frightened of anyone. She gave as good as she got and started most of the arguments in our house.'

'Yet she told strangers she'd run away because she was scared of being seriously hurt by him.'

'That's utter bullshit. Charlie mentioned he heard Mum and Roxy arguing over a boy she was seeing. She didn't take off because she was scared of Seth. She was more likely in a strop cos she couldn't get her own way and decided to give Mum something to worry about. She ran away twice – and one time was cos of some boy.' His face grew serious. 'Seth's tried to kill himself before. Don't keep him here. It might send him over the edge.'

Even if Seth had lost his temper and attacked his mother, without a connection to Gavin and Kirk she had no real grounds to keep him. Moreover, she still needed to establish why Roxy was in the house in Linnet Lane, and Seth didn't fit into that scenario at all. What was the sodding connection? Was Oliver somehow connected?

'Ever heard of Gavin or Kirk Lang?'

He pursed his lips as he thought. 'Not until Mum mentioned them on Sunday. She said they owned the house where Roxy died.'

'Have you ever been to a nightclub called Extravaganza in Armston?'

He shook his head. 'I'm not into that sort of thing. I don't dance.'

'What about Seth. Might he have gone?'

He rolled his eyes. 'No chance. He's a loner. I can't see him going to any clubs.'

'Have you any idea why Roxy was in the Langs' house the night it burnt down?'

'I left home three years ago and kind of forgot what everyone was like, including Roxy. I haven't a clue what made my sister tick, and we've all grown further apart since I left. All I know is Seth doted on Mum. He'd never have hurt her. He really, really loved her. Probably more than any of us.'

He'd been away for three years and admitted they'd grown apart. How reliable was he, and why was he so keen to have Seth exonerated?

'Does Paul know you're here?'

'Of course he does. He wanted to come with me but I talked him out of it because I thought it would be better for Seth if I came alone. He'll probably be stressed out, and besides, Paul's in fucking pieces at the moment.'

Natalie studied Oliver carefully. He seemed genuine enough but she'd learnt a long time ago not to take anybody at face value. 'How long did it take you to get here?'

'About an hour. I left barracks as soon as I got the news about Mum. I headed straight to the flat and then, when there was no sign of Seth, came here.'

'You were on exercise today?'

'That's right. We left camp at 5 a.m. and returned at 6 p.m.'

'You own a car?'

'Yes.'

'Were you on duty this weekend?'

A muscle flexed in his jaw. 'No, we had the weekend off.'

'What did you do?'

He shrugged. 'Went for a run, read, watched television, went for a drive. Hung about.'

'What did you do Saturday night?'

'Went for a drink.'

'With your friends?'

'Yes, we went into Nottingham and had a couple of pints and a curry.'

'Your friends can attest to that?'

'What are you getting at?'

'I'm just checking your whereabouts for Saturday and Sunday.'

'I was mostly around the barracks. Joined some of the guys in Nottingham on Saturday night for a few pints and a curry, like I said.'

'Why didn't you come home after you learnt of Roxy's death on Sunday?'

Her question caught him off guard. His hands clenched as he struggled to answer. 'Mum said not to, and to be honest, I was relieved. I didn't want to.'

'Why not?'

'I couldn't face everyone.'

'But they're your family.'

'I didn't want to, all right?' He blinked back tears. It was the first time he'd shown emotion. He tried to speak but couldn't. He lifted a hand to ask for a second to regain control, and when he had, she continued.

'I'd like the details of those friends so we can confirm this.'

'This is bloody ridiculous. I came to get Seth not to be accused of anything. I've lost my sister and my mum.'

'I'm fully aware of the situation but we have to check everyone known to the victims. I'm afraid that includes you.'

He released a long sigh. 'Really?'

'Yes, so if you wouldn't mind, I'll ask my officer here to take down the details and then you and Seth can leave.'

'You're letting him go?'

'For now.'

She left Ian to get the information they needed and wandered down the corridor towards the interview room where she'd find Gavin Lang. Her head felt fuzzy, her mind unfocused, and she

wondered if she was being overzealous in asking about Oliver's whereabouts. Then she reminded herself that she had a job to do, and gathering facts was a part of it. Chetwynd Barracks was only an hour away by car. If his whereabouts couldn't be confirmed, they'd have to dig deeper. She couldn't afford to discount anything, and Oliver could easily be covering up for his brother or himself. It was a sad fact but people lied, especially when they were cornered.

CHAPTER TWENTY

MONDAY, 2 JULY – LATE EVENING

Murray was pleased to see Lucy, who'd finally returned from the Stockwell Estate.

'Cold Chinese grub if you fancy it,' he said, pointing at the takeaway boxes on the desk near the door.

'Yum. Who doesn't love cold takeaway?' she said with genuine enthusiasm, hunting through the remaining unopened boxes and settling on sweet-and-sour pork. She picked up a plastic fork and stabbed at a piece. Chewing and making appreciative noises at the same time, she joined Murray by his monitor.

'What's happening?' she mumbled through a mouthful.

'Seth admits he was at the canal yesterday afternoon but didn't see his mum there. He suffers from depression and often goes there when he's highly stressed.'

'Well, according to Ellie, he's got a violent streak.'

'It doesn't make sense though. Why would he go to the Langs' house in the first place? Secondly, what the fuck was Roxy doing there? Thirdly, why would he burn down the house? And finally, what motive does he have for killing his mum? I can't work it out.'

'Buggered if I know. Where's Natalie?'

'With Ian. They've interviewed Kirk Lang and now Gavin. The fuckers kept us hanging about for their lawyer so she made them wait for her and spoke to Seth first.'

Lucy chased a piece of pork around the greasy box with her fork until she speared it. She waved it at Murray. 'You know what I think? I think Gavin and Kirk are shifty bastards who are up to no good. I still reckon they burnt down their own house for insurance purposes and somehow Roxy got caught up in it. There's somebody or something we haven't yet uncovered.' She chomped on the food and searched about for something to wash it down with.

'There's lemonade or tangy orange,' said Murray.

'Jeez! It's like being at a kids' picnic, which means you must have chosen the menu. You never did move on from fish fingers and chicken dippers, did you?'

She received a middle finger. Locating the bottle of lemonade, she partly unscrewed the top and allowed the foam to rush to the surface and recede again before unscrewing it completely. She poured it into a plastic tumbler, swigged it and then said, 'I'm going to see if I can get hold of Seth's medical history. I don't know who's lying here but if Seth is as violent as Ellie claims, he might be feeding us bullshit.'

*

Gavin Lang was on his feet as soon as Natalie walked into the room. The same lawyer who'd sat in with Kirk was with him, and he glanced at his watch to drive home Gavin's point.

'About fucking time!' Gavin snarled.

'I'm sorry about the delay. It couldn't be avoided.'

'Really?' His tone was harsh.

'Really,' she replied and pulled out a chair. 'Would you mind sitting down?'

'I've been sat for a bloody hour. Can we get this over with quickly? I've got to get to the club.'

Natalie requested the recording device be set into play and followed procedure by announcing her name and rank. Ian, who'd joined her, did likewise.

'It shouldn't take long. I wanted to ask you about Cathy Curtis,' she said.

'Never heard of her.'

'Do you recognise this woman?' Natalie slid the photograph of Cathy across the desk.

Ian explained what was happening for the purposes of the recorder. 'DI Ward is showing Gavin Lang a photograph of Cathy Curtis.'

'No.' He partly covered his mouth with his hand as he spoke, and Natalie knew he was lying.

'Could you make sure, please?'

'I don't recognise her.' He moved his hand directly in front of his mouth, a classic involuntary gesture of a person not telling the truth.

'She and a friend went to Extravaganza on Saturday, December the second.'

'Do you have any idea how many people pass through our doors? I see so many faces every week, I can't be expected to remember them all.'

'It was a night when you had free entry for women.'

'That doesn't help me in the slightest. We often run free entry nights for women. There'd have been loads more women than usual at the club on those nights.'

'According to her friend Megan, you spent some time with Cathy.'

'I don't recall that.'

'She said you were quite interested in her?'

'I doubt it,' he scoffed.

'What do you mean?'

'She was probably coming on to me and I was being polite. Happens a lot.'

Natalie's eyelids flickered in irritation. 'Again, according to her friend, it was definitely the other way around and you were

showing a lot of interest in her. In fact, so much so that Cathy felt uncomfortable and left the club.'

'Utter crap! I was only being civil.'

'So, you do remember her.'

'No. I don't. I'm only saying that I treat all women in a civilised manner. If indeed I did talk to her, she misconstrued events.'

'Apparently, you couldn't tear your eyes away from her cleavage.'

'For crying out loud! What is this? I don't know this woman, all right? If she was displaying and wiggling her tits under my nose, I might have glanced at them. I'm human, okay? I didn't try anything on with her or any of our clients. I don't need to. I've had plenty of girlfriends in my time. I'm in a healthy relationship, with Daisy, in case you've forgotten. I don't chase after women.'

'Are you categorically denying knowing or speaking to the woman in the photograph?'

'I damn well am. *If* I spoke to her, I don't remember it. Now, can I go?'

'In a moment. Could you tell me where you were yesterday evening between six and nine?'

'The tea shop.'

'You mean the tea room in Linnet Lane?'

'Yes… I was in the Vintage Tea Room in Linnet Lane with my girlfriend, Daisy Goldsmith, between six and nine,' he replied in a monotonous tone. 'I was upstairs in the flat.'

'Were you alone?'

'For some of the time. Daisy popped out.'

'Was your brother there?'

'No. He was with one of his friends then went to the nightclub to open up.'

Kirk had told her similar and she had the name of his friend to check out his alibi.

'What time did Daisy go out?'

'I can't be sure. I was asleep. It's been a stressful few days and I took a nap. She was there when I dozed off and gone when I woke up at about eight thirty. I watched a film and she returned to the flat around an hour later.'

Natalie had had enough of the bristling cocksure man opposite her. In spite of his attitude, his alibi wasn't watertight, and until she could confirm he was actually in the flat, he was a potential suspect. However, she needed reason to keep him detained, and unless they found a connection between him, Roxy and Cathy, there was little more she could do. It had been a long, frustrating and fruitless day and she'd had enough. She terminated the interview and sent Gavin on his way. Some days it was better to walk away for a while and wait for everything to settle so she could get a clearer picture.

*

Back upstairs, Lucy had unearthed some information on Seth. He'd been attending a community mental health centre for the past year. Natalie, back from interviewing Gavin, rubbed at her troublesome toe and grunted.

'Oliver insisted Seth would never harm either Roxy or Cathy and although Seth admitted he was at the canal around the same time as his mother, we can't establish a motive for attacking them, or a link between him and the Langs. Ian, where are you with Oliver's alibi?' Natalie asked.

'His friends confirmed he was with them Saturday night until gone midnight, and one of them saw him jogging around the barracks at five yesterday.'

'Okay. That's one more ruled out. We got anything else to chase up?' Natalie looked hopefully at Murray, who shook his head. She eased her shoe back on. 'Then fuck it. Let's call it a day.'

Tomorrow was another day. She hoped it would yield better results. So far, she had absolutely nothing to show for their efforts.

CHAPTER TWENTY-ONE

MONDAY, 2 JULY – LATE EVENING

Habib Malik drags his fingers through his dark hair, coating them lightly in the gel he's used. Like his dad always tells him, appearances are important, and after tonight, he's going to hotfoot it around to Nadia's house via the all-night grocery store for a box of chocolates and some flowers. Tucker would laugh his head off if he knew what he was planning and tell him he was a muppet for spending any money at all on a girl, especially frigid Nadia. Thing is he feels really guilty about Saturday night and he doesn't want to lose Nadia. Frigid or not, he really likes her and she's into romantic gestures. What can be more romantic than chocolates and flowers?

He rubs his hands together at the prospect of receiving so much money – five hundred quid. It's way more than he's ever had in his life. He's already decided what to do with it: he'll give some to Tucker – maybe a hundred – and then the rest is going towards his 'leaving home' fund. He hates Clearview, and every single penny he can save is one step closer to getting out and moving on.

He casts about the large field. It's a weird place to meet up, and from where he stands, he can make out the roof of the burnt house opposite, its timbers like a huge skeleton in the now fading light. No sooner does the sun disappear than the temperature drops several degrees, raising goose pimples on his arms, and he shivers but not from the cold. He turns away from the house, unable to look at it any longer.

Linnet Lane is silent – not one single car, bike or person in sight. He wonders if one day he'll be able to afford a house like one of those opposite, maybe with a girl like Nadia.

A rumbling of an engine alerts him to an oncoming car. He tries to force back the grin spreading on his face as the car slows. Easiest money he'll ever earn, and all he has to do for it is keep his mouth shut.

CHAPTER TWENTY-TWO

'Can't Dad take me?' Leigh's plaintive voice cut through Natalie's headache. She'd slept badly, plagued by feelings of inadequacy. She hadn't made progress on the investigation and was wondering what direction she should take next.

'He's got an interview on the other side of town. There won't be enough time to drop you off at school and get there in time for it.'

'But it means I'll get to school too early and have to wait about.'

'I know, sweetheart, but it isn't raining or freezing cold.'

'But I'll be, like, hanging!'

'Give it a rest, Leigh,' said David. 'You'll only be twenty minutes early. Your mum has to go to work too. Go on. Get ready.'

Natalie shot him a grateful glance. He looked as drained as she felt. A wave of guilt washed over her. She'd tossed and turned most of the night and undoubtedly disturbed him.

Leigh, still in her nightdress and large furry bear slippers, stomped upstairs to get ready. Natalie scooted up the stairs after Leigh. She needed a plaster for her toe. She'd rubbed it raw. That'd teach her to wear shoes that weren't properly broken in. She heard mumblings from Leigh's room and paused to catch the drift of the conversation.

'I really need your help. I forgot all about the stupid homework Felix set us and he'll totally freak if I don't hand it in today. I

already got a black mark for not handing in the last lot. I don't suppose I can borrow your answers, can I? No… Mum's dropping me off early. She's got some big case on… I know. Bummer. Look, if you photograph your answers and WhatsApp them to me now, I'll be able to copy them while I wait. Yeah. Sure. I'll put in a couple of deliberate mistakes so he won't guess. You're the best. Love ya, babe.'

Felix was the name of Leigh's maths teacher, one of the older teachers at her school, and it sounded like Leigh was about to cheat on her homework. Natalie couldn't do anything about it without proving she'd been eavesdropping. She examined her options. Both resulted in her rowing with Leigh. Things were tense enough at home without falling out with her daughter over copying another pupil's work. Leigh wouldn't be the only child at school to borrow answers from another, but she felt a pang all the same – her girl was gradually changing and becoming more teenager-like by the day. She smoothed down the plaster and pulled off a couple more strips in case she needed them then scurried downstairs to grab a cup of tea. David was at the table, eating a bowl of cornflakes.

'Did Leigh get her homework done last night?' she asked.

'I suppose so. She was in her room all evening. Why do you ask?'

'No reason,' she replied as she poured the last of the tea into her cup. 'Must be odd for her with Josh being off now.'

'I guess so.'

Josh hadn't appeared for breakfast. Even though he didn't have to go to school, he'd been up and about the last few days, and it seemed strange not to see him in the kitchen. She had no idea how he'd fill his days if he didn't get some sort of job.

'You seen Josh?' she asked.

'No.' David spooned in the last few flakes and then dropped the spoon into the bowl. 'Nat…' he began.

'Yes?'

He shook his head. 'Nothing.'

'Go on? What is it?'

There was a lengthy pause followed by, 'Are we okay?'

She took a sip of her tea. 'Course we are.'

'You sure?'

'Yes. Why?'

'You seemed distant last night.'

She knew what he was referring to. In bed, he'd tried to hold her but she'd rolled away from him. 'The investigation. It's got under my skin. I can't see which way to turn. That's all.'

'You sure?'

She nodded and finished the tea in two gulps. 'Better finish getting ready. We'll talk later if you like.'

Both knew that was unlikely but he nodded nevertheless.

'Fingers crossed for your interview today.'

'Cheers. I'm trying not to get too hopeful.'

'You should always be hopeful.' She slipped away before he could say any more.

The office was empty when she arrived at eight forty-five. She'd told the team to assemble at nine and that gave her fifteen minutes to decide what her plan of action would be. If she was honest, she didn't know which way to turn next, and her limited options involved talking to Roxy's friends and interviewing the staff at Extravaganza again. The fact Roxy had been at the Langs' house bothered her hugely because they hadn't yet established why she'd been there, and there were two more things that still troubled her: the first was that Ellie hadn't asked what had happened to Roxy or how she'd died, and the second was that Charlie had overheard an argument between her and her mother, seemingly over a boy. She speculated if it was somehow relevant and if somebody else – this boy – was involved.

A tap on the glass made her look up. Mike, unshaven, was standing outside. She beckoned him into the office, glad of somebody to talk to.

'Hey, how's it going?' he asked.

'Still not getting anywhere.'

'The footprints matched Seth's trainers. Did that not help?'

'It proves he was there but not that he had anything to do with Cathy's murder. He suffers from depression and the canal is his favourite place to go when he has a bad episode. It could be a coincidence he was there around the time his mother was killed.'

He gave her a look. 'But you don't believe in coincidences.'

'I know. That's what's bugging me the most. You haven't found anything that might have been used to strangle her, have you?'

'We searched the canal but there was no sign of anything that fitted the bill. I reckon the killer took it away with them. We have identified the fibres under her nails though. They're cream cotton twill. She wasn't wearing anything that matched them so you can assume they came from whatever was used to strangle her, or whatever the killer was wearing.'

'Cream cotton twill fibres – from?'

'Shirts, dresses, jackets, cots, tea towels, bedding, curtains… want me to continue?'

Her eyebrows lifted. 'That's quite enough to stump me, thanks.'

'Nat, I know it's tough, but we're all doing what we can to assist you. We'll get there in the end.'

'You know I appreciate that.'

He smiled and the wrinkles around his eyes deepened attractively. There was a brief silence before he lifted his hand and turned to depart.

'Mike!'

'Yes?'

'Thanks.'

'What for?'

'Reminding me why I'm doing this job.'

'I didn't say anything.'

'I know, but you are as dedicated an individual as I could hope to work with.'

He made a mock bow and left. His words had resonated with her. She didn't believe in coincidences. Cathy had gone to the canal for a reason, and if it had been to search for her son, she'd have told Paul that was where she was headed and not that she was going to Megan's. She'd taken Roxy's toy cat with her and she'd passed the house where her daughter had been found. Natalie suspected she'd been going to meet somebody else, and the fact she'd written Natalie's number on a piece of paper led Natalie to believe she'd uncovered something. Cathy might even have arranged to meet her killer.

Murray clattered into the room with a loud, 'Morning!'

She acknowledged his presence and asked, 'If I told you your best friend had died, what would be the first thing you'd say to me?'

'When? Where? How?' he replied with a slight hesitation.

'Exactly! Yet Ellie Cornwall didn't ask any of those questions, and I have a hunch she's still holding out on us.'

'Going to talk to her again?'

'Definitely. The Curtis boys too. Charlie overheard a quarrel between Cathy and Roxy on Saturday afternoon about a boy. I'd like to probe that.'

She was gaining pace, her thoughts lining up one behind the other. She now had a structure to her investigation and logic to her thought process.

'I'm still not sure about Cathy and why she was at the canal. If she'd gone looking for Seth, she'd have told Paul, wouldn't she?'

'Unless she suspected Seth was to blame and wanted to talk to him.'

'I hadn't thought of that.' She pursed her lips in irritation at not considering that possibility then came up with another theory.

'She took Roxy's toy cat with her and walked past the house where Roxy died. That sounds like the actions of a distraught mother – one who wanted to see for herself where her child had died. I can understand that. I'd want to do that if I were in that situation.' Her pulse increased as she reasoned that Cathy could then have headed to the canal to spend some time alone in her misery and was spotted. 'Someone might even have followed her there from Linnet Lane.'

Murray picked up where she was going with this new thought process. 'And that someone could even be Gavin Lang, a man with no alibi to confirm he was at his girlfriend's flat over the tea shop, within walking distance from where Cathy was murdered.'

'Exactly.' She reached for a marker pen, wrote down Gavin's name on the board and linked it to Cathy's. She added Seth's and said, 'Gavin and Seth were both in the vicinity at the time.' She tapped the desk with the pen in her hand, a confident *rat-a-tat-tat*. This was why she enjoyed being a detective.

Lucy bowled up next, full of enthusiasm, her hair still damp from a shower. She greeted the pair, dropped a canvas bag onto the floor and sat down, her body turned towards Natalie. Ian followed swiftly behind her and nodded a good morning to everyone. Natalie mused that since the evening with Murray at Extravaganza, he seemed to have returned to his former self.

Within a couple of minutes, Natalie was ready to begin.

'There's lots of loose ends we need to tie up before we can move on and we need to get cracking. So, with that in mind, Lucy, track down Ellie again. When we first told her about Roxy's death, she didn't ask where we'd found her friend or how she'd died. I'd have thought it would have been one of the first questions she'd have asked.'

'She could have been too shocked to ask, and she already told us she doesn't know the men,' said Lucy.

Natalie understood her reluctance, but teenagers, like many people, were secretive. She only had to think about Leigh borrow-

ing her friend's homework to know that. 'I know, and I might be reading too much into it, but she's already kept information from us so it's worth following up.'

Lucy looked doubtful but nodded all the same. 'Okay. I'll question her again.'

'I'm going to talk to Charlie. Murray, look into Gavin's story, will you? As we discussed earlier, he claimed he was asleep in Daisy's flat Sunday evening when Cathy was murdered and that Daisy didn't return until nine thirty. His brother was also out. Like you said, he was within walking distance of the canal. He had opportunity although motive is still a bit murky.'

'He did try it on with Cathy at the nightclub last December. Maybe there was more to it than that and they did have a fling and she dumped him or was even blackmailing him.'

'That's certainly possible and might go a little way to explaining Roxy's presence at their house – she might have known them through her mother. It's all very hypothetical so let's run a financial check on Cathy. Ian, see if there's been any odd activity on her accounts since last December. All clear on what we're doing?' With that she ended the briefing.

'Catch you later.' She shot out of the office and bounded down the stairs. She wanted to get to Clearview and tackle Charlie. Why he hadn't come out with this sooner, she didn't know, but she needed to ascertain who the mysterious boy in question was. This could be the vital piece of information she'd been hoping for, and boy, did she need it!

There was a sour smell in the flat. The curtains hadn't yet been opened and an aura of sadness rested heavily in the room. Shadows lingered in the gloomy corners like silent spectres. Oliver moved swiftly to the windows and let in some light, his face set stern.

'We had journalists here earlier. Told them to fuck right off. Bloody sharks.'

'Where's Paul?' asked Natalie.

'He went to work.'

'I'm surprised he wanted to or that his boss didn't give him time off.'

'He offered but Paul said he'd prefer to keep busy. It's pretty crap just sitting about here staring at each other not knowing what to say or do. He's having trouble holding it together. Charlie's in. He's not up yet though.'

'How are you bearing up?' Her concern was genuine.

'I couldn't sleep. I shared with Charlie and Seth. Slept on the floor. I couldn't face using Roxy's room. It's fucking awful being here. None of this feels real. It's even harder than I thought it would be. Everyone expects me to be the tough guy – the soldier – but…' The confidence he'd displayed yesterday evaporated.

She took in the dark semicircles under his eyes and spoke quietly. 'Have you spoken to the liaison officer?'

'PC Granger?'

'Yes.'

'She rang last night after we got back from the station. We said we were okay without her.'

'Are you, though? She's a trained, experienced officer. She really can help you deal with this.'

'No one can help us, can they? They can't change what's happened and they can't make it better. I lost a mate on operations in Afghanistan in 2016. We had to clear out all his personal stuff from his locker to hand back to his parents: photos, letters, clothes, his shaving brush and toiletries, the lucky rabbit's foot key ring that we joked about. We stripped his bed, got rid of his kit and erased all evidence he'd ever existed. It'll be the same here, won't it? We'll bury the pain and eventually get back on with our own lives. We can manage.'

'Talk to PC Granger. It'll help,' Natalie urged.

He gave a brief tilt of his head then said, 'I'll tell Charlie you want to talk to him.'

As she waited she glanced around the room. Since Sunday morning it had descended into a type of chaos. Crushed cans of beer were strewn on the table along with crisp packets, empty bottles of water and takeaway coffee cups. A pair of trainers, not Seth's, had been kicked under a small table, a hoodie cast onto the back of one of the dining chairs and the table covered in clutter. Cushions that had been plumped up proudly on the settees were now flattened and crushed where they'd been sat on or hugged tightly, or thrown on the floor next to newspapers. She caught sight of the headline on the front page of a local paper: *Teenager killed in arson attack on mansion.* The television remote control had fallen or been thrown onto the carpet, and several mugs had been left on a sideboard in between the ornaments that stood there.

Oliver was back. Charlie, in jogging bottoms and a tight T-shirt that showed off his muscles, trailed in his wake.

'Hi, Charlie,' she said.

He grunted.

'I'd like to talk to you about an argument you heard between Roxy and your mum. When did this take place?'

He shifted uncomfortably from one bare foot to the other. 'Saturday morning, before I went out.'

'Oliver said it was about some boy. Who were they arguing about?'

He flicked a look at his brother, who gave an almost imperceptible shrug.

Natalie spotted the exchange and pressed him further. 'This could be very important information. What exactly did you overhear?'

'I didn't hear it all – only snippets. I wasn't paying much attention to start with but Roxy got really loud and called Mum a bitch…

*

'You're such a bitch!' Roxy yells.

'For fuck's sake, Roxy, calm down. He's a bag of trouble and you know it. What the hell are you thinking of, hanging around him?'

'I'm old enough to make up my own mind. He's not as bad as you think.'

'Don't talk crap. You know exactly what he's like. Don't get involved with him.'

'I'm not going to be told who I can and can't see.'

'If you start hanging around with Tucker, you know what will happen. It'll end in tears. Let it go. There are plenty of other boys.'

'You don't get it, do you? I really like him.'

'Roxy, I'm warning you. Stay away from him. You know the consequences. Do you want that to happen?'

There's a long pause followed by a subdued response.

'No.'

'I'm sorry but you know I'm right.'

'Yeah.'

There's a pause and lower voices now.

'Who is this Tucker?' she asked.

'It's most likely Tucker Henderson. He's got a bit of a bad reputation around these parts. There's a rumour he and his mate Habib Malik set fire to the school art block.'

Natalie had heard about the fire but nobody had been charged for it. The fact the boys' names had been mentioned in connection to an arson attack rang alarm bells for her. She needed to talk to them urgently.

'Are they still at school?'

'No. They left last year. Neither of them work. They just hang about the place.'

Do you have any contact details for them?'

'No chance. Tucker's not one of my friends. He lives on the Galloway Estate in the same block as Habib.'

The Galloway Estate had the highest number of incidents relating to knife crime and drugs in the entire county. Tucker and Habib were from the worst possible part of Clearview. Natalie had to move in on them quickly.

CHAPTER TWENTY-THREE

David sat in his car with his head in his hands. He had absolutely no idea why he'd made up the story about having a job interview. Actually, he did know why: he'd wanted some attention. He'd wanted Natalie to be pleased for him. It was childish and pathetic and he wished he hadn't said anything.

He got out and stood beside his car, briefcase in his hand, looking like one of the regular, middle-aged businessmen walking to the nearby office blocks. He couldn't stay at home because Josh was there and it might slip out that he hadn't gone to any interview, so he'd put on a suit and left the house and now he was feeling like the biggest heel ever. What the fuck was happening to him? He joined the professionals making their way to work and for a fleeting moment recalled what it felt like to be part of that. He turned into a coffee house and queued to purchase a takeaway with the money he'd taken from the shopping fund. Natalie had left twenty-five pounds for household goods and shopping. He'd get it back. He ordered a flat white to go and handed over a five-pound note. The need to feel part of normal working life was acute.

Back on the street, he stopped at the newsagents next door for a local paper so he could hunt through the job sections. There might be something he could apply for. He picked up a copy of the *Gazette* and dropped it onto the countertop.

'Anything else?' the girl asked.

His eyes landed on the scratch cards next to the till. The twenty-pound note rustled between his fingertips.

'Two £20,000 Jackpots,' he said. He'd checked the odds and knew there was a 1 in 3.54 chance overall of winning a prize. *Gambler!* He winced at the voice in his head and waited for his change.

Back inside the car he drew the deepest breath, plastic cup balanced in the cup holder and cards in his sweaty palms. The throbbing in his temples was the blood pumping through his veins. *Idiot! You fucking idiot!* He lifted a ten-pence piece and scratched away at the surface, revealing the numbers. No win. He had to win this time. He was long overdue some luck. He asked the universe to listen to his request and rubbed again. There! Number twenty-one. He knew he'd win. It was only fifty pounds; however, his luck was on the turn and now he could replace the money he'd taken from the household kitty. In fact, there was even some left over and he could buy a nice bottle of wine for them to share when she got in. He'd tell her he'd done a short translation for somebody if she asked where the money had come from. He jumped back out of the car to claim his winnings and he already knew what he'd do with some of it. He'd reinvest and buy a couple more cards. Next time, he might win big.

CHAPTER TWENTY-FOUR

TUESDAY, 3 JULY – LATE MORNING

Following the morning briefing, Murray had driven to Armston and was now in the Vintage Tea Room, sitting opposite Daisy. The place was empty of customers but warm and filled with the delicious aroma of fresh baking. Daisy had some flour stuck to one cheek but he didn't draw attention to it. She picked at the corner of a red serviette that had been laid out on the table ready for customer use.

'I'd like to know what time you left the flat Sunday afternoon. Gavin said he was asleep when you went.'

'Four-ish.'

'And what time did you get back?'

She refolded the serviette and answered, 'Not too sure. I guess it was around nine fifteen or so.'

'And Gavin was in the flat when you left and when you returned?'

'Yes. He was asleep when I left and watching television when I got back.'

'Does he often go to sleep in the afternoon?'

'He doesn't normally get in until the early hours from the club, so it's quite usual for him to take a power nap. He flaked out after lunch. First, he dozed off in the chair but he was wrecked after

being up all night, what with the fire and everything, so he went to bed for a couple of hours. I left him to it and went out.'

'Where did you go?'

'Met a friend in town.' A flush climbed up her neck and she started to pick at the serviette again, worrying a corner of it.

'Can you tell me the name of the friend?'

'Why? I'm not under suspicion for something, am I?'

'I have to take down every detail.' He stared at her hard and waited. Eventually she broke eye contact with him but didn't answer. 'You're acting rather strangely for somebody who's been asked to provide some simple information. I only want to confirm you were with who you said you were with.' When she still didn't answer him he added, 'I can find out the hard way and have your phone and your car traced. I'll find out eventually.'

She put both hands to her forehead and inhaled deeply. 'Look, this can't get out. Gavin mustn't hear about it. Not yet. Not until we've told him.'

'Okay.'

'I've started seeing Kirk. It's not working out between Gavin and me but he's not easy to shake off. He's pretty keen on me and I've been trying to find the right moment to break up with him. Kirk and I met up yesterday and discussed what to do but we're leaving it for a while longer before we break the news.'

'Were you with Kirk all afternoon?'

'Yes, from just after four until nine. We met up at the marina in Barton-under-Needwood. I told Gavin I was out with friends.'

'How did he seem when you got in?'

'In what way?'

'Worried, hyper, miserable?'

'He was a bit annoyed I hadn't got back earlier cos he'd fancied a meal out but we got a takeaway delivered instead and watched telly. He was normal.'

'Did he tell you what he'd done all afternoon?'

'No, but he was still in his lounge pants and top he was wearing when he went to bed, so I figured he'd not done much.'

'It must be tricky having both men living with you here,' he said.

'That's changed. Kirk's staying with a friend until the insurance money comes in and he can rent somewhere. He's not going to share with Gavin. It'll be really difficult once Gavin finds out about us.'

Murray made a note of what she'd told him. A thought flashed across his mind – would Kirk and Daisy deliberately burn down the house so Kirk could free himself of living with Gavin? It seemed extreme. He'd ask Natalie for her thoughts on the matter.

'Why do you want to know where Gavin was?'

'Cathy Curtis was found dead in the canal down the road from here. She was Roxy's mother.'

'The girl who was in Kirk's house?'

'That's right.'

'Shit! What's going on?'

'That's what we're trying to find out.' He had another thought. 'You used to work at the nightclub, didn't you?'

'Yeah.'

'You were a hostess there.'

'That's right.' Her voice was hesitant as if expecting another bombshell.

'Do you know Sandra Bryton and Crystal Marekova?'

'Ye-es.' Her eyes narrowed as she spoke.

'You friends with them?'

'No.' She shook her head emphatically.

'But you know them.'

'I saw them at the club. I served them drinks but I'm not friends with them.' She wrinkled her face up as she spoke.

'Is there something you want to tell me about them?'

'No. I just didn't get along with them, that's all.'

'Why are they VIPs?'

'They're good at bringing in new customers.'

'Why would they do that?'

'They get VIP treatment for bringing in business – it's an incentive.' A timer pinged in the background. 'My cakes are ready,' she said.

'They lap dancers?'

'Why are you asking me this?'

'It's part of our investigation.'

'Yes, they're lap dancers and clubbers – good-time girls. That's all.' She pushed her fringe away from her forehead testily, but some strands clung to the dampness there.

'One last thing. Would you say Gavin was a bit of a ladies' man?'

'He flirts with customers sometimes but it's a front. Girls fancy him and he gives them the charm but he takes relationships seriously – really seriously.' Her face and intonation suggested she was finding Gavin intense. 'I have to rescue my cakes.'

Murray tried one more question. 'You don't think he was seeing anyone on the side, do you?'

She threw back her head and laughed. 'I wish. It would make my life a lot easier. No, fat chance of that.'

'Where is Gavin? He's not upstairs, is he?'

'No, he and Kirk have gone to London.'

'Why?'

'They're visiting some old friends and doing some networking.'

'Do you know where?'

She wiped at her cheek, felt the dried-on flour there and rubbed at it. 'No. I wasn't invited.'

'Any idea when they'll be back?'

'Later today, tomorrow? I really don't know. Gavin said it depended on how it went.'

'What about the nightclub tonight? Is it open?'

'They'll have arranged for somebody to be in charge if they're not back.'

'What time did they leave?'

'Quarter to eleven. You missed them by about twenty minutes.'

Murray wound up the interview and left the tea room. The doorbell tinkled merrily and fresh air replaced the warm scent of vanilla. He had new information regarding Daisy and Gavin but he was unsure if it helped in any way. He checked his watch and headed towards the canal on foot to establish how long exactly it would take him to reach it and see if there were any cameras that might have picked up a man headed that way on Sunday evening.

*

Having rung Tanya to ensure the Curtis boys received professional help, Natalie called Ian.

'There's nothing unusual about her finances. I can only see a monthly pay check and child benefit going into her current account. I don't think she was blackmailing Gavin unless she was receiving cash,' he said.

'We'll consider that option again, if we think it's relevant. At the moment, I'd like to find out more about Habib Malik and Tucker Henderson. Get hold of Lucy, tell her about them and email her their photographs so she can ask Ellie about them, and then join me at Tucker's flat.'

It was a twenty-minute drive from the flat on the Stockwell Estate to the other side of Clearview to the Galloway Estate. The barren areas between the large apartment blocks reminded Natalie of post-apocalyptic wastelands she'd seen in sci-fi films, with rusted, burnt-out cars and vans by the side of the road and small tribes of hollow-eyed youths gathered in front of boarded-up shops. She parked away from prying eyes in a side street and waited for Ian to arrive.

Ten minutes later and Natalie was becoming impatient. Ian couldn't be much longer. She tried his mobile only to have it go to answerphone, so she left a message. 'Ian, I'm going inside. I'm parked on Flint Street. Catch me up.'

The pedestrian underpass to the estate stank of piss and Natalie walked quickly through it, her footsteps echoing noisily behind her, hoping she didn't come across any troublemakers. She ought to have waited for Ian but her haste and desire to speak to Tucker and Habib had spurred her on.

She emerged into the bright sunlight and squinted ahead. The building she wanted was to her right, but to reach it she had to pass a group of young men who eyed her suspiciously. She increased her pace, eyes on the entrance.

'You're not welcome around these parts,' shouted a voice behind her.

She continued regardless.

'I said, you're not welcome.' The man had suddenly caught her up and brought two of his friends with him.

She spun on her heel and glared at them, then held up her ID. 'Welcome or not, I'm here on official business.'

'Coppers shouldn't be walking about on their own. It's dangerous around here.' He cocked his head to one side. He was about the same size as Murray, head and shoulders above her and lean like a basketball player, with dangly arms and long legs clad in tracksuit bottoms. She estimated him to be about Josh's age.

'Do you know Roxy Curtis?'

The long-limbed boy continued observing her through heavy-lidded eyes. 'Never heard of her.'

Natalie rooted for the photograph of the girl and showed it to him. He shook his head immediately. 'Don't know her.'

'She was seeing Tucker Henderson.'

He turned to his friends. 'You know anyfin' about Tucker 'n' a girl?'

The second boy gave a dramatic shrug. 'Tucker? He ain't got no girl.'

The tallest boy moved closer. 'See. We don't know nuffin' about no Roxy.'

'Then move away and let me do my job.'

The youth stood his ground for a while longer, then, languidly, took a small step to one side. 'Not stoppin' you. Just checkin' you out.'

'You checked me out now, so excuse me.' She moved away, determined to maintain a steady pace and an air of authority. Her heartbeat, however, had accelerated. She was foolish to be here alone. Her rank and occupation were no guarantee of her safety in these parts; in fact, they were more likely to cause friction or aggression. She opened the entrance to the flats, aware of the group behind her, and pulled out her mobile.

Ian answered. 'Just parking up.'

'There are some kids outside the block. I'll wait in the entrance for you. Don't challenge them. They're spoiling for trouble.'

No sooner had she ended the call than the door opened and the boys trooped in.

'Tucker's not in.' The taller one, the leader of them all, was moving towards her, hips swaying.

'How do you know?'

'He was out when I called for him.'

'What time was that?'

'What does it matter what time it was? I tell you he's out.' The boy advanced, closely followed by his friends.

Natalie took a quick breath and stood her ground. She didn't want this to turn nasty. 'Okay. Thanks. I'll try him later.' She began to walk towards them but they blocked her path. 'Could you move out of the way?'

The leader gave her a cold look and Natalie felt her heart jump in her chest.

'Okay, break it up!' Ian's voice was loud. The youngest of the boys shuffled away, immediately joined by the second. The tallest remained where he was, his eyes on Natalie. 'I said, break it up.' Ian had reached them both. The boy said nothing, and blinking once, he moved away lazily to join his friends.

'I won't ask again.' Ian took a step forward and the boys, one by one, left the building.

It was only after the door shut with a thud and she watched their backs retreating that Natalie released her breath. 'Shit! That was a bit uncomfortable. Good thing you turned up when you did.'

'Did they threaten you?'

'They were trying to. Not sure how far they'd have gone if you hadn't appeared.'

They watched the youths disappear from view before climbing the filthy staircase. Used condoms were identifiable among small mounds of takeaway cups, plastic bottles and cigarette ends shoved into corners.

'This is awful,' said Ian. 'How can anyone live in a place like this?'

'I don't think many of them get a choice.'

'It's bloody foul.' Ian stepped onto the second landing. The flat they wanted was four doors along. Natalie tried the bell but was met with no response. She rang again and hammered on the door but was met with silence. They moved to the door at the end of the corridor, home to Habib Malik. She pressed and held the doorbell but nobody answered the door. Neither boy was at home.

*

Ellie's mother, Jojo, had up until now been quietly supportive of Lucy's questioning, but as her daughter dissolved yet again into tears, she demanded the interview end, and Lucy had to dig deep for patience. She tried again, ignoring Jojo's protest.

'Ellie, we know Roxy was seeing Tucker Henderson. She must have told you about him?'

Ellie's head shook from side to side. 'I don't know anything,' she wailed.

Her mother stood up. 'I don't see how this can be helping. My daughter's clearly upset by all of this. She doesn't know anything. You're wasting your time.'

'Please sit down. I won't keep you much longer.' Lucy played it cool. She was waiting on some vital information to persuade Ellie to talk. The woman dropped back down again and took her daughter's hand in her own, made soothing noises and ignored Lucy, who was relieved when Ian rang her again on his way to the Galloway Estate to join Natalie. He had managed to contact Boo's mother at work and email her the photographs of Habib and Tucker. She could tell by his voice that he'd come up trumps. It gave her the leverage she needed. Boo's mother had identified the boys. She faced the girl again, voice serious.

'We can't waste any more time, Ellie. We have a witness who saw you and Roxy last Thursday, in the hallway of your apartment block with Habib Malik and Tucker Henderson. They went so far as to say you all seemed very close and noticed Tucker had his arm around Roxy. There's no point in denying it any longer.'

'Ellie?' Her mother's voice was cool now and Ellie swallowed hard.

'She was frightened her brothers would find out about her and Tucker. They hate him and Habib, and if they'd found out she'd been seeing him, they'd have probably killed them. I already told you about Seth. He's mental. He and Charlie almost killed Habib a few years ago. They're racist and kicked him half to death. Roxy didn't want the same thing to happen again so she was keeping it secret.'

'Did she go to see Tucker on Saturday night?'

'She was supposed to meet him but her mum found out and stopped her.'

'Did you know she told her mum she was on a sleepover with you?'

Ellie's eyes filled again. 'No. When her mum busted her, she decided to stay with friends in Armston and still try to see him.'

'So you *did* speak to her?'

She sniffed miserably and issued a soft, 'Yes, on Snapchat. I told her to spend the night with me but she'd already made plans to stay with her friends.'

'Who were these friends?'

'Some women she'd met a few months ago who told her if she ever needed a place to hang out at, she could stay with them.' Ellie twisted a tissue around in her hands as she spoke.

'Are they called Crystal and Sandra?'

Ellie's eyes filled again.

Lucy spoke more firmly. 'Are their names Crystal and Sandra? This is really important. We need to know.'

Ellie's bottom lip trembled violently and then she spluttered, 'Yes. They are.'

*

Natalie was halfway back to Samford when she received a call from Superintendent Aileen Melody. 'There's been a young man found in Linnet Lane. There's also a suicide note. It's linked to your investigation.'

'Who is it?'

'Teenager by the name of Habib Malik. He appears to have hanged himself from a tree in a field opposite the Langs' house. He was found an hour ago.'

'Oh, fucking hell! I didn't expect that. I've been hunting all over for him.'

'Then I'm sorry to be the bearer of more bad news. There's to be a media conference at five and we need to give them clear details of where we are in this investigation.'

'Are we sure he committed suicide?'

'I'm at the crime scene and I think there's a chance he did, but also a question mark over his death. How far away are you?'

'Ten minutes tops. I'll let the others know.'

Ian was close behind her in the squad car; she used the communications unit to let him know there was a change of plan then rang Murray and Lucy to inform them of the latest development. This had sent the investigation spiralling in another direction and

she wasn't sure if they were getting closer to finding any answers or simply further away. She fervently hoped it was the former.

The small paddock, now cordoned off with crime scene tape, was almost directly opposite number ten. It was approximately two acres in size and empty apart from one gnarled and twisted oak tree close to the opening, wide enough for a tractor to pass through. Tall hawthorn hedging planted around the perimeter shielded the field from the road. It was only after Natalie had entered the field that she could appreciate how large and old the tree was, with a huge trunk and thick, sweeping branches.

The teenager had been cut down and was laid out on a ground sheet, being checked over by Pinkney. Aileen looked on as he examined the boy's eyes and neck. Natalie joined her superior, who spoke as soon as she arrived.

'A rambler found him.'

Pinkney studied one of the boy's smooth-skinned hands and examined the tidy, clipped nails closely, then repeated the act with the other hand before shifting position and giving Natalie a clearer view of the boy. Habib's thick dark hair was shaved at the temples and gelled into place. He'd obviously taken care with his appearance; his chin was clean-shaven and his eyebrows had been groomed into two neat arches.

She dropped her eyes to his neck and the thick nylon rope that had been used to cause his death. She'd attended a lecture in her early years of policing and learnt that falls of more than two metres almost always resulted in decapitation. She was relieved that hadn't happened to this boy. It was bad enough seeing him lifeless, let alone mutilated.

'As you would expect, there are abrasions around his neck, most likely from the rope, but there are also other marks and light bruising on his wrists, upper arms and ankles.' He pointed at the

marked tissue on the boy's bicep. 'These might have occurred while he was trying to set himself up or some time before death, but given their colouring, I would suggest they are recent. I'm going to need more time before I can give you a definitive answer on that score.' He lifted the noose to search for further markings. It had been cut above the knot, as was usual in these circumstances.

'Can you turn the rope around so I can see the knot?' Natalie asked.

Pinkney obliged. It was a simple slip knot. The boy was in a rigid state of rigor mortis, which suggested he'd been dead for between eight and twelve hours and had come to this location the night before. She caught the eye of the forensic photographer.

'I'd like to look at the crime scene photos of him in situ.'

The officer gave her the camera so she could run back through what he'd already taken. She peered closely at the pictures of Habib, a slim, olive-skinned young man in a short-sleeved, dark-patterned shirt and jeans, dangling from the branch, his feet several centimetres above the ground, then glanced back at the tree. He'd thrown himself from a branch about three metres above the ground. The rope was still attached to it. She gave the camera back to the officer and studied the tree thoughtfully. It would have been easy enough for him to clamber up it. There were plenty of places to gain a foothold, choose a branch, tie a rope around it then put his head through the noose and jump. That thought sent a shiver through her. What a terribly calculating and desperate way to die. She wondered how long it had taken for him to stop jerking and fighting, and for his air supply to finally be cut off. Hanging didn't always cause instantaneous death. Sometimes, victims could thrash about for a long time before finally breathing their last.

She turned away. Ian was also puzzling over the scene. 'Considering he came here to kill himself, Habib's dressed quite smartly, isn't he?'

Natalie had thought the same. He'd been wearing a new shirt, the creases still crisply visible, and his hair had been gelled. Had he really come here to end his life? Natalie wasn't convinced.

'Has he messed himself?' she asked Pinkney. Often suicide victims soiled themselves.

'Doesn't appear to have,' came the reply.

Natalie clucked quietly to herself. That didn't seem right. She'd once attended a suicide in a home where the victim had not only wet themselves but suffered an erection.

'What about the note?' She directed her question to Aileen, who passed her a plastic bag. Inside was what looked like a torn page from a school exercise book. Natalie read the few words written in blue biro.

I KILLED ROXY AND HER MUM. I AM SORRY. FORGIVE ME. HABIB.

Natalie released a small sigh. 'I'm thinking out loud here but this note seems very brief... almost too impersonal. However, we have come across suicides before where no note was left, let alone a brief one. I don't know what to think. It just doesn't feel right to me – he was racked with so much guilt over killing Roxy and Cathy that he hanged himself yet left no explanation as to *why* he murdered them. We'll put a handwriting expert on it to see if he wrote it.'

Aileen was in agreement. 'Any other initial thoughts?'

'Well, Habib was seen with Roxy and her friend, Ellie, and another boy – Tucker Henderson. We'll find Tucker and talk to him. I'll work on the premise this is a suspicious death.' Natalie snapped a photograph of the note on her mobile.

'Yes. Do. I have to get back to HQ but I must be kept up to speed with this. We have to let the media know what's happening so make sure I have all the facts before the press conference at five. I'll hand that note to Forensics for examination.'

'I'll get a sample from Habib's folks to do a handwriting comparison.' Natalie returned the note.

Aileen gave the boy on the ground one last look and departed. Natalie turned her attention once more to the tree.

'Why would he come all this way with a length of rope and a note to hang himself?' Ian asked.

'It's close to where Roxy died.'

Ian blinked several times, processing the information, then rubbed the back of his head. 'I don't get it. Why did he kill Roxy and her mother?'

'I'm having difficulty understanding that too.'

'Maybe Roxy's death was an accident. He could have taken her along to help him torch the Langs' house and she got trapped inside.'

'But she was asleep, or relaxing on the settee, when the house was set on fire. She wasn't trapped.'

Ian let out a hiss of exasperation at his own theory. 'Yeah, of course. Oh, this is so bloody confusing.'

She walked towards the tree and studied the branches again. Habib was slightly built. He could undoubtedly have climbed the tree, yet the more she thought about the possibilities, the more certain she became that the boy hadn't come here to kill himself. She turned at the sound of Murray's voice. He was talking to Pinkney. Mike had turned up too and made a beeline for her.

'I've spoken to Aileen. Is there some doubt over how he died?'

'You ever climb trees as a boy?' she asked.

'When I was about ten. Not done it for a good few years.'

'Me neither. I do, however, remember getting scraped a lot, trying to get up there. That tree is old and the bark is thin. If Habib scrambled up it to tie a rope over a branch, then leapt off, he'd have knocked off sections of bark from the trunk and branches. He'd have got dirty and maybe even grazed himself. He'd have hesitated for a while, getting up courage to jump... sat on the branch with a

noose around his neck and then, after jumping, he'd have dangled even for a short while, kicking out. It's a natural reflex… a survival instinct. He'd have clawed at the noose and undoubtedly knocked against the trunk. However, there's no sign of dirt or damage on his clothes, shoes or hands, Mike. There'd have been stains, tiny particles of bark present on his skin or under his fingernails, even traces on his shoes. There's nothing that I can see.'

'Maybe they're not visible to the eye. We'll check and we'll examine this entire area,' he said and left her to reflect further.

Ian, who'd been listening, added his thoughts. 'You're right. I always got filthy when I climbed trees. The bark's dusty with age. There's no residue on his hands or clothes at all.'

Murray was now approaching and Natalie met him close to the teenager's body. He shook his head in sorrow.

Pinkney was packing away his medical kit and looked up. 'I'm done here and need to get him back to the lab. There's a few things I'm unhappy about and need to investigate.'

'Does that mean you don't think he killed himself?' asked Natalie.

'I think there's a very good chance he didn't take his own life.' Pinkney latched his medical case and then crouched by Habib again. He traced a finger gently over the dark bruising on the teenager's neck. 'To start with, these abrasions are inconsistent with what I'd expect in these situations.'

'So how did he die?' Murray had moved forward and was now bent over the body. Natalie joined him.

Pinkney replied, 'Asphyxia.'

'As you'd expect if he hanged himself,' said Ian, who then apologised quickly. 'Sorry, I was thinking out loud.'

'That's true but I've had the misfortune of coming across several hanging attempts similar to this one, and in all those cases there was evidence of an inverted V bruise from the ligature. This lad doesn't have that V-shaped bruise. Add to that fact, the bruising sustained

to the neck area is very deep in places and there are numerous abrasions. I would suggest Habib was strangled first and then this was made to look like a suicide attempt.'

Natalie dropped down. 'Show me.'

Pinkney rolled the boy over. The bruising was dark and patterned across the nape of his neck, but as Pinkney had said, there was no V-shaped bruise. 'There's straight-line bruising, as you can see, and that is invariably linked to ligature strangulation. I'll be more certain once I carry out an autopsy. I'll arrange it immediately.'

The team moved away so the body bag and stretcher could be moved into position. Mike was back and had caught the tail end of the conversation.

Natalie had several requests for him. 'I need you to examine that tree and this area in particular. If Habib didn't commit suicide, we need to establish how the perpetrator managed to string him up. The boy weighed approximately ten stone, and if he was already dead, that's quite a dead weight to carry up a tree. How did the killer manage to do that, let alone create the scene so it looked like Habib had killed himself? It can't have been easy. There must be some evidence here to help us.'

'We'll do what we can. For what it's worth, I don't think the perp could have hauled a body up the tree easily. They must have used some form of pulley or propped Habib up on some steps or a chair somehow.'

'Then there's a possibility we're dealing with more than one killer,' Natalie replied. 'Ian, arrange canvassing in the area again. Somebody might have spotted Habib last night. He looks to me as if he was dressed for a night out. Maybe he was picked up somewhere else and brought here, so see if anyone noticed any vehicles parked up around here. Murray, you and I are going to visit Habib's parents, then Tucker Henderson.'

CHAPTER TWENTY-FIVE

The serious-looking woman in her thirties who opened the door screwed up her face on seeing Natalie and Murray on the doorstep.

Natalie spoke as she flashed her ID card. 'I'm DI Ward and this is DS Anderson. Would it be possible to talk to Mr Omar Malik, please?'

'He's having his lunch.'

'Are you Mr Malik's sister, Fatima?'

'I might be. Why?'

'We understand Mr Omar Malik lives here with you.'

'What's this about?'

'Would you mind if we came inside?'

The woman understood something in Natalie's tone and showed them into a small, untidy kitchen, where a man dressed in overalls had a sandwich in one hand and was scrolling through messages on his mobile phone with the other. He put down his food immediately when Natalie and Murray entered and craned his neck to look up at them. He had the same high cheekbones as his son but the remainder of his face was covered by a thick beard and moustache.

'Mr Malik, I'm afraid I have some bad news regarding your son, Habib.'

The man bit his lip then asked hoarsely, 'What's happened?'

'I'm very sorry indeed. He's dead,' Natalie said.

Fatima's hands flew to her mouth and she released a loud gasp. Omar nodded to himself and spoke again. 'How did he die?'

'We aren't sure yet.'

The man looked at his phone. 'I've been trying to reach him. I sent three text messages. I thought he was with his friends. You say you don't know how he died but you must have some idea. I need to know.'

'I'm really very sorry. He was found hanging from a tree but we are looking into his death. We don't have any answers yet. I understand this is a dreadful time for you, but we really need to ask you a few questions.'

'Hanging? You think he killed himself? No. Impossible. He wouldn't do that.' The man balled his fists and pressed them to his lips, eyes now moist.

'We're investigating his death as suspicious, sir,' Natalie said.

'Yes, suspicious. He wouldn't take his own life. Not *my* son!' His voice rose and Fatima rushed to his side. He pushed off the hand she placed on his arm. 'He wouldn't, would he?' His question was aimed at his sister, whose head shook from side to side.

'We've arranged for an officer to come and help you through this and she'll be here soon, but in the meantime we must ask you some questions.'

'What questions?' His head snapped up as he spoke.

'About your son, sir. Can I ask you how well he knew Roxanne Curtis? You might know her as Roxy.'

'I know her. I've come across all the family at one time or another. Two of them – Charlie and Seth – they're bullies. They set on Habib back in 2014, when he was only thirteen. They hurt him badly. Kicked and bruised him and he couldn't walk properly. He wouldn't tell me what had happened at first, and when he did, both my late wife and I wanted to press charges, but Habib begged us not to. They're a despicable family. Habib avoided Roxy. She

was frequently around these parts, hanging about like a bad smell, but he didn't like her. She's untrustworthy – deeply untrustworthy. I can imagine that you think everyone who lives on this estate is a junkie or a criminal, but not all of us are. Some of us are here because this is where we have been housed. We can't afford to move away and we stay away from trouble: the drug addicts, the alcohol abusers and the louts who steal and fight. We live our lives like decent folk, raise our kids and behave like civilised humans. Habib was a good boy. He kept out of harm's way and away from people like Roxy Curtis.' His voice was thick with emotion.

'Sir, were you aware that Roxy was found dead in the early hours of Sunday morning, in a house fire in Armston-on-Trent?'

'I was not aware.' He shook his head heavily. 'Why are you asking about her, then?'

'Because we believe your son and Tucker Henderson were friends with her and might have known why she was in the house when it was set alight.'

He waved a hand at her. 'This makes no sense. My son is dead and you come here asking about some girl? He wasn't friends with her. If he was with her, it was her doing. She latched onto a few of the boys from these flats. She and her friend were often here.'

'Which friend?'

'I don't know her name. A tall girl with cropped blonde hair and a bad attitude.'

Natalie thought he was possibly referring to Ellie, who matched the description. 'What about Tucker?'

'Tucker lives four doors away. Of course, Habib was friends with him!'

'But Tucker has a reputation for getting into trouble,' she insisted.

The man snorted. 'Tucker pretends to be tougher than he is. He likes to think he's the hard man around this block but truth is, he isn't. He and Habib stuck together and looked out for each

other. It's wise behaviour. If you are alone on this estate, you can run into trouble. Who told you that about Tucker?'

'It doesn't matter, sir.' There was no point in saying the revelation had come from Oliver and Charlie Curtis. It appeared there was some rivalry between the two families.

Natalie aimed her next question at the woman, Habib's aunt. 'Did you know where he was headed last night?'

'Yes. To see Nadia, his girlfriend.'

'What's Nadia's surname?' Murray asked, notebook ready.

'Fryxell.'

Murray threw Natalie a look of surprise. There was a sergeant named Fryxell who worked at Samford HQ.

Natalie continued. 'How long has he been seeing Nadia?'

The woman looked over at her brother, who cleared his throat and said, 'About three months or so.'

'What time did he go out?'

'Seven, I think,' he replied.

'Did you realise he hadn't come home?'

'Not until I came home, which was about an hour ago. I was working overnight,' he replied. 'That's why I've been texting him. I was trying to find out where he was and when he'd be home.'

'Was anyone else in the flat last night?'

Fatima replied, 'Me, my husband and our children. We were here all night but I didn't know Habib hadn't come home. He hadn't returned by the time we went to bed at ten but that wasn't unusual. He sometimes is at Tucker's until quite late. This morning I took the children to school and went shopping afterwards. I got back at midday and checked his room then but his bed was made and so I thought he'd got up and gone out. I never imagined for one second something terrible had happened to him.'

'There was a note left behind at the scene,' Natalie said. 'We'd like to take a sample of his handwriting with us for comparison purposes.'

Fatima disappeared to Habib's room to look for an exercise book or notes he would have written.

Omar trained sad, damp eyes on Natalie and spoke again. 'Tell me honestly, do *you* think Habib killed himself?'

She shook her head. 'No, sir. I don't think he did.'

'Then find whoever did this to my son.'

A liaison officer arrived at the flat soon afterwards, and leaving Omar and his sister in their care, Natalie and Murray tried Tucker's flat one more time. This time, they were in luck. The seventeen-year-old was at home with his mother, a heavy-jowled woman in her mid-forties, with mousy hair scraped back from a round face that already bore deep frown lines – the signs of a difficult life. After breaking the news to him, they sat with him in the sitting room and asked him about Roxy.

'Shit! For real?' Tucker scratched at his shoulder, leaving raw marks on his bare flesh. The hooded vest he wore exposed his biceps and the elaborate design of skulls, gravestones and bones tattooed the length of his shoulders and upper arms.

'I'm very sorry but he's been identified.'

'Fuck.'

'Tucker, we need your help. He left behind a note saying he'd killed Roxy and her mother.'

'That's total bollocks! Habib couldn't kill anyone. He couldn't even fight! He'd run a mile in the opposite direction rather than get involved in a fight. Isn't that right, Ma?'

'That's right,' she replied, speaking to Murray, who had his notepad in his hand. 'They're one of the nicest families on the estate.'

'And there's no way he'd top himself. No way!'

His mother added her own thoughts. 'I've known Habib since he and his family moved here, almost six years ago. Tucker's right, he wouldn't have killed himself. He's been through a lot – bullying,

torments and he even lost his mother to cancer three years ago – but he came through it.'

'He was bullied?' Murray asked.

Tucker nodded miserably. 'We were in the same class at school and he was always picked on.'

His mother spoke again. 'They've been inseparable for years and Tucker's always looked out for him. One time, some little bastards almost kicked Habib to death but Tucker stepped in and saved him. Poor kid. He was always being picked on.' It was the same story his father had told them. The Curtis boys had set on Habib.

Natalie directed her next question to Tucker. 'What can you tell us about Roxy Curtis?'

'What do you want to know?'

'What was your relationship with her?'

'I didn't have a relationship with her. Her brothers are shitbags. They're the ones who kicked the crap out of Habib. Called him all sorts of racist names and worse.'

'When was the last time you saw her?' Natalie asked.

'She was round and about here last week. I saw her with Ellie. I can't remember which day. They're like groupies, trying to hang out with lads from the estate. I think she's copped off with most of the lads here at one time or the other. Bit of a slag.'

'Tucker!'

'It's true, Ma. Everyone knows it. They're both slags. Roxy chases after everything with a dick.' He picked nervously at a spot on his chin.

Natalie continued. 'Did *you* get off with her?'

'Only once. A couple of weeks ago in the park near her place. We shared some smokes and she and I fooled about for a while but then she cleared off back to her place and I came home with Habib.'

'And you haven't met up with her since?'

He scratched the spot so hard a scarlet pinprick of blood appeared. 'No. No way.'

Murray looked up from his notepad, pen in the air. 'You're saying the last time you spoke to her was two weeks ago?'

'That's right.' He turned from Murray to Natalie.

'What about last Thursday when you were seen in the hallway of the block of flats where Ellie lives?'

'Oh yeah, shit, I forgot about that. Was that Thursday? It was only for a few minutes. We didn't hang about. Had a cigarette and left.'

Natalie wasn't convinced but Tucker was still talking, getting increasingly upset. 'Shit! This is mad. Habib's dead? He wouldn't have committed suicide. I know he wouldn't. He was my best mate and he'd have told me if he'd even been thinking about it. Some fucker had it in for him. It'll have been one of the shitheads on the estate.'

His mother admonished him again but he jumped to his feet. 'It's true! You know what he was like. He hated confrontation, and everyone around here loves a bloody good fight. I should have been with him, then it wouldn't have happened.'

'Did he have run-ins with many people?'

'Of course he did. We both did. This is the Galloway Estate! You can't walk down the path without somebody having a go at you. Somebody's taken it too far.'

'Who do you think would do such a thing?'

'There's plenty to choose from but Roxy's brothers have always had it in for him. Fuckers! I bet they're behind it. I should have been with him.'

'You couldn't look after him twenty-four-seven. He didn't need a bodyguard,' said his mother quietly.

'But he did, didn't he? He fucking well did,' Tucker replied. 'Look what's happened to him.' He thumped the wall hard with a balled fist.

'Pack it in! You'll smash through the wall,' his mother snapped.

Natalie kept talking to the boy, who stared angrily at his mother. 'Tucker, did you see Habib yesterday?'

'No. I've not seen him since Saturday.'

'What time was that?'

'We went to the youth club for a bit but there wasn't much going on so we went to the amusement arcade and messed about on the machines.'

'Where was that?'

'The arcade near the old bingo hall on Pine Way.'

'Near where the Curtis family lives.'

'It's a fair way along from their place.'

'How long were you there?'

'A couple of hours. Then we hung out in the park and came home at about eleven, I guess.'

'Anyone see you?'

'Probably. It was packed but there wasn't anyone I recognised.'

Natalie made a note to check the cameras along Pine Way and inside the arcade. 'And the park?'

'Empty apart from us.'

'Did you set eyes on Roxy that night?'

He shook his head.

'What about Ellie?'

'Nope. Didn't see her either.'

'She was at the youth club. I'm surprised you didn't see her there.'

He rubbed again at the angry red spot. 'She wasn't there when we were.'

'Are you telling me the truth?'

'Absolutely. Ellie wasn't there.'

Natalie would get his alibi looked into. For now, she and Murray still had to talk to Nadia Fryxell, Habib's girlfriend, so they took their leave; however, Natalie wasn't convinced by his story. No matter what he might say, his body was telling a different one.

*

Sergeant Gretchen Fryxell was on leave and at home in her semi-detached house in Armston-on-Trent. She was wearing shorts, a T-shirt and floral gardening gloves and looked completely different out of her uniform. Both Natalie and Murray knew her from work, where she worked in narcotics – a solid, square-faced woman with a permanent frown.

'Hi, Murray, Natalie. What brings you here?' She patted the head of her wire-haired pointer, who'd accompanied her to greet the visitors.

'I'm afraid it's official business. Is Nadia in?' Nadia was the same age as Josh and had recently finished her GCSE exams.

'She's sunbathing in the back garden. What is it?'

'Habib Malik. He was found hanging from a tree in Linnet Lane, opposite a house that burnt down on Saturday night.'

'Oh Lord! Habib? She'll be devastated. Do you want me to break the news to her?'

'Actually, we need to talk to her. We think his death's suspicious.'

'But you just said he hanged himself.'

'No. I said we found him hanging. We aren't sure he committed suicide.'

Gretchen pulled off her gloves. 'I'll tell her and then bring her inside. Could you put the kettle on, Murray? The teabags are in the pot marked tea. She takes two sugars.'

The kitchen was brightly lit by the sun streaming through the windows, intensifying the orange and red of the splashback tiles that were under the overhead cupboards and behind the large sink. Murray filled the kettle and reached for the pot. The mugs hung from hooks under an ochre cupboard. Gretchen clearly liked colour in her life. The place was quite a contrast to the sombre flats they'd visited on the Galloway Estate. From her vantage point, Natalie observed Gretchen traverse the freshly cut lawn to where a long-limbed girl wearing a turquoise swimming costume was laid out on a sunbed. She crouched down, took the girl's hand in hers and

spoke to her. Nadia sat up and the magazine she'd been reading tumbled to the ground. Gretchen sat down on the bed beside her and enveloped her in a motherly embrace. In the kitchen, the kettle bubbled and whistled.

Natalie watched as Gretchen helped her daughter put on a towelling robe, as if she were a toddler unable to dress herself, and marvelled at a mother's love. She understood it. There was nothing she wouldn't do for her children. Gretchen was protecting hers, helping Nadia deal with the shock. 'They're coming inside.'

Murray stirred the tea and placed the mug on the table. No sooner had he set it down than Gretchen entered, her arm around Nadia even though she was a head and shoulders taller than her mother. The girl's teeth were chattering in spite of the warm day.

'Sit down, love. Drink the tea. It'll help,' said Gretchen, and she pulled out a chair for her daughter. 'This is DS Anderson and DI Ward. They work at Samford like me. They're going to ask you a few questions about Habib. I want you to try and answer them all as thoroughly as you can and help them find out what happened to him. Will you do that for me?'

The girl nodded and Gretchen gave her forehead a kiss.

Natalie gave Nadia a small smile. 'I'm so sorry about Habib. How long have you known him?'

'Six months but we've only been seeing each other seriously for the last three.' She grasped the mug tightly.

'Were you supposed to see him last night?'

'No. We hadn't arranged anything.'

'And you're certain of that?'

'Definitely. I went out with Mum to the cinema.'

'That's right. We went to Tamworth and had a pizza afterwards. We returned about ten.'

'Did you text Habib or speak to him?'

The girl nodded. 'We were on Snapchat for ages yesterday morning. I didn't speak to him after that. I kept my phone turned

off in the cinema. I texted him after the film when we were eating and he seemed fine. He said he was in the middle of something and couldn't talk but he'd have a nice surprise for me later. I tried to get hold of him today but he didn't answer and I thought he was out with Tucker. He couldn't mean this, could he, Mum? This isn't the surprise?' Her voice trailed away and the teeth-chattering began again.

Her mother prised the mug from her curled fingers and covered both hands with her own. 'No, love. He said "a nice surprise". He had something else in mind.'

Natalie had picked up on the way Nadia had spoken Tucker's name and asked her,

'How do you get on with Tucker?'

'He's okay.'

'I get the impression you don't like him too much.'

'I don't dislike him but I didn't like the way he pushed Habib about. He was really bossy. Sometimes, he'd behave like he owned him – click his fingers and say, "Come on," and Habib would follow him like a dog. I think he was scared of Tucker.'

'Did he say anything that made you suspicious?'

'There were a few times. It didn't matter what we were doing, if Tucker texted or rang him, he'd drop everything and go. It happened once when we were in town together. We'd not been there five minutes when Tucker sent a message telling him to meet him urgently. He said he had to go and we argued about it. I thought Tucker was deliberately trying to stop us seeing each other but Habib wouldn't have it. He said I was way off, and if he could stay he would but he had to leave. I didn't get it. I told him if he left I wouldn't see him again. He came to the house to apologise the next day and explained he owed Tucker for looking after him when he was younger, and we made up.'

That was a possibility. Tucker and Habib had been friends for a very long time.

'Did he mention anyone who was out to harm him?'

'No. I know he wanted to move away from Clearview. He was hoping to get an apprenticeship at Rolls-Royce and move to Derby. He'd applied and was waiting to hear back. He hated Clearview and the Galloway Estate. He said it was like living in a ticking time bomb.'

CHAPTER TWENTY-SIX

Natalie, who was driving her own car and had sent Murray on ahead to HQ, stopped off at a petrol station to refuel, grab something to eat and ring Aileen to tell her what they'd uncovered so far. The fact was, it was insufficient. The Curtis family had been involved in altercations with Habib and Tucker in the past, and there appeared to be a rivalry between the families. They still hadn't established a connection between Roxy, her mother, the Langs and Habib. Her superior sounded vexed but there was little more Natalie could give her. Until they made a significant breakthrough, they could only work with the evidence they had. Aileen would have to appease the press the best she could.

She chugged the cold bottle of water and peeled back the cellophane on her cheese sandwich. It tasted bland but she ate it anyway and took advantage of having a couple of minutes to herself to ring home. Leigh would be home from school, and having interviewed Nadia and Gretchen, she had a desire to have a few words with her own daughter. Leigh picked up the phone.

'Hi, sweetie. How was your day?'

'Okay. Why?'

'Just wondered.'

'It was okay. It was school. Can't wait for the holidays.'

'Won't be too long. Listen, I was wondering if you'd like to go and see *Ocean's 8* at the cinema with me.'

'I've seen it already.'

'When was that?'

'The other day on DVD.'

'It's out already?'

'Yeah.'

There was a spike in her daughter's voice that indicated she wasn't telling the truth. It was unlikely the film was on DVD yet. One of her friends had probably got hold of a pirated copy. However, Natalie hadn't rung for a row; she'd wanted to feel that special maternal bond. 'Well, how about we watch something else then?'

'Yeah, okay.'

It wasn't quite the response she'd hoped for but it was at least something.

'You choose a film you fancy seeing and we'll go this coming weekend.'

'If you're not busy.'

'Leigh, busy or not, I'm due a day off and I'm going to spend some of it with you.'

'Okay.' The voice sounded more cheerful. Natalie had succeeded and it felt good.

'Is Josh about?'

'No. He's out and Dad's dead annoyed with him.'

'Is Dad there?'

'He's working in his office. Are you coming home for tea?'

'I'll try. It might be a bit late so keep mine warm for me.'

'It's chicken salad!'

'Keep it cool for me then.'

'Ha!'

'See you later.'

'Yeah. Bye, Mum.'

The chat had both cheered and troubled her. Learning Josh had riled David was slightly worrying. David didn't often lose his rag with the boy. If anything, he was the patient one and she was far more likely to fuss or nag.

Since finishing his exams, Josh's personality had started to change and he was becoming increasingly aloof. She forced the last of her plastic-tasting sandwich into her mouth, started up her engine and blew out her cheeks with a noisy exhalation. She'd find out what was going on later. Everything and everyone close to her had to take a back seat while she was working an investigation, and sometimes that felt too great a burden for her to bear.

*

When Murray returned to the office after talking to the Fryxells, he found Ian talking on the phone and Lucy back at her desk.

'Where's Natalie?' Lucy asked.

'She had to appease Aileen. I think the big boss wanted something to tell the press but we haven't got anything new. What about you?'

'Ellie said Roxy and Tucker were an item.'

'Not what Tucker says. Reckons Roxy fancied him but he didn't encourage it.'

'Not the same version I was given. Ellie also says Seth and Charlie attacked Habib a few years ago, when they were all at school.'

'Ah, that's interesting cos Tucker told us that same story.'

'Ellie spoke to Roxy briefly on Snapchat before she went off to find Crystal and Sandra.'

'And Tucker didn't see Ellie at the youth club. Great!'

'Maybe he didn't,' Lucy said with a light shrug.

'Do me a favour, Lucy. One of them is shitting us.' He pulled out a chair and was about to sit down when he said, 'You'll never guess who Habib's girlfriend is.'

'Go on.'

'Gretchen Fryxell's daughter.'

'Fuck me! Gretchen the bulldog?'

'That's the one. Lives in a really nice house in Armston. Her daughter's lovely. Doesn't look anything like her mum.'

'That's a blessing then, isn't it?' Lucy flashed white teeth for a brief second.

Ian spun around and interrupted their conversation. 'That was one of the technical team on the phone. They're processing Habib Malik's mobile and they've just found out that he purchased several packs of Xanax over the last few months. It's a benzodiazepine medication used to treat anxiety orders: panic, depression and agoraphobia.'

Murray spoke up. 'That makes sense. He got beaten up as a kid, seems to have been bossed about by his best friend, lost his mother to cancer and wanted desperately to get away from the Galloway Estate. I can see why he'd need it. It also supports the theory he killed himself – a teenager with mental health issues could well intend on taking his own life. If we didn't already suspect he'd been murdered, that information would only make it seem more likely he'd killed himself.'

'Surely he'd be on prescription drugs if he had an anxiety disorder, not buying them himself?' said Lucy.

'True but plenty of people read up about conditions online and self-medicate. It's reasonable to assume he bought them for himself.'

'I suppose so,' Lucy replied.

Ian continued, 'There have been a few cases of kids buying drugs off the Internet and selling them on. If Habib wasn't getting them for himself, he could have been doing just that.'

'Let's not jump to hasty conclusions,' said Lucy. 'We should see what Pinkney comes up with first, and if there are traces of the drug in his bloodstream. It's more important we focus on why he was killed.'

'I'd say dealing drugs was a possible reason,' Ian insisted. 'Somebody could be exacting revenge. He lived on the Galloway Estate, Lucy! It's not exactly Beverly Hills there.'

'Beverly Hills? Where'd you come up with that? You watch too much television,' scoffed Murray.

'You know what I mean. All sorts of rough kids live there. Loads of them are into drugs.'

Lucy rubbed the bridge of her nose. 'Okay. Let's consider it an option.'

Murray spoke up again. 'Anyway, that aside, Natalie wants us to talk to the Curtis boys again. Somebody's not being straight with us and we need to get to the bottom of the incident surrounding beating up Habib. If Seth and Charlie did have it in for him and Tucker, we might have to consider their involvement in his death.'

'I'll come with you.' Lucy pushed back from her seat and made for the door.

Murray stood up again and hesitated before speaking to Ian. 'You okay here?'

'Of course. Why shouldn't I be?'

'Just checking,' said Murray. He put a friendly hand on the man's shoulder.

'I'm okay. Really.'

Lucy, who'd observed the friendly gesture, called out in a cartoon voice, 'Miss you already!' and blew Ian a kiss.

'Fuck off!' Ian replied with a laugh.

'Reckon you can manage for half an hour without him?' she joked as she and Murray made their way downstairs. 'I'm beginning to worry about you two. I'll have to tell Yolande to watch out and that she has a love rival.'

'Like he said, "Fuck off."'

She laughed and bounded ahead of him.

Natalie was coming up the stairs and almost bumped into them.

'We're going to talk to the Curtis boys,' explained Murray.

'Ellie reckons Habib was victimised by them,' said Lucy.

'That's what we've been hearing too,' Natalie responded.

'My interview notes with her are on my desk if you want to go through them. Some of what she told me contradicts what you learnt.'

Natalie readjusted her bag on her shoulder and let out a sigh. 'Thanks. I'll read them. I might try and get hold of Gavin and Kirk again, ask them about Habib.'

Murray shook his head. 'Daisy told me they've gone to London and isn't sure when they're back. Could be tonight.'

'Why are they in London?'

'Some networking event and visiting friends. Oh, and I also found out Daisy and Kirk are seeing each other behind Gavin's back. They've not told him yet but are going to. Kirk is now staying with a friend and isn't going to move back in with Gavin once the insurance money comes through. It crossed my mind that Daisy and Kirk might both have been involved in setting fire to the house so they could create a situation where they'd be together, but it seems extreme and now Habib's dead as well, I'm not so sure.'

'I can't work out why they'd want to kill Cathy or Habib, or why Roxy was in that house, but it is possible Daisy and Kirk arranged to burn down the house to claim insurance money then move in together. Jeez – people and their bloody secrets!' said Natalie, rolling her eyes. 'Okay. I'll ring Gavin and Kirk or I might even try the nightclub later and see if I can track down the elusive duo. Let me know how you get on.'

Natalie bent over her desk and rested her forehead in her hands. She'd read Lucy's interview notes. All the damn lies: Ellie, Roxy, Tucker… they were all doing her head in. Ian was tapping at his keyboard; the clicking penetrated her brain and distracted her. She admonished herself for being oversensitive to the noise. It didn't

usually trouble her. She was tetchy and tired, and in the corner of her mind was a reminder that Josh wasn't behaving as he usually did. She had no idea why he'd suddenly changed and wondered if any parent ever understood their teenage children. The internal phone rang and she lifted the receiver. Mike was on the line.

'I stopped off at the technical department to see if there were any new developments… and there are. Habib set up an account and purchased Xanax but the delivery address isn't his home address. The drugs were sent to number eight-seven, The Towers, Galloway Estate.' It was Tucker's address.

'How did he pay for them?'

'Debit card.'

'In his name?'

'Yes. And cash was put into his current account the day before each purchase.'

'He was getting money from somebody, putting it into his account then using it to buy the drugs?'

'That's right.'

'I don't know if that's helpful or has clouded it further, but thanks anyway.'

'I have more. We've examined the area around the oak tree where we found his body. There's definitely evidence of activity in as much as there is significant bark deposit at the foot of the tree where it fell away from the trunk, presumably because it was kicked or knocked by whomever tied the rope around the branch. There are bald patches on the branch where the rope was tied, but we've examined Habib's clothing for any bark residue and found very little. He definitely didn't climb up the tree. Somebody did, but not him. We still can't fathom out how he was strung up. There's nothing to indicate a pulley was used. If it had been, we'd have had significant patterns of wear and tear on the branches – they're old and quite brittle in parts – but there's nothing. We can't find any prints or marks that would indicate somebody used steps or even a ladder. It's proving testing.'

'Okay. We'll work with what we've got for now and wait for Pinkney's report.'

Mike sounded so weary and flat, she wanted to say something to lift his spirits, to prove she understood and appreciated his dedication, but Ian was nearby so she could only thank him again and return to her thoughts.

*

Lucy and Murray were on the doorstep of the flat at Pine Way. Charlie Curtis stood in front of them, his legs planted and hands tucked under his armpits. There was nothing obeisant about his stance.

Lucy appealed to him again. 'We need to ask you a few questions about Habib Malik,' she said. She sensed him bristle at the name. 'Can we come in?'

'I don't have anything to say.'

'That may be but we need to speak to you and your brothers. Are they in?'

The gate opened behind them and Oliver, in running gear, appeared. He pulled up short. 'What's going on?'

'We need to talk to you all.'

'Charlie, fuck off out of the way and let them in,' said Oliver, wiping sweat from his forehead.

Charlie took a step backwards and let them in, and once they were inside, he muttered something inaudible to his brother, who responded with a sharp nod and took charge of the questioning.

'What's this about?' he asked. He hadn't yet shaved and his face was dark with stubble, his cheeks reddened by exertion. The brothers had similar muscular physiques: both clearly worked out. He picked up a grubby tea towel from the back of a chair and wiped his head and face with it.

'Are Paul and Seth in?'

'Paul's at work,' grunted Charlie.

'And Seth? We'd like to talk to you all,' Murray said. At over six foot he had height on the boys and was matched in terms of physical stature. He stared hard at Oliver, who eventually spun on his heel and left the room to get his brother. Charlie folded his arms, hostility still emanating from his pores.

'How are you bearing up?' asked Lucy, hoping to diffuse some of it. It worked.

'We're coping.'

'Has PC Granger been around?'

'Yeah, Tanya's cool.'

Lucy offered a smile. It was good he was on first name terms with the liaison officer.

Oliver returned with Seth, a thin, pale beanpole next to his brother.

'Hi Seth,' said Lucy.

'Hi.'

'We want to ask you about Habib Malik,' said Murray, and he caught the look that flashed between Charlie and Seth. 'You and he had some history, didn't you? You didn't get along.'

'He's a little turd.' Charlie clenched and released his fists several times. He really had issues with the dead boy.

Oliver leant against the table, tea towel in his hand, and maintained a silence.

'Can you tell me what sort of thing he got up to that got you angry?'

No one replied. Seth looked uncomfortable. Murray decided to push him.

'Seth, you got something you want to tell us?'

The boy looked to Oliver for guidance. Oliver gave a little nod. 'Go on. Tell them what you told me last night.'

'A couple of weeks ago, I saw Roxy in the park with Tucker and Habib. They were all smoking and having a good laugh.'

'How did it make you feel seeing your sister with them?'

The fists clenched tight. 'I wanted to hit them both.'

'But you didn't confront them?'

'No, I didn't.'

'It made you angry. Is that right?'

Seth nodded. 'Yes. She knew they had it in for us but she was there with them. She even snogged Tucker.'

'Did you tell your mother or Charlie about this incident?'

'No. I didn't.'

'He didn't say anything until last night,' repeated Oliver.

'Did he tell you, Charlie?' Murray asked. The boy shook his head. Murray turned his attention back to Seth.

'Did you decide to confront Habib or Tucker alone? Maybe tell them to stay away from Roxy?'

'No!'

'Even though you were angry with them?'

'No! I told Roxy I'd seen her and she got mad at me. She said she didn't give a shit what I thought about Tucker or Habib because she really liked them both, and if she wanted to go out with Tucker, it was her business.'

'Where were you last night, Seth?'

'Home.'

'What about you, Oliver?'

'Charlie and I went out to the local gym and worked out then hung out with some of the guys we met there. Got back at about eleven. Seth was already in bed when we got back.'

'Can you prove your whereabouts?'

'Sure. We checked in at the gym at seven, did a two-hour session, and I can give you the names of the guys we were with after that. What's this all about?'

'All in good time,' said Murray. 'Seth, was Paul here with you?'

'Only for a while but he kept bursting into tears over Mum and Roxy, so in the end, he went to the pub. He cries all the time. We can hear him at night. It's horrible.'

'It must be. It must be really difficult for you all,' said Lucy, aware how still all the boys were, almost rooted to their individual spots, like rabbits in headlights. She wondered if it was a sign of guilt.

'What did you do after Paul went out?'

'Laid on my bed and thought about Mum and Roxy. I wished none of this had happened and everything would go back to how it was before.'

'You didn't go out at all?'

'No.'

'You didn't contact anyone or chat to anyone online?'

'No. I don't have many friends.'

'Why do you all hate Tucker and Habib so much? What happened for you to fall out?'

Charlie growled, 'They're scum.'

'Why do you say that?'

Oliver answered, 'They sold drugs to schoolkids.'

May 2014

Habib spins around and kicks at an empty plastic bottle that is rattling around in the breeze. The park is empty apart from him and Tucker. It looks bleaker than ever today – paint peels from the swings, and the chains that hold them are rusted. The roundabout where Tucker now sits, propped against a gunmetal-grey bar, is covered in stains and graffiti etched into its wooden floor – a reminder of just how shit it all is here. Tucker stubs out his fag, adding to the stained floor, and says, 'Look, it wasn't our fault.'

'Of course it was our fucking fault! We shouldn't have got involved with Art.'

'You wanted to do it too!' Tucker snaps back and scowls at his friend.

Habib studies his trainers, worn and shabby. He knows why he agreed to sell drugs for Art's mob – because he wanted the money. Life

has been the biggest crock of shit ever recently. He has no friends other than Tucker and he's really low. Mum's not well and he has no idea if she's got something serious or not. All he knows is he hates living in fucking Clearview. The money they get from Art helps make it more bearable. They can buy cigarettes and go to the arcade and generally lose themselves for a while.

'Let's not fall out over it,' he says.

'Good.' Tucker hops from the roundabout and yanks on the rail, sending it spinning. He comes across and fist bumps his mate. 'We weren't to know it was bad. Besides, I heard Baz was going to be okay.'

Baz is the boy who bought the E from them and ended up in hospital. At first they were scared rigid he'd die. However, it wasn't their fault, they'd reasoned. Art was to blame. He'd given them the gear to sell and you didn't argue with Art. He and his gang owned Clearview. It was their patch for dealing, and if he singled you out to do a few deals for him, you did it.

'What do we do now? Own up?' Habib asks.

'You out of your fucking mind? We say nothing.'

A shout takes them by surprise. 'You two. We want a fucking word with you! You nearly killed Baz.'

It's Charlie and Seth Curtis. Charlie's best mates with Baz and he's one mean fucker.

'Leg it!' yells Tucker, and he sprints towards the far side of the park and a fence he knows he can jump over to reach the main road. Habib's behind him and slower. The brothers are too quick for them, and Seth reaches Tucker with extraordinary speed, bowling him over. He pushes him against the grass with one strong hand. His face is scrunched up in anger. Seth lands a punch to his nose and pain explodes across his face.

'You bastards. Baz is on life support thanks to you. You're going to pay for this.'

Tucker kicks out and twists and turns wildly to escape Seth, finally breaking free from him, and hurtles towards the road. Screams halt him in his tracks. Habib is curled into a ball by a tree and Charlie is

kicking him with heavy boots, over and over again. Habib is begging him to stop but Charlie is apoplectic with rage, cursing and kicking simultaneously. Seth has doubled back and is joining in. Habib howls in agony.

Tucker acts without thought. He thunders back towards the boys and jumps on Charlie's back, tightening his grip around the boy's throat until he starts pulling at Tucker's hands. Tucker doesn't let go. Charlie spins around to loosen the boy on his back but can't shake him off. He's choking and spluttering and Seth tries to assist but can't and Tucker squeezes more tightly still until Charlie falls to his knees. Seth's face is now pure concern.

'Charlie?' The fight has gone out of him. He's worried about his brother, and still Tucker crushes Charlie's windpipe until he sees Habib struggle to his feet, then he lets go and kicks Charlie hard in the crotch. Seth, concerned for his brother, doesn't chase after them, and Tucker puts an arm around his friend and helps him hobble away towards the flats.

Oliver finished recounting the story. 'I wasn't involved but I knew about it.'

'This true?' Murray asked Charlie and Seth, who nodded simultaneously. 'Why didn't any of you report it?'

Charlie answered, 'That's not how we do things in Clearview. We look after our friends and family. Baz almost died. Seth and I handled it our way. Tucker and Habib were too scared of us after that to sell anything again.'

'Do they sell drugs nowadays?'

Charlie shrugged. 'I don't know. We don't have anything to do with them.'

'Do any of you take drugs?'

'No fucking way!' said Charlie, almost spitting out the words. Seth shook his head. 'Never.'

'What about medication for depression, Seth?'

'I take Prozac.'

'Ever tried Xanax?'

'No. I was on Lexapro but Prozac suits me better. Doctor said not to mess with the meds or I could get worse, so I don't.'

'What about Roxy?'

Seth looked towards Charlie, who gave a slight nod of his head. Taking it as a signal, Seth sighed heavily. 'Yes, she took drugs – a bit of weed, the odd E, maybe other stuff.'

Oliver shook his head sadly. 'I had no idea.'

'How could you know? You've not been around for ages,' said Charlie, accusingly. 'You've been away nearly three years and we've probably only seen you half a dozen times.'

'Are you having a go at me?' said Oliver, squaring his shoulders.

Murray prepared himself to break up a fight but Seth yelled at the pair. 'Shut up! Just shut up, both of you.'

Oliver's eyes opened wide at the sudden outburst but he offered a quiet, 'Sorry.'

Charlie muttered an apology too.

'So, what happens now?' asked Oliver. 'You going to charge these two for fighting with Habib and Tucker?'

'No, but we would like to know all your movements last night.'

'What's happened?' he asked more cautiously.

'Habib's been killed.'

*

Natalie finished speaking to Lucy and Murray. Oliver and Charlie Curtis's whereabouts checked out. They'd been at the gym and then gone out with some of the guys they'd met at the gym – a couple of personal trainers who worked there. Seth, however, had no firm alibi and Paul had been at the local pub. The landlord had confirmed Paul had been in although he wasn't certain what time he'd left.

She told them to head home, dismissed Ian and clocked off herself for the day. As she gathered up her keys, she glanced at the time: it was six forty-five. It was much later than she'd hoped to leave. She had no appetite for the chicken salad waiting for her or a desire to sort out problems between Josh and David. She wanted to drop by the nightclub and see if she could speak to Kirk and Gavin Lang. She'd tried their phones again to no avail, but a barman at Extravaganza who'd answered her call to the nightclub had been certain they'd be returning from London around nine thirty, so first things first, she'd head home and see her family.

CHAPTER TWENTY-SEVEN

TUESDAY, 3 JULY – EVENING

A low murmur coming from the television set in the sitting room indicated at least one person was in.

Natalie called a hello, hoping for some response, and heard a soft, 'Hi, Mum!' She headed towards it. Leigh was curled up on the settee in her favourite spot, hugging a large cushion. *Emmerdale* was drawing to a close. Leigh was addicted to soap operas and could not only name all the characters in every soap but knew every detail of their personal lives. If there were GSCEs in soaps, Leigh would pass with an A*. Natalie was way behind on the storylines but didn't mind a half an hour of television drama that took her away from the real-life dramas she dealt with on a daily basis. She entered the room in time to find Leigh open-mouthed.
'Good episode?'

'Brilliant! I can't wait to see what happens next.' She lifted the control and flicked through the channels.

'Josh in yet?'

'I haven't heard him.' She tuned into BBC One. 'You want to watch *EastEnders*?'

'I'll grab some food and come back.'

Leigh snuggled further back into the settee like a contented dog. Natalie left her to it and trudged through to the kitchen.

David appeared from nowhere. 'I didn't hear you come in,' he said.

'I shouted.'

'Oh! There's some salad in the fridge. It was a bit too warm to cook. I was going to do burgers but Josh went out.'

'I heard. Leigh said there'd been an argument.'

'That's right. He's getting too big for his boots.'

'Where's he gone?'

'I don't know. Alex's, I guess.'

She opened the fridge door and lifted out a plate of food. David had covered it with cling film for her. She peeled it off. David pulled open a drawer and passed her a knife and fork.

'Thanks.'

'I don't know what's got into him. Ever since he finished school, he's morphed into a bolshie teenager. I can't get a full sentence out of him.'

Natalie knew what he meant. Josh was becoming increasingly uncommunicative. 'He's probably concerned about his exam results. He's got ages to wait until he gets the results and you know how much he wants to go to sixth form college,' she reasoned. 'His routine's been broken and he's probably missing it and his school friends.'

'I can't see that being the case. He talks to them every day. He's never off the fucking Internet.'

'Not the same as going to class with them and actually hanging out with them, is it?'

'Bloody Internet! It's killing communication skills and it's full of dangers.'

Natalie couldn't face one of David's rants. Once he started moaning, he'd not stop for ages. 'That's the world we live in, David. Kids today live online. Their friends are online. He's sensible. He won't be up to any trouble.' She poured some salad cream onto the lettuce to make it more edible and ate a forkful. There was more to it than this. David was probably finding it increasingly difficult to connect with their son. Josh was growing up and away

and coming to the end of his childhood. He'd just finished school and the next step would be A-levels and then university. 'What was the argument about?'

'About him being an idle toerag and staying in bed until after lunch.'

'Fair enough.' She tried the chicken. It was dry and sucked all the moisture out of her mouth when she chewed it. She swallowed and washed down the lump with a mouthful of water.

'I don't know what's wrong with him. Lazy shit. I wasn't like that at his age.'

'I suppose he thinks he has no reason to get up.'

'Are you defending him?'

'I'm reasoning why he might not feel like getting up.'

'Sounds like you're defending him. There's no excuse for laziness. When I was his age, I used to be up at seven without fail. Holidays or not. My father wouldn't stand for such idleness.'

It seemed difficult to imagine Eric, David's father, being so strict, but she let it go. David was pacing the kitchen, irked by the whole business.

She pushed the plate to one side. 'Maybe when he has a job…' she began.

'He didn't get the job. He got a text earlier to say they'd filled the position.'

'Oh! That's a shame. Well, he needs to try other places. There must be something.'

'There's not a lot for people who are qualified let alone a sixteen, soon-to-be seventeen-year-old, waiting on the results of his GCSEs. I don't think he's going to be able to find any work.'

'Surely he could clean cars or do some gardening for people!'

'Well, why don't you put that proposal to him because he isn't listening to me at the moment. I'm hardly a shining example of productivity, am I?' There it was! David was in a self-pitying mood

again and his authority had been challenged. That was what this was all about.

'Okay, I will. What time's he due back?'

'I don't know.'

'Have you texted him to find out?'

'No, Natalie, I haven't.'

Natalie collected her phone and rang Josh. David stood arms folded and waited. Josh picked up.

'Hey. You okay?'

'Fine.'

'You at Alex's house?'

'Yes.'

'What time do you plan on coming home?'

'Dunno. Twelve?'

'I have to go out again. How about I pick you up on my way home at about ten thirty?' She'd make sure she was done with the Langs and the nightclub by then.

'Ten thirty? I don't have to get up for school.'

'No, but we all have to get up early and I don't want to have to wait up too late for you.'

There was a lengthy pause then, 'Okay.'

'Thanks. See you later.'

'You're too soft with him,' David said.

'What?'

'You should have told him to get his arse back home. How dare he dictate what time he comes and goes. This isn't a fucking hotel.'

'Can you hear yourself?'

'He's turning into a spoilt brat and you're not helping.'

'I'm picking him up and bringing him home. How is that not helping?'

'Ten thirty is too late.'

'What time do you suggest?'

'Nine is plenty late enough.'

'Then you should have made sure of that before he went out!'

'Maybe we should get him his own door key so he can simply come and go as he pleases.'

She wasn't going to argue any further. She threw him an icy look and went to join Leigh. There was enough melodrama on the television without adding to it.

Leigh had gone upstairs to "mess about online", leaving Natalie to watch a film that she couldn't get into. She'd tried Kirk's and Gavin's mobiles again but both had gone to answerphone. Frustrated and tired and in a moment of weakness, she'd rung Mike.

'Sorry to bother you but I wanted to check to see if you'd found anything else,' she said. She winced at her lie. What she'd really wanted was to hear his voice.

'I'm afraid not. I've called it a day. Best to start again after a night's sleep and when I'm feeling fresh. Less chance of making mistakes.'

'That's how I feel.'

'Yet here you are gone eight at night, talking to me about work!' She could hear the teasing in his voice and it made her smile.

'I'm too transparent,' she replied. *Shit!* She was flirting. She knew she was and she shouldn't be.

'No, Nat. You're many things but not transparent. You're like an onion with its many layers and some days I feel like I haven't yet reached the real you.' His voice was sultry and sexy and made her heart beat faster.

'You know me well enough.'

'Well, enough to know something's bothering you if you've rung me after hours… and it isn't work.'

He'd sussed her. 'David and I are in disagreement about Josh. David thinks he's being a lazy little shit and I think he's behaving like a normal teenager.'

'How so?'

'He didn't get up until after midday. David thinks he should be more switched on.'

'He hasn't got any reason to get up, has he? His exams are over. The way I see it, he'll have plenty of days to get up at the crack of dawn and go to work, just like we do. A fucking lifetime of early starts to the day, so he ought to be making the most of his youth. Besides, it's a well-known fact that teenagers need more sleep than adults. Their confused brains need rest.' She could hear the smile in his voice.

'David's got a point though. Josh has been really uncooperative recently, argumentative and even a bit... sluggish... dopey.'

'Aftershock from his exams. Josh isn't dopey at all. He's a very smart kid.'

'Yeah.'

'Takes after his mother.'

'That'll do. Flattery will get you—' She bit her tongue and immediately regretted her words. 'I shouldn't have said that. I'm tired and behaving like a—'

He spared her any further embarrassment by interrupting her apology. 'Don't worry about Josh. I was a right so-and-so at his age. He's full of rampant hormones and frustration. He's in no-man's land until his exam results come through and he's stuck at home every day with nothing to stimulate him. He'll adjust once Leigh has finished term and you start to do holiday activities with them.'

'Thanks. I feel better about it now. Sometimes, you're so close to the problem you can't deal with it.'

'Well, just remember when I am going through hell with Thea, you'll be the first person I'll ring.'

'I'll be happy to dispense advice although I can't guarantee it'll be the right advice.'

'I'm sure it will be. As for your investigation, I'll crack on again tomorrow, so try to put it aside and enjoy your family time.'

'Thank you.' She was reluctant to hang up but David appeared. 'It's Mike,' she mouthed.

'Hi, Mike,' he shouted.

'Say hi back to David for me. See you tomorrow.'

It was almost nine fifty by the time Natalie reached Extravaganza. The bouncer was quick to tell her that Kirk and Gavin weren't in but she refused to accept his word and demanded she see for herself. He allowed her entry and told her where she'd find their office. It had been many years since she'd been in a nightclub and this was a far cry from the last one she'd visited. Its artistic, modern design was undoubtedly cool, and with music she couldn't identify hammering in her ears, she decided she was getting very old indeed. This was way out of her comfort zone. There were already about fifty to sixty people in the place and she traversed the floor in the direction of the sign for the toilets, edging past energetic dancers and circumnavigating a group of young women clustered near the door who looked like they'd stepped off a millionaire's yacht in sequinned halter tops, shorts and sunglasses.

There was no sign of Gavin or Kirk in their office so she back-tracked and headed to the bar, where a lanky young man asked what she wanted to drink.

'Nothing. I'm looking for Kirk and Gavin Lang,' she said.

'They're not here. They've gone to London.'

'I spoke to Rick earlier, he said they'd be back at nine thirty.'

'They're definitely not in. Hang on, I'll ask Rick.' The man disappeared through the door marked 'Party Room', leaving Natalie alone by the bar. The neon flashing lights and pounding music vibrated through her body. She didn't fit in with the younger crowd, jumping about in time to the rhythmic beat. She'd never really been a nightclub person. David most definitely wasn't. Booths were filling up with young men and women dressed in outfits

she'd expect to see on the catwalk, and she unconsciously tucked her blouse further into her black trousers. She was the dowdiest person here.

The music merged seamlessly into another track that sounded remarkably like the first. The deejay on the platform gave an enthusiastic cheer to introduce the track change and was rewarded with squeals from the dancers on the floor. She tapped a beer mat impatiently against the bar and waited for the young man to return. Eventually he did, with another man, in his late twenties with a trimmed goatee beard, by his side.

'You Rick?' Natalie asked, raising her voice over the hubbub.

'Yes, sorry. I should have let you know. I spoke to Kirk earlier. They've got held up at some VIP event in a new nightclub and aren't coming back now until the morning. Want to leave a message for them?'

'I already have. They're not answering their phones.'

The man shouted, 'If it's anything like this place, they won't be able to hear to speak so they'll have turned them off. I leave mine in my locker. No point in having it on in here. Do you want me to tell them you came by?'

'It's okay. I'll talk to them in the morning.' She'd already wasted twenty minutes at the club and had to collect Josh from his friend's house. She'd ring Daisy and make sure Gavin hadn't come home sooner than expected but just not turned up at the club.

She returned to her car and left the club car park, driving into Armston itself and down a street filled with pubs and restaurants. It was a warm evening and she lowered her window to cool off the car interior. She preferred fresh air to air conditioning, and as she drove along she caught snippets of laughter coming from those who'd taken advantage of the fine weather to come out for a drink or a meal. A group of revellers outside the Green Man laughed collectively, the hearty laughs carrying to the interior of her Audi. Good weather seemed to bring out the best in people. There was a

time she and David would have driven to the nearest pub on a fine evening and sat outside for a meal – but that was before the gambling. She pulled up to the traffic lights at a junction, her indicator clicking like a metronome. She supressed a yawn. It would only take ten minutes to reach Josh and she'd be home by eleven. She glanced right as she waited and caught sight of a man and woman walking along the pavement. The woman's bobbed hair was blonde to the halfway point when it became strawberry-red. The couple stopped briefly in the gloom of a doorway, and the man caressed the woman's bare shoulders then slid his hands down her back to rest on her backside before pulling her towards him and kissing her. Natalie remained transfixed, her mind buzzing like an angry, trapped fly. What the fuck was Mike doing here? And with Crystal!

She ought to chase after him and tackle him about it, but she still had to ring Daisy to confirm Gavin hadn't returned to the flat, and she needed to collect her son. Fuck Mike! She'd deal with him tomorrow.

CHAPTER TWENTY-EIGHT

WEDNESDAY, 4 JULY – MORNING

Natalie strode into the office determined to make headway. She'd had a lousy night's sleep with thoughts see-sawing between her son, who she'd picked up after her fruitless visit to Extravaganza, and Mike Sullivan.

Josh had seemed sluggish, as if he'd been drinking, but she could detect no smell of alcohol on his breath. He'd been reluctant to talk to her but she'd kept up the conversation in the car on the way home…

'Speak to me,' she says.

'What about?'

'Don't play games, Josh. You and your dad. What's been going on? He says you've been backchatting and rude. That's not like you.'

His chin juts out. 'He called me a lazy git and went off on one at me.'

'And why do you think he did that?' Natalie is trying to get Josh to see things from his father's perspective. He's a bright lad. He'll be able to work out why David has got so upset.

Josh, however, seems confused, his eyes unfocused. 'Because I didn't get up until after twelve but I was tired. I'd been playing on my PlayStation and I didn't go to sleep until about five. It's not like I had to get up for any reason. I told him that and he started shouting at me.'

'Okay, so you were upset at his reaction and he probably overreacted.'

'It was more than that.'

'Josh, we need to sort this out. It's understandable that you feel at a loose end at the moment but falling out with your father isn't going to make for a pleasant summer.'

'No. It wasn't about me sleeping in late. It was later when I told him I hadn't got the job. He tore into me and said my attitude sucked, and if I wanted to turn out a failure, then that was fine.'

Natalie is shocked. What was David thinking? He shouldn't have been so harsh. Then Josh adds something else that makes her realise the problem is worse than she suspected.

'I was really pissed off then. I told him I was going out but he said I should clean up my room and help him with dinner instead, and be useful instead of taking everything for granted. That made me madder so I texted Alex and said I'd meet him. Dad didn't notice me leave, he was sitting in the kitchen drinking whisky and staring at his phone. He didn't even look up.'

'We'll sort this out tomorrow. He was probably having a bad day. You know what it's like when other things make you feel low. You lash out at the people you love the most. He won't have meant any of what he said. He's finding life tough at the moment. It'll be forgotten tomorrow.'

'He shouldn't take his frustrations out on us.'

'That's what we all do. Families take the emotional punishment because we care about each other.'

He blinks at her and she wonders once again if he's been drinking. She asks the question casually. The answer is bitter and defensive.

'No, I haven't. Don't you start on me too!'

'It's just that you seem a bit woozy. You're not coming down with anything, are you?'

'I'm tired. It's been a bad day.'

'Of course. Well, get some sleep and don't stay up all night playing games.' She gives him a smile. She wants to ruffle his hair and hug him but he's prickly and she's already managed to get him to talk to

her; physical contact is a step too far. She follows him upstairs to bed and observes him walk about his room zombified before shutting the door – and her – out of his life again.

She was almost relieved to be at work, where her mind would be so focused on the investigation, she'd have no time for other concerns.

'Morning, everyone. We've got a shitload to get through today. Is there anything new before I get started?'

Ian spoke up. 'The toxicology report for Roxanne Curtis has arrived. Although the body was badly charred, they tested her blood, saliva and urine and discovered traces of alcohol and Xanax, indicating she consumed both within twenty-four hours before death.'

Natalie grunted at the news. The investigation was coming together at last.

Ian continued. 'From what I can gather, alcohol intensifies the sedative effect of Xanax. She'd have been out for the count when the blaze started.'

Natalie digested the information without moving from her spot at the front of the office then began with, 'Okay, let's start with this latest news. We know Habib and Tucker sold Xanax and that Roxy was with them two weeks ago, so we should consider the possibility they supplied her with the Xanax. Of course, that doesn't help us uncover who committed the arson attack on number ten Linnet Lane. There are a few possibilities: the Langs burnt or had it burnt down for insurance purposes, or somebody with a vendetta against them set fire to it. Whatever the reason, we still don't know what the fuck Roxy was doing there. I hardly think she broke into the house alone and decided to have a drink and drug-taking party on her own, so there's every chance she was inside with somebody else – someone who might have been able to disable the alarm system and who escaped the fire and left her behind. What are your thoughts?'

Murray started with, 'Well, there was no sign of a break-in, so she might have been with Kirk and Gavin and died of – I don't know – let's say an overdose of Xanax and alcohol. They panicked and set fire to the house to hide her body.'

Natalie made a note on the whiteboard, jotting down the suspects' names and circling Roxy's name before saying, 'The only thing wrong with that theory is that there are other less extreme ways to dispose of her body rather than setting fire to their home.'

'Unless they saw it as an opportunity to get the insurance money,' Ian added and earned a respectful nod from Murray.

She wrote 'motive insurance' next to their names then continued. 'Okay, now let's consider other options. Habib and Tucker purchased Xanax online and presumably sold it on. Two weeks ago, they met Roxy in the park near her home and, more recently still, at the block of flats where Ellie lived. According to what we've discovered, Habib and Tucker had issues with Charlie and Seth, so why would they hang out with Roxy – sister to the same boys who beat them up? I can only imagine she either didn't care about what had happened in the past with her brothers – after all, she was a bit of a rebel herself – or she had good reason to be with them. Assuming Seth and Charlie are telling the truth, we know Roxy took drugs, and if she was hanging around Habib and Tucker, it might have been because they were supplying her with Xanax.' She paused and looked each of her team members in the eye. Judging by their faces, they were following her train of thought and coming to the very conclusions she'd drawn.

'If all of that is true, then that opens up the possibility that Seth and Charlie once again took matters into their own hands. Roxy bought drugs that made her drowsy and died in a fire. They might blame Tucker and Habib for her death. They might have killed Habib.' She wrote all the information on the board, and beside the names of Seth, Charlie and Oliver she wrote 'motive revenge'.

'Then we have the mother, Cathy Curtis, strangled close to Linnet Lane on Sunday evening. Seth was there although he claims not to have seen his mother. Gavin Lang's whereabouts for that time period are questionable. He was at the flat above the tea room but both his girlfriend, Daisy, and Kirk were out together and can't vouch for him. The flat is within walking distance of the canal. He might have met up with Cathy or followed her there and killed her. I don't know why he'd do that. All I do know is he lied to us when we asked about her, denied knowing her, yet was all over her at the nightclub in December.'

'Maybe Cathy knew something about him we have yet to uncover,' suggested Lucy, who was met with nods.

Natalie added this information to the board then placed the palms of her hands on the desk and continued. 'I couldn't reach Gavin or Kirk Lang last night, so I went to Extravaganza, where a member of staff informed me they'd stayed overnight in London. I rang Daisy immediately afterwards and she confirmed that. Gavin had rung her to say he was staying over and would be back today. I refuse to piss about with this pair any more. I want their whereabouts for Monday night when Habib was possibly killed, firmly established. I want to know why they were in London with their phones switched off, and if that means hauling their arses down here, then do it. I also want Ellie Cornwall and Tucker Henderson brought in for questioning. I'm not putting up with any more duplicity, lying or fucking about. These kids know more than they've been letting on, and we're going to get to the bottom of this. Somebody get hold of Pinkney. He must have a good idea by now of how Habib died. Forensics are supposed to be giving our investigation priority so I'm going to see exactly what they've found out to date. We need to get a fucking move on. I want some answers. Have you any questions?'

When there were none, she gave a curt nod and walked out of the office, leaving the team lost for words.

Upstairs she swiped her pass and gained entry into the forensic lab, a clinical white room that reminded her of her school science laboratories. There were several white-coated officers working at various benches. She recognised the black-haired Darshan even while he was wearing his face mask. He was working on the other side of a glass partition and raised a hand in greeting. He said something to his companion – Mike. Mike pulled away and Natalie could see what the men had been examining. It was Habib, who was laid out on the table. Mike came through the side door, tugging at his rubber gloves.

'Can I have a word in private?' she asked.

'Sure.' He ushered her into a side office and closed the door behind them.

'This is a pleasant interruption.' He smiled and relaxed against a desk. 'Habib was brought in about ten minutes ago. Pinkney sent through the autopsy. Did you get it?'

'It hadn't come through when I left the office.'

After leaving the office, she'd spent five minutes standing next to the coffee machine wondering how best to handle Mike. It was none of her business if he chose to see, embrace or have sex with another woman. He was single and separated, yet she couldn't shake the feeling of regret. She'd watched the traffic rumbling past and decided she felt low because she felt let down. Mike had admitted to having feelings for her. She'd been gradually edging herself in his direction even though she'd been trying to put her family first. If she was honest with herself, she was disappointed that he'd been charming and flirtatious on the telephone, then only a couple of hours later been intimate with one of the nightclub's dancers.

'Well then, to summarise, the internal findings confirm what we suspected. Habib was first strangled and then hanged to make it appear as if he'd committed suicide.'

It came as no surprise to her. 'Will you run tests for drugs in his system?'

'Pinkney sent blood samples for immediate analysis and they came back clean. No alcohol or drugs in his system.'

'I want to double-check he hadn't taken any Xanax.'

'He'd been buying it online so he was tested for it.' Mike cocked his head in puzzlement but she continued.

'Check him again. I want to be absolutely positive.'

'The handwriting expert got back to us a few minutes ago and confirmed the handwriting on the suicide note doesn't match Habib's. The boy definitely didn't write it.'

'Most likely the murderer did then.' She stood as if expecting more.

'Righto. I'll get back to you if there's anything at all. I've pulled my officers from other cases and put everyone on this investigation. We're working flat out to assist you.' He didn't get the thanks he expected, and his brows knitted together. 'Nat, what's up? Why did you really come here?'

She looked into the distance, unable to voice what she really wanted to say.

'Is Josh okay?'

'I don't know. He was weird last night.'

'In what way?'

'It doesn't matter. I'll sort it.'

'Look, if I can help…' he began, but she shook her head to silence him.

'I went looking for Gavin and Kirk Lang last night.' The words tumbled out. He didn't respond. 'I saw you with someone.'

Mike stared fixedly at her then said, 'What do you expect from me, Natalie?'

'I thought…'

'Thought? You're married to David – my best friend. You have a family you love. I haven't asked you for anything because I know you can't give it to me. I'm not going to behave like a monk or moon about like a lovesick teenager. I'm a grown man, Natalie.

I have needs and desires. You aren't in any position to judge or condemn me.'

'I'm not.'

'Then why bring this up? So what if you saw me with a woman. What do you want to hear? That she means nothing? That you're the only woman for me?'

'Shit, no!'

'Then what?'

'I wanted you to know I'd seen you.'

'Great! Big deal. I was with another woman.'

'She's been charged with soliciting in the past... and you're a police officer. I don't need to spell it out.'

'And it's nobody's business what I do in my free time – nobody's! Even if she's been had up in the past, it doesn't necessarily mean I paid her for sex, does it?'

'Did you?'

'Whether I did or not is not your concern so butt out.'

'Mike, don't get defensive with me. I told you I saw you, that's all. I haven't reported you.'

'Really? That's big of you.'

'Back down, Mike!'

'I'm not the one with a face that looks like it sucked lemons. Want to know what I think? That you are green-eyed about it. You didn't like seeing me with someone that wasn't you. I can't put up with jealousy. It's childish and pathetic. It fucked up my marriage. I don't react well to demanding, needy women, so if that's all, I've got work to do.' He snatched up his gloves.

'Hold on just a moment! I'm not jealous and I'm not needy. *Needy* is the last fucking thing I am. So, before you stride out in a fit of childish pique, let me be clear about this. I'm fully aware you're single, and you and I aren't in any kind of relationship. As you pointed out, I'm married, and if I remember correctly, you're the person who advised me to stand by David. The woman you

were with last night is not only a prostitute but one of the two women who looked after Roxy when she ran away on Saturday. I came to give you the heads-up and to say that I haven't mentioned what I saw to anyone else. Your private life is exactly that, but I don't want my investigation compromised because you're fucking one of my witnesses, understand?'

He maintained an icy demeanour and then through gritted teeth said, 'Understood,' and strode out of the office.

CHAPTER TWENTY-NINE

WEDNESDAY, 4 JULY – MORNING

Natalie had spent an uncomfortable hour updating Aileen before reading Pinkney's report on Habib Malik. She read the last sentence and stared again at the whiteboard. All the names up there were somehow connected. It reminded her of a dot-to-dot book she'd been given as a child. She'd drawn neat lines from number to number but it was only once she'd drawn the final lines that she'd recognised what the picture was. After completing several pictures, she'd become more adept at guessing before she'd found the final numbers. How she wished she could see the final picture on that board. It was there. She just couldn't make it out. She pulled out all the notes she'd made on each victim. Was the key to this Roxy Curtis? It had all begun after her body had been found. The communications unit burst into life. Murray sounded exasperated.

'Finally got hold of Gavin and Kirk. They attended some red-carpet event at a nightclub where they used to work. They were out until the early hours and then crashed out at a friend's house and have only just picked up their messages. They're now on their way back.'

'How very convenient,' muttered Natalie from her desk.

'Should take them a couple of hours to get to HQ. I'm on my way to the Hendersons' flat to bring in Tucker.'

'Roger that,' said Natalie.

Ian glanced in her direction. 'Just got an email update from the technical team. There's a CCTV camera along Pine Way close to the amusement arcade, where Tucker and Habib apparently hung out on Saturday night, and it hasn't picked either of them up.'

'So they might not have been there. I wonder where the fuck they were?'

The office fell silent again. Natalie's thoughts fell firstly to Tucker, who she needed to talk to again, and then to Crystal and Sandra. Should she interview them again too? She couldn't think about the two women without thinking about Mike. For a split second he'd reminded her of David when he was backed into a corner. Bloody hell, the two men in her life were both letting her down at the moment. Needy! Nothing could be further from the truth. She hunted for the case file and read through the notes on Crystal and Sandra. Although they were both lap dancers, she couldn't help but wonder if they were still working as prostitutes too; after all, not only had they been had up in the past for soliciting, vice squad had been investigating the nightclub.

Ian interrupted her reading with a loud, 'Fuck me!'

Natalie stiffened in anticipation of what he'd uncovered. Another line was about to connect the dots on the board. It turned out to be a significant one.

'Tucker is related to Kirk and Gavin Lang!'

'Impossible! They spent their youth in foster homes. They don't have any relatives.'

'Oh yes they do. Well, sort of do. They were in foster care with another boy called William Henderson for several years. He's Tucker's father, or rather, he was. He was killed in a motorway pile-up in 2008. I suppose they're Tucker's uncles of a fashion.'

Natalie scrambled to her feet. This was a significant breakthrough. She put Tucker's name up on the board and studied the picture. It was beginning to take shape at last – Tucker might

know the men and he hadn't been where he'd claimed to be on Saturday night.

'This changes the course of the investigation, and it gives us someone we can place at the house with Roxy.'

*

Lucy couldn't locate Ellie. She wasn't answering her mobile. She wasn't at home or school, and her mother, who was at work, didn't know where she was either. A faint thrumming began in Lucy's temples. *Could she be in any danger?* She was on her way out of the block of flats for the second time that morning when she spotted Boo's mother, weighed down with shopping bags, approaching her. Boo danced merrily by her side. She broke away when she saw Lucy and skipped towards her.

'Hi, Boo,' said Lucy.

'Hi. I've got an ear infection. I don't have to go to school today.'

'Does it hurt?'

'No, but if I shake my head, I go dizzy,' she replied.

'Then I suggest you don't shake your head.'

'That's what I told her,' said her mother, who'd reached the door.

Lucy held it open for her and received a strange look for the small kindness.

'What are you doing here?' she asked before passing through it.

'Looking for Ellie.'

'We just saw her,' said Boo. 'Didn't we, Mum?'

Her mother shushed her.

'I really have to talk to her again. Whereabouts did you see her?'

The woman gave a soft shrug but Boo wobbled her head from side to side and sang, 'Ellie's in the park.'

'Boo! Go upstairs… now.'

Boo gave Lucy a cheeky grin and scampered inside.

'I really need to find her. I'm worried about her,' said Lucy. It was enough to get the woman to issue her with directions.

'Walk along Pine Way until you reach the old bingo hall and it's on your left. She was sitting on a swing. That was about five minutes ago. She might still be there.' A nod signalled the end of the conversation and Lucy held onto the door until the woman had gone through. She caught sight of Boo waving at her before she bounded up the stairs. The kid was a ball of non-stop, fun-loving energy. Would Spud be like that? The thought made her smile to herself.

Ellie was alone in the park on a swing hanging from rusty chains. She was smoking a cigarette that she hastily stubbed out when she saw Lucy approaching. A backpack was propped up beside the frame. She didn't speak and lowered her gaze. Her red-rimmed eyes gave away the fact she'd been crying.

Lucy dropped onto the swing next to her and pushed off with her heels, allowing herself to swing backwards and forwards gently. 'Not done this for a few years,' she said and then halted the movement. 'I think I was quite a bit thinner than I am now. I can hardly fit onto this seat.' She wriggled into position and tried again. She stopped the pendulous movements and brought the seat back in line with Ellie's. The girl hadn't upped and left.

'It's pretty hard when you lose a friend, isn't it?'

Ellie studied her trainers.

'You can't keep everything to yourself, Ellie. It'll make you ill.'

'You don't understand.'

'Believe me, I do understand. I know what it's like to wish you'd said the right thing the last time you saw that person, instead of being rude to them. I know what it's like to wish you'd been there when it had happened and that you could have done something to stop it. I know what it's like to wake up feeling light and cheerful, looking forward to sharing your day with them, only to suddenly be hit with the realisation that they're not there any more. I understand. It's different for each of us but death is a huge issue

and we have to deal with it in our own way. What you must never do is keep your feelings bottled up.'

'What makes you think I'm doing that?'

Lucy lifted her legs and swung backwards and forwards. 'You're not at school. You ought to be. You should be there remembering Roxy for the fun person she was. You and your friends should be sharing memories because doing that helps you to heal. Sitting alone does not. It messes with your mind.'

Ellie stared at the road beyond. A huge car transporter drove past followed by a line of cars. Lucy counted twenty of them before Ellie spoke. Her voice seemed to come from far away.

'Roxy and I used to come here a lot. It's really for little kids but Roxy loved these swings. She wanted to swing all the way round the bars on them – like a circus performer. I used to video her trying to do it. Some days, we'd have a bet on who would do it first and both have a go but we couldn't do it no matter what we did. One day, I was videoing her and she got really high… I mean, really high, like the swing was going to go right over and I started screaming, "You're doing it!" then, suddenly, she let go and fell off and landed in a puddle of water. I thought she'd broken something, but she jumped up and pointed to the wet patch on her bum and said, "I've wet my knickers!" I'd videoed the whole thing, so we watched it back and couldn't stop laughing.' She stopped talking and swallowed. 'It was really funny. I have lots of funny memories of her.'

'Then you need to keep sharing them. She'd like to know you were talking about her.'

'Yeah. She would.'

'I used to talk to my friend all the time. Like they were still there, even though they weren't. It made it feel like they weren't really gone.'

'I needed to Snapchat her this today. It hurt so badly when I knew she wouldn't answer.'

'What did you want to tell her?'

'Everything. About how scared I am. How much I miss her and about Habib.'

'I'm sorry about Habib. Who told you?'

'I heard about it on my way to school. I was outside in the yard. They were saying he'd hanged himself.'

'We're not sure yet how he died.'

'I couldn't go into lessons. I had to get away. I came here because I wanted to be near Roxy. We used to sit here for ages just talking. I didn't know what else to do.' Ellie rested her hands on her lap and tears filled her eyes as she whispered, 'I think Habib was murdered.'

'Then you know how important it is that you come to the station and talk to us.' Lucy set her swing off again.

A silence fell between them, punctuated only by the soft groans of the rusty chains as the two swings moved backwards and forwards in tandem, until Ellie turned to face Lucy and said, 'Yes. Okay.'

CHAPTER THIRTY

The interview with Tucker wasn't going well. Not only was he refusing to cooperate, his mother was proving to be a distraction.

'He hasn't done anything wrong!' she wailed for the umpteenth time.

'Mrs Henderson, could you please keep quiet? Your interruptions aren't very helpful. Tucker, we don't want to have to caution you but if you continue to withhold evidence, we'll be forced to do so.'

'Why? He's only a boy!'

Natalie spoke to the lawyer, a man in his early thirties with googly eyes, a high forehead and a receding hairline. 'I suggest you ask your client's mother to refrain from interrupting us further or I shall request she is removed from this interview.'

Tucker took matters into his own hands. 'Ma. Go outside. You're doing my head in.'

'I'm not leaving you alone. They'll accuse you of all sorts if I'm not here to protect you.'

Natalie bit back an acerbic retort. The general public often had warped ideas of what went on in interview rooms. She probably expected Murray to launch at her son with a truncheon and beat a confession out of him while Ian held him pinned to the floor. She'd had enough histrionics from the woman. She spoke to Murray.

'Would you please take Mrs Henderson to the interview room next door and arrange a cup of tea for her?'

'I'm not leaving my boy with you.'

'He has a lawyer present. We're recording the interview. Nothing untoward is going to happen. Please try to calm down. He's not been charged with anything. We're asking him to help us with our enquiries.' Her words seemed to find their mark and the woman finally stopped carrying on.

The lawyer spoke quietly to Tucker, advising him to answer the questions.

'Wait outside, Ma. It's best if you go.' Tucker cocked his head briefly to drive home his request.

She stood up reluctantly and shuffled to the door. 'I think I should be here.'

'Ma! Just leave it, will you?'

Once she'd departed, Ian started the recorder, introduced everyone present in the room for the second time, and Natalie tried once more to coerce Tucker into giving her the information she desperately needed. She laid it on the line once more about how he would be charged if he didn't cooperate.

'Tucker, do you know Gavin and Kirk Lang?'

'Maybe.' His anxiety once more manifested itself in his actions and he raised a hand automatically to his collarbone – an indicator he was nervous.

'They were fostered into the same family as your father.'

He remained silent.

'You do know why you're here, don't you?'

'Not really.'

'We're investigating the suspicious deaths of your friend, Habib Malik, Roxy Curtis and her mother, Cathy. Habib was your best and closest friend. You and he were seen with Roxy on several occasions. Roxy's body was found inside Gavin and Kirk's house,

and Habib was discovered in the field opposite it. I suggest you make life easier for yourself and answer my questions.'

His lawyer spoke to him again and eventually he tilted his face to the ceiling and said, 'Yes, I know them. They were my dad's foster brothers.'

'Have you known them long?'

'Since Da passed away. They came to his funeral and chatted about them all growing up together. I didn't see them again until they moved up to Staffordshire.'

'Did you start seeing them regularly once they'd moved to Armston-on-Trent?'

'No. Only once soon after they first arrived. Not since then. We're not like them.'

'What do you mean by that?'

'They're flashy, showy, rich go-getters from London. We're ordinary and pretty poor by comparison, and we live in Clearview. They were Da's mates, not ours.'

'When was the last time you saw them?'

'Two years ago, maybe. I can't remember exactly.'

'Where did you see them?'

'At their house. They invited me around to watch their swanky television. I guess they felt sorry for the *poor* kid who'd lost his father. They didn't ask me back.'

'Why not?'

His face screwed up contemptuously. 'They thought they'd done their duty. And I spilt a drink on their posh settee.'

'You're talking about their house in Linnet Lane?'

'Yeah.'

'They didn't stay in contact with you or your mother even though they live in Armston?'

'No. I think they felt they owed it to Da to try and be nice to us to start with, but then they gave up once they saw where we lived and what we are really like.'

'Why would they do that – try and be nice?'

'Da stuck up for them a few times when they were all kids. He used to be handy with his fists. I think he helped them out when they got into bother.'

'Bit like you and Habib? You looked after him too when he got into trouble.'

'Yeah.' He began to gently rub along his collarbone and Natalie knew she was getting somewhere with the boy. Although there was now an opportunity to get him to open up about Habib, her primary concern was the Langs. They'd maintained their friendship of sorts with Tucker's father, had been to his funeral and had possibly tried to befriend Tucker.

'Would I be right in saying you've never been back to their house since that day?'

He slid his fingers along his clavicle towards his shoulder and back in a slow rhythm, giving himself a gentle massage as he did so. She'd seen him perform a similar action before when she'd interviewed him. It was yet another nervous tell.

'I've not been back.' There it was again, a more anxious kneading this time, the sign he was feeling uncomfortable.

'Did Roxy know Gavin and Kirk?'

'I dunno if she did or didn't. She never told me. I didn't have much to do with her.'

'Apart from recently when you were kissing her in the park?'

Another quick rub. He was becoming increasingly uncomfortable and it was time to dig deeper.

'Can you explain why you and Habib were buying Xanax online?'

'Who told you that?'

'We have Habib's mobile. There are text messages from you in which you tell him how much and when to buy the drug, and instructions of where to meet him to collect the money to put in his current account.'

'What messages? That's bullshit. I never sent any messages.'

'It's a common misconception that people think if they delete messages or use applications to hold private conversations, we won't be able to find them, but our technical team can. Nothing online ever disappears, Tucker. For the benefit of the recorder, PC Jarvis is showing Tucker transcripts of text messages between him and Habib Malik.'

Tucker pushed the sheets of paper away. 'Fuck, man! This is out of order. Ma was right. You are trying to make out I did something when I didn't.' He glared at the lawyer. 'Make them stop. Tell them to let me go.'

'I'm afraid he can't do that. You need to answer the questions. This is evidence you purchased these drugs, and traces of this same drug, Xanax, was found in Roxy's blood. Unless you want to find yourself charged with manslaughter, Tucker, you really should tell us what you know.'

'Can they do that?'

His lawyer spoke to him in a hushed tone. Tucker squirmed on his seat and shook his head then scrubbed at his neck again.

'Tell me why you were buying Xanax, Tucker.'

Tiny bubbles of sweat began to form on his upper lip. He let out a hefty sigh. 'Way back when we were at school, we got in with some really badass blokes who paid us to sell some gear for them at school. It was only harmless – a few pills, some coke. Anyway, it must have been bad cos one of the lads, Baz Hill, had a major reaction to some E we sold him. He began thrashing about soon after he took it and spewing and, well, he ended up in hospital. Baz was Charlie Curtis's best friend, and when he heard who'd sold him the E, he and his brother came after us. They started to beat the crap out of both of us but I got away. They really laid into Habib. I got him away from them, and we didn't sell any more after that, but the Curtis boys made sure we knew they were watching us.

'Habib was paranoid after that. I mean really fucking scared that they'd go for him again and this time kill him. His mum had just got sick with cancer and that made him worse. He became depressed and got dead panicky about all sorts of things. His dad didn't know anything about it all but I did, and I had mates who took Xanax to help them chill out. I told Habib about the drug and he bought some and it helped him cope with all the shit that was going on in his life.'

This wasn't the explanation she wanted but he seemed relieved to get things off his chest so she didn't interrupt. At last she had some truth. This was the same story Charlie and Seth had told Lucy and Murray.

'It was my idea to make some money. Neither of us have jobs and it's fucking hard having no dosh. Habib wasn't keen after what happened last time, but I convinced him we'd only sell a few Xanax pills. It was coming up exam time and there were loads of kids shitting themselves about them, so I asked about and told them we could get our hands on legitimate pills to help them through – make them calm and breeze the exams.

'I charged them £1 per pill or £2.50 for a 3.5 milligram bar and took the money upfront. When we collected enough cash, we'd put it into Habib's bank account and he'd buy the Xanax in bulk and get it for a cheaper price. We made a bit of extra money for ourselves that way. We didn't do any harm.'

'What about Roxy? Did you sell her any Xanax?'

'Fuck no. We didn't sell her it.'

'So how come she had it in her system? You have to come clean about this. You're looking at manslaughter.'

'I didn't sell her any! She didn't even know about us selling it. We only sold to the same crowd. We were really careful who bought it and how much they bought. The last thing we wanted was another kid, like Baz, almost dying, and I'd be mental to sell

anything to one of the Curtis family. They'd definitely kill me if they found out.'

'It sounds very suspicious and slightly too convenient. You admit that you and Habib sold Xanax to schoolchildren and yet you don't know where Roxy obtained her pills.'

'It's the truth.'

'It might be but it doesn't help you much. I need facts.'

'Like what? I didn't give her the fucking pills. She had them with her…' He stopped, realised he'd revealed something important and waited for Natalie to pounce. She did.

'We know you weren't at the amusement arcade. You lied about that, Tucker. Were you with Roxy the night she died?'

His answer was a drawn out, 'Yes.'

At last, she was getting somewhere. 'Tell me what happened on Saturday night.'

It was a full minute before he answered her. He laboured over his explanation. 'Habib and I met up with Roxy and Ellie. They'd been chasing after us for ages. It was obvious they wanted to go further.'

'Have sex with you?'

'Yes.'

'I arranged for us to meet up, have a few drinks and then… you know.' He looked at the lawyer. 'I didn't kill anyone.'

'Go on,' said the lawyer. 'Tell them what you know.'

'I've got a key to Gavin and Kirk's house – it's a copy and they don't know I have it. When I visited them that time I told you about, they had to go out to get some food. I snooped around the place while they were out. Man, it was huge. They had everything: sound systems, televisions in every room, even in the fucking bathrooms. They had one of those spa baths with water jets and gold taps and walk-in wardrobes! Jeez! Anyway, I came across some house keys in a sort of jar thing with a lid so I took them, and the following day, I had copies made. I let myself back into the house and replaced the original keys where I found them.'

'What about the house alarm?'

He snorted. 'Kirk punched out the code that time they took me home with them. I was stood right behind him and saw it – 950316. I remembered it. The stupid fuckers never even changed it!

'I didn't do any harm. They had everything imaginable! Every fucking thing. My dad had nothing, just rented a crappy flat in Clearview, and they were his foster brothers, so I figured it was okay for me to go around to their house when they were out and watch their telly and pretend the place was mine.' His cheeks inflated as he released another sigh.

'I told Roxy and the others about the house and they wanted to see for themselves. Roxy said she'd like to *do it* there. She was mad keen to see inside so I agreed. Roxy knew a couple of the nightclub lap dancers so she made sure Gavin and Kirk were at Extravaganza and that we'd have the place to ourselves for a few hours. We took booze with us and set up in the entertainment room. Roxy was pissed off because she couldn't smoke – Gavin and Kirk would've known somebody had been in if they smelt stale smoke, so she pulled out a bag of yellow pills and suggested we try them instead. I knew they were Xanax. She'd got them from some dealer outside the nightclub, the same fucking nightclub Gavin and Kirk own. Anyway, we took them and got high and had sex on the settees: Habib and Ellie, me and Roxy. We finished the alcohol and Roxy dozed off. Ellie had to go home, so Habib went with her. I tried to wake up Roxy but she told me to fuck off, she'd leave when she was ready to go, and went straight back to sleep, so I left her.' He suddenly dropped his head into his hands.

'Fuck! I was wasted. I was so wasted I left her asleep on the settee. I didn't think anything bad would happen. I really thought she'd wake up and leave.'

'That was the last time you saw Roxy?'

'Yes.'

'Have you any idea what time that was?'

'No. I was high as a kite – I could barely find my own way out of the place. I remember straightening the cushions and taking the empty bottle with me. I saw Ellie and Habib up the road. They were standing there, talking or arguing, I don't know. I was going to catch them up but I didn't want Ellie giving me a hard time about leaving Roxy behind, so I headed in the opposite direction to a different bus stop to them, and caught a night bus home.'

'You were sober enough to remember to tidy up but not to help Roxy out of the house that you'd broken into?'

'I didn't break in!'

'Technically, you did. It was unlawful entry. You also had sex with a minor, a girl under the influence of alcohol and drugs.'

'But I didn't give her the drugs. She brought them with her.'

'You've committed serious offences, Tucker. Your lawyer will be allowed some time to talk to you and your mother in private, and then we shall be back to charge you officially.'

Tucker put his hands on his head. 'But I didn't kill her!'

'I'm going to leave you for the time being. When we return, we're going to continue our interview and we're going to also talk about Habib. You might want to tell your lawyer everything you know before that happens. Interview suspended at 11.50 a.m.'

CHAPTER THIRTY-ONE

Ellie Cornwall had broken down and begged Lucy not to involve her mother. Even though she had to have an adult present, she didn't want it to be her mother. Lucy had been obliged to inform Jojo that her daughter had voluntarily come to HQ and was assisting them with enquiries, and that an appropriate adult would be with her during her interview.

Lucy ended the phone call with the assurance that Jojo could wait for her daughter at the station, and then headed to the interview room to join Murray and Ellie. Ellie was hunched in her chair next to a social worker who'd been brought in to be an appropriate adult. She looked up when Lucy came in. 'I spoke to your mum. She's on her way here but she'll wait in reception for you.'

'She angry?'

'I'd say more concerned about you than angry,' Lucy replied. 'We'd like to record the interview so we have all the correct facts. Would you be okay with that?'

'Yes.'

Murray pressed a button and the machine emitted a beep.

'That's the recorder starting. We have to say who we are so anyone listening knows who's in the room and who's speaking. 'DS Carmichael,' she said. 'DS Anderson,' said Murray. 'Clara Jakes,

social worker.' The diminutive woman gave an encouraging nod at Ellie, who said her name aloud.

'Thank you, Ellie, for coming in. I'm going to start by reminding you of our conversation in the park. You told me in the park that you were frightened. Is that right?'

'That's right.'

'Why are you frightened?'

'I'm scared of being killed.'

'Is there a good reason that you might be killed?'

'Yes.' The girl's lips began to tremble.

'It's okay, Ellie. You're safe. You're here with us. We can help you. Tell us why you're afraid.'

'My mum doesn't need to find out, does she?'

'That depends on what you tell us.'

'You won't tell her everything, will you?'

'Ellie, we need your help. Your best friend, her mother and a boy you both knew are all dead. If you saw something that can help us find whoever is responsible, then please help us.'

Ellie's eyelids fluttered. 'I'm not sure.'

Lucy jumped in before the girl could change her mind. 'What would Roxy tell you to do?' It was cruel but the right call to have made.

'To tell you.'

Lucy said nothing more but waited for the girl to begin, and once she did, the words tumbled quickly.

'We were all in the house in Linnet Lane on Saturday – me, Habib, Roxy and Tucker. Roxy really wanted to sleep with Tucker. She'd been crazy about him for ages and she finally got off with him in the park a couple of weeks ago. She fixed up for us to double-date with him and Habib because she knew I fancied him. Tucker had a key to the house…

*

Roxy's waiting for them by the house. She's really excited to see the three of them arrive. 'I thought you lot were going to wimp it,' she says with a cheeky grin.

Tucker puts his arm around her and kisses her on the lips, squeezing her bum as he does so. He pulls away with, 'As if. Been looking forward to it. You checked it's clear? You speak to them friends of yours?'

'Crystal and Sandra? Yeah, they've gone to the nightclub to work. Gavin and Kirk are there tonight. It's a busy night so they won't be back any time soon. I spun them a really sad story.' She pulls a dramatic face and begins to blink back tears. In a halting voice, she shows them how she convinced Crystal to let her stay the night. 'Please help me! My mum has thrown me out and I have nowhere to go. I'm so frightened!'

Tucker laughs quietly. 'Bloody hell! You're a good actress.'

'Well, had a lot of practice, haven't I? Convinced my mum I was at Ellie's so we got all night to mess about, after Ellie goes home to her mummy.' She laughs.

Ellie scowls at her. She's a bit annoyed she hasn't got the same freedom as Roxy. Her mum will be home in the early hours and she'll have to be back by then.

'They'd all go ballistic if they knew I was with you,' Roxy drawls.

'I'm not scared of your brothers,' he replies.

'You fucking should be. They'll murder you if they find out about us.'

'Can you two shut up and let us in? Someone will see us,' says Habib, pulling Ellie closer to him. He's had his arm around her since they left the youth club and she can feel the heat rising from his body. He smells lovely – all clean and sexy.

'We'll go in first and double-check,' says Tucker, and while the girls wait on the driveway outside, they unlock the entrance and disappear into the darkness.

Roxy slips her arm through Ellie's. 'All right, babe? It's going to be mega. Isn't this the poshest place you've ever seen? And we get to do it here.'

'I'm not sure. I like Habib a lot but I'm not sure I'm ready for sex,' Ellie whispers.

'You're plenty old enough and he's gorgeous. Besides, he hasn't done it with that snotty Nadia Fryxell yet, and you'll be his first proper girlfriend. He'll probably dump Nadia afterwards.'

Tucker reappears and hisses at them to come inside. Roxy squeezes her friend's arm and they sneak in. The place is massive and Ellie is overwhelmed by it immediately. She's never seen a house like it, and when Tucker opens the door to the entertainment room, she gasps. It's like a private cinema with massive settees and a ginormous flat-screen. Tucker leaps onto the settee furthest away; Roxy squeals in delight and hurls herself down beside him. Habib is more grown up and takes Ellie by the hand, leading her to the other settee.

Tucker lifts the control and snuggles back like he owns the place. 'What d'ya fancy watching? They've got Sky.'

'Anything,' says Roxy, unscrewing the lid on the bottle of vodka she's brought with her and taking a good slug before passing it around. 'Got any fags?'

'Yeah, but we can't smoke in here. They'd smell it as soon as they got home,' Tucker replies and takes the bottle from her.

She pulls a moody face then suddenly smiles wildly. 'Good thing I brought these then,' she says and waves a bag of pills at them.

'What the fuck are those?' he asks, taking the bag and examining the contents. 'Hey, Habib, she's brought some Xanax.'

Habib gives a thumbs up.

'They any good?' asks Ellie. She's never tried them.

Habib looks at her with dark eyes that make her insides go liquid. 'Sure, I've taken them a few times. They're not dangerous. They make you calmer... like you're floating.'

Roxy's already swallowed a couple with the vodka, and Tucker flicks two into his mouth then throws the bag across to Habib.

'I'm not sure...' Ellie begins.

'They're fine… trust me,' Habib replies. 'Look.' He downs one with the vodka and passes the bag to her.

She takes one and swallows it with a slug of vodka too, then they repeat the procedure. A film is chosen and the bottle passed around and then a second bottle opened. Before much longer she feels Habib's mouth on her neck as he covers it in kisses, and her earlier inhibitions depart in that instant. She wants nothing more than to be his girlfriend, and judging by the noises coming from the settee next to them, Roxy and Tucker have gone beyond heavy petting. She doesn't glance over. Habib's hands are on her and she is lost in the moment.

It is only when they've had sex and are spent that the mood changes. Habib pushes her arm off him and suddenly seems more aloof.

'What's up?' she says, searching for the romantic mood again.

'Nothing. It's just I shouldn't have gone so far. I didn't intend to. I like you a lot but I didn't mean for this to happen.'

'What did you expect to happen?' she hisses.

'Make out a little, not go all the way. I have a girlfriend.'

'You didn't give her a thought when we were shagging.'

'I got carried away – the pills, the booze…'

She is furious. How dare he treat her like this? She looks for her bra and blouse, suddenly ashamed to be seen naked. Roxy and Tucker are fast asleep, spooning like two naked lovers, and now she's even angrier with Habib.

'You fucker! You used me!'

'I didn't. I never meant for us to go this far… you encouraged me.'

'What? Oh, that's it! You are a complete wanker. Roxy! Wake up. We're going.'

Roxy murmurs something unintelligible.

'Roxy!' She pulls on her jeans and slips her sandals back on, then crosses the room to Roxy and Tucker. Her friend is out for the count. She tries again. Tucker comes to and mumbles they'll follow on in a few minutes. Habib asks her to wait for him. He's getting dressed. He tells

Tucker to get a move on. Ellie tries to wake Roxy again who brushes away her hand and rolls over. Tucker is now on his feet, searching the floor with vacant eyes for his clothes.

'Roxy! We're going. Come on!' The girl doesn't reply. Ellie tries again but Roxy only mumbles goodbye. Fuck her! Fuck them all! Ellie checks to make sure she has everything and makes for the door, but Habib is there, blocking her way.

'Get out of the way,' she demands.

'You can't go on your own. I'll walk you to the bus stop.'

'What? You feeling guilty or something?'

'Yes.' The solemn look on his face halts her in her tracks. 'I'm really sorry. You're really lovely, Ellie.'

She begins to bristle again. How dare he give her compliments but tell her he isn't interested in her?

Behind them Tucker is pulling on his socks. 'Wait up. We'll come with you.'

She doesn't want to spend another minute in the house. Roxy still hasn't come to and she isn't going to hang around to wait for her.

'It's the pills, Ellie. I shouldn't have taken them. I wanted to spend time with you and get to know you. That was all. Can we at least be friends?' Habib pleads.

'Are you for real? Fuck off out of my way.' She barges past him, down the hallway and out through the huge entrance into the cool, where she stands still for a moment and inhales the night air. Then she hastens down the driveway and across the road onto the other side, distancing herself from the house, Habib and the memory of what she's just done. It's darker here beside the bushes that line the road and she feels hidden and safe. She remains close to the foliage and collects her muddled thoughts. It's quiet. Nobody is about. She can walk to the bus stop and catch the night bus alone. She doesn't need any protection. She heads away from the house, Habib and from Roxy, who is to blame for all of this. A rustling sound behind her causes her to quicken her pace.

A voice hisses, 'Ellie, wait up.'

She ignores Habib, who catches up with her and tries to converse as if nothing has happened between them. She continues up the road, heartsick at what has happened. Habib pulls at her wrist and draws her to a halt and speaks to her again, but she isn't listening. She wonders what she ever saw in him. He isn't that good looking and there are plenty of other nicer boys than him at school. Time halts for a while as she studies his face, his large nose, the over-gelled hair and the pathetic look he is giving her, and she decides that she's been an idiot. She doesn't acknowledge him and walks off again, takes the road on the right that heads to the church and back to the bus stop where only a few hours earlier she'd arrived. She is angry at that Ellie, the girl who was excited at the prospect of getting serious with Habib. She wishes she could turn back the clock. Habib has caught her up again. This time he sounds surprised.

'Did you spot who I just saw headed towards the house?'

She wants to ignore him but she is curious. 'No. Who was it?'

'I'm pretty certain it was Roxy's stepfather.'

'What would he be doing here?'

'Maybe he's found out about her and Tucker. He'll kill her if he sees them together.'

'You're mental. How could he know? You were seeing things. Or making it up. Just leave me alone. I don't want anything to do with you ever again. Go back to your girlfriend.'

Ellie shook her head as if to clear it. 'When I found out Roxy had died, I knew it had happened at the house. I thought you were going to say she'd overdosed. I didn't dare ask what had happened to her in case you saw how scared I was. Then I found out there'd been a fire, and I thought maybe Roxy had lit up a fag and accidentally set fire to something and wasn't able to get out of the house in time. Then… her mum died… and then Habib died and now I can't get it out of my head that I'm going to be next.'

The girl dissolved into gasping sobs.

'It's okay, Ellie. Take deep breaths. You're perfectly safe.'

'If Paul saw Habib, he'll have seen me too. I know this doesn't make any sense but it does to me.'

Murray was about to intervene but Lucy shot him a quick look. Ellie trusted her. She'd confided in her. Lucy had to see this through to the end. 'Ellie, listen to me. Nobody is going to hurt you. We won't let that happen. Do you understand?'

The sobs eased a little although the panic was still visible in her reddened face, scrunched up like a hungry baby's screaming for attention.

'I didn't believe Habib. I figured he was winding me up. Now I do. He even said Paul was probably hunting for Roxy, and if he found her with Tucker, he'd murder her. I just thought he was being an idiot.'

'You didn't see Roxy's stepfather on the road or near the house?'

'No… but if it was him and he killed Roxy because of her being with Tucker and then went after Habib, he'll come after me.'

'No, Ellie. He won't.' The girl was hysterical and what she was saying made little sense. It was unlikely Paul knew about Roxy and Tucker, let alone that the teenagers were in the house in Linnet Lane. There were too many question marks hanging over that theory: why would he set fire to the house, how did Tucker escape and why was Roxy left behind? She spoke evenly to the girl. 'You've done the right thing to tell us. We can make sure nothing happens to you.'

'Please don't tell my mum about Habib, about what we did.'

'I don't think she needs to hear that information from us, but you're going to have to explain why you were at the house Saturday night.'

The girl snuffled into a tissue.

'Is there anything else you can tell us?'

'I don't think so.'

'Did Roxy ever say she was scared of Paul?'

'No. It was Seth who scared her, but all her family hate Habib and Tucker. I think they really would have killed her if they'd found out she'd slept with Tucker.'

These were a young girl's theories based on stories from her best friend, but there was still enough here to cause concern.

'We talked about this before, but did Roxy mention anything about where she'd got the drugs?'

'Crystal and Sandra. She said they were really cool and knew where to get something that would help us enjoy the evening even more.'

It seemed they'd uncovered another small piece of the puzzle. It was possible that Crystal and Sandra had supplied the Xanax that Roxy had taken along to the house. The next step would be to talk to Paul Sadler.

Lucy gave the girl a smile. 'You've been brave talking to us. Roxy would be proud of you.'

Ellie nodded and then, hunching over, again began to cry softly.

As soon as they were outside, Murray spoke. 'I'll deal with Crystal and Sandra.'

'Good idea. I'll let Natalie know what's happened.'

'Good work.'

'You reckon? Poor girl is in a lousy state.'

'She opened up to you. She'll feel better now she's confessed about what happened. It took a lot for her to tell us about Habib. I think you pulled it off well.'

'There's hope for me, then?'

'In what way?'

'As a parent.'

'I don't know why you worry about it. You'll ace it.'

'We'll see about that.'

CHAPTER THIRTY-TWO

Tucker was now in a holding cell waiting to be charged for drug possession with intent to distribute and having sex with a minor. Natalie had given the command to bring in Paul Sadler. Messages were piled up on her desk but she had little time to deal with them because Gavin and Kirk Lang had returned from London and turned up at reception. She put aside the document marked 'urgent' and headed back downstairs.

Natalie and Ian were going to deal with Gavin first. As she headed into yet another interview room, Natalie felt like she was running on a treadmill that was slowly increasing in speed.

The whites of Gavin's eyes were pink, and not even the strong smell of aftershave could disguise his sour breath: the aftermath of a heavy night of drinking mixed with black coffee.

He made no apology for being out of contact and started on the defensive. 'I hope this hasn't been a wasted trip. We're busy people.'

'Too busy to answer your phones,' Natalie answered coldly.

'I already apologised to DS Anderson. We were networking all afternoon and night. It's not a good look to be on your mobile in those situations. We're here now, aren't we?'

'Thank you for coming in. I'd like to ask you about Paul Sadler.'

'Who?'

'Does that mean you don't know who he is?'

'Can't say I've come across the name.'

'Paul is Cathy Curtis's partner.'

'Cathy?'

'Don't fuck me about. Cathy was at the ladies' free entry night on December the second. You were very interested in her.'

'Oh, that Cathy. She was interested in *me*.'

'So you claimed last time. Do you know her partner?' She lifted a photograph of Paul up so he could see it.

His reaction was unexpected. He put his hand to his chin and rubbed the length of it. 'Yes. I know him.'

'How do you know him?'

'He's one of the dickheads who used to come into the club.' His use of a derogatory term led Natalie to suspect there'd been some trouble.

'You said "used to".'

'That's right. He was a nuisance so we banned him.'

'What did he do?'

'It doesn't matter what he did.'

'Did he challenge you about flirting with Cathy?'

'No! I wasn't flirting. I keep telling you that. I didn't even know she was his partner.'

Things didn't add up for Natalie. Why would Paul go to an expensive nightclub in Armston when he claimed to rarely visit the town? He definitely didn't seem the clubbing sort. There could only be one reason he wanted to visit Extravaganza: lap dancing.

*

Crystal sat on the kitchen stool and rested her head in her hands. Murray felt like a giant in such a tiny space. If he lived here, he'd spend all the time knocking into cupboards, the fridge, door handles or the cooker every single time he turned around. He'd asked about Roxy again and told Crystal she'd been in possession of Xanax, pills they believed to have come from the club.

'Have you any idea who gave them to her?'

She emitted a painful sound, a low moan that lasted an age.

'Did you give the pills to her?'

'Give? No. No way! I stupidly left some in my spare room in the top drawer in a bag. She took them. I didn't say anything when you asked about her. She was dead. It didn't matter that she'd stolen some pills. At least, I didn't think it did.'

'Can you prove she took them?'

She let her hands fall to her knees in one tired gesture. 'No.'

'You know how this really seems to me, don't you?'

'I would never give a child any pills or drugs. That's all I can say in my defence. Anyone who knows me, knows I wouldn't.'

'When did you realise they were missing?'

'Not until the police wanted to check the room. I went to hide them and discovered they'd gone.'

'Why would she take them?'

'She chanced upon them.'

'No. She told her friend that she knew somebody capable of getting her something to help her "enjoy the evening more".'

'That could mean anything.'

'She came looking for you. She must have thought you'd be able to supply her.'

'I don't know why she'd even think that unless…'

'Unless what?'

'The first time we met her, under the bridge. We took her to McDonald's and then she came back here. She went to the toilet.' She shut her eyes to try and think back. 'Shit, I can't remember properly. It was months ago but Sandra had some gear she'd bought.' Her eyes opened and she continued. Murray watched for signs of fabrication of the truth but nothing gave her away. He had little reason to doubt her words. 'It was quality gear and she gave me my share. I took it to the spare room and put it in my drawer and… I remember Roxy standing in the doorway. She'd turned the

wrong way out of the toilet and had come up the corridor instead of down to the kitchen.'

'It's not a huge flat!'

'I know but she was upset and I thought she was confused. I walked back to the kitchen with her. Do you think Roxy overheard us talking?'

'She might have caught a drift of your conversation if she was still near the kitchen when you were talking.'

'That's the only explanation I can come up with.' She looked him straight in the eye and he believed her. It made sense. Voices would carry easily from the kitchen to the hallway, and if Roxy had lingered, she might have picked up on the conversation and then heard Crystal in her room, opening drawers.

'Let's try it out,' he said. 'I'll go into the hallway towards the toilet. You say a couple of sentences in a normal voice and then go to your room and open the drawer you used to stash the drugs.'

She complied. Murray, now in the toilet halfway down the hallway, soon heard a muffled, 'This is a really stupid idea but I hope you can hear me. Can I stop talking now?'

'Try the drawer,' he called. Within a minute he heard the sound of a drawer grating against a rung as it was being hauled open. It was possible Roxy had heard the same noise. He emerged from the toilet and joined Crystal, who was trying to get the drawer back into place.

'It sticks,' she said as she shunted it back and forth before getting it to slide shut. 'You heard me?'

'Yes. Where did Sandra get the gear?'

'I can't tell you that.' She moved away from the chest of drawers and dropped onto the single bed.

He saw the resigned look in her eyes and knew he could push her further. 'Roxy's dead. Her mum's dead too, and now one of her friends is dead. No one need know you told me. Come on, Crystal.'

'It was from one of the bouncers at the club.'

'Which one?'

'Clark, but you didn't hear that from me, right?'

'I understand. Thank you. We'll look into this.'

'I don't know what else to say. I didn't give her any drugs. She stole them.'

Murray studied her distraught face. She sat like a broken doll, shoulders slumped, all energy gone. 'Do you know this man?'

He took out his phone, pulled up the photograph of Paul Sadler and passed it to her.

She let out a snort. 'Yes. He involved in this?'

'We don't know.'

'It wouldn't surprise me if he was.'

'Why wouldn't it?'

'Because he's got a really nasty streak in him.'

'Tell me more about him.'

'Why should I?'

'Because at the moment, I'm the only person preventing you from being charged for possession of drugs, supplying a minor and possibly even manslaughter.'

'You are kidding me? I didn't give her any drugs! I told you what happened.'

'Help me out, Crystal, and we'll clear everything up.'

'You wouldn't charge me? You know I was telling you the truth. She overheard us. She saw me in here!'

'I don't know that for sure. You could be making it all up.'

'Oh, come on!'

'Just give me some information. That's all I want.'

She deflated further on the bed, seemingly shrinking into herself. The words sounded like they were being dragged from her lips. 'It was at Extravaganza. He was one of our clients.'

'Clients in what way?'

'Any way they like,' she replied.

*

Natalie was on the same track as Murray. Back at HQ she thought she had Gavin on the ropes. 'Did Paul pay for dances?'

Gavin cocked his head to one side and released a weary, 'No comment.'

'Why did you really bar him? Was it something to do with the girls?'

'No comment.'

She sat back and glared at him. He wasn't going to crack and she'd have to try all over again with Kirk. A firm rap on the door prevented her from losing her rag with the man. She was called outside and handed a phone. Murray was on the other end and updated her on what he'd just found out from Crystal. She strode back inside the room with renewed energy.

'My officer's been talking to one of the girls who works at your club – a lap dancer, although I understand the girls offer more than dances.'

He lifted his hands to his temples. 'This is not relevant to anything. What they do is their business.'

'What they *do* happens to be on your premises, so let's stop pussy-footing about. I'm investigating three deaths. I don't give a shit what goes on in your club. I don't care if the girls are screwing your punters. I'm not looking into what goes on there. I can, of course, hand all this information over to the vice squad, get your place shut down and charge you with perverting the course of justice. So, if you'd like me to make your life hell, then carry on behaving like an arsehole.' She glared at him. He released a slight sigh, a sign of resignation, and she pounced. 'What did Paul Sadler do that made you throw him out of the nightclub?'

Gavin rubbed his lips together, his head moving from side to side as he fought his conscience. Finally, he acquiesced. 'The fucker roughed up one of the girls. She'd already complained to me that he got very aggressive during sex sessions, but some guys can be like that. I told her I'd sort it out. I had words with him and warned

him not to try that sort of thing with them again, but he did and we banned him from coming back.'

'Which girl?'

'Sandra Mallory. She's been off for a while so you haven't met her.'

'Did he have sex with any of the other girls?'

'Crystal once, but she refused to go with him again.'

'That was it? You didn't threaten or hurt him in any way?'

'We warned him that we'd tell all his workmates and family what a sexual deviant he was. It was only words. We've used that sort of threat before. The punters usually run a mile. They don't want their mums or wives to know what fuck-ups they are. I thought that was the end of it. He was such a weedy guy. All fucking macho in the bedroom with a young girl and a bloody wimp when up against real men.'

'When did this happen?'

'Three weeks ago.'

'I asked you if anyone had reason to set your house on fire and you didn't mention him.'

'I didn't think he had the balls to do that! We throw people out regularly for all sorts of reasons. He was such a wimp, he didn't even register on my radar.'

'Why did you say you didn't know Paul Sadler when I asked you earlier?'

'I didn't know the bastard was called Paul Sadler. He told everyone his name was Mark. Do you think he set fire to our house?'

'I don't know yet; however, I do know that Tucker had a key to your place.'

He threw his hands up with a loud, 'Tucker? How the fuck did he get a key to our house?'

'He told us he stole a set of house keys from a jar and had a copy made.'

'Why did he do that?'

'He wanted to drop by when you were out and watch the television.'

'You're joking!'

'That's what he told us.'

'I don't get it. What on earth made him do that? This is madness.'

'It would have helped if you'd mentioned him to us when we first asked you about who might have access to your house.'

'He never entered my mind. We've not clapped eyes on him for a couple of years. Besides, why would he burn the place down? We didn't do anything to piss him off. In fact, the opposite. We had him around once.'

'Why only once?'

'He stole fifty pounds from a wallet Kirk left out on the top. I was pretty certain he'd taken it and was going to challenge him about it, but Kirk persuaded me to let it drop. It wasn't important. We just didn't invite him back and he never reappeared. We simply forgot about him.'

'He might have resented the fact you didn't invite him back.'

'It was bloody ages ago. If he did and he's responsible for the fire, why would he wait until now? Why not torch the place back in 2016?'

'Okay, take me through it all properly. Explain why you invited him around.'

He released a sigh and rubbed a hand over his face, as if to erase the sudden irritation he was feeling. 'We were fostered together for a while with Tucker's father, William, who was like our older brother. We got on quite well but we didn't stay in touch much after we left that home – just the odd phone call, catch-up now and again. We knew he was married, had a kid of his own, and then we found out about the accident and went to his funeral. Kirk felt sorry for William's boy, Tucker. It reminded him of how we were – fatherless – so after we moved here permanently in

2016, he suggested we make an effort to get to know Tucker, for his dad's sake. We invited him to the house but he was a prickly, rude, horrid little shit.'

'Have you noticed anything missing from your house the last few months?'

He rubbed a hand over his chin again and blinked in disbelief. 'I can't think of anything. I suppose he could have stolen things, but if he did, I didn't notice – maybe the odd misplaced game for the PlayStation, but they reappeared and I thought the cleaner had moved them. Shit! It could have been him. The sneaky little bastard. I can't believe it! Do you think he's responsible for the fire?'

'We're investigating all possibilities.'

'It was a goodwill gesture and look what's happened. We should never have bothered with him.'

Natalie was inclined to agree but she was somewhat annoyed by the man's continued lack of concern over the deaths of Roxy, Cathy and Habib. These people meant nothing to him. He'd not mentioned them once. She'd leave him to stew for a while. It might make him reflect on what had happened.

'If you wouldn't mind waiting here, I'll be back later.'

'Can't I leave? I'm not a suspect.'

'I'd rather you stayed put. As I said a moment ago, we are investigating all possibilities, and something new has come to light. We've obtained a financial report for the nightclub. It showed a substantial loss of earnings and we've learnt that you are, in fact, in a great deal of debt. We still can't ignore the possibility that this could be deliberate arson for insurance purposes.'

He released another hefty sigh and sat back in his chair.

CHAPTER THIRTY-THREE

David drained his whisky glass. The amber liquid had slipped down nicely and he was feeling the rosy after-effects of drinking a good brand. Of course, he wouldn't be able to share that knowledge with anyone and had poured all the contents of the Macallan single malt that had set him back almost fifty pounds into an empty bottle of blended Scotch from Aldi that had cost eleven pounds. Natalie didn't like whisky so she'd be none the wiser.

His luck had held out and one of his further scratch cards had rewarded him with a hundred pounds so he'd treated himself and bought a DVD for him and the kids to watch. He poured another glass and scowled for a brief moment. Josh had poo-pooed the video and gone to his room instead. Still, Leigh had seemed please by his choice, and they planned to watch it together when she finished her homework. He'd replaced the kitty money and even bought Natalie a bottle of wine. It was nice to feel like a good father and husband. He had half an hour before Leigh would be down. He ambled into his office and pulled out his phone. He'd put the remaining winnings from the cards into his online casino account and felt like a quick flutter on roulette. He was on a winning streak. It seemed a shame to not see it through.

*

Natalie was discussing the results of the interviews with her team.

'He has means and motive,' said Ian, speaking of Paul Sadler.

'You reckon he'd burn down the house, knowing Roxy was inside?' Murray played around with some paperclips, stringing them together into a long chain. Natalie had noticed he fiddled a lot when he was getting frustrated – foot tapping, twiddling pens and messing about with stationery items. 'Tucker's got a motive too. He might have accidentally set fire to the house and now be covering his own back. Habib was going to grass him up, so he killed him. Not sure why he'd kill Cathy though.' Murray scowled at his own theory.

'We can't even be certain that Paul was actually in Linnet Lane. We only have a statement from a very frightened girl who can't recall seeing him that night. Habib may well not have seen anyone. He could even have been spooking her, winding her up or coming up with some nonsense to take her mind off what they'd been doing. I agree Paul has motive to burn down the house but he'd have to know where the Langs lived first. He had an alibi. And then there's the whole matter of Cathy. Why would he kill her?' Natalie put her hands behind her head then dropped them quickly. She could smell her own armpits. It'd been a long day cooped up in stuffy interview rooms. She'd not gleaned any new information from Kirk, who'd been as dumbstruck as his brother to discover Tucker had been letting himself into their house while they were out. Both men had offered up alibis for their whereabouts at the time of Habib's murder and she'd let them go for now. She had a sudden urge to freshen up. She collected her bag, containing make-up and deodorant. 'Back in a minute. Ian, check through those messages and make sure there's nothing else urgent.'

She spotted Mike in the corridor, striding towards her, head down, but dived off into the ladies' rather than speak to him again. She stared at her sorry reflection with a sigh and unclipped her

hair, searching in her bag for a brush. The door opened and closed with a bang and she looked up to see Mike reflected in the mirror.

He held up both hands. 'I'm not here to fight. I saw you come in and I wanted to apologise. You're absolutely, one hundred per cent not needy and I was a complete dick to say so.'

'Yes, you were.'

'That's all.'

'Okay.'

He paused by the door, his hand resting gently on the handle. 'You didn't mind me being with another woman?'

She rested her hands on the sink. 'Part of me did but I don't have any claim on you. You're not a possession.'

'That's the most sensible thing a woman's ever said to me.'

'You just don't know the right women,' she replied, glad that any tension between them had lifted.

'Maybe I do.'

'Don't, Mike.'

'Don't Mike, what?'

'Don't flirt with me.'

He gave an almost imperceptible nod and left. She ran the tap and waited for hot water to come through before holding her hands under it until they turned red and the veins rose up on the backs of them. She needed to wash away the smell of the day and get ready for the evening and her next interview with Paul Sadler. This wasn't over yet.

Paul Sadler had the dishevelled appearance and smell of a homeless man with sunken cheeks and hollow eyes, and stubble covering his cheeks and chin. He admitted to having been thrown out of the nightclub and, between tearful break-downs, confessed he'd got carried away and hurt one of the prostitutes at Extravaganza.

'She encouraged me to be rough with her, even said she enjoyed being tied up tightly and spanked hard, and when I did those things to her, she said I was too rough, that I'd forced her to do things she didn't want to do. She started screaming and I covered her mouth with my hand but she bit it. I didn't mean to hurt her but she was hysterical so I slapped her, maybe a little too hard. Gavin must have heard all the noise and rushed into the room with his brother, and they went crazy when they saw the blood. I tried to explain it was an accident, but they wouldn't listen to me. They frogmarched me naked down the back staircase, tossed me into the yard, chucked my clothes out after me. They took a photograph of me lying there and threatened to distribute it to everyone I knew if I went back and to tell my friends and family what I really liked doing to women. I didn't return.'

'Did Cathy know about your trips to Extravaganza?'

He rested his elbows on the table and slouched forward, his face a picture of misery. 'She had no idea about them. She'd have gone apeshit if she'd found out.'

Natalie wondered if Cathy had found out about his visits and challenged Paul. He seemed close to the boys – he was still living with and looking after them – so maybe he couldn't face her leaving him and taking them away. She dragged herself away from such wild speculation. Facts. She needed facts.

'Paul, remind me again where you were on Saturday night after Roxy went out.'

'Home. With Seth and Charlie. We played video games. I went to bed with Cathy. We told you that before when you asked. I was at home all night.' His eyes widened as he spoke and he leant closer to her, both indicators of his innocence.

It was true. They had little to no evidence to prove Paul had been elsewhere that night.

Natalie tried a different approach. 'You were spotted on Linnet Lane that night.'

He pushed himself upright, brows pulled low on his forehead. 'Impossible! I wasn't there. Someone's mistaken. I was at home. Ask the boys.'

It was hopeless. Their potential suspect had an alibi for that night. Although he had motive, they couldn't prove he was at the scene of the crime, and a dead boy couldn't act as a witness.

Meanwhile, upstairs, Ian and Lucy were searching for information on Paul and hadn't come across anything useful. Ian stopped working to reply to a text. It was the fifth that had come in while they'd been in the office and Lucy couldn't help but say something.

'You got a new text buddy?'

'It's Scarlett.'

'Is it back on with you two?'

'Might be.'

'That's good to hear.'

'Maybe. Maybe not.'

'What do you mean?'

'It'll be on again but only if I quit my job.'

'What do you want to do?'

'I'm torn. I spoke to Murray about it and he says I should stick to my career. It might not work out with Scarlett and I'll be left wishing I hadn't given up something I love doing.'

'Sound advice from the big man. I'm with him on that.'

'But I love her and Ruby too. What if I do this job and grow weary of it and wish I'd never turned my back on them? It works both ways.'

'I'm more of a follow-your-heart person. Things shift and change all the time. You can't legislate for the future. You think too deeply.'

'Think? Shit! You've just reminded me. Natalie asked me to check her messages and I haven't done it yet.' He leapt to his feet and scurried to the desk, leafing through the pile of notes and documents. He stopped at one and raced to the phone, dialled a number.

'Hi. Yes. You left a message for DI Ward. Really? Uh-huh. Okay. Can you send a link across to the email? Thanks.'

He scooted to his desk and tapped at the computer keys. 'There!'

'What have we got?'

'There's a small surveillance camera attached to St Mary's church. It picked up some strange activity on Sunday morning.'

'Why didn't we get hold of this earlier?'

'When I asked about it, I was told it only covered the church grounds and the gates were padlocked, so it wasn't a top priority. It turns out the camera wasn't set at the correct angle; something had knocked it off balance. The church warden noticed it earlier and alerted the team, who then checked it.'

Lucy pulled up a seat to examine the footage that had been sent through. The first shot was of the church footpath, verges neatly trimmed. It slowly moved left to right, sweeping over the gravestones. Lucy could make out inscriptions on the tombs, and flower arrangements and small ornaments on one grave. The picture continued and the camera now settled in position. They could now see the top of the wall and the footpath beyond. The timeclock counted the minutes and seconds, and at 12.43 and 15 seconds, the front tyre of a motorbike came into view. Lucy held her breath as the bike halted. There was nothing for several minutes, merely flashes of movement that indicated the driver was there. Without warning the camera began to swing back.

'No!' said Lucy, straining forward to see the person who was now walking past. She glimpsed a dark figure moving away, with what appeared to be a can in their gloved hand. The camera rested on the footpath.

'Shit! That's not much to go on, is it?'

'It's something. The technical team are trying to establish the make of bike.'

'Remind me which bikes the Curtis boys own.'

'They both have 125 cc bikes. Charlie's is a Yamaha YZF-R125 and Seth owns a Honda CB125.'

'When we went around on Sunday morning, Charlie's Yamaha was in the yard. Paul worked on it that afternoon after Cathy left. That could be Seth's bike.'

'But who's riding it?'

'It could be any of them except they all claim to have alibis for that night.' Lucy scraped back her chair. 'I'll run it past Natalie and let her decide what to do.' She thundered down the stairs towards the interview room, tapped on the door and asked if Natalie could step outside for a minute.

Several minutes later, Natalie presented the fresh information to Paul, who shrank in horror. 'I wasn't there. It isn't me. I don't own a motorbike.'

'But Charlie and Seth do. You could have borrowed theirs.'

'Charlie's had been misfiring all week and wouldn't run properly. I was working on it. You know that. Seth wouldn't let anyone borrow his bike, not even me. The keys to it are on his key ring, which he hangs onto. He's very protective of his bike. I couldn't have used either bike, and after I finished playing video games with the boys, I went to bed.' His shoulders began shuddering again. 'Cathy confirmed it. She knew what time I went to bed. If only she were here to tell you again!' He wiped his hands up and down his face to clean them of tears and snot.

He was a snivelling wreck; a broken man. Natalie wasn't sure which way to turn. They had little to nothing to place him at the scene of the arson attack, or at any of the crime scenes. Was she barking up the wrong tree? Had Seth duped them and driven to St Mary's church, parked up and taken a can of petrol to the house to set it ablaze? Was Habib wrong about who he'd claimed to have seen?

She studied the whimpering man in front of her. Gavin had called him weedy and a wimp yet he'd attacked a young woman,

Sandra M, at the nightclub and broken her nose. His ex-girlfriend had claimed he could be violent but had withdrawn her complaints. There could be another side to this man. If Cathy were alive, would she reconfirm his whereabouts or would she say that she'd been mistaken, got the time wrong, or maybe even covered up for him? She made an instant decision to search all of Paul's flat. They still had the warrant they requested when searching for the Adidas trainers. Maybe they could uncover something that would help place one of the Curtis family at the scene: identify the bike from its tyre or, ideally, retrieve the receptacle that had contained the petrol.

CHAPTER THIRTY-FOUR

WEDNESDAY, 4 JULY – EVENING

The afternoon dragged into evening. Social services were dispatched to arrange for the Curtis boys to find alternative accommodation for the time being. Paul was still being held for questioning but continued to bleat his innocence. Tucker was cautioned and sent to a cell for the night. Reluctantly, Natalie wound it up for the day. As much as she would have liked to press on, they were all only human, and they needed some time to recuperate.

*

Drawing up onto her front drive, Natalie realised she was glad to be home. No matter what troubles they'd faced or what problems still lay ahead, her home was her sanctuary. The thought of sitting down with her family with a glass of chilled wine was tantalising, and for the time it took to walk inside from the car, she felt relief at being here.

A burst of laughter came from the sitting room that lifted her spirits. There hadn't been enough light-heartedness recently. Leigh was having a fit of giggles. The sound warmed her heart. She glanced in and spotted David in his favourite chair, a glass of whisky balanced on the arm of it. He caught sight of Natalie and paused the film.

'Hey, Mum!' said a pink-cheeked Leigh, squirming about on the settee to focus on her. 'We went to McDonald's after school and then we bought this DVD, *Humor Me*. It's hilarious.'

'It's about a grown man who has to move in with his ageing father. It is pretty funny,' said David.

'I'll come and watch it with you. I need a quick shower and a glass of wine but not in that order.'

'I'll get it for you. I bought a bottle today and put it in the fridge in case you fancied a glass.' David eased forward to stand up.

'No, stay there. I won't be long.' She was pleased at such thoughtfulness.

'You sure?'

'Yes. Carry on.'

He flopped back into the cushion and set the film off again. A cloud of giggles followed her to the kitchen, where she reached for the wine and poured a large glass. It was cool and refreshing and tasted slightly of lemons. Perfect! After another mouthful she topped up her glass and, taking it with her, padded upstairs to the bedroom. Josh's door was slightly ajar. She poked her head into his room to say hello but it was empty, the computer paused on a game he'd been playing. She was about to move off when the bathroom door opened and he stumbled out then hesitated when he caught sight of her.

'You okay?'

'Of course I am.'

'Josh, look at me.' She placed the glass on a chest of drawers, her desire to drink it forgotten.

He faced her, eyelids flickering as if struggling to stay open. His pupils were dilated, his speech very slightly slurred. She lifted a hand to his forehead to check for a temperature and he flinched.

'I'm not a baby,' he grumbled.

'Are you sure you feel all right?'

'Yes.'

'Have you eaten today?'

'Yes.' His sulky response was out of character.

'Have you been drinking?' she asked cautiously.

'No!' He breathed out exaggeratedly into her face.

His reaction caused further concern. He didn't smell of alcohol but it was apparent to Natalie that he wasn't himself. Of the two children, Josh was always most alert, better behaved, less volatile and the one she'd come to rely on to behave sensibly, yet he was behaving cagily, his whole stance suggestive of somebody who was guilty – but of what? Her maternal instincts kicked in first. He might actually be sickening for something and these were warnings of some underlying serious condition or illness. She smiled warmly and put a hand on his upper arm.

'Sorry. I'm just being an over-concerned mum. What have you been up to today?'

'Not much.'

'Did you go out?'

His brows knitted together. 'No. Yes. I did for a while.'

His confusion caused more red flags. She hadn't asked a difficult question.

'Come and sit down for a sec,' she said, walking to his room.

He dropped his head. 'I don't need another lecture.'

'No one is giving you a lecture.'

'Dad does… every day.'

'Sit down.' She dropped onto the edge of his bed and patted the crumpled duvet.

He chose the chair by his desk.

'Josh, are you unhappy?'

'No. Of course not.'

'It must be weird having no school to go to and hanging around with Dad all day.'

'It's okay.'

'You're not worried about your exam results, are you?'

'No.'

His eyelids half-closed, causing her to react with, 'Have you taken any pills or medication from the cabinet?'

'No.'

'You seem out of sorts. I want to check there's nothing that might be making you act this way. Have you taken anything?'

'Act in what way?'

'Please don't avoid the question. Be straight with me, Josh. I can forgive anything but just be honest with me. That's all I ask.'

'I don't know what you're talking about.'

'I think you do.' She knew her children and husband, and all the indicators that they were being economical with the truth or hiding something: Josh's was a physical reaction that gave him away – a reddening he couldn't control; Leigh would squint into the distance as if she'd spied a tiny bird on the horizon; and David had numerous tells – scratching, suddenly humming tunelessly or head-rubbing. She'd given birth to this boy and lived with him for almost seventeen years. She knew him inside out, and now, seeing him sat with floppy limbs and a scarlet flush spreading up his neck, she knew he was keeping something from her.

'What have you taken, Josh?' Her voice was firmer this time.

'Nothing.'

She stood up in one movement and pulled out the bedside drawer.

'What are you doing?'

'Looking for whatever you've taken.' She rifled through playing cards and notes and tangled earbuds.

'Get off my stuff! This is my room. It's my private space. You can't do this!'

She ignored his protests and continued searching. Josh yelled at her to stop and David appeared.

'What's all the noise about?'

Natalie looked up. 'Josh is on something.'

'Don't talk daft!'

'David, look at him. He can hardly sit up straight. He's not been right for a few days.'

'He hasn't taken anything. He's tired, that's all. He's been glued to that computer most of the day.'

'He couldn't remember what he'd done today.'

'I get like that too. It's called boredom. Calm down. He hasn't taken anything.'

'I don't need to calm down because I'm not worked up.' She put the drawer back carefully. She stared at Josh, who couldn't meet her eyes. 'I'm concerned about you, Josh. That's all.' She left them both in his room and headed for the shower. When she emerged in her robe with a towel around her damp hair, she found David in the bedroom, leaning against the wall.

'What were you thinking of?'

'He's showing signs of drug abuse,' she said.

'He's showing signs of a teenager who spends too much time online. It's little wonder he's sluggish. He's never off one device or the other.'

'I want to search his room.'

'No. I won't let you do that. While you were in the shower, I talked to him about it. He said he wasn't taking any drugs, so we're going to leave it at that.'

She pulled the towel from her head and patted her hair dry. She was sure Josh was lying to them both. David took her silence to mean she'd accepted what he'd said.

'You need to separate work and home life. You'll only make matters worse if you pursue this. We'll keep an eye on him.'

She wanted to disagree. Her boy needed protecting from himself but she accepted she'd handled it badly. She'd been more like a police officer and less like a mother. There was probably a better way of dealing with such matters, and she wished somebody had written a handbook on bringing up teenagers because at the moment she was stumped.

CHAPTER THIRTY-FIVE

THURSDAY, 5 JULY – MORNING

Leigh had been her usual grouchy morning self, David frosty, and there'd been no sign of Josh when she'd left the house. Natalie kicked her car door shut and marched into headquarters determined to resolve the investigation. At least it was something over which she had control.

As she'd stared at the ceiling wondering how best to handle Josh, her thoughts had jumped to the case and she'd had a thought, one that had caused her to ring Murray at eight o'clock and ask him to head to Armston before the morning meeting.

She headed straight upstairs to Forensics to see what, if anything, had been found. The news wasn't great. A unit was still at the flat in Clearview and had nothing to show for their searches.

Darshan looked over his rimless glasses at her, his expressive eyes full of apology. 'As you can see, the more the technical team enhanced the image of the motorbike's tyre, the grainier it became. While it was possible to identify the letters "P" and "I", indicating it's a Pirelli tyre, they really couldn't get sufficient clarity to determine a tread pattern. Pirellis are popular tyres and on both the Honda and the Yamaha belonging to the Curtis family. We've also tried here. We took tyre casts but we can't match them, even using the latest cross-referencing software. Sorry, Natalie.'

It was a blow but one she'd half-expected. 'No sign of any container used to carry petrol yet?'

'None found so far.'

'There has to be something.'

'Unless they disposed of all evidence.'

Natalie suspected he was right. If any of the family had been involved in the fire or the murders, they'd have got rid of everything that might implicate them.

She stood outside the laboratory, mobile in her hand, waiting for Murray to ring. A group of white-coated officers, like a group of young doctors, approached and greeted her. She acknowledged them and paced back down the corridor. Sunlight streamed through the floor-to-ceiling windows that overlooked the road and bounced off her shoulders. Outside it was another brilliant blue day, the sort of day that ought to be spent beside the sea. She could never think of sunshine without thinking of the seaside and ice cream and walks along a sandy beach. The phone rang at last.

'I'm emailing you a photograph,' Murray said. 'Your hunch was correct.'

'You know what to do next then, don't you?'

'That's an affirmative.'

She waited for the email alert, opened the attachment and then bounded down the stairs to join her other officers.

Paul sat hunched over like a toad in the corner of the holding cell. Natalie searched her soul to find some sympathy for the man but found none. Ordinarily, she wouldn't be down here talking to a suspect, she'd leave such matters to the officers, but she wanted to sow extra doubt in his mind and add to the pressure he was undoubtedly feeling.

'We're going to question you further. You have the right to legal representation,' she said.

'I don't know any lawyers,' came the tired reply.

'There's one on-site and I strongly advise you to take up his offer to represent you.'

'You've found out something, haven't you?'

'I'm not at liberty to discuss anything with you. I wanted to ensure you knew your rights.'

'Are you going to charge me?'

'You'll be brought upstairs shortly.'

She turned on her heel and hoped she'd given him enough to weaken his resolve.

Natalie, Ian and Lucy were all present during the interview. It took much the same format as the previous one with Paul denying any wrongdoing. Natalie decided to use the information she'd received earlier from Murray.

'I'd like to go back to Sunday afternoon, soon after Cathy had gone to visit her friend. You claimed to have been working on Charlie's motorbike. Is that correct?'

'Yes.'

'What was wrong with the bike, exactly?'

'It had a bad misfire and an oil leak.'

'Could it still be ridden?'

'No. It was likely to break down or seize up completely.'

'Is it working now?'

'Yes. I fixed it yesterday. I had to find something to do to take my mind off what's happened.' The tears started again.

'It is a Yamaha YZF-R125 bike. Is that correct?'

'Yes.'

'And it takes Pirelli Sport Demon tyres. Is that also correct?'

'Yes, and so does the Honda. They're popular tyres. Why are you asking me this?'

'Just answer the questions, please. When did the leak on the Yamaha become apparent?'

'I don't know.' The answer was sharp and quick. He suddenly tucked his hands under his armpits. 'Why?'

'You told us you went to bed at about midnight the night Roxy died. Cathy confirmed the time.'

'Yes.'

'Tell me, Paul, how did she know what time it was?'

'There's a clock by the bedside. She must've looked at it.'

Natalie studied his face, waiting for him to realise he was being backed into a corner. His forehead began to glisten slightly. She reached into a file and pulled out the photograph printed from the email Murray had sent her. She studied it before passing it across the table. Paul kept his hands clamped under his arms.

'For the recorder, DI Ward is showing the suspect a photograph numbered JB8,' said Ian.

'This is a photograph of the bedroom you shared with Cathy. Which side of the bed do you sleep on, Paul?'

He dropped his head. 'The left.'

'You sleep on the left-hand side of the bed. You can see from the picture that there is no bedside table or place to rest a clock or phone on the right-hand side. Cathy couldn't have seen the time from her side of the bed.'

'She could see it from her side of the bed.'

'No, Paul, she couldn't. That is a Lexon Flip alarm clock and it only shows a display when you hover your hand over it.'

'I must have done that. Yes. That's it. I remember. She asked what time it was and I told her.'

'I have no doubt that you told her the time. It just wasn't the correct time.'

He was about to protest but she silenced him. 'I was asking about the oil leak on the Yamaha. These are stills taken from CCTV footage of a motorbike that drew up beside St Mary's church in Armston at 12.43 on Sunday morning.' She began to lay out all the photographs so Paul could see them.

'DI Ward is now showing the suspect a series of photographs JB9 through 14,' Ian added.

'The tyres on this bike have been identified as Pirellis.'

Paul said nothing.

'In this photograph you can make out a person wearing what appear to be leather motorcycle gloves, carrying a container, which we believe to be a jerrycan.'

'It wasn't me,' he said, his words mere whispers.

'First thing this morning, one of my officers went to St Mary's church and examined the area where the bike drew up. He found oil stains where the bike had been standing.'

'It wasn't me.'

Natalie swigged the black coffee that Lucy had brought back from the machine and stared at the clock. It was almost ten. This was now turning into a long waiting game yet she was sure Paul would crack. He was back in the holding cell. The evidence they had was flimsy at best and all she could hope for was a confession. She drained her cup and waited for the internal phone to ring.

They all used the time to hunt for more information and she trawled back though the case notes hoping to find something else they could use. She was surprised to hear a gentle cough and looked up to see Darshan.

'You might find this useful. I've been going through the computer we brought back from the flat and Paul purchased this off Amazon.' It was a 2.5 gallon no-spill poly gas can. 'It can take just under ten litres of fuel,' said Darshan.

'That's quite a hefty thing to carry on a motorbike. How would he have managed that?' asked Ian.

'Saddlebags, backpack or my guess is strap it down on the back seat with bungee straps,' said Darshan.

'Have you told Forensics?' Natalie asked.

'I rang Mike immediately,' he replied with a small nod.

'Thank you. This is exactly what we needed.'

Ten minutes later, presented with the evidence, Paul was willing to confess. He dragged his hands over his grey face.

'I admit that I set fire to the house in Linnet Lane. I wanted some payback – for the humiliation, for treating me like scum. I bought the petrol can and planned to burn down their fancy house while they were out. I made sure both Charlie and Seth could give me an alibi, and after they'd gone to bed, I sneaked out. I wheeled Charlie's bike down the road, started it up there and parked up at St Mary's church. I didn't want the engine to rouse anybody on Linnet Lane. I carried the can to their house. I'd planned on wetting rags and stuffing them through the letter box but the door to the entrance opened when I pushed on the letter box, so I poured the petrol all over the floor, set it alight and ran.

'Believe me, I had no idea Roxy was inside at the time. How could I possibly have known she'd be there? I haven't been able to eat, sleep or even think about it since. I can't live with myself for what I did.'

'Habib saw you when you approached the house. Did you spot him?'

'I didn't see a soul. I was fully focused on getting to the house, starting the fire and getting back home as quickly as possible. I planned it so nobody would be inside. I didn't want anyone to die!' he wailed.

'You deny seeing Habib?'

'I swear I didn't see him.' He rested his hands either side of his temples and stared at the table with haunted eyes.

Natalie continued, undeterred by his evident upset. 'What happened to Cathy? Did she find out what you'd done? Did she threaten to tell us?'

'Cathy? I didn't kill Cathy. I had nothing to do with her death. I loved Cathy.'

The lawyer spoke quietly. 'I think we're quite clear on this matter. My client is admitting to arson and the possible manslaughter by misadventure of his stepdaughter, Roxanne Curtis.'

'I am not giving up.' Natalie was sticking to her guns. They'd tried comparing Paul's handwriting to that on Habib's suicide note but it had proved inconclusive. In spite of similarities in letter formations, the expert couldn't say with complete certainty that Paul had written the note.

Aileen Melody was once again the voice of reason. 'You have to make the decision to charge him accordingly. We can't wait about indefinitely. If he isn't responsible for the deaths of his partner and Habib Malik, then we are wasting valuable time.'

'There'll be something. I'm sure of it.'

'You have ample evidence to convict him of the arson attack.' While they had forensic proof that confirmed Paul was behind the arson attack, they had nothing that placed him at the other crime scenes. 'I'm giving you until one o'clock to make the call.'

Natalie was dismissed and headed directly to her car. The frustration had become a physical mounting pressure in her chest and she needed to get away for a while. She tore down the lanes towards Armston, knowing she wouldn't be much help but needing to be at the flat in Clearview. There was something they were missing. Her phone rang and she put it on speakerphone.

'Mike, I'm headed in your direction.'

'That's timely.'

'What have you found?'

'Meet me where we found Habib.'

She pulled up behind the white forensic van right outside the field where they'd found Habib. She paused for a second to survey the remains of Gavin and Kirk's house. Normally, in such tragic circumstances where a person – especially a child – had died, floral tributes would have been laid out, but she was saddened to see there was nothing to show anyone cared. A flash of red caught her eye and she crossed the road to better examine it. It was a small, heart-shaped balloon with a message that read, 'To the best friend in the world. Swing high until we meet again. Love you forever. Ellie.' She thought back to what Lucy had told her about the swings in the park where the two girls had made plans and laughed together, and a lump rose in her throat. She swallowed it down. Now was not the time for sentimentality. As she turned away she spotted Mike by the open gate and crossed to join him.

'I found the bungee leads used to strap the petrol can onto the bike in the back of Paul's van along with these, caught up in some ripped dust sheets.' He lifted a small plastic evidence bag containing grey particles.

'And they are?'

'Fragments of bark from an oak tree. Come with me.'

She followed him into the field where a ladder was resting against the tree trunk. Remnants of a dust sheet had been tied to both the top and bottom of the ladder to cover the feet. Mike explained his theory. 'Paul's an aerial fitter and I'm pretty certain he'd be expected to cover up the rubber feet on his ladder so they don't mark walls when he clambers into loft spaces, hence the dust sheets. It's been bugging me how Habib was strung from the tree

and why we couldn't find any evidence to indicate how he got there. I think the killer prepared the rope so it was hanging quite close to the trunk. He wrapped torn pieces of dust sheet around the ladder feet and then strapped Habib to the ladder, using the bungee cables and more pieces of ripped sheeting. Then he propped both the ladder and the body against the tree. The ground was dry so the ladder didn't leave any marks and the thick material protecting the feet prevented obvious indentations in the bark.

'There is no other way this could have been accomplished. It's really difficult to raise a dead body up a tree by tying a rope around it and hauling it over a branch, or by standing on a step and lifting it into a noose without assistance, and besides, we'd have found some forensic evidence to suggest that was what had happened. However, it is possible for a killer to tie a body to a ladder and extend that ladder little by little until it is high enough for that person to climb up a few rungs, slide a prepared rope around their victim's neck and then cut them free from the ladder. The body would swing sideways and come to rest in a position that would make it appear the person had committed suicide.'

Her heart thudded against her ribs and she was keen to get back. 'Is this Paul's ladder?'

'It is.'

'You have the sheets and samples of bark and can prove unequivocally that he committed this crime?'

'Unless somebody else had access to his van, then yes, I can. We can test the bungee ropes for Habib's DNA too.'

'What about Cathy? How can I prove he killed her?'

'I can't help you there. We simply don't have enough evidence for you to point the finger at anyone.'

'Okay. I'll work with what I've got. Thanks for this.'

'I'm only doing my job.'

'And it's appreciated.'

She dashed for her car, glancing one last time at the house opposite. She couldn't bring the girl back to life but she had at least found the person responsible for her death. She too had done her job, except there was still one final line to add on this particular dot-to-dot drawing before it would be completed.

CHAPTER THIRTY-SIX

THURSDAY, 5 JULY – AFTERNOON

The office was stuffy, having heated up thanks to the sun shining directly through the window. Natalie squinted and drew the louvre blinds to shut out some of the dazzling rays that bounced off the whiteboard and showed up every fleck of dust on the dark desktops. Below her the never-ending traffic rumbled along but behind the double-glazed windows she heard only slight stirrings from her team as they waited for her to begin the brainstorming session. Ian sat with a notepad in front of him. Murray was once again fiddling with items on his desk while Lucy sat upright, hands on her thighs as if ready to jump up at any moment, like a cat poised to strike. They had Paul's confession that he'd set fire to the house in Linnet Lane and substantial proof that he'd killed Habib, but they still had insufficient evidence to link him to Cathy's death. Natalie returned to the front of the room and nodded at Ian, indicating he should continue.

'I could talk again to the man who saw the motorbike near Linnet Lane. Maybe he was wrong and it wasn't Seth's bike that he saw,' said Ian.

Lucy was quick to disagree. 'No, he gave us the last two letters of the registration and it was definitely Seth's bike. Plus, Seth admitted he was at the canal. The witness definitely saw Seth.'

Natalie stared at the names on the board, her forehead creased in thought. There had to be a reasonable explanation. There was

one possibility, which she tested on her team. 'What if there were two bikes and the witness only happened to spot Seth's?'

Murray flicked at a pencil, propelling it into a circle, and after it came to a halt, he said, 'Wasn't Paul working on the Yamaha? His neighbour heard him swearing at it.'

Lucy nodded in agreement. 'Unless she was mistaken about the time, but she was playing with her kid outside and she was quite clear about them going inside to eat.'

Natalie chewed at her thumb, ideas now mounting up. 'What time exactly did she hear Paul swearing?' she asked, sending Ian scurrying for the notes.

'Six thirty or seven.'

'It wouldn't take long to reach the canal. Fifteen minutes by bike. Maybe Paul arrived shortly after Seth left.'

'What about the text Cathy sent Paul?'

'He could have sent it himself from her phone.' It was falling into place. Then she had the lightbulb moment. 'Lucy, get me a name and number for Paul's neighbour.'

It took a few minutes to find the information but soon Natalie was speaking to Heather Collins. 'It's DI Ward from Samford Police. You might remember I spoke to you a few days ago.'

'I do. There's been police crawling all over the house. I heard they've all been arrested.'

'I wouldn't believe everything you hear. I need to ask you a question.'

'Okay.'

'Can you think very carefully about this? You told us you heard Paul swearing and you took Tommy inside.'

'That's right.'

'Did you hear anything else at all?'

'Like what?'

'Did you hear an engine start up?'

There was a pause. 'No. I don't think I did.'

'How about a loud squeak?'

There was another hesitation, then the voice at the other end lifted. 'Oh, you mean his gate. It always squeals. I wish they'd put some bloody WD-40 or something on it. Actually, yes. I did hear it. It made that noise just after he shouted, "Fucking bitch!" I was almost inside by then. He was in a right lather.'

After hanging up, Natalie stared at the board and made her announcement. 'I think Paul Sadler's been messing with us. He wasn't swearing at the bike he was repairing. He called it a "fucking bitch". I know cars, bikes and ships can be referred to as female, but I think he was talking about Cathy. He was angry with her and fixed the bike quicker than he said he did – and what Heather overheard was him venting as he left the yard with the bike. Now we need to prove my theory.'

She looked into the corridor, heart hammering. She almost had him. A figure was fast approaching the office. It was Mike.

'Natalie! The dust sheets. They're made of cream cotton twill. I think one might have been used to strangle Cathy.'

With the evidence mounted up against him, Paul could deny the accusations no longer. After another lengthy interrogation, he hung his head in shame. 'I didn't mean for any of this to happen. I only wanted to pay those bastards back. I didn't know Roxy would die. I was sick when I found out – properly sick. My world imploded and I didn't know what to say or do. I had to stay calm, pretend it wasn't me who'd caused the fire, but Cathy was astute. She put two and two together so quickly. I don't know how she did it. Maybe she knew me too well, could see I was hiding something, and she went through my computer history and found out I'd bought the jerrycan.'

*

Paul doesn't know where to turn or what to do next. He's screwed up in ways he never imagined possible. What the fuck was Roxy doing inside those bastards' house? He's killed his stepdaughter. He's got to sort out Habib and he has a plan to silence the boy. He'll offer him a stupid amount of money to keep quiet about seeing him. The kid will do anything for cash; he has few morals in spite of his shy demeanour. He leans over the toilet bowl again and throws up. He only just held it together while the police were at his flat. He can't break down now. They have no way of knowing it is him. He has to play it cool. He stares at his face and wipes the sweat from his brow. He can't seem to stop perspiring and Cathy's been giving him strange looks. She senses he's keeping something from her. She's no idiot but even she can't guess what he's done, can she? He bluffed her when he got back, told her it was just gone midnight when it was actually almost two o'clock. She is his alibi for that night, and besides, she loves him. She'll believe in his innocence, won't she?

He hastens out of the bathroom. Cathy's been surprisingly calm since the news of Roxy's death while everyone else has acted in their own ways to the tragedy. Charlie has gone to his girlfriend's house and Seth's buggered off somewhere and now Paul feels strangely left out. He loved Roxy too but they've seemed to forget that.

He walks into the sitting room and Cathy, who's at the computer, shuts it down suddenly. The movement is quick and in contrast to how she stands up and meanders to the kitchen, avoiding eye contact with him.

'I'm going to look for Seth. I'm worried about him,' she says.

'I'll come with you.'

'No. I'm going alone. He'll be upset and confused. He needs me.'

The words hurt. She's shutting him out. As she disappears to collect her bag, he checks the computer and finds the last page she was on. His blood runs cold. She's been searching for a phone number for DI Ward at Samford Police Headquarters. He checks what else she's been looking at and sees she's been searching through the computer's history and that she's discovered what he ought to have deleted but never thought

to – the website from which he bought the jerrycan. He should have deleted his browsing history but he never imagined the police would knock on his door. Not in a million years.

He races after her and catches her putting on her wedged sandals. 'Is everything okay?' he asks, testing her.

'Fine.'

That one word tells him all he needs to know. Cathy suspects him. She may love him but she'll never forgive him for Roxy's death, accidental or not. Moreover, he can't trust her to keep quiet.

She doesn't kiss him goodbye and leaves him standing in the doorway, knowing the police will come back, and the next time, they'll take him away. He won't let that happen.

The fucking bike is still leaking oil. He was lucky to have got back home earlier from Armston before it broke down. It is an easy enough fix. He sets to work and gets angry firstly with himself then Cathy. He can't let her tell anyone what she suspects. He doesn't want to hurt her but she's brought this on herself. Why couldn't she keep her fucking nose out? It would've been all right. They'd have pulled through. Roxy was a pain in the arse at times anyway. Always arguing and carrying on. They'd have got over her. Next door, the little brat is squealing and shouting. He's a noisy little fucker. In spite of the high-pitched, excitable screams coming from the yard next door, he resolves the issue with the bike and wipes his hands on a cloth.

He hears the kid's mother chatting loudly on her phone. 'I know, hasn't he grown?'

He rolls his eyes then something switches on in his head. He can use this moment. Fucking Cathy! She's put him in this position but he can make this work. He throws a spanner onto the floor and curses loudly then picks it up and bangs it against the metal toolbox. 'Fucking thing! Why won't you untighten?'

'Speak soon, babe.' The woman hangs up.

He smashes the spanner against the box once more so it rings out loudly, and he curses.

The child is quiet for a moment and he hears the woman talking quietly to him. He's attracted their attention. He wheels the bike to the gate. Cathy has fucked things up big time. This isn't his fault. None of this is his fault. 'Fucking bitch!' he says loudly and opens the gate.

Natalie picked up her case files and cast a final look at Paul Sadler. He remained seated with his head bowed, as he had done ever since she'd revealed their findings to him and he'd finally confessed to killing Cathy and Habib. He was no longer a sobbing mess. He was blank-faced, sucked dry of all emotion, a defeated man – a killer.

His sole intention had been to destroy the Langs' house and instead he'd destroyed lives – lives of those he professed to love, not to mention others affected by the deaths of Roxy, Cathy and Habib.

He'd murdered Cathy in cold blood, sent himself the text message from her phone, and then gone one step further to cover his tracks. He'd arranged to meet Habib, promising to pay him £500 to keep quiet about seeing him in Linnet Lane. The meeting point was the field, where he first strangled the boy with plastic aerial wire and then strung him up, unobserved and unnoticed by the people who lived on the street.

Natalie held the phone to her ear and let Gavin Lang rant. 'What a vindictive and stupid bastard! Burnt down our house just because we threw him out of the club? I hope he gets locked up for a long time.' She had told Gavin what he needed to know. Paul Sadler had torched their house and in so doing had accidentally killed his stepdaughter.

Gavin carried on, 'Fucking Tucker. He's to blame for this too. If he hadn't broken in with those kids, nobody would be dead.'

Natalie understood his anger however, she was done with the Lang brothers.

'What's going to happen now? Do we even get an apology off you for hassling us?'

Natalie grimaced at the remark. 'We conducted our enquiries and you assisted us. We didn't hassle you, as you put it.'

'Yeah, right. Like we had a choice. So that's it, then? I'll have to let the insurance company know about this. We're still waiting for our claim to be processed.'

'You can reaffirm that you were a victim of an arson attack and a person has been charged.'

'Good. We need to get things moving along. All of this has been a right bloody nightmare.'

Natalie could imagine his face as he spoke, the superior attitude that irritated her each time she'd interviewed him. A woman and two teenagers were dead, yet Gavin believed he and Kirk were the victims in all of this. 'Unfortunately, it isn't quite over. I believe the vice squad are interested in what goes on at your nightclub.'

'Oh, shit!' Gavin fell silent at last then ended the call.

Natalie flopped back in her chair. She was drained. The investigation had been intense, dramatic and troubling. Paul had ruined lives and because of his actions, three young men were without their mother and sister. She hoped they'd recover from their loss – Seth would find it the hardest. She doubted if Seth or Ellie, for that matter, would ever get over what had happened, even with the counselling they were both now undergoing.

CHAPTER THIRTY-SEVEN

Aileen was waiting for Natalie in her office. Paul Sadler had been charged and Aileen had been able to give the press a statement announcing that an arrest had been made. Natalie expected her superior to be pleased with the quick result, but one look at Aileen's face told her otherwise.

'Sit down, Natalie.'

She did as bid.

Aileen remained with elbows on her wide desk, fingers loosely interlocked. 'First off, I'd like to offer my personal thanks for resolving this investigation so promptly, professionally and with such dedication. It's an honour to work with such disciplined officers. I'm fully aware of how much energy and time went into this and I couldn't have asked more from you or your team.'

Natalie bowed her head in acknowledgement. She couldn't take all the credit. Murray, Lucy, Ian and Mike had all played their part.

'This will soon become public knowledge but I wanted you to hear it from me. I'm being moved on. It's been on the cards for a while and there's a new rising star who'll be replacing me. I wanted you to know that I think you have huge potential. You are an outstanding officer and I see no reason why you shouldn't consider furthering your career. Your children are getting older and increasingly independent. You should make the most of this time and opportunity. Your success rate hasn't gone unnoticed.'

Natalie sat numbly. She'd heard rumours and whisperings that Aileen was going to be replaced but they'd been quashed in recent weeks. This was a shot out of the blue and she realised how much she'd grown to respect the quiet, no-nonsense woman. She would undoubtedly miss her.

'That's all I wanted to say. There'll be a formal announcement in the next day or two. You capturing Paul Sadler in record time has at least allowed me to leave with my head high. Thank you for that. Please keep this information confidential until it becomes official. That's all.'

Natalie stood up, unsure of how best to react. She wanted to say something meaningful or even embrace the woman, but all she could do was extend her hand and say, 'It's been a great pleasure to work with you, ma'am.'

The lights were off in her house. At least tonight she wouldn't wake up concerned about the investigation. The loose ends had been tidied up. It had been a tough but mercifully brief investigation and she could keep her promise to Leigh. They would go to the cinema this coming weekend. She also had some bridges to build between her and Josh. It was almost half past eleven and the house was in darkness. She tiptoed upstairs and stopped suddenly by Josh's room. The door was ajar and his bed empty.

She checked the bathroom and downstairs, and even glanced in Leigh's room but she was alone, curled up under her duvet. She tried Josh's mobile number. It went straight to answerphone. She rooted around his room to see if anything was missing and if her son had, like his sister earlier that year, run away.

She hastened to the bedroom she shared with David. The smell of stale alcohol pervaded the suffocating room. David was flat on his back, mouth open, deep in slumber. She bent over him and shook him hard. He came to with grunts of confusion.

'David, where's Josh?'

David could barely focus on her; his eyelids blinked furiously, his face fuzzy with sleep. 'Natalie?'

'Josh isn't in his room. Where is he?'

David sat up, his face reflecting the confusion. Natalie noticed he'd buttoned up his pyjama top incorrectly and the collar was skew-whiff. A half-empty tumbler of whisky was on his bedside table. It didn't take great powers of deduction to work out he was still half-cut. 'I don't know.'

'Was he in his room when you came to bed?'

'I assumed he was. He went up to his room after dinner. I thought he was on his computer, as usual.'

'But you didn't even go in and say goodnight to him?'

David rubbed his hand over the top of his head. She knew the answer without him having to say it.

'For fuck's sake! You knew I was worried about him. You said you'd keep an eye on him.'

David didn't reply.

'Did he say anything to suggest he was going out anywhere or that he'd run off?'

'No.'

'Did you two argue?'

'No. He's hardly spoken to me today.'

She left him and headed back to Josh's room, where she fired up his computer and prayed he hadn't logged out of his social media sites. He hadn't and she was able to access his Facebook profile, where she found messages from his friend Alex. She only read the first few, the most recent sent that evening at eight:

Alex: Got the details. Starts at 10. You still up for it?

Josh: You bet.

Alex: Gonna be wicked.

Josh: Can't wait.

It sounded like they could be going to a party, but the fact Josh had sneaked out rather than tell them where he was actually going, suggested he was up to something that she and David would disapprove of. Alcohol, drugs and teenagers could be a bad combination, and while she was no prude, she only had to think of Roxy, Ellie, Tucker and Habib to be concerned for her own son. It was the dishonesty that set her pulse racing.

She shut off the computer and started downstairs.

David was on the landing in bare feet, his face contorted in confusion and despair. 'Where are you going?'

'To find our son.'

'Wait for me.'

She stopped mid-stride and without turning around said quietly, 'No, David. I don't want to be with you at the moment.' She descended rapidly and he raced after her and pleaded with her as she put her shoes back on, but she ignored him. She picked up her car keys again and left without saying another word. She didn't trust herself to speak to him. What she really wanted to say would ruin everything.

She jumped into her car and headed towards Alex's house. She'd try and raise his parents and see if they had any idea where the pair had gone. She tossed her mobile onto the passenger seat and it flashed as it landed, notifying her of an unread message. She picked it back up and, steering with one hand, opened it. Mike had sent the briefest of texts:

Excellent result.
Congrats.
Mike

It was enough to make her ring him. He'd been there for her when Leigh had gone missing and he would be the one person who

could probably help her find Josh. He picked up immediately and she explained the situation.

'Where are you?'

'I'm almost at his friend's house. I'm hoping his parents know where the boys are.'

'You think he's at a party?'

'A party or maybe even a rave. The message from Alex said he'd got details and it started at ten.' The house was within sight.

'Whatever it is, it can't be too far away, unless the boys got a lift to it. I'm still at the lab so I'll get in touch with the technical division and pick their brains. If there's a rave going on, we might be able to find out where it's taking place.'

'Would you? Thank you, Mike. I'll try Alex's folks and ring you back.'

She tumbled out of the car and raced towards the dark house. Her footsteps set off the neighbour's dog, who began woofing – a bored, repetitive bark. She rang the doorbell. Soft chimes reached her ears and the dog increased its yaps. It was a clear night and a cool breeze coiled around her, chilling the bare skin on her arms, causing the hairs to rise. She rubbed at them and rang the bell once more. There was no reply. She tried a third and final time, and when no one appeared, she hastened back to her vehicle and drove towards Samford.

'Mike, Alex's parents aren't in.'

'Don't panic. We're on it.'

'I don't know where to start.'

'Come to HQ. We'll fathom it out together. We've got the technology here. I'm trying to get a triangulation on Josh's phone.'

She drove, heart pounding, towards Samford. She hoped she wasn't having a knee-jerk reaction to the sudden change in Josh's temperament, but he was her child and she had a duty to protect him. It was not only the strong maternal instinct that was driving

her, it was the reminder that drug abuse could have terrible consequences.

Mike was waiting for her in the car park and jumped into the passenger seat. 'We got a hit on his phone. He's in Samford. I've got one of the lads hunting on social media. We suspect it's one of those pop-up raves where the location isn't given out until the last minute so it can't be raided or shut down. Somebody will have blabbed on social media. They always do. They get stoned and start posting about it. Head towards the Omega Industrial Park. That's the area where we picked up the last transmission from his mobile.'

She drove at speed, the road a black blur punctuated with traffic lights that were all on green.

'I'm reacting badly, aren't I?' she said as she floored the accelerator along a derestricted section.

'I don't think so. He slipped out, late at night, without telling you where he was going. He's put himself into a potentially dangerous situation, and at the end of the day, he's sixteen. I think you're completely right to hunt him down. If it were Thea out there, I'd have the entire station searching for her.' His words hit home and she was grateful for them.

His phone rang. He answered it and grunted thanks. 'One of the team thinks he's located a warehouse party on the Omega Industrial Park. There've been some photos posted on Twitter, and he's certain that's where they were taken.'

They were only three minutes away. The estate was enormous, with vast warehouses spanning several acres each. It would be quite a task to work out which side road to take and locate the warehouse being used. However, Mike was on it. He spoke assuredly, instructing his colleagues to check for empty warehouses then obtaining directions. He kept a level head when they drew a blank at the first warehouse and directed her around the labyrinth of the roads around the estate to another warehouse, and then a third where they could hear loud music.

'Stay with me,' said Mike. 'We'll find him together.'

They entered through a side door and straight into a seething mass of bodies. The air was thick with perspiration and sweet, sickly aromas she associated with cannabis. The noise made her eardrums vibrate. Mike grabbed her hand and leant into her ear, cupping it and shouting, 'Stick with me.'

Together they pushed past the throngs of young men and women catapulting themselves around the floor to a manic beat. Mike's hand was warm and large and enveloped hers. She drew comfort from his presence and strength and turned her head this way and that, attempting to locate her son. They attracted little attention from the party-revellers who were too engrossed in the music and dancing to notice two adults in their forties. A wild-eyed young man chugged a large bottle of water, the contents spewing down his neck and missing his mouth. It was unbelievably hot in the warehouse and damp patches were once again forming under Natalie's armpits. Mike glued his fingers around hers and pulled her deeper into the warehouse. The tempo of the music quickened and there were cheers from the crowd, who raised arms and bounced as if on a giant trampoline. She looked up at grim-faced Mike, who stood head and shoulders above most here and who was scouring the room for Josh. It was hopeless. They would never find her boy here. As those thoughts crossed her troubled mind, her eyes locked onto a figure she recognised and she tugged at Mike's arm. 'Alex!' she yelled and pointed.

The boy was loose-limbed, his arms flinging up and outwards like an uncontrollable marionette's as he danced on rubbery legs in front of two girls who grinned and prodded each other and laughed at his antics.

Natalie dropped Mike's hand and made a dash for the boy, seizing him by the wrist. 'Where's Josh?' she shouted.

He stared with glazed eyes.

'Where is he?'

One of the girls tapped her on the shoulder and yelled, 'Are you looking for Josh?'

'Yes.'

'Toilets.' She made a sign with her hands to indicate it was because the boy had drunk too much alcohol and pointed to the far side of the room.

'You know he's only sixteen?' said Natalie of Alex whose birthday was a month after Josh's.

The girl spoke to her friend and they backed away, disappearing swiftly into the crowd. A blinking Alex spun around 360 degrees and back.

'Where'd they go?'

'They left. You're coming with us,' she said to Alex, and once again, taking his wrist, she manoeuvred him in the direction the girl had indicated. He'd become instantly subdued, head low. Mike walked the other side of the boy protectively as together they shuffled past the revellers.

Mike waited with Alex while Natalie shouted Josh's name and thumped on each of the cubicles. The last door opened to reveal her son, on his knees, hands on the cistern, head over the bowl.

'Fuck. Josh! Speak to me.'

He emitted a groan then heaved noisily. She squeezed in beside him, pushed his fringe away from his face as he heaved again. There was nothing left to bring up.

'What's he taken?' she yelled.

Mike shook Alex's arm to make him reply. 'Nothing.'

'Don't bullshit me. What's he taken, Alex?'

'Just a popper.'

'Do you mean Ecstasy?'

'Yes.'

'How many has he taken?'

'One'

'Josh, can you hear me?'

'Yeah. I'm okay.'

'Can you walk?'

'Yes.'

She put an arm under his armpit and helped him to his feet. She couldn't stop the hot, angry tears from running down her face. Her resolve and calm had abandoned her. Mike came forward and helped Josh out.

'You gave us a scare,' he said.

Josh managed to look shame-faced. 'I'm really sorry, Mum.'

She couldn't speak for sorrow. He was all right but a line had been crossed and he was no longer her little boy. She'd found him this time but how much longer would she be able to look out for him? He'd be studying for A-levels in a few months and then probably going on to university, and she'd have no control over what happened to him. She'd warned him about the dangers of drugs yet still he'd taken them. What more could she do? She wiped the tears away and drew a breath. He was safe and there was still a chance for them to talk this over and establish why he'd been so rebellious. He might yet respond to reason.

'I can manage now. I don't feel sick any more,' he said.

'Alex, where are your parents?' Natalie asked.

'Out for the night.'

'You'd better come home with us then.'

They pulled up on the road outside her house. Josh and Alex had fallen asleep on the back seat, slumped against each other. Mike had ordered an Uber to take him from Natalie's to his house. She turned off the ignition and waited for David to appear at the front door, but when he didn't, she spoke.

'There was no need to arrange a taxi. I'd have run you home.'

'You have enough to do. You have to deal with the boys.' He glanced at his mobile. 'And Uri will be here in two minutes. Now that's what I call prompt service,' he said with a quick smile.

'I couldn't have done this without you.'

'Yes, you could. I just helped you find him quicker.'

There was a pause during which all they could hear was the heavy breathing coming from one of the sleeping boys.

She cleared her throat and spoke quietly. 'About the other night. I *was* jealous. I'm as bad as every other woman you've known. I was angry and hurt and yet I had no right to feel like that. I shouldn't have laid into you.'

His eyes crinkled. 'That's generous of you. You didn't have to admit to that.'

She turned around to check the boys – completely dead to the world – and whispered, 'I did because I want you to know how I feel about you. I can't keep up the pretence any longer. I need to move on but first I shall have to talk to David. I don't want to do anything behind his back. I want to do it properly.'

He didn't respond, and for a moment she thought he was annoyed by her sudden outburst; after all, she'd kept him at arm's length for such a long time. Then he slid his hand on top of hers, fingers curling around her own, and leant towards her. She faced him and he dropped a light kiss on her lips before pulling back.

'If you're sure.'

'I'm sure.'

'Then I'm happy with that decision.' He looked at her for the longest moment then headlights appeared in her rear-view mirror as his ride approached.

'I'll see you tomorrow,' she said.

'You bet.'

He opened the car door, illuminating the interior and rousing Alex, who shoved Josh off him and yawned. A light popped on in the sitting room of her house and David's white face peered from

behind the curtains. She told the boys to go inside and stood by the car door as Mike got into his taxi with a wave.

The front door opened. David's voice was behind her but she continued to watch the taxi until it disappeared from view, then faced her house. Like her son, she'd crossed an invisible line. Life was going to be very different from here on in.

EPILOGUE

David sits in the dark beside Josh's bedroom window, which overlooks the road. The curtains haven't been drawn and he can see any vehicle approach. Each time he spots headlights, he peers out hoping it is Natalie and Josh returning.

He is a dismal father and husband. He's let them down time and time again. How many more times is this going to happen? He wipes his eyes. He's cried enough since Natalie went out in search of Josh. He feels impotent. He should be with her yet part of him tells him she's overreacted. The boy will be okay. He's a resilient teenager who is testing his boundaries. How many teenagers don't do that? So, the boy's slipped out unawares to some party. It isn't the end of the world. Yet it is because it matters to Natalie.

He hears an engine and recognises Natalie's car as it pulls up behind his own. He leaps to his feet to greet her then comes to a sudden halt. It isn't Josh who is sitting in the passenger seat. It's Mike. What is his best friend doing in his wife's car?

Deep, rhythmic pulsing fills his ears and he moves to one side, so Natalie is not aware of him.

They appear to be talking. He watches, twisting the wedding band that encircles his finger and praying silently. The streetlight illuminates the car sufficiently for him to see Mike kiss her and his heart explodes into tiny fragments. He can't catch his breath. He stands in horror until another car appears and Mike gets out. David can now make out his son and friend who stretch and yawn and fumble for the door

handles. He moves swiftly, a mask of fatherly concern now in place. He is still, for the moment, a father and husband and he will fight his corner to maintain that role.

A LETTER FROM CAROL

Hello, dear reader,

My sincere thanks to you for buying and reading *The Sleepover*. I hope you enjoyed reading the book as much as I did writing it. If you'd like to keep up to date with all my latest releases, just sign up at the following link. Your email address will never be shared and you can unsubscribe at any time.

www.bookouture.com/carol-wyer

We're already on the fourth in the Natalie Ward series and I find myself deeper in love with all the characters, especially Natalie, although I have a fondness for all of them… well, with maybe one exception – David – but nevertheless, I feel sorry for him. This was such a pacy book to write and I found myself, at moments, holding my breath. I had to actively remind myself to breathe.

The foundation for *The Sleepover* came from real-life events and an article I spotted in a newspaper. The underlying theme is secrecy and hiding the truth from people, even those we love the most. How many people really tell the truth? How many children lie to their parents, and how many spouses lie to their partners? My research raised many concerns that I am sure you will share with me, but it also gave me the opportunity to create a tale that I hope you found engaging.

Do you ever really know anyone?

If you enjoyed reading *The Sleepover*, please take a few minutes to write a review, no matter how short it is. A few words will suffice and I would truly be most grateful.

I hope you'll join me for the next book in the DI Natalie Ward series, which will be out on 6 December 2019.

Thank you,
Carol

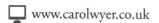 www.carolwyer.co.uk

 AuthorCarolEWyer

 @carolewyer

ACKNOWLEDGEMENTS

Sometimes saying thank you doesn't seem enough and this is one of those occasions. During the writing of *The Sleepover*, I found myself dependent on a number of individuals to guide and assist me, and experts who ensured the book was factually correct.

I am incredibly grateful to Nigel Adams, a retired fire officer and forensic fire officer consultant, who helped me hugely with my description of a house blaze by providing very useful documentation and talking me through what being a fire officer entails. He also introduced me – albeit online – to Kai, the West Midlands Fire Investigations search dog, who I urge you to seek out on Twitter. I learnt a huge amount from Nigel, much of which I couldn't put into the book, but which opened my eyes further to the bravery and dedication of those who work in the fire service.

Thanks go to members of the CWA for answering my barrage of questions, and to Stuart Gibbon, a former senior police officer who has not only written books that crime writers like myself keep by our laptops at all times for reference but who is always available to answer any police-related query.

Further thanks go to the entire team at Bookouture, without whom there would be no book – that includes all those who had eyes on this book, those who formatted it and everyone involved in marketing and public relations.

Finally, special and sincerest thanks go to my amazing editor, Lydia Vassar-Smith, whose clever suggestions changed this book from a good one to one I am extremely proud of. Thank you.